AN EQUATION OF ALMOST INFINITE COMPLEXITY

Also by the Author

The Day Immanuel Kant was Late:
Philosophical Fables, Pious Tales,
and Other Stories

j. mulrooney

An Equation of Almost Infinite Complexity

CASTALIA HOUSE

An Equation of Almost Infinite Complexity

J. Mulrooney

Published by Castalia House
Kouvola, Finland
www.castaliahouse.com

Editor: Vox Day
Cover: Castalia House

ISBN 978-952-7065-29-7

God made the land and the waters,
He rides on the wind and the storm.
The Devil sails lost on the ocean.
The angels will keep him from harm.
The sailors are dreaming of riches
While the merchants dream of the sea.
Tonight I will go to bed dreaming
Of one who does not dream of me.

My bonnie lies over the ocean
My bonnie lies over the sea
My bonnie lies over the ocean
Oh bring back my bonnie to me.

—Traditional. Adapted by N. Scratch

The Lord said to Moses on Mount Sinai, "Seven weeks of years shall you count—seven times seven years—so that the seven cycles amount to forty-nine years. Then, on the tenth day of the seventh month let the trumpet resound. On this, the Day of Atonement, the trumpet blast shall re-echo throughout your land. This fiftieth year you shall make sacred by proclaiming liberty in the land for all its inhabitants. It shall be a jubilee for you....

"Do not make him work as a slave. Rather, let him be like a hired servant or like your tenant, working with you until the jubilee year, when he, together with his children, shall be released from your service and return to his kindred and to the property of his ancestors....

"...He shall nevertheless be released, together with his children, in the jubilee year."

—Leviticus 25: 1, 8–10a, 39b-41, 54

Yet now ... on that day whereon I rose from the dead I grant unto all you that are in torment refreshment for a day and a night for ever. *And all they cried out and said: We bless thee, O Son of God, for that thou hast granted us rest for a day and a night: for better unto us is the refreshment of one day than the whole time of our life wherein we were upon earth...*

—The Apocalypse of Paul, chapter 44
(trans. M.R. James)

Contents

1 The Devil Moved In   1

2 Party with the Devil   23

3 The Party Breaks Up   41

4 The Furnace   55

5 Loves of Thisbe   59

6 Loves of Thisbe, the Prequel   69

7 Abandon Hops   83

8 The Little Black Book of Death   91

9 The Society for Equitable Assurances on Lives and Survivorships   103

10 The Job   115

11 In Which Thisbe Learns of a Minor Detail   123

12 Other Job Seekers   127

13 New Colleagues   137

14 Thisbe Does Not Fear Her Passion   153

15 Cooper is Investigated   159

16 Legal   169

17 Thisbe and Julius   181

18 Thisbe and Dean   187

19 Tourism   193

20 Sridhar   209

21 The Ice Storm   215

22 After the Storm   225

23 After Cooper's Arrest   235

24 Cooper Tells Thisbe   249

25 Abby and Julius   257

26 In Which Thisbe Discovers Something of Interest   265

27 Two Bars in Toronto   271

28 Visiting on Cooper's Street   281

29 A Party at the Fiery Furnace   291

30 Another Visitor   301

31 Dying Changes a Person   307

32 Back to Work   313

33 Black Mass   321

34 The Zombie Love Drug   335

35 Another Death   343

36 A Job Offer   351

37 Journalism   355

38 Maconochie   359

39 Police and Perquisites   367

40 More Journalism   379

41 Gardening   387

42 Julius Ascending   391

43 Pearl Beyond Price   397

44 A Deal is Struck   403

45 A Contract Fulfilled   413

46 Unseasonable Weather   419

47 Cooper's Life Then   427

48 In Which We Take Leave of Old Friends   445

The Last Chapter:
    An Equation of Almost Infinite Complexity   459

Chapter One

The Devil Moved In

When the devil moved in next door, Cooper Smith Cooper had the same question everyone else did: how would it affect the property values? Even Cooper would admit, he was tempted to put the For Sale sign on his lawn too, just like the Grigsons. His neighborhood was a prosperous suburb in the northeast corner of North York, and even though it was well away from the housing projects and the worst parts of Scarborough, it doesn't take much. Mr. Grigson said, "I don't think he's a good influence," and Mrs. Grigson said, "We're happy with what we got for it," which, since they had purchased in 1987 for a small fraction of the current asking price, was undoubtedly true. But Mr. Grigson couldn't resist adding, confidentially, "I think we got out just in time. You should think about it, Cooper."

"Thank you sir," he said. "I will."

As it turned out, their fears were unfounded. The new neighbor soon had a perfect putting green lawn and well-tended begonias, nicer even than Mrs. Mazur's, who is particular. As Mr. Keiter, the English teacher at the high school, said with pardonable pride, "We here in the suburbs are very tolerant, and in this respect perhaps superior to our foremothers and forefathers." If there were odd noises and shriekings from the house at odd hours, they were easy to overlook. After all, the Smythe girl had a rock band that lasted three years, and nothing coming out of Mr. Scratch's house—they had learned to call him that—was as bad as Caitlin Smythe's band playing *Ironic* or the latest bilge by that April Levine.

Cooper would sometimes remember his conversation with Mr. Grigson in the endless years after he took over as the devil. He would change the title on the business card from "Prince of Darkness" to "Prime Minister of Darkness", giving the job a more democratic flavor. Relaxing at a beach resort or waiting for an interview in the greenroom of a television studio, Cooper would wonder whether he had made the right choice. He would become nostalgic and remember the girl he had been in love with when it all happened. He never admitted the possibility that he had been duped. After all, once a decision has been made, what good is regret?

But all that was in the future. Cooper was unemployed when Scratch moved in, and perhaps he should have sold. The lawsuits were dragging on, and he had to borrow money. He also had too much time on his hands. He loafed around the house and jumped any time the phone rang, always thinking it would be his lawyer calling to tell him he had become a millionaire. One Sunday after church, the call came: Goohan, a red-faced Irishman from Trenton, Ont., his lawyer.

"They talked about you in church today. 'How beautiful are the feet of him that cometh over the mountains,' and all that," said Cooper. "I hope this is an early Christmas present."

Goohan, always deadpan, grunted something unintelligible by way of answer and then asked Cooper if he had a job.

"Goohan, you Santa Claus! You're phoning to tell me that I've just become a millionaire and I don't have to work?"

There was not even a pause on the other end. "No, I'm phoning to tell you that you've just *not* become a millionaire. The whole enterprise is collapsing and we're just another creditor in a long line. We're going to get *nada*."

"Nada? What's that?" Cooper trembled with confusion. Did Goohan just say 'Not become a millionaire'? Was that sarcasm?

"Zero. Zilch. Zip. Null set. Naught. Nuffin'. Noodle."

"Noodle?"

"Nothing."

"Ah. I'm not sure I understand."

Like all lawyers, Goohan regarded his clients as dolts. Still, he resented repeating simple facts. He said: "No. Money. For. You."

"Oh." Cooper drummed his fingers. "Ah." It was so unexpected that he had no questions ready, no idea what to say or do next. "Mm." His overwhelming thought was to get off the phone without betraying to his lawyer that he was disappointed. He did not want to appear foolish: to be the sort of person who indulged in frivolous hope for things that did not happen. It occurred to him that an American would get angry, would rant and rave. He toyed with this idea, but said only, "Well. I guess that's that."

"Yes," said his lawyer. He seemed to be expecting something else. "They have no money."

"So there's nothing to get?" Cooper ventured.

"Yes, that's right. Nothing. The whole place has imploded financially. The banks are picking over the flesh now. Suppliers are waiting to drink the blood next. Baby vultures like us have to wait until it's all over, and by then the bones are stripped clean."

"Any marrow?"

Goohan, on the other end of the line, was either rolling his eyes or considering the point. Cooper was just beginning to feel hopeful when Goohan said, in that tone that indicates a considerable amount of eye-rolling has just been completed: "No. No marrow."

"No, I didn't suppose there would be," Cooper said with what he hoped was ease. He was glad that Goohan was not there in person, since he felt that he was blushing. "Well," he said. "Isn't that interesting," he said. "Too bad," he said. "Easy come, easy go,

I suppose," he said. He ventured a little laugh, blasé, unconcerned, nonchalant: "Ha ha." It flopped into the phone like a goony bird landing. He wished Goohan would pick up the conversation. "Well," he said. "I don't suppose there's too much to talk about then."

"Right. Just the matter of my expenses."

Which was how Cooper learned that total failure did not, in the case of the legal profession, result in any discount to the customer.

He did not have time to worry about it, however, because he was leaving for Banff with a particularly interesting snow bunny that afternoon. He had used frequent flyer miles to upgrade their seats. Disappointment, attentive stewardesses, and free alcohol proved to be a bad combination. When they arrived at the hotel, his date went to the bathroom to reapply her makeup. By the time she came out, he had fallen into a deep and discordant slumber. When he awoke alone in the police station that night, he had no recollection of checking in nor even where he was. "Drunk and disorderly," explained a helpful guard.

A call to Goohan got him returned to his hotel the next morning. For the rest of the weekend the concierge tsk-tsked every time he passed, and one of the girls at the front desk giggled. He hoped he had at least been amusing but was too embarrassed to ask. In his grog-beclouded memory, he saw himself singing a great many verses of "The Road to Mandalay" and "Waltzing Matilda", then riding down a curving staircase on a luggage cart. There had been some unpleasantness about a Mountie's hat as well. His date did not return and did not answer calls from his cell phone. By Saturday afternoon it occurred to him that she might be screening her calls, and he tried her from the anonymity of the hotel phone.

"Hello," came her voice. There was the sound of glasses clinking, music playing, and people talking.

"Abby," he said, realizing he was not sure of her name. He checked his pocket hastily for their plane tickets. Yes, he had the right name. She was a journalist, he recalled. "Abby," he said.

"I can't come to the phone right now," said Abby's voice. "Please leave your name and number at the sound of the, um, the tone, and I'll get back to you soon. Okay. Beep. That was the tone. Oh stop it," she said, and giggled.

Cooper began to leave his message: "Abby, I've been looking for you everywhere, I don't know what's going on, our flight leaves tomorrow and–" But her phone had hung up.

He wanted to think that it was just like her to record a new phone message at a bar surrounded by people although he didn't actually know her well enough to judge. Two hours later, he called her on his cell phone again. This time her message had no glasses clinking, no music, no 'Oh stop it'. She's fixed the message, he thought with approval. Then he noticed that this new message sounded in every way identical to her old pre-glasses-clinking message. He concluded that there was a seventy percent chance that she was avoiding him. Despite his loneliness, he found consolation in the fact that he was so knowing and jaded.

He got out to the slopes and did his best to look dashing. He thought he saw Abby going down a hill while he floated in the chairlift above, but she disappeared in a cloud of snow. Later, he saw the same coat on the next hill, but again it disappeared before he could catch up.

On the day they were to leave, he still had not seen nor heard and became worried. He left the plane ticket he had bought for her with the concierge at his hotel. "Her name is Abby, she's about twenty-five years old and very chic, you'll see that right away, very lovely, and she's got that kind of stylish hair with the little swoop where it goes down and…" He found himself telling the concierge a lot about Abby and stopped when he realized he was no longer talking about Abby but about himself and his ruined lawsuit and his previous job that had evaporated out from under him and his time in actuarial school and his job in the slaughterhouse. The concierge was a skinny woman with bright yellow hair and resembled a floor lamp. During Cooper's long disquisition she smiled with the sincerity of a polar bear listening to a seal's description of its mother's tragic childhood in Frobisher Bay, and Cooper realized that she had been on duty the night he arrived.

Cooper did not see Abby again until he was seated on the plane to go home on Sunday night. She arrived late, looking stunning but breathless, and collapsed into the seat beside his.

"Oh, hi," she said.

"Where were you?"

"Oh, I had a wonderful time with you," she said, patting his arm. "Something came up with my, ah, a family situation I needed to take care of. It was really wonderful the way you put up with me. It's just that I'm just so tired, I really need to sleep." She closed her eyes and was silent and untouchable from Banff to Toronto.

On his return he was surprised to discover that his financial situation was dire. He sat at his table drinking beer at eleven o'clock in the morning and discovered that he had enough money for, at most, three months. He had already sold his Range Rover and most of his stocks. He had skipped three mortgage payments. On the computer, he pulled up a long letter he had written to his bank manager, a Mr. Ravi Akkakumarbalapragada, explaining that he would soon be a millionaire, that he appreciated Mr. Akkakumarbalapragada's and the bank's patience, that, in the world of high finance and subtle legal dealings, which was Cooper's life and Mr. Akkakumarbalapragada could not possibly understand, events that seemed to proceed slowly could suddenly unravel with astonishing swiftness, and that if only Mr. Akkakumarbalapragada would wait patiently for a little longer, he would be making a wealthy friend for the bank. The letter, dated four months earlier, oozed condescension.

In front of him now was Mr. Akkakumarbalapragada's letter. Unlike Cooper's, it was polite and proper. It advised him that, as no money was forthcoming, the bank was beginning foreclosure proceedings. Cooper's problem was that there was no money to come forth.

He needed a job. He had put his name in with a few headhunters during the lawsuit, but hadn't been serious. He had had a couple of short jobs as a consultant, working on actuarial tables, but always got bored, started boasting, and got into trouble with management. Work was hard to take seriously with visions of easy cash from judge and jury dancing in his head. Now he sat and stared out the window. Perhaps he could call the last place he had worked. But no, when his boss accused him of not caring about deadlines, he had said, "Good point," and toddled out the door to cheers and curses. Cooper pushed past triumphs aside. He pulled up his résumé and started tinkering with it: perhaps Book Antiqua was the font he needed. From next door came the sound of voices shrieking, or perhaps power tools, as Scratch fired up his recurrent orgy.

Cooper put the house up for sale and spent the next eight weeks working regular hours—eight to six with a break at lunch only to exercise and eat—looking for work. He called friends, relatives, acquaintances, former colleagues. "Rui? Rui, how are you? It's Cooper. Yes, Cooper. No, Cooper. Cooper. Yes, that's right. Rui, I'm just checking in to see if– Cooper. Yes, *that* Cooper. No, no, I never went there. Is this Rui Doniello?" He created three different résumés targeted at the three fields he thought he had the most to offer ("While it has been some time since I have done public relations, I look on this as a long term career opportunity and am willing..."). He made sure he was on file in every company in the city. He posted copies of the résumés on all the internet sites.

When Book Antiqua didn't work, he went to Bookman Old Style and Arial again. Once when he was feeling crazy he tried Corsiva. But by that time, the economy had gone to hell and no one was hiring. No one was buying houses either.

He was not boastful by nature, but he had spoken a little too much about his expectations for the lawsuits. "No, I'm not working, I'm hoping I don't have to do that anymore," he might say, or he would smile smugly and say something like, "We'll just see how it plays out." Now that was all over. Just a few months ago his friends had envied the sheer arbitrariness of his coming wealth. As they learned that he was living on his capital and waiting for his money to come in, they said, with ill-concealed sour grapes, "Cooper should really have a job. It's not good to have nothing to do." They said the same words now that his hopes were dashed, but this time with deep inner satisfaction. They pretended that they had always known nothing good would come of litigation. While they had avoided Cooper before because he was going to be rich, they avoided him now because he was poor, but with happier hearts. Meanwhile, Mr. Akkakumarbalapragada's bank lurked in the night, ready to pounce.

Cooper looked back over the last several months and tried to conclude that he had been given bad advice. When that didn't work, he tried to conclude that all his friends had betrayed him. When that didn't work, he tried a few other things—blaming his lawyer (no good, Goohan had been hopeful but careful to make no promises); blaming his parents (but they had retired to Florida and seemed disappointed to hear he was involved in a lawsuit); blaming his girlfriend (he didn't have one); blaming the world economic situation (promising, but pretentious and too impersonal to be satisfying). He tried fluoride in the water, the Trilateral Commission, the New World Order, the Americans, Islamic fundamentalists, Jews, Nazis, the Bilderbergers, cheeseburgers, foreigners, women,

men, homosexuals, furriers, couriers, lawyers, the government, Walmart, Bill Gates, the Pope, left-wing journalists, conservatives, Bohemians, evangelical Christians, AIDS, repressed homosexual yearnings, unremembered child abuse, television advertisers, radiation from cell phones, starchy diet, and the failure of his personal assertiveness training to render a positive new direction in the level of his personal assertiveness, if that's a fair way to say it. Though theologically imprecise, it was more right than wrong to say that Cooper was an insomniac suffering through another dark night of the soul.

His next door neighbor was planning a party. "You should come over and get to know me," said Scratch. "After all, the devil you know is better than the devil you don't." He laughed, a mild hissing sound: "Tss, tss, tss." He added, "I make that joke every time." Scratch was calm, imperturbable, quiet. He seemed always at ease, always to have time. He was a chubby and ill-defined fellow, short, barrel-chested and broad-stomached. One foot was always covered in an orthopedic shoe and he had a slight hitch in his outward-kicking walk. The top two buttons of his sports shirt were undone so that the grey hair on his chest was on display. He wore gold chains on his neck and glasses that got dark when the sun came out. He smoked strong American cigarettes that brought a tear to the eye and a spot to the lung. A little low class: Cooper could never make up his mind whether Scratch looked like an Italian from Greece, New York, or a Jew from Miami, Florida. But when he spoke, all that was forgotten. He seemed like a centered wise man out of a Hollywood movie, who is always Indian (either type: American or sub-continental) or Oriental, or black: Morgan Freeman, or James Earl Jones without the big voice. He had that same slow insightful way about him so that he might mention something about a seed growing into a tree or the sun rising after it sets, but in just the sort of a way that made you stop and say, "Heavy duty." It was said he had a cricket behind his stove that he would neither hurt nor put outside since the nights were growing colder.

Cooper and Scratch stood in the narrow driveway between the two houses. "I see yours is up for sale," said Scratch.

Since there was a large For Sale sign beside them, Cooper felt it would be impolite to deny this. "A victim of the economy," he said. "Need to downsize."

"Ah," said Scratch. "The downsizing of the economy may reflect the shrinking imagination of a certain kind of business executive."

Cooper had to stop listening for a second to absorb this statement. It occurred to him that he wished that he had said it. But as he and Scratch continued to chat, it turned out that, aside from pithy profundities and a little howling from his basement, Scratch was the best kind of neighbor: a networker. It turned out that he knew someone who knew someone who knew someone who was taking over a division of the Society for Equitable Assurances on Lives and Survivorships—the Seals life insurance company.

Scratch: "It was while we were discussing the removal of risk from life and its relationship to the divorce rate. He said, if I recall, that there were no original thinkers."

"Who did?" asked Cooper, wondering whether risk had in fact been removed from life.

"Oh, I don't think you'd know him. An acquaintance. Always after me for something. His phrase was, 'All they want to do is add a column fifteen digits to the right of the decimal point.' Do you know what that means?"

"Not really. I'm an actuary. Everything we do is statistics. The job is all about adding a new column behind the decimal point." He thought for a moment. "I don't know what being a creative actuary would mean."

"Fraud?" suggested Scratch.

Cooper thought. "Could be," he admitted.

Scratch's tip was good. Despite its quaint name (or perhaps indicated by it), Seals was an ancient and powerful insurance company. A name Scratch gave ("Thournier") got Cooper past the usual Human Resources cerberuses and straight to the department he wanted. They asked for a résumé, and Cooper spent a day working on it. It was not easy. Per Scratch, he was supposed to be a risk-taking actuary, but what did that mean? Chartered accountants got to count money all day—a job replete with sex and glamor. Cooper counted people—no risk in that at all, let alone sex.

As far as Cooper knew, the main actuarial controversy of his day had been settled, with the big companies plunging cheerily into the securitization of life insurance policies—the practice of bundling policies and selling them to some other company to administer. The insurance company's sales people could be sympathetic and kind to their clients to win their business; then their policies were bundled and sold to people who sprinkled ground glass on their Cheerios and bred puppies to be eaten at the Yulin festival, people who could protect insurers from the adverse impact of their reckless generosity. Securitization was immune to business cycles and attractive to outside investors. Unfortunately, this selling of relationships had arrived and blossomed from a tiny eccentricity into universal practice without any help from Cooper.

The only actuarial controversy he had participated in was how to smooth the curves as a cohort started to die off. Actuaries sometimes run into statistical illusions. For example, of the 50,000 people in some demographic group (American coalminers born in the Caribbean, for instance), no one dies at the age of 92 because only four people live into their 90s and they die at the ages of 93, 95, 96, and 101. Statistically, this creates the illusion that Caribbean-American coalminers cannot die at the age of 92. There are a few different ways to fix this, and, though Cooper could no longer remember why, actuaries sometimes got quite hot about using one method instead of another. It was difficult to make the whole teapot-level fooferah into an epic tale of visionary brilliance. After many attempts and several hours, Cooper ended up on the same résumé that he always used for actuarial jobs—but this time, he printed it out in Palatino Linotype.

After faxing in the résumé and letter, he spent some time with the *Moscow Puzzles* ("Tests of Divisibility") and then turned to the depressing chore of paying the bills and balancing his checkbook. The overdraft was almost at its maximum, and there were bills for which there would be no money. Cooper puttered about for an hour cleaning up and watering the plants.

Just when he was thinking he really should have used Arial, the phone rang. Thournier, a woman with a surprisingly youthful voice, wanted him to call for a phone interview the next week. For the first time in months, Cooper felt that the great world of money and jobs was again opening up to him.

Cooper's phone interview was the day of Scratch's party. The interview began as well as phone interviews usually do—which is to say, it was uncomfortable, awkward, and unclear. But things got rolling when Cooper, acting on Scratch's tip, said that he was interested in innovation and new techniques. This seemed to perk some interest on the other end of the line, and he was asked to elaborate. Cooper mentioned his curving methodology and how it could fix those tricky end-of-life calculations. There were snotty chuckles, and Cooper realized that he was playing into his worst stereotype—another actuary buffing up the fifteenth decimal place. He changed tack: computer modeling, chaos theory, stochastic analysis.

"An electron," he explained, "cannot be said with certainty to be in any exact place at one time. However, we can say with certainty that it is in a general area. This is what we mean by stochastic analysis. We don't work with electrons, but in actuarial science, the goal is to find enough stochastic slices of time to overlay, one on top of the other, to rule out certain periods of time. As each stochastic band is overlaid, more of the window of the lifespan is eliminated, and we can find a precise time of death. So for instance, people live anywhere from a few seconds to, on the outside, 121 years. But chain smokers, paradoxically, live from thirteen and a half to ninety-six." It occurred to him that he was not sure what the word 'stochastic' actually meant.

"Why thirteen and a half?" came a voice from the phone.

"Simple. We have not been able to find a chain smoker younger than thirteen and a half. I don't know how old you are if I know you're a chain smoker. But I know that you're at least thirteen. I know you're not ninety-seven. If I can add to the list of facts that you've been in the army, I know that you're at least fifteen and a half if you're male, seventeen if you're female."

Voices on the phone mumbled: "But the recruiting age is…"

"He means people lie about their age and join despite being officially too young, eh?"

"Ah."

The mumbling pleased Cooper: someone at least was listening. He continued. "Of course some of these things are definitional. If you change the definition of chain smoker slightly, a kid named Artie Pernalli becomes the youngest chain smoker at eleven years old. And if you change it just a little bit more—loosen it, a few less cigarettes—there's a forty-two-way tie at the age of eight among children from Montreal and Gertrude Faluken of Eyebrow, Saskatchewan."

Cooper was pleased that he was able to cast such trivial points in terms that made them sound original and interesting. There was nothing in what he described that was not already built into the actuarial tables of every insurance company. He had just used five-dollar words to make his pedestrian observations sound original. But now the female voice named Thournier called him on this.

"Cooper, this is all very well, but I don't see how calling it stochastic analysis makes it any different from what every actuarial table everywhere has always done. You cut the population into demographics and overlay those on age cohorts, and you get a good picture of what your risk levels are. This is all junior actuary stuff. What's different?"

Cooper, like many sons of the middle class, had grown up coddled and did not have practice responding to direct challenges. He panicked. In one of his short consulting engagements, a brilliant tiny Sikh named Rajiv (but who, for reasons Cooper never learned, was called Pablo by everyone) had propounded certain original and far-fetched theories, much to the amusement of Cooper and his coworkers. Now, rather than admit that he had merely been spiffing up old ideas with coats of fresh blather, Cooper took the irrevocable step. He passed on Pablo's claims as his own. "The difference is that with the information available to us now, we can make enough overlays to tell you when people will die."

"What? Within what time frame? With what accuracy? What's our risk?"

"You heard me. When they die. Period."

"When who dies?"

"I haven't built the computer model yet. But I'm telling you that your models are out of date. With the Internet, with one-to-one marketing that Internet companies use, with online banking and transactions, we can harvest information heretofore" (heretofore? Cooper asked himself) "impossible to get. We can tell you, by individual, the exact day any particular person is scheduled to die."

"How?"

"It's an equation. It's all just equations.

"What do you mean?"

"I'm talking about the Holy Grail." Holy Grail? Cooper asked himself.

There was the same question on the other end: "Did he just say 'Holy Grail'?"

"I'm saying that, if you give me a team and the computers to do it, I can create the equation. The factors are out there. We need to put them together. It can be done. I can do it."

"By individual. The exact day any particular person will die."

"That's right."

"But that would take an equation of infinite complexity. There aren't enough data points in the world to support it. And what about unmeasurable factors, preferences and things like that, that get people into trouble? What about simple things like just because no one has died because of factor x doesn't mean no one ever will? No one's been killed with hotdog tongs, let's say—"

"Now wait a minute—"

"—but that doesn't mean that one day some fluke mishap won't end the life of some poor slob."

Other voices joined in: "What about randomness?"

"There was a murder with hotdog tongs six years ago on Manitoulin Island."

"Really?"

"How did they do it?"

"It seems that there was this old-fashioned restaurant-pharmacy, and the owner liked to breed gerbils…"

"What I want to know is why you know about this murder."

But the hotdog tong murder story was interrupted. "And what about evolutionary factors? People are changing. Our children are taller than us, and we were taller than our parents, who were taller than their grandparents. When you're casting into the future, you can't possibly anticipate things like that."

"And besides…"

"I want to hear about the hotdog tongs!"

Thournier cut through the yacking. "Just because all the statistics say 'Mr. X is expected to die on Thursday afternoon,' that doesn't mean that Mr. X won't die within two weeks either way."

Cooper, who had been trying to interrupt for some time, finally succeeded. "Now Ms. Thournier. Everyone," he said. There was quiet. "You've all said a lot of things. I've listened patiently, and now I think it's time that I get a chance to respond. I think that's only fair." An older actuary he knew, Ferdie Meisenthal, had said these things when his idiotic ideas were assailed, and Ferdie's phrases rolled out of Cooper as if he had invented them himself. He had always hated Ferdie Meisenthal. "Flukes and randomness bedevil any statistical discipline. There are ways you can accommodate them, but will they catch you up once in a while? Sure. That doesn't invalidate the whole exercise. If our actuarial tables were five percent more accurate—even one percent more accurate!—how much would we save? Millions. Billions. When a new application comes in, we shouldn't just assign a risk level. We should know that date when we set the prices. The real date. The trajectories we're talking about are so far-ranging that the tiniest improvements result, over time, in huge financial rewards. Huge!" He had forgotten the point he needed to make next, and so belabored the current one. Then he remembered the other thing he wanted to say. "There's no such thing as an equation of infinite complexity. That's an illusion caused by our limited perspective. Every equation has a finite number of factors."

Someone at a distance from the phone was definitely blowing a raspberry. It was suddenly cut short.

A new voice came on the line, Indian, heavily accented: "The argument," it said, bouncing up and down as voices from the subcontinent often do, "is whether the equation is an equation of infinite complexity or an equation of *almost* infinite complexity." Every voice on the other end of the phone hushed. Cooper had heard the voice earlier during the call. This was Sridhar, the mathematician in the crew. His small clarification had momentarily been interpreted as an endorsement.

Cooper, feeling that he had come dangerously close to making himself a bad joke, grasped at this straw. "Exactly. Exactly right. An equation of almost infinite complexity. That's what we're building. There will be modules for cultural factors, hereditary factors, heuristic factors. There will be randomizations, which, we hope, we'll be able to keep to a minimum. It won't be easy. But that's what I'm offering. An equation of almost infinite complexity." Top that, Pablo, thought Cooper.

There were shufflings and mumblings coming to Cooper through the phone, but nothing he could discern clearly. There was a sudden utter silence, as if the other end had hung up. Cooper could not believe it. He stared at the phone. He shook it and held it to his ear. Nothing at all. It was as if it were a cell phone that had been turned off. Just when he thought he had been getting somewhere, they hung up on him. He cursed Pablo silently. He said aloud with disgust: "An equation of almost infinite complexity. What crap."

The dead phone suddenly came to life. "Sorry, we had you on mute. Did you say something, Cooper?" came one of the voices.

"No, nothing," stuttered Cooper, terrified.

"I thought you said 'An equation of almost infinite complexity, what crap.'"

"Oh. Um, no." Cooper thought. "A little side conversation. Nothing important." He was blushing.

"We're discussing something over here. We'll be another minute."

"Okay," said Cooper.

"But Thisbe, I thought he said—" came another voice, cut off suddenly as the mute button was again pressed and the phone went dead in Cooper's hand.

Cooper was in an agony of suspense. They had heard him call his own presentation 'crap'. How could he have forgotten that office conference phones had mute buttons? He spent long sorry minutes meditating on the importance of this interview. His mind raced. He knew that he was a good actuary. He would be useful to Thournier. Why had he risked everything to babble about Pablo's half-cocked science fiction? He had laughed at it just a few months before. He needed a job. If he could write Akkakumarbalapragada and tell him that he was employed, the foreclosure proceedings might slow down. Now he wouldn't even get a face-to-face interview.

The phone came alive again with a pop that made Cooper's ear smart. Thournier's voice said, "We would like you to come in for an interview. I know this is short notice, but tomorrow is the best day for us. We'll want a presentation of how you'll achieve this 'equation of almost infinite complexity.' " She said it as if the words disgusted her. "A project plan, high level, nothing too detailed. I think it should contain a timeline, an outline of the modules you think we need to create, what resources you think you'll need to achieve this..." She was angry. Cooper had won. He assured Thournier that tomorrow was no problem and got off the phone.

Cooper swelled happiness. He would write to the bank immediately. He would write to Pablo and thank him if he could find him again. He would send Scratch a thank you card as well. He felt he wanted to dance, to sing, to find someone short and ugly and punch him in the head, to find a beautiful woman and kiss her smack on the lips.

There was just one problem. Unless God performed a miracle, Cooper hadn't a hope in hell of delivering the equation.

Be that as it may, he created his presentation easily enough. He read it over and felt that he was done with it. He went to the bathroom, then watched a documentary about a woman who wrote poems about her cats, her expenses paid by grants the government gave to artists. Some time during the documentary, he thought of something else he might say and went back to the presentation to add it. Looking at the slide, he realized that what he thought was a single bullet point was in fact a better way of thinking about one of his topics, and he began to rewrite the slide. As it turned out, changing the slide meant he had to change the slides that led into it, and also the slide after it. He was almost done when he realized that his entire new approach was susceptible to a simple criticism that rendered it invalid. His initial draft had been correct. He tried to undo his changes, but realized that his backup version had been overwritten by the latest incorrect version. Then he read it over again and it all fell into place as it was. He was ready. He could relax.

Feeling mildly exhilarated, he decided to walk around the block. It was a cool autumn afternoon with the threat of rain in the air. That was all right: he still had a good trenchcoat to wear to his interview the next day. The second Mrs. Rulen—mousy, pale and flat-chested as the first had been—stood on her front lawn bagging leaves. She wore loose-fitting jeans and dirty yellow gloves with red flowers on them. Her wiener dog barked at Cooper but did not attack. Cooper bent down and put out a nervous hand for the dog to sniff. It growled. Cooper put the hand in his pocket.

"Oh, Lindsay, be quiet," said the second Mrs. Rulen.

"Hello," said Cooper.

Lindsay was also the name of the first Mrs. Rulen: "A real female dog," explained the second Mrs. Rulen. She smiled as if she had been naughty. Cooper, uneasily focused on the growling dog, could not quite catch the joke but smiled anyway.

He continued his walk. A car pulled up beside him, slowed down, and then stopped. He was always a fearful of muggers, but he saw that he had nothing to worry about. The car was an expensive foreign model, and as the passenger side window slid down to permit the driver to speak to him, he saw that a lovely young woman was the car's only occupant.

"Hello," he said.

"Hi," said the woman. "I'm wondering if you could tell me how to get to–" and she named the street on which Cooper lived.

"Sure," he said. "You need to turn around. You just passed it. Do you know if you wanted to be east or west of Wallingford?" It occurred to Cooper that she was somehow familiar.

She did not know.

"I think the numbers to the left start at 486. So if you're less than 486, you want to go right."

She bestowed upon him a smile that dazzled. Her eyes were green, her hair a dark brown. "Thanks!" she said. She pulled into the driveway directly in front of him, stopped, noticed he was facing her, granted him another glorious smile and wave of her hand (thin, elegant), put her car in reverse. She drove off.

Cooper walked home with a lighter step, feeling that if only it had been raining and he had taken a tap-dancing lesson or two, he might give Gene Kelly a run for his money. Giving directions was not exactly the same thing as saving a fair damsel from a fire-breathing dragon, but it gave him a feeling that any dragons who happened around had better watch out. He had a serious interview that he was already prepared for and beautiful women in fancy cars were slowing down to ask his advice. Things were picking up.

As he came around the block, he noticed that the beautiful woman's car was parked almost directly outside his house. It was all he could do to keep from running the rest of the way down the street. But when he got to his home, it was quiet. Instead, he noticed that Scratch's driveway was full, and he remembered: Scratch was having a party.

Cooper had made up his mind not to go but now decided otherwise. After all, he had promised Scratch that he would bring a salad. He went upstairs to make sure that he had clothes for tomorrow. He checked the refrigerator and found a limp and discolored head of Boston lettuce. Picking at it, he was able to salvage some tolerable leaves and threw them into a metal mixing bowl. Some crumbling croutons were in the pantry, so he added those. There was a surprisingly small amount. He found that everything went bad before he got around to eating it. He added a few more lettuce leaves and covered them with salad dressing to disguise the discolored bits. To keep it fresh, he covered the salad bowl with a shower cap taken from the ski resort hotel. If he left the salad on the counter with the shower cap over it, he could probably make it to the living room before anyone knew that he had brought it.

His work as a chef done, he sat down to his presentation to check it one more time. It made no sense at all. He could not follow any of his own thoughts, though he recognized them as words he had just written. He began to panic. He started a completely new presentation, realized he was too upset to do the detailed work, and concentrated on creating the correct structure. When he looked up again, an hour had passed and it was time to go to Scratch's. He decided not to go. He stood up, walked around the room, and sat down again. He realized that he had promised to bring the salad. Could he bring the salad over and then simply leave? He decided that this would be rude. Besides, the party would clear his head. He realized that he had an opportunity to chat with a beautiful woman. He went to the window to check for her car. It was still there. He was not ready for his interview, but that was all right. He could go to Scratch's for an hour or even two and start fresh with plenty of time left before tomorrow.

Chapter Two

Party with the Devil

Scratch and Cooper were separated by a driveway only wide enough for a single car, the houses having been built in the 1930s before the standard lot sizes had been established. He made his way around the tightly parked cars. His salad looked a little pathetic, but there was nothing for it. He would abandon it in the kitchen as quickly as possible and hope that someone else brought a nice salad that people might confuse with his. He rang Scratch's bell. Through the wooden door chimes tinkled out "You are my sunshine, my only sunshine." A loud shriek came from somewhere below his feet in the basement.

A delicate man with long yellow hair, greasy and lank to his shoulders, opened the door. He wore beige walking shorts and a black T shirt with faded sparkly letters on the front that said "Pardyhardy!" On his feet were heavy brown Kodiak work boots with a green patch and untied laces. "Yeah?" he said, and when he opened his mouth, his teeth pointed in several different directions. "Who the hell are you?" The evening was cold, and his breath, smelling of peanut butter and beer, smogged the air.

Cooper was taken aback. "I—That is—um," he bumbled. If the man was strange, the house he stood inside was stranger. Scratch's house and Cooper's had been built to the same plan, yet it was nothing like his. Instead of a small alcove and a narrow passage with a dining room on one side and living room on the other,

Scratch had taken out the interior walls and the doorway opened into a great room of magnificent proportions, with massive pillars that went all the way up into the second storey. Though Cooper saw nothing unusual about the exterior roof line, the ceiling inside was a curved arc above the pillars. The corridor between the pillars was marked by candles, so that Cooper felt most as if he had opened the door on a church.

But instead of saints or crosses, a full-sized bronze statue of a naked woman stood in the alcove. Her form was not sensual to Cooper's eye since though the sculptor had made the general shape of a woman, he had left his thumbprints everywhere so that the skin was not smooth. She was standing on one leg, bent way back and holding a bow, which she appeared to be aiming directly above her at the ceiling. Although there could be no mistake, Cooper looked behind to see if he had come to the right place. There were nothing but ordinary suburban houses separated by their narrow driveways. Inside, people were milling about, some with drinks in their hands.

"You coming in or what?" said the man in the door. "Leaves are blowing in."

Cooper went inside and introduced himself. "Cooper Smith Cooper. From next door. Mr. Scratch invited me." He held his salad low and to the side to prevent anyone from looking at it too closely.

The doorkeeper grunted.

Feeling brave, Cooper said, "And you are?"

"Gormley," said the doorkeeper.

"Well then," said Cooper, meaning by this to put Gormley in his place.

Although he had come only a few minutes after the time Scratch appointed, the party was already well under way. Over Gormley's shoulder he could see some people he recognized and some he did not. Had he gotten the time wrong? "Am I late?" he asked.

"I don't know. When did you have your last period?" asked Gormley, who then dissolved into an ugly mass of laughter, his pale face crinkling so that it resembled a ball of tinfoil someone has tried to smooth out, his teeth as crinkly as the rest of his face. "Urf urf urf!"

Cooper edged past the still chortling Gormley to the spectacular interior. The first order of business was to get rid of his incriminating salad. He found a great wooden door on the side of the huge central hall and opened it. The kitchen behind shocked him in its suburban ordinariness. It looked exactly like his own kitchen, including a similar model gas stove from the 1980s and the wood veneer cabinets. Like the great room, it was crowded with people. Cooper said hello to Mrs. Mazur and the second Mrs. Rulen, who were talking about a sermon, and also about sugar beets.

Cooper saw Scratch, dressed in a black shirt and brown pants, gold chains hanging around his neck, bullet head bobbing and nodding. He was skipping from counter to oven to sink in the extreme stages of preparation. Cooper pushed his sad little shower-capped bowl onto a counter beside a magnificent piece of painted clay pottery, filled to the brim with some walnut, apple, cheese, strawberry, and lettuce creation. Gesturing vaguely in the direction of both, he called to Scratch: "I've left a salad."

Scratch, distracted, waved. Then, noticing it was Cooper, walked over. Cooper preempted him: "I had no idea things were getting started so early. So many people," he said by way of compliment.

Scratch shook Cooper's hand. "Thanks so much for bringing the salad. I was worried there wouldn't be enough. But if the many bring a few, their few becomes a many." He picked up the little metal bowl.

"It's not much..." said Cooper, turning bright red.

"Oh, I'm sure it's just—lovely," said Scratch, peeling back a bit of the shower cap. The salad had settled during Cooper's trip between the houses, and covered only the bottom part of the bowl. It appeared large enough to feed no more than two hungry gerbils and a hamster, assuming one of the gerbils was on a diet and the other had recently had his stomach stapled.

A pockmarked man appeared, vaguely familiar to Cooper. He was fortyish, short, broad-shouldered, with a high forehead made prominent by a receding hairline. He was not good-looking. "Ah, more good things from the earth," he said ebulliently. He took the bowl from Scratch and removed the shower cap.

"Mr. Cooper just brought this," Scratch said, as the man was saying,

" 'When the coffee is drunk, only the dregs remain.' Parmenides."

"Julius," said Scratch, introducing the pockmarked man to Cooper. "Came with Thisbe."

They stood together, contemplating Cooper's salad. There was no disguising its poverty.

"Fresh vegetables," Julius said, "are proof that there is no God." Cooper goggled at him a little. This was not usual party conversation. Where had he seen Julius before? "Vegetables have no flavor. They go bad before you can eat them. They do not delight the tongue with tactile interest. Many grow underground, where worms are their playmates. There is nothing comely that we should look upon them. And yet, they are required for good health." He took the metal bowl from Scratch's hand and swung it about, holding it up for contemplation as if he were Hamlet and the bowl Yorick. "And why are vegetables necessary for health? Shall I tell you?" He took a leaf of greasy lettuce between his fingers. It flopped like an old dishrag. He threw it into the sink with fussy disgust. "Vegetables are required so that all shitting which must needs be done, shall be done. They clean," his voice dropped an octave, "the bowel." He took the bowl and swung it with a long arm, dumping all its contents into a garbage can with a flourish.

He handed the empty bowl back to Scratch, who handed it to Cooper, who, red-faced, placed it back on the countertop beside the painted clay pot. "Vile," Julius said. He took the shower cap, placed it on his own head, and swept magnificently from the room.

Cooper and Scratch looked at one another. "Julius," said Cooper.

"Julius," said Scratch. He began to say something else, but Mrs. Mazur came by and Scratch interrupted himself to greet her. She said, "The service was wonderful."

"Thank you," said Cooper, uncomprehending. Service? All he had done was left the salad on the counter. But he said, "I love walnuts with apples and cheese, don't you?"

"Because there's someone here you should meet," Scratch was telling him.

"Oh?" said Cooper. "By the way, I talked to the people at Seals. Thanks for the tip." But Scratch had already turned to talk to a woman Cooper did not recognize, then bustled off to respond to a beep from the oven. Cooper, interested in whom he should be meeting, caught up and asked, "Who should I meet?" He was hoping some of Scratch's life insurance friends would be there in case tomorrow's interview didn't go well.

"Hm? Oh," said Scratch. "Well, have you met Death?"

"What's that?" Cooper said. He wasn't sure he had heard.

"Death."

Cooper was not sure he was going to enjoy Scratch's friend, whom he imagined was a skinhead with a motorcycle and an arm full of tattoos. Goths made Cooper uncomfortable, although most of them were gentle and weak. Or perhaps this Death was punkrocker who had changed his name. A friend of Cooper's once followed a band whose lead singer had legally changed his name to Johnny I Shitforbrains.

Scratch said, "Death. Gormley. I don't think you've met him before."

"Gormley. You mean the man at the door? What's his first name?"

But now Scratch was talking to the second Mrs. Rulen. "Yes, I agree about the punch. It's actually your recipe, couldn't you tell? But I didn't have cointreau, so I used…" Cooper followed Scratch as he wandered through the kitchen. He handed out trays of *hors d'oeuvres* and sent some guests to the nooks and crannies of his home.

"The house is impressive," said Cooper. "I like what you've done with it."

"I had a decorator," said Scratch. "But you were asking me about something?"

Cooper said, "People I should be meeting. You said something about that."

"Did I? I was thinking about what Thomas says about the orders of angels. First there are the seraphim, who are the highest and burn with love for God. Then come the cherubim, who know God with perfect knowledge. Do you know what this means?" asked Scratch. He opened the door to the dining room. Cooper again was amazed. Although the room connected to the kitchen through the same door his dining room did, this room looked like something out of a modernist catalogue. The floor was all in flat black tile. There was a severe brushed steel table, surrounded by asymmetrical black leather chairs, each a unique design. Above the table was a light fixture of thin pastel-colored ropes hanging from the ceiling, each with a tiny pinprick light in the end. The table was full of Cooper's neighbors and others, some awkward and some relaxed, some eating with chopsticks, others with black metal knives and forks.

"Thomas is saying," said Scratch, "that love is greater than knowledge."

Cooper, taking in the room around him, had no idea what Scratch was talking about.

Cooper, having lost Scratch, looked about for the lovely woman without finding her. As he stood in the dining room, there came the howling noise that so often rose from Scratch's basement. It began suddenly, an almost inhuman wailing at a high, intense pitch, hoarse yet piercing. There was no lead in. It was as if someone had dropped the needle on a record player in the middle of a heavy metal guitar solo, except unlike heavy metal records this anguish sounded as though it was made by a human being. The sound got under Cooper's skin so that he wanted it to stop, he wanted to put his hands over his ears and keep it out. In fact, the second Mrs. Rulen was doing just that. Cooper was reminded of a new mother he had known who said, "Kids' crying doesn't bother me, but when it's your own kid, you can't stand it."

Cooper had left the kitchen, walked through the dining room, and come into the room of pillows and silks that he decided to call the living room. Everyone—Scratch's house had filled up with guests—seemed to have the same fingers-on-the-blackboard reaction to the scream that he had. People were stopped, listening, frowning, annoyed, upset, nervous. Then, just as it had begun, it stopped.

The house was quiet for several seconds, so quiet that it was possible to hear the cricket chirping behind Scratch's stove, its high-pitched voice chanting, "Freeze dry, freeze dry, freeze dry." Everyone was straining to hear if there would be a follow on, another scream, a cry for help, a voice, the sound of death... Nothing came. Then, from below them, a slam, a whacking, and the buk, buk, buk of someone walking slowly up a staircase. Cooper, who, no matter what Scratch had done to the place, had some idea where things were, pushed his way over to the kitchen just in time to see Scratch appearing through the cellar door he knew would be there.

"I hope that didn't bother anybody," he said to the room generally. "It's an old house, and some of the mechanicals get a little noisy now and then."

"What the hell was that? Your washing machine?" said a man Cooper did not recognize.

"Furnace," said Scratch. "Old and footsore, noisome, an old soldier ordered to the wars again but remembering still the promise that his last battle was the one that would secure the lasting peace."

The party-goers stared at Scratch.

"It complains when it comes on." Spoken with Scratch's easy calm, the tension dissipated, and everyone began to talk again.

Cooper wandered about. Scratch's taste was so consistent in its inconsistency that it shocked Cooper. Every room was perfectly what it was—medieval hall, 1980s kitchen, ultramodern dining room, Asian parlor—yet none of the rooms spilled over into each other. There was no linoleum in the great hall, no candles in the Scandinavian dining room, no brushed steel in the Sears catalog kitchen.

"Another Jane Austen movie, *Mansfield Park*?" Mr. Keiter, who taught English at the local high school, was saying. His house neighbored Cooper's on the other side.

Julius, no longer wearing the shower cap, said, "Whenever I've got a few spare minutes, I've always got my nose in Jane Austen's latest."

"*Pride and Prejudice*," said Keiter, pompous as a Women's Studies professor talking to a grandfather who has admitted a preference for summer dresses. "*Mansfield Park*."

"With Jayne Mansfield and Brad Park," said Julius.

"*Sense and Sensibility*," intoned Keiter.

"*Fridge and Frigidity*," said Julius, unintimidated. He leaned over and took in the small circle of people listening. "Her new one," he explained.

"*Emma*," continued Keiter.

But Julius was rising to his theme: "*Fridge and Frigidity*. Jane Austen takes on miscegenation. It starts with the Fridge—that's William Perry, remember, defensive lineman for the Chicago

Bears, big three hundred pound black guy—and he's asking Emma Thompson,"—imitating an African-American—" 'Woman, you got any mo' dis heah fried chicken?' And she says,"—here Julius affected a high squeaky British female voice—" 'Yes. It's in the Frigidaire!' But," and he switched to his usual speaking voice, "she's really disgusted, see, because he's such a fatty."

The others at the table responded. "Oh, I like Emma Thompson. She was so good in *Sister Act*." The new conversation sent everyone off after movies.

"Do you like Jane Fonda?"

"No."

"She was good in *Barbarella*," contributed Mr. Rulen.

"Yes, you can't take that away from her…"

Julius continued, appearing only slightly amused so that Cooper—who did not know Jane Austen from J. K. Rowling—was not sure whether he was completely joshing. "Well, *Fridge and Frigidity*. It's Jane Austen's tragic story of how a glandular eating disorder tears lives apart. But there's a psychological aspect as well. The tragedy is, the more she repulses him, the more he's driven to eat. But the more he eats, the more she repulses him. In the BBC version, the Fridge is played by George Foreman…"

"There's a very nice wog as manages the bank at Parkway," mumbled Mr. Rulen. "Polite. That's the British influence." He scratched the side of his nose. "Name is completely unpronounceable, fifty-seven syllables, as bad as the Spaniards…"

Cooper turned from the conversation to find Scratch beside him with a tray. "I don't follow movies myself," Cooper said by way of apology. "But what a room," he told Scratch. "Wowie."

"Feng shui, actually," said Scratch. "Or at least, that's my excuse when things are misplaced. Tss. Tss." He winked generally and began handing buns to the people in the room. "Croissant?" he asked. "Shrimp coming as well." He paused, and said to one of Cooper's neighbors, "You become what you hate. That may be the secret hidden in the saying, 'Love your enemies.'" Scratch turned to Cooper and said, "You should meet Thisbe too."

"Thisbe Two?"

"Yes, Thisbe–" and he said a second name, but Cooper could not hear it as a roar of laughter came from around the table. He looked to see if he could pick up the joke but could not. Julius looked only mildly amused, though it seemed that people were laughing at something he had said. Cooper turned to ask Scratch for Thisbe's surname, but his host was already talking to someone else and then retreated back to the kitchen.

Cooper wandered back to the great hall with its candelabra and stone. He found the first Mrs. Rulen, a painted wonder of cosmetic surgery, with skin screwed so tight behind her ears that her face was as smooth as the face of an over-inflated blow-up doll. Her chest had formerly been a flat prairie, as inviting to a lover as the strip of the TransCanada highway that goes from Manitoba to Alberta, which is to say, the sort of place where you go as fast as you can and still fall asleep. Now it had all the topographical wonders of an expensive mountain resort. Cooper looked at her undeniable attractions and thought how foolish were those who claimed that love was more than sex. For he felt quite tenderly toward the first Mrs. Rulen—she of the formerly mousy brown hair, formerly flat chest and formerly sagging face, who had been left by Mr. Rulen for the equally timid brown-haired spinster down the street, now the second Mrs. Rulen. The first Mrs. Rulen, made noble by her status as victim, was made notable by her status as D-cup, bleached into blondeness and liposuctioned to delectability—and yet, Cooper knew that he did not care for her, would never care for her, and that, if she had remained her sagging and mousy self, he would not feel tenderly toward her in the least. He had not had an affair with her, thinking he would do much better when his money came in. Now that it was not coming in, it occurred to him that perhaps she might be as good getting as it got.

Then he saw the woman he had come for: the woman of the green-eyed smile and the foreign car. He didn't know her name. In the great room, reaching up to light a high candle, a petite yet well-developed female, lithe of limb and luxurious of lash, with unmistakable wide green bright eyes that shone with candlelight. Even at a distance, the eyes reminded Cooper of the mint jelly that had accompanied his lamb chop the night before. She wore smart business clothes: tight slacks and a white blouse with a tailored paisley vest. Just as the baby boomer, who excoriated his father for his gas-guzzling status-seeking Cadillac in 1972, discovered a deep appreciation of the safety, four wheel drive, and sheer practicality of a Hummer in 2012, so Cooper, who a minute before had pish-tushed true love in his heart, found himself smitten on a nearly first-sight basis. It was to be his tragedy that he remained true to this love through each sling and arrow that an outrageous fortune would chuck his way. He said: "Yowza."

The first Mrs. Rulen accepted this as a compliment due her.

"Hello," said Cooper stepping past her to the green-eyed beauty. "Can I help you with that?" For the new woman was not tall enough to reach the high candelabra. Cooper, much taller, took the flaming punk from her and lit the wick.

She thanked him, then did a double take. "Well," she said. "This is the second time tonight you seem to be here just when I need you."

Cooper, feeling a deep inward satisfaction that she had recognized him, pretended that he was just now recognizing her. "Hm? Oh! Oh, I remember. Directions. The BMW."

"Yes, that's right. I should have picked you up."

Cooper relished the unsavory associations of the phrase while pretending not to notice them. Was she flirting? "Oh, I always enjoy a walk outdoors. Fitness, you know," he said. "But I had no idea you were coming here."

"Have you been here before?"

"Been here before?" he asked. Then he understood. "Oh! At first, when you asked if I'd been here before, I thought you meant that feeling that the French call, for reasons you have to speak French to understand, *déjà vu*. I don't speak French, do you?" Then he said, "No, this is my first time. I really like what he's done with the place."

"It means 'already seen.' You're familiar, though. Why are you familiar? Were you at the service?"

"That's the third time someone has mentioned service. Do I look like the waiter?" Cooper said, bantering.

It turned out that this was the right thing to do because she answered quietly, with a note of apology, "This is the first time I've actually been over here. He used to have a church on Church Street. Storefront place. Downtown. You don't call it a service then?"

"Oh," said Cooper, seeing the light. "I don't know. I'm Catholic. We call it Mass. But what do you mean, his church?"

"Didn't you know? That's what he does for a living. He's a preacher."

"He's a what?"

"A priest, is that the right word then? He runs a church."

"What do you mean he runs a church? Who's 'he'? Scratch?"

"Just so. He runs a little church. The lease ran out on Church Street, and it was very small, so he's started doing it right here. I don't know for how long, I've missed a lot. Of course with the open house following the service tonight, it's a little more crowded than usual. Mrs. Garfield—that's her there—" and she pointed to a lady Cooper did not know, "got me coming. She was one of his first members. I think you call them members. I'm new to churchgoing myself. What's it like being Catholic?"

"It's all right," Cooper said, though he had been Catholic so long he had not thought that question could be asked, let alone answered. He was thinking of Rui Doniello, whose father used to make fun of Protestants. Cooper found it hard to tell them apart from Catholics, though he recalled someone mentioning that Presbyterians insisted on crucifixes without any Jesus on them. He supposed it had something to do with keeping the wood useful for building tables and rabbit hutches and such.

She was saying, "I've tried a lot of things, but never going to church before." Looking at her, with her lovely outline and her lesbian vest, Cooper could see what she meant. Since he, like most of his generation, felt vaguely that the primary purpose of religion was to prevent sex, he was somewhat disappointed that he was meeting her just when she was trying it. Then she said, "Sometimes I worry that church is just another enthusiasm, like all the others."

He didn't quite know how to take this, but it sounded hopeful. He asked, "Does he have a Jesus on his cross?"

"I don't remember," she said, "I think so. Why?"

"He may be a Catholic after all," Cooper said, with an air of authority.

"Oh, I think he is. Or wait. Are they different from Protestants? You always hear them mentioned together."

But Cooper was on firm ground here. "No. No, there's a big difference."

"What is it?"

Here, Cooper had to admit, he was stumped. "Rui's father used the word 'heretical,' but I don't know what hair has to do with it."

"Does that mean the funny haircuts those monks used to have? Where they make a bald spot in the middle?"

"You know, I think it does. In Latin. Only come to think of it, I don't know if he meant Protestants or Catholics were. Heretical, I mean. He was a Catholic."

"Oh," she said. Since they had exhausted their total store of knowledge, the woman changed tack: "Well, you should really come next time. I'm sure there's a Jesus on the cross, a big silver one now that I think of it. We can ask to see it. He's a very interesting speaker, I can't get over how much I've..." She went on about Scratch. Cooper heard none of what she said. He watched the tip of her long nose, which moved up and down of its own accord, just a little, when she spoke. It was charming. She gave off a delightful odor, of soap and scent and shampoo and just a hint of the intoxicating sweat of a young woman. He found himself wishing that she were paying less attention to how interesting Scratch was and more attention to him. There was more in her talking, he thought with bitterness, than admiration for an "interesting speaker." But he felt better when she lowered her voice and, for the second time, took him into her confidence. "It's because of Mr. Scratch that I've decided on a new plan. I haven't told it to anybody yet. But I feel so strong when I'm near him..."

But they were interrupted by Julius, who arrived clapping a familiar hand on the woman's shoulder. "Hey, hey," he said.

Cooper was disappointed. Of course when you meet a beautiful woman and begin a nice conversation, it means that she has a boyfriend.

"Oh, I'm sorry," Julius said. "Julius." He held out his hand to Cooper.

"Cooper. I'm Cooper," he said, limply shaking Julius's hand. "You're the Jane Austen fan," he said, trying to preempt any conversation about his salad.

Julius laughed.

"Cooper?" said the beautiful woman, looking quizzically at Cooper. "Jane Austen fan?" she said, giving Julius the same look.

"My heroine. Jungle Jane herself. Inventor of the Austin-Healey roadster."

The woman regarded him with skepticism.

Somewhere Mr. Rulen was saying, "It's not that they can't work, mind you..."

"Cooper!" came a new voice. "Well, Cooper, how are you?" It was Keiter, patting Cooper's back with phony old-friend jocularity. They were not old friends, but rather neighbors who did their best to torment one another. When Cooper was away on vacation one summer, Keiter trained his new puppy to do its business on Cooper's front lawn. When Keiter had friends over for a Sunday afternoon barbecue, Cooper spent the afternoon splitting firewood in his backyard with a high-decibel chainsaw. Keiter had double incentive to say hello to Cooper now: to meet the pretty stranger and annoy his neighbor at the same time. "Hello, Mr. Keiter," Cooper said. "Mr. Keiter, this is–" but Cooper realized that he did not know the name of the woman.

"Cooper? Cooper, would you come here for a minute?" Scratch came bustling out and took Cooper by the arm. "Excuse us, please," he said.

Cooper, who had just been about to learn the name of the beautiful woman, hid his disappointment and did his best to be polite. "Yes sir," he said. He was looking over his shoulder, but the woman was now laughing and talking to Keiter and Julius and did not appear to notice that Cooper was leaving.

"Cooper, if you could help me with the plates. All work that needs to be done is honorable. And while I've got you, there's something you need to see. It's a book, you might like it, and you'd really be doing me a favor if..."

Cooper was not listening. He looked in despair at the beautiful woman standing between Keiter and Julius, then passed into the kitchen with his captor. Scratch babbled pleasantly about the shrimp, the uptick in the profits of the insurance industry, the Seals company in general. Cooper helped dry the dishes. Scratch pointed to a little black spiral-bound notebook on the refrigerator. "Take a look at that. You might find it helpful to your project." It killed Cooper that Scratch could think a book could be more interesting than stealing a beautiful woman from under Keiter's nose.

Mr. Rulen was standing in the hallway, apparently alone, but still speaking in his mumble: "You can only do so much against your genetic makeup. It's all in Darwin, actually…" Cooper realized that he was speaking to someone behind the bathroom door.

After finishing with Scratch, he again found the beautiful woman. She was sitting on a couch, Keiter as ubiquitous as a vowel in the word "ubiquitous."

"It's Greek, I think," the woman was saying.

Keiter was saying, "Working as an educator."

"Mr. Keiter teaches grade nine at the high school," explained Cooper, willfully oblivious to Keiter's attempts to imply that he lectured at Trinity College.

She asked Cooper what he did.

Keiter jumped in: "Currently a victim of the economic downturn."

"But in line for–" Cooper began.

"For the proceeds of a trumped-up lawsuit," interrupted Keiter.

"Actually, I'm just between jobs," Cooper said confidentially. "Interviewing tomorrow, in fact."

Cooper was gratified to see that the woman appeared sympathetic. "Are you a teacher too?" she asked. "You're a few months late, I suppose…" She meant that the school year was under way.

"No, no. I'm actually an actuary–"

But Cooper's last words were drowned out by Gormley, who was standing nearby and hollered, "Yeah, he's late! Get your period yet?"

The woman looked at Cooper and said: "?"

"Exactly," Cooper agreed.

"Urf urf urf," laughed Gormley.

Gormley was trying to screw the cap off his beer bottle. He had exhausted the usual method of holding the bottle in one hand and turning with the other and now held the bottle between his thighs and tried to turn the cap with two hands.

"Can I get that for you?" Cooper asked. Gormley handed it over. There were tiny greasy flecks of rolled black dirt where he had held the bottle. The top popped off easily in Cooper's hand. He gave it back to Gormley, who looked at the bottle and at Cooper, a question in his eye. Cooper shrugged.

Gormley continued to stare.

"Trick to it," Cooper lied.

"Hey, Cooper," said Keiter, "What's your interview for? Are you going back to selling goofballs to children again?"

"Cooper?" said the woman. "What did you say you did for a living?" she asked. She turned an attentive eye on Cooper, which pleased him.

But Gormley, who had finished a long swig, again interrupted everyone with his loud bleating voice. "What's the trick?" Cooper didn't know what he meant until Gormley held up his bottle.

"Oh, I don't know, strong grip, I think is all. Anyway," he said, addressing the woman, "I'm actually an actuary. An alliterative actuary," he said, trying for but not quite achieving the I'm-clever-but-don't-take-myself-too-seriously cuteness that gave Alan Alda his ten-year run and would inspire David Letterman's I'm-clever-but-don't-take-myself-too-seriously cynicism.

"Did you use to wrestle?" Gormley asked, still on the topic of Cooper's amazing ability to open beer bottles.

"No. No, I didn't. I'm an actuary."

"Seriously?" said the woman.

"Arm wrestler?" Gormley asked.

"No, just natural ability, I guess," said Cooper. "Yes, seriously," he said to the woman.

"And your name is Cooper?"

"Cooper Smith Cooper. Eats so much rice they named him twice," said Keiter, patting Cooper's belly. "My name is Jorge." Pronounced as if Spanish, though Keiter was a sandy-haired Teuton whose parents hailed from Kapuskasing, Ontario.

"Yes," said Cooper to the woman. He had thought Keiter's name was George.

"I thought there was something familiar about you," she said. This was a line Cooper had seen friends use when trying to start conversations with women. He was surprised that it was being used this time by the woman, and accompanied by a perilous twinkle in the eye. It was the sort of look that a mugger, having paid his debt to society and out bowling with friends, gives to the prison guard kegling in the next lane. Cooper, sensitive but wrong, fancied that it might be an invitation.

"I used to work at—" and Cooper named his old firm.

"You have a presentation for a Ms. Thournier tomorrow?" She pronounced it "thorny-er."

Cooper was delighted. "Yes, exactly. Do you work for her?" He held out his hand to shake hers. "Can you believe that she pronounces her name 'Thornier'? Should be 'Thoorn-yay,' *non*? It's like a joke name. 'There once was a girl named Thornier.' Can you imagine having a name like that in high school? I guess it's better than 'Nancy Tucket,' but not by much," said Cooper, with the chipper lightness of tone he used for clever anecdotes.

She ignored his hand, bristly as a porcupine on Saturday night when it orders a mai tai and discovers that last call was five minutes ago. She said, "You're that asshole on the phone today."

Keiter was full of glee. He said, "Not only that. He's also that asshole standing right here in person."

Gormley guffawed so that he snorted on his in-breath: "Hwaaahk!"

Chapter Three

The Party Breaks Up

"Oh *Coo*per," yodeled the first Mrs. Rulen. She had not been part of their conversation, but came tottering over on high heels, her long legs a wonder of sinew and muscle beneath her short skirt. "I really need to get going. Do you think you could walk me down the street?" She turned to the woman, Keiter, and Gormley. "I just don't know what the world is coming to, there's so many things that go on, you just don't know who to trust, and it's all since that Vatican II. Oh, thank you Cooper dear, would you get my wrap, I think it's in the hall closet..." Her overdone perfume eradicated the more subtle smells of the lovely woman.

Cooper was forced to retreat with the first Mrs. Rulen. "Scout's code. Always there for a damsel in distress," said Cooper by way of goodbye. He tried a smoldering look. It failed to come off. "Very nice to have met you," he added, retreating into his habitual Canadian deference.

The lovely woman gave him a cool smile. "Bye," she said, turning a cold shoulder away from him. Julius had appeared again.

"See you soon," Cooper called as he headed toward the door. "You'll still be here when I get back?"

Gormley followed Cooper with a new beer bottle and handed it to him. "Open that one," he said, and belched. "Boy," he said, taking the open bottle back from Cooper, "Did *you* strike out."

Cooper did not think so. The woman was a little shy. He decided that she did not want to appear too partial to him in front of Julius. She knew about Seals and the evil Ms. Thournier. He would see her again. It was too bad she had a boyfriend, but he could be patient.

It was a cool fall night with that sort of northwest wind that lets everyone know the weather is just going to get worse. Leaves rustled on the ground like auditors stirring up copies of form 5000-S2 T1 General, Schedule 2. The first Mrs. Rulen made her goodbyes in an exaggerated way that matched her implants ("*such* a *lovely* time…"). Cooper, full of the mysterious green-eyed woman, felt ridiculous walking the first Mrs. Rulen home. He also felt that it was hazardous. She seemed to have several more hands than other people of Cooper's acquaintance. Long nails slid along his arm. "Do you know," she whispered into his ear, "what Scratch said to me?"

Cooper, wishing she would move away, said, "Nope. What?"

"*He* said he *would*n't help me. *You'll* help me, *won't* you, Cooper?" She leaned against him. A hand was on his back and snaking lower.

Not knowing what else to say, he said, "Sure, Mrs. Rulen."

"*Please.* Call me Lindsay," she husked. Another hand was touching his left buttock. "*Cal*endar reform." She stopped short. "You don't know *what* I'm *talk*ing about! Admit it."

There was nothing to do but admit it.

Like many enthusiasts, the first Mrs. Rulen mistook incomprehension for interest. With a pat, touch, and pinch, she described her plan for a rationalized calendar in which every month would be 28 days. "A thir*teen* month calendar with a leap month added every *twenty* years. It would save *lit*erally *bill*ions of dollars!"

This rang a bell. She had become a real estate agent after her divorce and asked him to help her with mortgage tables. But Cooper was not a good teacher. From their sessions together, the first Mrs. Rulen had concluded that the different number of days in each month was the real problem, and had built a castle of nonsensical reform to solve it.

"Why is Scratch not helping?" Cooper asked.

She pouted. "*He* says he *can't*. *He* doesn't know *where* to take it."

"Imagine that."

"He *must* know *some*one!" she whined. "The *pope* needs to *fix* this schmozzle!"

"If it's anybody it's some ministry in Brussels," guessed worldly Cooper. "The IASB?"

"Cooper, *real*ly," said the first Mrs. Rulen. She had done research, she explained, by which she meant she had found websites that agreed with her. The *cur*rent months had been man*i*pulated by Roman *em*perors (Caesar Augustus *steal*ing a day from February so that *his* month would be as big as uncle Julius's), so of *course* the pope had authority. "The *new* month will be between July and August, when it's *nice* out, so people will *love* it. And the *pope* will love it because we're going to call it—*Fran*cis!" This last said with the air of a philosopher concluding a syllogism.

They were past the house where Mr. Rulen now lived with the second Mrs. Rulen and all the way to the first Rulen house. Cooper, desperate to change the subject, interrupted. "What did you think of the party?"

The first Mrs. Rulen stopped for a second, then switched tracks as thoroughly as Cooper. She became seductive and pouty again, ran her long nails over his arm and said, "I had *such* a nice time. There are a *lot* of ways to have a nice time." She looked at him with bumptious invitation.

They were at her door. Cooper asked, "What was the name of the woman who came with that Julius fellow?"

She gave him a look. "I *don't* know." Her mouth fell open. "I don't have *any* idea." Warming to her theme, she said, "I don't *care*." She shouted, "I don't know *what* she has to do with *any*thing!" She swung an open hand at Cooper, a long nail scratching his cheek. "Good *night*!" She slammed the door before Cooper could say another word.

Cooper marched briskly back to Scratch's. His face smarted, but he was pleased. He had gotten rid of the first Mrs. Rulen, perhaps permanently. The annoyance with which she responded to questions about the woman proved, beyond any doubt, that the new green-eyed woman was attracted to him. Women, he reflected, were insightful about such things. If the first Mrs. Rulen felt jealous, she must have seen something—some subtle sign. Cars were pulling out of Scratch's driveway when he returned, but her BMW was still there. He waved some goodbyes, rang the doorbell and whistled along with "You are my Sunshine."

He made a circuit of the amazing house looking for the woman and did not find her. It took him some time—the interior was much bigger than his—and he was nervous that he had missed her. He looked out a window: her car was still there. Then across the great hall he saw her putting on a trenchcoat. He caught her eye. He raised his hand to wave and called out, "See you tomorrow." She turned away without acknowledging him. He walked up to her and said, "It was nice meeting you. I never did find out how you're related to Seals."

"I can balance a ball on my nose and clap my hands," she said coolly.

Cooper did not know how to take this, but smiled and laughed as if appreciatively: "Ha. Ha."

Julius said to her: "Don't try to be clever. You'll just hurt yourself."

She made a grimace that might have been a smile and walked

out the door. Julius said, "You seem to have a red stripe on your face. Wrestling with the natives?"

"Um," responded Cooper with more brevity than wit. He stood at the door and watched them pull away from the curb.

He went to the kitchen, where Scratch was wrapping some dishes with cellophane and handing them out to some remaining guests. "Goodbye Cooper," said the second Mrs. Rulen, a plate of cookies in her hand. "What happened to your face?"

"Oh Cooper," said Scratch. "Did you manage to meet Thisbe? She's the lady I told you about."

"I don't think so," Cooper said, realizing that he had lost a networking opportunity and, worse, that it was getting late and he had a presentation to write. "By the way," he asked with calculated casualness, "What was the name of that lady who came with Julius?" He was thinking of the way she had smiled when she recognized him at the candle. He followed up with "And I have an interview tomorrow," so as not to appear too eager.

Scratch was delighted. "Really! You see, Cooper, this is why the Mishnah says, 'Thank God for evil and praise him.' After suffering comes joy."

"I hope so," said Cooper. Although the lovely woman had mentioned a cross, it seemed Scratch was Jewish after all.

Responding to his previous question, Scratch said, "Thisbe. That's the lady you were supposed to meet. She's sharp, isn't she?"

"Thisbe? Yes, a regular skewer," Cooper said, pleased.

"Did you have that stripe on your face when you came in?" Scratch asked.

So he had met the right person after all. He had bonded with her. And she worked for the company at which he was interviewing. So many ideas and questions flooded his mind that he couldn't get any of them out. As Scratch seemed to expect something more, Cooper said: "I didn't know you belonged to a church. Which denomination?"

"Oh, we're really non-denominational," said Scratch. The stragglers had left, and he was now placing cellophaned leftovers in the refrigerator. "Church sounds so grand. We're very informal."

"Oh. I'm Catholic, myself," Cooper said, feeling that it would be rude not to disclose his own allegiance.

"That's too bad," Scratch said.

Cooper was surprised at this. "Pardon me?"

"I said, It's too bad you're Catholic."

Cooper was just wondering whether or not to take offense at this when Scratch continued. "Because if you've got your own church, you may not feel the need to come to ours."

"Oh," said Cooper. "I see." There was a pause which felt awkward to Cooper, though it did not seem to bother Scratch. To fill it, he said, "You're recruiting new members then?"

"Nothing so formal. Always on the lookout, though. You'd be welcome any time."

Cooper had the impression that Scratch was not acting much like the devil. He would have to check his dictionary. Perhaps he was missing something.

Keiter came into the kitchen. "Why is there a shower cap on the bronze woman's head?" he asked.

"The bronze woman's head? You mean Erubis? The woman with the bow?"

Keiter nodded.

"It's more original than the usual hats and jackets visitors leave on her, I suppose," said Scratch.

Cooper was able to shed light: "They keep salad fresh. I take them from the hotels. The little coffee packets too."

"Do you take the towels?" Keiter asked, censorious.

Cooper looked at Keiter. "Of course not," he said. "They're not complimentary. And, they're rough."

"Did you have a nice time, Mr. Keiter?" asked Scratch.

"Sure," Keiter said.

There was a piercing shriek from the basement. With one exception, Cooper had not noticed these during the party, perhaps because the noise of the people talking drowned them out, or perhaps because the house had been warmed by the crowd and the furnace did not come on.

"The doctrine of hell is one of the most cruel and useless inventions of mankind," Keiter said to Scratch. It seemed a challenge.

"Oh, I couldn't agree more," said Scratch mildly.

They began to wax philosophical, something that always bored Cooper, particularly as he wanted to ask about Thisbe again. "The liberal idea of Progress, like its conservative mirror image Nostalgia, is attractive to an imagination that does not care to look closely into particulars," Scratch was saying. Cooper took a quick spin around the house, but, aside from the two in the kitchen and Gormley, it was empty. The clean-up was nearly done—Scratch was finishing a few dishes in the sink while he talked. Gormley sat down beside Keiter and began to root about in his left ear, stopping occasionally to examine the product before he rolled it between his fingers and flicked it away. Cooper was wondering how to ask Keiter if Thisbe had mentioned him at all. He thought about asking Scratch for her home phone number. She seemed grouchy at the end of their conversation. Cooper decided this was likely because of Julius's silliness, and was a good thing: she was getting tired of her goofy boyfriend. He decided to ask casually about her during his interview tomorrow ("I believe another member of the staff, Thisbe…?"). He needed her last name from Scratch.

But Cooper could not get a word in edgewise. Scratch may have impressed lovely young Thisbe, but now he and Keiter were banging away on each other with great whacking words like "existential," "ontological," "angst," "transcendent," "prelapsarian," and "eschatological." Cooper didn't understand most of the words, let alone follow the sentences, and consequently had a hard time breaking in. He had thought it would be better to ask for Thisbe's number in a casual sort of way, a kind of "Oh who was that interesting girl she asked to borrow my copy of *Northanger Abbey*" sort of thing, but it looked like he would not be able to. He did learn one fact: Keiter had once been an Anglican priest. Cooper would have assumed Anglicanism paid better than teaching school, but apparently not.

He wandered through the bizarre house and back again. Keiter, Gormley, and Scratch were sitting in the kitchen around the linoleum table. Keiter was by the refrigerator. Cooper brushed past him to get a beer. There were none left. Keiter was saying, "I studied a fair bit of comparative religion at one time."

Then a surprising thing happened. Gormley reached over and touched Keiter, and the schoolteacher fell off his chair. Cooper, just closing the refrigerator door, caught him.

"Mr. Keiter," said Cooper. Then, more urgently, "Mr. Keiter!" He was holding Keiter under the armpits. Keiter's head was down. Cooper lifted as he called his unresponding neighbor. "Keiter!" Keiter's head lolled on his neck. His face rolled around towards Cooper. The jaw was slack, the inside of the mouth dry. The eyes were open but the eyeballs had rolled up so that only the whites were visible.

"He's having some kind of a fit!" Cooper yelled. He was so shocked that he loosened his grip. Keiter fell to the ground, his head flopping forward and bouncing on the floor like a bowling ball released too high. "Ooh. Sorry about that," Cooper mumbled. He was about to pick Keiter up but thought better of it.

"Call nine one one," he said, as if to himself. "Call nine one one."

Gormley looked at Cooper with an unreadable expression, neither happy nor sad—abstracted, perhaps. Cooper would later remember that he had noticed it, though he did not then know what to make of it. There was no time. "Call nine one one!" he hollered at Gormley with relief. Yes, this was the right thing to do, he had it now. He hollered again. "Keiter's having some kind of fit. Call nine one one!"

"Don't bother," said Gormley. "He's dead."

"Gormley," said Scratch. He was still seated.

"Mr. Keiter," Cooper said, leaning over to help him up. "Mr. Keiter?"

He did not answer.

"Mr. Keiter," Cooper said, kneeling beside him. "He's not moving. Help! Hello, Mr. Keiter!" Cooper spoke to Keiter in a loud and slow voice, enunciating every word, as if Keiter's hearing were the problem. Keiter lay on the ground, now rolled over on his back and staring with fixed gaze up at the ceiling. Cooper could not believe what was taking place. "What's going on? Mr. Keiter," he called.

"Gormley," Scratch was saying.

"I know," Gormley said, sheepish but also irritated. He stood up and paced about, eventually standing beside Cooper.

"Hey, Keiter," Cooper called again. He tried to sit the dead man up, but Gormley's big work boot was standing on Keiter's outstretched wrist. "Excuse me," Cooper said to Gormley with some impatience.

"What?" Gormley barked, as if it were not his fault. But he moved his foot.

"Now now," said Scratch. "There's no excuse for impolite behavior."

"Help me," Cooper said. Gormley, with some grumbling and a little bit of spilled beer, helped Cooper get Keiter to a chair. "He's having some kind of fit!" Cooper cried again, though by now he knew.

"I don't think so," said Scratch calmly.

"A fit," snorted Gormley. Cooper couldn't tell if he was laughing or not.

"Look at him. His eyes are rolled up, he's not responding, he's obviously having," he began frantically, but stopped. "He's not breathing," Cooper said quietly. Realizing what he was saying, he became frantic again. "He's not breathing! Do you know CPR? Do you?" He looked from Gormley to Scratch, both of whom shook their heads. "Is there a phone? Where's the phone? I need a phone!" He did not remember seeing one in Scratch's house.

Scratch and Gormley moved Keiter to a chaise longue on the deck outside, giving him a long laceration above the wrist when his arm caught on the door. Keiter was wearing a golf shirt with three buttons, two of which were already undone. Cooper undid the third. He hesitated, grabbed Keiter's nose, hesitated again, thought better of it, and finally tried to blow air into Keiter's lungs. Nothing happened. He laid Keiter back and yelled at Gormley and Scratch to try the Heimlich maneuver. By this time three or four neighbors had congregated and stood on Scratch's deck. Someone was giving directions to a 911 operator. Apparently no one wanted to touch the body. Keiter's eyes were closed—had Scratch done that?—and he appeared to be asleep. No one knew of a doctor in our neighborhood, but Mrs. Mazur was a retired nurse, and someone fetched her. She was old and slow, and arrived just before the ambulance did. Red streaks flew up and down the wall of Cooper's house as the ambulance lights spun in Scratch's driveway.

"This man is dead," Mrs. Mazur announced, querulous. "You don't need a nurse. You need …"

"Step aside please, ma'am," said a white-uniformed EMT.

But his diagnosis was the same. The police arrived, and a Sergeant Maconochie took statements from each Gormley, Scratch, Mrs. Mazur and Cooper while the EMTs moved Keiter to a gurney and covered him with a sheet. "We'll take him to the hospital," they told Scratch and the police.

"Please," said Scratch.

"Thank you," said Sergeant Maconochie.

Scratch and Gormley were strangely unmoved by the whole event while Cooper was beside himself. He babbled pointlessly to the police, recounting the evening's story at length, including helping Thisbe with the candle, Keiter's flirtation, Thisbe's identity, the first and second Mrs. Rulenses. He gave a great many details that would be no earthly use to the police, but they heard him out with stoic politeness. He reached the part where Keiter fell over:

"I was just looking in the fridge and I don't even remember what we were talking about, when Mr. Keiter—right after he was touched by Mr. Gormley—fell off his chair and into…" Cooper stopped.

Maconochie, by now used to him going on, noticed only that the flow of words ended. "Yes?"

"That was when Mr. Keiter collapsed."

"I see. Did you notice anything in particular about the way Mr. Gormley touched him?"

"No. Not sure what you mean…"

"Was he pushing Mr. Keiter so that he fell?"

"No. Not that I saw. He was just beside him."

"No reason to think that Mr. Gormley had anything to do with this death?"

"No!" Cooper practically yelled.

"Is there anything more?"

But now Cooper was distracted. "Hm?"

"Is there anything else you have to say about the death of this man?"

Cooper had begun with the aftermath of Keiter's death and told the story in a roundabout way, and realized that he truly had nothing more to say. He said: "No! No. That is, everything happened as I told you. There's nothing more."

The policeman said: "That cut on your face looks new. How did you get that?"

Cooper went on a long convoluted explanation, in which he touched on Thisbe and the first Mrs. Rulen and Thisbe again, imparting a great deal of speculative information about romantic relationships and the insight women have into the minds of other women, so that Maconochie could not understand exactly how he had been cut and had to ask several times for clarification. "And so Keiter was flirting with one of the ladies, and you were jealous, and the other lady also became angry and cut you as part of this romantical triangle," Maconochie summarized.

Cooper did his best to straighten out the policeman's geometry, but Maconochie seemed under some misapprehension even after Cooper's best efforts. "It wouldn't be a triangle anyway since there were four of us."

"And what were the four of you doing?"

"Talking at the party. But, as I said, there were undercurrents."

"Undercurrents that led to violence, such as that cut on your face?"

"Well, yes."

"And what other violence did these undercurrents lead to?"

Eventually Maconochie grew tired of trying to follow Cooper's explanations, and Cooper, tired and sick of the obtuse policeman, gave up trying to make it clear. He did not want to think about Maconochie at all. For he had realized that Keiter collapsed when Gormley touched him, and his mind was full of the fact that Scratch had said that Gormley was Death.

Eventually the paramedics, the police, the neighbors and Mrs. Mazur were all gotten rid of. Cooper was sitting out back on a plastic lawn chair eating potato chips with Scratch and Gormley. The chill fall air was welcome after the excitement and tedious police questioning. In the distance he could hear the barking of a dog, and beyond that the roar of trucks on the 401.

"Gormley did it, didn't he?" he asked Scratch. For even though Gormley was there, Cooper couldn't bring himself to ask directly.

"Did what?" asked Scratch.

"Keiter."

"Keiter?"

"Keiter."

"Oh. Keiter."

"Keiter."

"He means Keiter," said Scratch to Gormley.

"Jesus," said Gormley.

"Yes, but he means Keiter," said Scratch.

"Hm?" Cooper said.

"Well," said Scratch.

"Well what?" said Gormley. He had been slouched in another of the green plastic lawn chairs, but he suddenly stood up and said, "I got to take a dump," and disappeared through Scratch's sliding glass door.

"How does he do it?" Cooper said. He longed for Scratch's deep philosophical perspective.

Scratch said, "I imagine he sits on the toilet, like everyone else." He handed Cooper a casserole dish covered over with tinfoil. "Would you take this downstairs to the refrigerator?"

Cooper took the dish and made his way to the basement stairs.

"Bring me back a beer!" came Gormley's voice from behind the bathroom door.

Chapter Four

The Furnace

Scratch's basement was empty except for the mechanicals: hot water heater, an old refrigerator, a gigantic ancient furnace. There was also a comfortable rocking chair. The furnace filled an entire corner of the basement, a pale green hulking monolith, at least six feet around, with eight arms that spread in all directions into the ductwork that circulated heat through the house. There was a small door, about three feet square, padlocked shut on one side. A tiny pilot light within the furnace's heart could be seen through thin bars on the door. Cooper remembered as a boy seeing a similar monstrosity inside his grandmother's house, long since replaced with a smaller ninety percent efficient model.

He went to the refrigerator to put back the food that Scratch had given him. He was still shaken by Keiter's death, and he took a beer and opened it. He might have thought no more about the furnace, but it suddenly turned on with a shriek and clanking that startled him. He looked around. The fire inside the monster blazed up and dazzled his eyes; and he saw, so certainly that he could not doubt it, the image of a person shrieking inside the flames. Just as the baby boomer, engaging in fornication with the eighth woman he does not care for, sees, at the instant of consummation, the flash of bored contempt on the face of his partner, gone so quickly that he pretends it might have been passion, just so did Cooper see the fast-disappearing person behind the bars. He went to the furnace and peered inside.

There was nothing out of the ordinary. There was flame in the furnace's heart, but that was not unusual—stories of greenhouse effects aside, it had been a cold autumn, with temperatures dropping to freezing at night. Scratch's great hall upstairs was cool, even damp. No wonder the furnace came on. Strange how the mind plays tricks on one, Cooper told himself without conviction. He shook his head as if to clear it. He could not have seen, he told himself, what he just saw.

The death of Keiter had rocked him. He had never cared for Keiter—a schoolteacher, a neighbor, someone with whom he had nothing in common—but he had never before been present at a death. It was bizarre and frightening, almost ridiculous. It was rude. People didn't just die like that. They died in old age homes, or in car wrecks. It put him in mind of a wedding reception he had attended where the dinner was a roast pig like you saw in cartoons, a real piggy-looking pig with an apple in its mouth. Cooper's date could not eat, and Cooper knew how she felt. There was something just not right about meat looking like the animal it came from. Proper meat came in styrofoam containers. Just so, it was not right for a man to die while visiting.

Cooper had now been standing in the basement for several minutes. The beer bottle he had retrieved from the refrigerator was tepid in his hand. He returned to the refrigerator to exchange his warmed bottle for a cold one, closed the door and turned to the staircase.

"Hey, Cooper," came a voice from behind the furnace.

Cooper nearly jumped out of his pants. He was so startled that he shouted, threw the beer bottle into the air, and only by a sheerest luck managed to catch it again before it struck the cement floor. "Don't do that!" he yelled over at the furnace. For now, it was clear to him, some practical joker had been hiding behind the furnace all along and was having fun with him. "Come out from over there," he said, breathing hard but struggling to achieve a conversational tone.

"No, you come over here," hissed the voice from the furnace.

What now? Cooper thought, wondering who on earth was playing this foolish trick. The voice was a man's, and Cooper was disappointed. If a woman had tried to seduce me down here, that wouldn't be such a bad thing, Cooper thought, remembering a scene from a late night movie on cable. Excepting perhaps the first Mrs. Rulen, there had been no time in his life when a woman had tried to seduce him, though according to the late night movies on cable, it happened pretty often.

He went over to the furnace. No one was there. He made a circle around it. No one was still there. "All right, where are you hiding?"

No one continued to be there. Then, a low hiss. "Psst!"

"I'm going upstairs. This isn't funny. You're not funny," he said, addressing the room in general.

"Oh, there you are," said a voice right beside Cooper, so that, for the second time, he was startled and jumped. This time he was not lucky, and when he threw the beer bottle it bounced off the furnace with a hollow clong. The metal cap landed on his big toe and made him jump again, this time with pain, and the fat part of the bottle shattered against the cement floor. Cooper, hopping, brought his foot down on a shard of the bottle and the glass cut through his shoe and grazed his foot. He hardly noticed. The voice shushed him with terrible earnestness: "Shh!"

Cooper, standing on one leg and holding the beer-wet foot in his hand, saw a small person, perfectly formed but less than twelve inches high, shushing him from out of the flames of the fiery furnace.

"Mr. Keiter? Mr. Keiter, is that you?"

It was.

Chapter Five

Loves of Thisbe

Thisbe pulled the car into traffic. "Songs about lovin' and livin' and good-hearted women…" sang the countrified radio.

"Songs about chintzes and blintzes and sprained arms in splintses," sang Julius. He turned the radio off and sang with a Nashville accent: "Get your tongue out of my mouth baby, I am kissing you goodbye." He spoke: "You can't improve on that one, really." He went back to the radio song: "Songs about sneezes and cheeses and snot when it freezes…"

"Julius," said Thisbe, mock-annoyed, shifting gears and passing a car on the right with a stomp on the accelerator.

"I'm just one rhyme short for you: 'Songs about frisbees and Thisbes.' I suppose I could add 'how-did-you-miss-me-s' or something like that."

" 'Bar Mitzvies'?" Thisbe suggested.

"No one was ever elected Pope by offending the Jewish vote. To judge by the number of Holocaust movies, the world is now seventy-five percent Jewish."

"Julius…" said in a warning.

"I know, I know. Even the nephew of the king must be careful."

"You aren't the nephew of the king."

"True. I got my job on merit. I blackmailed a politician." Julius was in a government ministry, a job which he claimed combined the best of banking ("hours: ten to three"), teaching ("we do nothing between June and September") and prostitution ("that little thrill you get when the hand drops into your pants is actually us, reaching for your wallet").

"Mm hm."

"Blackmail is just as much a job skill as dating the boss's daughter or having large breasts. You get what you put in. That's my motto."

But Thisbe changed the subject. "It's too bad you weren't there for the service."

"I can't go to Scratch's service. I'm an atheist."

"Julius, it would be nice if I didn't have to go alone to these things."

"You weren't alone. I came along after the service. Remember, I come from a family of atheists. In fact, a family of Catholic atheists. The kind who believe you have to be punished for your sins even if there is no God. My folks should actually be Unitarians, the church specifically designed for atheists with children. But I've progressed. I maintain an independent posture toward the World to Come. To the extent that I dabble, I believe that Allah is God and Mohammed is his prophet. In the meantime, I like German beer, country music, and the Montreal Expos, or, as we call them in English, the Washington Naturals. Women dig me."

She understood that all this was male bravado, perhaps not particularly well done. "Why Mohammed?" she said, following his irrelevancy despite herself.

"Well, first of all, Mohammedans become cross when you disagree with them. You say to a Moslem, 'I beg to differ,' and the next thing you know a pleasant young woman in a burkha comes to the door and detonates a nail bomb hidden in her purse. The suicide bomber is Islam's one truly original contribution to world culture this last four hundred years."

"Uh huh." Thisbe was tired of this.

"But more importantly," said Julius, sensing he was unappreciated, "A refinement on Pascal's wager. Pascal says that since you know you're going to die, there are really two possibilities: you die and it doesn't matter what you did; or you die and it does. He says you should believe in God because you don't lose much by wasting an hour a week being Christian, and if God does exist, you could gain Eternity. It's always worth betting on a long shot if the upside is pretty snappy—eternal life, for instance. Like a lottery ticket that costs less than you'd notice spending and could win you a million spondulix. I mean, why not invest a few hours?"

"So why won't you come to church with me then?"

"As I said: a refinement. I took Pascal one better. He's right. You should do at least the minimum if you might get eternal life. But what *kind* of eternal life? That was my question. Christian eternal life is endless contemplation of the Godhead. So that's pretty good. Better than a visit to the proctologist, for instance, although some of my gay friends might disagree. But at least better than waking up and finding yourself the cheeseburger course in an eternal Satanic McDonald's, which is what my ancestors believed."

"But you don't believe it."

"In what, proctologists? Of course I believe in them. I've got the stretch marks to prove it. But that's not what we were talking about."

"Jesus, Julius."

"Yes, him I don't believe in. Nor that eternal contemplation stuff. Why believe in eternal contemplation of anything? Islam takes Christianity one better. Instead of contemplating God, when an Islamic man gets to heaven, he gets—"

"You've got to be kidding."

"Babes! By the truckload. Gallons of them. Talk about your world's great religions. It's sort of like Calvin's doctrine of Total Depravity. But—a very optimistic kind of Total Depravity."

"It's chauvinistic. Do the women get truckloads of men?"

"If you're betting on an afterlife, go big or stay home is my advice."

"What about the women?"

"Oh, they're all virgins."

"No, the women who get to heaven."

"What about them?"

"Listen. I think I've found something here and it would be nice if you were supportive. And, it ticks me off that you can't show up on time."

Thisbe, just thirty, had been a freshman at the university twelve years ago. At the time, she showed some promise as a violinist and thought she would have a career as a performer. She read Ayn Rand, and the crude worship of achievement had impressed her then as something great. Eyes wide, she felt she was escaping her backwater high school and going to the mighty university, where she would find intellectual rigor and challenge, that she would learn side by side with others devoted to the Good, the Beautiful, and the True.

In those days, she thought that she had found these things. After the stultifying atmosphere of a suburban high school, where there was little for an intelligent teenager to think about, the free-wheeling life of university went off in her like an explosion. She felt newly created, and by a simple mistake believed that she had created herself. She bounced back from her losses with courage and grace and learned confidence from her triumphs. She discovered that she was desirable. After an ugly duckling high school career (a funny wart on her shoulder had turned out to be a malignancy, and the successful chemotherapy kept her sickly, bald, and sequestered through grades ten and eleven), she had developed into a knock-out, or what passes for one in university, viz., a skinny girl with a big chest. Virginal less because of moral compass than lack of opportunity, she decided (largely on the authority of her first year psychology textbook, which was, after all, a third edition) that it was foolish to be squeamish about sex, and she forced herself to relax while a drunken anthropology major deflowered her in the bathroom at a frat party.

She began sleeping with men, and by disciplining herself, learned to enjoy it. This had the old-fashioned consequences of a venereal disease and a surprise pregnancy, both of which were cured at no cost to her through the marvels of medical science and the university's student health insurance program. In those days her trajectory was still rapidly upwards. She thought that she would become a concert violinist. She won two small competitions and finished second in an important one.

But she was on the verge of becoming cynical. After two years, she had been at the university long enough to realize that many of the people she had first admired were not what she had thought. The musicians took beta blockers before their auditions and slept with the jurors to improve their chances at competitions. The activists were more interested in media coverage than they were in changing the world. The intellectuals were cynical careerists who cared neither jot nor tittle for the knowledge about which they wrote. Instead of loving their work with perfect love, they hated their own minds and thought only of the careers their scratchings might bring.

All were happy to take a good-looking young woman to bed, where they talked about love but did not believe in it. She said to Meghan Evans, "They don't even care about sex. They don't want to screw us. They just want to have something in their lives that reminds them of porn." This comment had more intelligence than sensitivity, as Meghan Evans was so unattractive that she could not remind even a university professor of porn. Thisbe came to see the university men as cowards, time servers, and bureaucrats. None were confident in their own strength. Instead, their goal was to undermine others so that they would appear better. Like children, they thought, "If I could break his arm, my arm would be stronger." Instead of climbing mountains, they stood on stepstools and belittled the world around them for being short. Or, as her friend Abby Bruler put it: "What a package of wieners."

But before Thisbe fell completely into brutality, she met Julius. She found herself beside him in summer, building houses for the Habitat for Humanity. As they taped drywall in the dust of a hot June afternoon, her pockmarked coworker told her that he wanted to be a painter. "But I discovered a peculiar thing," he explained. "Only the unsuccessful artists spend all day working on art."

"What do the successful ones do?"

"They spend all day working on grants."

"Grants?"

"Arts grants. Applications for dough from institutes and the government."

"And you?"

"I discovered that I could paint like crazy."

"Yes."

"But that I was terrible at writing grant applications. No talent for it at all."

"And so?"

"So I've chucked it. There's no point being second-rate."

In those days, Thisbe admired Julius. Despite his smartass exterior, he had insight. She was impressed with his critique of the bureaucratic world of arts careers and adopted his categories: Grants versus Art. She saw in Julius one of those who walked the road less traveled. As they measured and taped and sanded and vacuumed through that summer, she became convinced that she had found a man committed to truth telling. He was noble: funny and tragic and sad. He was not just empty self-promotion, he would not call Lady Gaga an important musician just to avoid listening to Mozart, or write pointless and incomprehensible essays praising the pointless and incomprehensible Jackson Pollock when anyone could go to the AGO and see the Rembrandt. His decision to honor greatness—even if he might not achieve it himself—found an echo in her own questing heart.

That had been eight years ago. She was young, and she did not yet see that Julius's retreat from art might be caused by the very cowardice that it claimed to critique. Yet he played an important part in her life, for her misunderstanding of him saved her from the convenient cynicism that poisoned so many of her professors and classmates. She lived with him on and off for a year, seeing in him, especially in that first heady summer, the possibility that there were great things to be done. The fact that Julius was not as interested in great things as she believed was less important than her reinvigorated conviction that greatness was the thing.

They had had hard times. He was unfaithful to her once or twice with a bimbo from Victoria College. As it turned out, this did not annoy her much because she had been toying with the idea of an affair herself. But then lightning struck, and one day she dropped him faster than a baby boomer called to war dropped patriotism: she discovered the man who would be the love of her life. His name was Dean. The love of her life lasted two years. When that was over, Julius and Thisbe got together again.

Six more years had passed. She thought she was happy. For she had revised her opinions of Julius. Though realizing that he had neither talent nor the burning desire for truth that she had once credited him with, she no longer felt that those things were important. Julius, to her new thought, was a good man. Despite his cynicism and grief, despite his smartass style, he was someone who understood the limitations of life, someone whom, if she did not love, she might learn to love. There were times when she awoke in the middle of the night and felt him in the bed beside her. She would stare up at the ceiling in the dark room and think, this is what I need, not my violin and crazy impossible passion, but simple faithfulness. Whatever else befell, Julius was always true to himself, true to her. She needed to be more like him. Remembering her old self, full of enthusiasms and a hero worship that had left her disappointed and despairing, she felt ashamed. Julius was the right sort of man. He was limited, yes. But he was steady and true. She felt that she had matured, that she had been pounded into nothing inside some crucible of love and come out a better woman. Or, as Julius might have sung, paraphrasing Johnny Cash: "I've been flushed from the bathroom of Dean's heart."

Thisbe's mind was wandering, and she almost missed their street. The tires squealed a little as she made the quick turn into the driveway. "Jesus," said Julius. The country station was singing, "Believe me baby, I lied," and Thisbe, catching only this bit of the silly refrain, felt that the singer was singing about her life, and tears welled so that she had to tilt her head back to prevent them from overflowing and running down her face. She drove the car into the condominium's parking garage peering out the bottom of her eyes.

She looked at Julius and felt grateful to him. Scratch had preached that there is rarely glory in people, and those to whom glory is given get there only through the doggedness of faithful service. She heard in this the story of her failure and Julius's success. Whatever else he might say or do, she felt that Julius would not waver. If he wanted to say something, he said it. When he said he loved her, she would take him at his word. Scratch had said that she must never envy the successful because the only free man was the one who could tell the Queen to go to hell if he pleased. "And the successful can never do that. Success means the enslavement of the successful to the people who made him a success." If Dean would not be there for her—and, not having heard from him in years, she felt that she had finally accepted that he would not—she felt that Julius was the solid thing that she had found for herself in this world. The limited life of the faithful and the free would be hers.

She parked the car in their spot. Julius's big hand groped her thigh. He liked to begin in a public place, then stop suddenly, then begin again, then stop, then finish on the floor in the living room. "Julius," she said. For it was a fact of their relationship that the better disposed she felt toward Julius the less she needed sex with him.

She turned off the car. Julius's hand continued on her thigh.

"Julius," she said again.

"Thiz," he said. His hand continued on her thigh, so nifty its movements that she was becoming interested. Then he said: "You know why I was late? I saw someone we know on television. You won't believe it."

"Julius, stop," she said. "Who?" She removed the car key and dropped it in her purse.

"I had the business news on. My boss was going to be on—all this corporate governance nonsense—and I felt obliged to watch him. But after his segment came the teaser for the next. It was Seals, and I saw him in the background."

"Julius…" His hand continued its magic path. His chatter was just enough to distract her from the feeling rising in her body. In the back of her mind, it occurred to her that, whatever else she thought of him, Julius did know how to get a woman going. She stopped that train of thought. "Julius," she said, in her cold professional forceful don't-mess-with-me voice. But his hand continued, and she did not stop it, and her body rose into his touch.

He pushed towards her, scrunching her against the door. He panted into her ear. "What I saw on TV was your new boss. Dean. Of all the gin joints in the world—did you know a gin joint is a marijuana cigarette soaked in the demon rum?" He had backed off to make his joke, but now pushed forward again.

"Julius…" She felt the door handle on the small of her back.

"All right, all right. But this is true. They've hired your old boyfriend to be your new boss. Dean."

The door opened suddenly, and Thisbe fell out of the car.

Chapter Six

Loves of Thisbe, the Prequel

Dean was brilliant, handsome, exotic, and accomplished. He had come from the Wharton school of business to do a doctorate in mathematics, something that was continually interrupted by consulting engagements during which some Fortune 500 company would fly him to an office in Texas or Washington DC or Seattle or Silicon Valley and pay him $75,000 for two months while he figured out some problem that, apparently, no one else could figure out for them. When he was not studying or working, he was a good enough trumpet player to substitute in the opera company orchestra (an aunt was on the board) and sometimes played professionally in theater pit orchestras. He was also the love of Thisbe's short life.

They had surprised each other. He was not interested in art or aesthetics or greatness, he did not seek the love of women. He was only driven to succeed in all he did. She was not interested in a new boyfriend or business or the second-tier musicians who hung about the edges of professional theater. In some ways, the attraction each held for the other was inexplicable. Yet for two years, they carried on a scorching love affair, Thisbe completely under the domination of this egoist. Dean's friends and relations said, "A music student? He could do better." But when they met her, they saw that she was alert and intelligent and lovely and admitted that there was nothing not to like if she was Dean's choice. "She's young," they would say, "but so quick. And so charming."

For their part, Thisbe's friends—musicians, students, bohemians—were fascinated and appalled by Dean. "Is he nothing but a success machine?" they would ask. Then they would meet him. He would turn his handsome sad-eyed intensity on them and listen carefully to everything they said, returning well-considered and interested replies, and they too found nothing to dislike.

With Dean, Thisbe felt she had found the other half of her own soul, someone who could complete her. Her life before him evaporated like a dream forgotten on waking. She had been living with Julius at the time, and she left all her things in his apartment and never went back for them. Even the friends who had warned her of Julius's mediocrity and infidelity were surprised at how perfectly Thisbe forgot him. "He's a nice guy," they would say in defense of Julius, but someone used the word "irrelevant," and that stuck too.

While everyone likes their friends to be lucky in love, Thisbe and Dean were too much. Their togetherness, their intensity, their indestructible delight in one another was hard to take. "When they invite me, I feel like they don't really care if I say yes or no," said Meghan Evans, and everyone knew what she meant. Abby Bruler, younger but sharper, said the same thing more precisely: "It's as if no one else is in the world but them." They were destined for marriage, or, if that was too old-fashioned for such an heroic couple, at least for some lifetime arrangement.

But as the first year waned and second waxed, there was a change. Where before the two had been inseparable, each seemingly made more gloriously themselves by the other, signs of a more ordinary love appeared. This was noted with approval. Thisbe and Dean might bicker; or Dean might decide not to cut his business trip short. He would spend an extra night in Seattle to avoid taking a redeye. Instead of two weeks in Bora Bora for Christmas, they stayed home so that Dean could work on his thesis. Thisbe's friends began receiving phone calls from her again, sometimes even when Dean was in town. "It's more realistic," said Meghan Evans.

Because Thisbe's friends believed that, after an initial peak, the love affair was subsiding into something more solid and steady. They had, they told each other, seen it before. The lovers lose the first overwhelming fascination and their relationship dwindles into something more regular. There was a certain satisfaction in this since no one likes to have their middling infatuations exposed to the unforgiving glare of real love. But in predicting for Thisbe and Dean the stability of an average love, they were all wrong.

Over the next months, everything crumbled away. Dean became distant and aloof with Thisbe. He refused to come out when her friends were going to be present. If he did run into her friends, he was openly contemptuous, calling chubby well-meaning Meghan Evans a "fat pinko parasite" and stylish Abby Bruler a "gold watch socialist" who "wouldn't know a workingman if he raped her."

Thisbe's initial promise as a performance major evaporated, in part because the obsessive focus required for musical glory had transferred to Dean. There should have been no shame in this. As Julius had pointed out years before, practicing six or eight or ten hours a day, as violin majors are apt to do, smacks of an unbalanced mind. But as her friends realized, this was a disappointment to Thisbe, who had hoped for greater things and who, such a short time before, had shown promise of achieving them. It was therefore with a particular shivery thrill that they discovered that Dean, arguably the cause of her disappointment, mocked her in her decline. She fell out of the performance program and graduated with the commonplace *cum laude* in music education. At a party celebrating the end of Thisbe's four years, Dean referred to her revised major as "the refuge of the talentless."

Dean's comments caused a sensation among her friends, who were delighted to think ill of the man who had aroused their suspicion all along. Their gossip, stifled by the perfect love in their midst, now burned up the phone lines. Dean was a control freak. Dean was an egoist. Dean was bipolar. Dean had deep psychological problems that manifested themselves in a desperate will to succeed and an initial charm, which later turned into bitter resentment against regular people for the normal, well-adjusted lives they led and he never could. Dean was a jerk, a goof, a nut, a screwball.

The breakdown came on a stormy night in June, when Thisbe waited two hours for Dean in a restaurant, leaving numerous messages on his cellular telephone. She gave it up and went home in the rain to shower and weep in front of an old movie on television. Dean called.

"Oh my God, I was so worried. Please don't ever do that again. Don't let me not know where you are like that…"

He cut her off. "Please don't call this number again. My cell phone is for work."

"I know, I know. It's just that you hadn't called and I was so worried…"

"I don't know what you were worried about. I didn't come because I don't want to see you anymore. I would appreciate it if you would stop bothering me."

She could not speak, for despite the difficulties of the previous months, she had not yet admitted that she was to lose him. His words stunned her. She felt a growing panic, but fought against it. She realized that he would hang up if she did not say something, so she quickly said, "Dean, wait." She was surprised at her tone, which was commonplace and controlled.

She succeeded, because he did not hang up. He said, "Yes, what is it?" He was impatient.

"Are you having a bad day? I don't want to put any pressure on you, you know that." Without thinking, she had adopted the tone of a mother speaking to a peevish child. She was pleased, realizing as she spoke that any other tack—emotional appeals, anger, sarcasm—would have ended the conversation immediately. "I just want what's best."

"Hm," he said in a way he had, thoughtful and amused. She felt her words had made an impression. "You may want what's best, and then again you may not," he said. She realized that he was mocking her: she wanted what was best, meaning him. "The fact is that I don't want you. I would appreciate it if you would stop phoning. In fact, I would appreciate it if you left me alone completely."

"Dean–" and now she could not stop the emotion pouring into her voice. Though the night before she had told Abby Bruler all about Dean's recent inattentiveness and even cruelties, she realized that she did not care, that she loved him and wanted him no matter how he behaved. "Oh Dean, I–"

Again the brutal interruption. "Please stop this emotional nonsense. That sort of thing never helps. I have no time for you now."

"Dean!"

"Nothing about you is of any interest to me. Please respect my wishes and leave me alone. Goodbye."

"Dean!" she fairly shrieked.

He hung up.

When Meghan Evans heard about Dean's final break with Thisbe, she said, "That man sold his soul to the devil a long time ago." As we shall see, gentle reader, she was absolutely right.

By this time Thisbe had graduated and was thrown out into the world. At first she could not adjust. She disappeared to live like a hermit in a cottage her parents owned some hundred miles north of Toronto. She was energetically unhappy and found meaningless lovers among the transient vacationers at the lake. She worked odd jobs to buy food and tried her hand, without success, at poetry. She did better with music and found herself writing songs for a rock band. The chords were crude and the melodies cruder, but the band liked her and even let her sit in to warble along on fiddle. The words they supplied were about redemption through love, either imagining a happy couple finding each other and realizing that their love will save them from the tawdriness of the world; or about the destruction of love, and how the tawdriness of the world must overwhelm the lives of those engaged in love affairs. A demo tape was well-received by a small record company, but then the lead singer of the band was hospitalized after driving his car into a moose, and she heard no more from them.

When the early frosts of autumn came, she left the un-winterized cabin to return to Toronto as a transient herself, spending a week or two with her parents, then moving to stay with friends, then back to her parents: a week on a married couple's couch, a few nights on a dorm room floor, a road trip to Saskatoon, house sitting for an aunt and uncle while they spent a month in Florida, then back to her parents. She lived day to day without purpose, plan, or means, a savage in despair.

She fell into a job at an insurance company. She discovered that it paid well. She discovered that she liked being able to buy things. The insurance people did not care about art or achievement or philosophy. They did not care about anything at all, it seemed, except vacations and money. They were pleasant and unpretentious, intelligent and yet less imaginative than a pragmatic Scottish slug. Thisbe had not known such people could exist. They adopted her as one of themselves, and if she sometimes mentioned music or philosophy or her violin days, they were willing to overlook it. They liked her. She liked them.

She had been a bossy, scolding child, always knowing what needed to be done next, and this characteristic served her well in business. Her unhappy and unsettled life made her mean, and this gave her a reputation as someone who Got Things Done. She was clever and covered up her lack of formal business education by being quicker than the people she dealt with. She discovered that a great deal of effort was expended doing things for reasons that were unclear to everyone, and her lack of training was less a handicap than she would have guessed. If her life was in a funk, her career was not. She was promoted to manager. She was twenty-six years old.

One night at a bar she saw Julius again. It was a patent set up. Meghan Evans, whose breast had been grabbed by Julius at a party, and who since then had always had a soft spot for him, practically forced Thisbe out with her. They sat drinking beer and listening to a blues band, whose music, like the music of all blues bands, was as intoxicating for the first three songs as it was boring for the next fifteen.

"Oh, look! It's Julius!" shrieked Meghan over the music. She noted with displeasure that Thisbe, thin and slouched forward at the little bar table, hardly looked up from her beer. Peanut shells crunched under Meghan's feet as she went to get Julius. She was nervous lest he reveal that she had asked him here explicitly to meet Thisbe. "She's not doing too well," she called in his ear.

"The perfect man turned out not to be so perfect after all," said Julius, for no one needed to mention the name of the man for whom Thisbe had lost everything.

"He's an asshole," said Meghan with self-conscious crudity.

"I guess youthful Thiz is feeling the pip."

"What?"

"I said it sucks to be Thisbe right now."

"Yeah." There was something in the way Julius spoke that made Meghan uneasy. They had been separated from Thisbe by the terrific noise the band was making and a knot of dancers, and were slowly making their way back to the table. As they sat down, Meghan saw Julius smile, a thin V crossing his pockmarked face. She realized: Julius is here for revenge. Even as this thought struck her, she adjusted to this new not uninteresting reality. Perhaps this was no more than Thisbe had coming.

"Thisbe! How are you?" bellowed Julius. The noise in the bar created a dispensation from the usual physical distance politeness demands, and Julius used it to pull his chair so close to Thisbe's that their thighs touched as he talked. "How are you doing? Long time no see."

Meghan was happy that Julius was not letting on that they had planned the meeting together, when he overdid it.

"How's Dean?" he called, interested, carefree, spontaneous, fake. For everyone knew the story, and it had by this time been two years since Dean had left.

Meghan winced.

Thisbe did not. "I don't know," she said. "We split up."

She had spoken at a regular volume so that Julius made her repeat it, although it seemed to Meghan he must have heard well enough—she had spoken in a pause between songs. This time Thisbe yelled, "I don't know. We– split– up!"

"That's too bad," he said, delighted. "What happened? I thought things were going so swimmingly. But you know what they say: 'Women are from Heaven–'"

"Julius," said Meghan. For to her credit, she enjoyed the idea of cruelty more than its reality.

"'–Men are from Uranus.' How you like that crack?"

But Thisbe was so sunk in herself that she did not notice. "He got tired of me I suppose. I don't know what happened. I don't know. I'm pretty tired of myself, if you want to know the truth."

"It's only quarter past ten," said Julius. "Much too early to get tired of yourself."

Thisbe looked at him for the first time. Meghan did not know how to interpret the look. Thisbe had always been a private person, an observer, a scold who wanted to argue ideas but careful what she revealed about herself. Just as Meghan was deciding that Thisbe must hate Julius, her face broke into its first smile that night.

"Yeah," she said, and it was as if someone had flipped the switch from Depressed to Charming. "Much too early."

That was four years ago. Now she was thirty years old and back living with Julius. She had thought that she was happy just a few minutes before. She had hurt her hand on the parking lot asphalt.

"Are you all right?" Julius was saying, coming around and untangling her from the car door, helping her up.

"Fine." Julius had his arm around her. She did not want this and pulled away. Then she realized that she might appear rude, so she said, "Wrenched my back."

"The way you fell out the door there, it was like you just disappeared, you were there and then you were–" but Julius was looking at her strangely.

Now that she was reconciled to her life, Dean was back. Thisbe could not believe it. Of all the gin joints in all the towns in all the world, Julius said. And even as she thought of this, she thought, It's fate. It had to be this way. He's come back and my life will begin again. She said to herself, I hate him. We had something and he destroyed it. He is cold, arrogant, heartless, wicked.

She fought against the strong feelings. They would help nothing. But she was overwhelmed. Even the sexual tingle aroused by Julius's cunning hand was confused. She felt her thighs rubbing together as she walked. Julius was of no interest to her. She fairly flew into the condominium they shared and was texting people she worked with before the door closed behind her. When Julius turned on the television, she almost shouted at him when he skipped right past the news station and went to music videos. "Leave the news. It might be on," she said. She could barely control her voice, and she realized that she was being rude to Julius. But she could not stop herself. She phoned the first person who responded to her text. "Is it true?" she asked.

What was she talking about?

"Dean. Dean Darwin. Is it true? That he's accepted a job with us?"

The voice on the other end of the phone did not know.

Thisbe was beside herself with anxiety but had just enough composure to say, "Oh, we saw something on the news. Just wondering. See you tomorrow."

She could not think who else would know. She flopped down on the couch, defeated. Julius's hand touched her thigh. She jumped. "Oh! You scared me," she said.

"I've been right here," said Julius.

"Sorry. Don't know why I'm so nervous," she said, making an effort to smile.

"Sure," said Julius. "It's not like your old boyfriend came back or anything."

"Oh Julius," she said. "I don't know why you're thinking—" But even as she tried to comfort him, she forgot him. She realized that the IT people might have updated the human resources system. She would be able to look up Dean, even find out where and with whom he worked. She was in the middle of a sentence when this thought struck her, and she could not remember what she had been saying. "I've just got to check something for work," she said, leaving the room.

"You might want to put a band-aid on that hand."

She waited with impatience for her computer to fire up, making it take longer by nervously double-clicking on icons and not waiting for them to open before double-clicking on something new. She stared at her computer screen, one leg jiggling up and down, a quick nervous short movement.

"Thisbe," said Julius, and again she jumped, her hand leaping involuntarily to her throat.

"Don't do that!" she said.

"Sorry. So. What work do you have to do?"

"Work? Oh. Oh, I'm just expecting an email," she said. "I'd forgotten about it."

"Okay." But instead of going, as he usually did, Julius pulled up a chair behind her to watch.

Where before she had forgotten him, now that he was seated behind her and could see what she was doing, she was acutely aware of his presence. "Julius," she said. She turned around. "What are you doing here?" It was the first time she had looked at him since they came home.

His face was pockmarked. His head was too long now that his forehead reached so much higher than it used to. He had wide shoulders, but his chest had slid down into his belly. He looked at the world with an askance glance, he called it, his head slightly cocked to one side, the result, a friend in medical school had told them, of some ligament tightening. She saw that he was holding his jaw and shoulders tightly. Was he getting emotional?

"Julius," she said. "I don't think that you have anything to worry about. He didn't come back for me, that's for sure," she said, while inside she reeled with the hope that that was exactly the reason he had come back.

They watched some news and one of the late night talk shows, where the ever-cool host affected to be a shocked small town boy while interviewing a sexologist. Thisbe brought out coffee and leaned on Julius's shoulder, but he ignored her and then leaned forward for the remote control so that she had to sit without touching him. She regretted her excitement over Dean and told herself that that was all over. She recognized her excitement for what it was: smoke without fire. Her mental picture of Dean made no allowance for the changes the years had brought. He was probably boring and watched sports on television. Paunchy and balding. She wanted to ask Julius what he had looked like. She started to ask: "Julius."

"Hm?"

She realized that it would be a mistake and she quickly changed the question already forming on her lips. "I'm supposed to go to Scratch's on Wednesday?"

Though her hesitation was barely perceptible, he somehow knew that she had intended to ask about Dean. He turned and looked at her with a cold glare. "I remember," he said. He turned back to the television.

She knew that he was remembering that she had left him for Dean once before. She thought of arguing with him but stopped herself. If she said, "I'm not going to leave you for Dean," he would answer, "Who said you were?" Nothing would be helped.

Her eyes grew heavy and she leaned against him. He moved away again. She stood up. He did not acknowledge her "Good night" or the kiss she left on his cheek. "Hm," he said, as if he were concentrating on the television—though she noticed that he was staring at a commercial about soap.

As she lay in bed, she wondered: What did she want? She had just been saying to herself that Julius was a good man, a kind man, and that asking for more than that was wrong. Now along came Dean and her thoughts went crazy. She remembered one of her Ayn Rand novels, in which the heroine—always a proxy for Ayn Rand—leaves a good man for a better one. In the novel she simply explains to the good man that good must give way to the better, and everyone understands and accepts the situation. She recalled—and even now, lying alone in the dark years later, it made her roil with shame—she had said such things to poor Julius when she left him for Dean. At the time, she believed that what she had done was right. If ever she thought about how Julius felt, she had not cared. She had been too absorbed by Dean, too in love, too much overwhelmed by their relationship. She did not want to lose herself so completely again. She had grown to like her new self, older-and-wiser, seeing much and expecting so little. She accepted the world and its limitations, its disappointments. Even as she said all this to herself, she fell asleep dreaming of Dean.

She awoke confused and in the dark to the feel of a man's hands on her body. She did not know where she was at first. She thought that she was with Dean and panicked: what would Julius think? Her body, warmed by Julius's earlier ministrations, rose towards her lover. They groped and bit at each other in the dark in a confused mixture of rage and longing.

They finished on the floor of the bathroom amid streams of whispered obscenities, collapsing exhausted on the cold tiles. Julius rolled away. Thisbe cleaned up alone in the bathroom and felt sore, tired, and miserable. When she returned to bed, Julius stared at her eyes. She looked slightly beside him, pretending not to notice.

"Well?" he said.

"Good night," she said.

She lay beside him in chaste astonishment and disgust until sleep once again sank her into dreams of Dean.

Chapter Seven

Abandon Hops

"How did you get in there?" Cooper asked Keiter. Keiter stood, perfectly formed but less than a foot tall, peering out at Cooper through the grate in Scratch's furnace.

"Cooper. Get me out of here."

"How?" asked Cooper. "Are you really in there? You look awfully small."

"I don't see why you have to go making personal comments," said Keiter.

"Sorry."

"Right. Now get me out. I'm hot."

"Of course you're hot. You're in the furnace. Come out of there."

"I can't. The door's locked."

"Nonsense. It– Oh." Cooper noticed again the large padlock to one side of the barred door.

Keiter's small hands reached through the bars. "Open the lock," he hissed, pointing at it.

Cooper looked around on top of the furnace for a key, but there was none. He checked the top of the refrigerator. No key. He checked the windowsills, the top of the hot water heater, any nook, niche, or cranny he could find in the basement. "No key!" he said.

"Hurry, hurry, I'm burning up," hissed Keiter.

Cooper, looking at a small dusty shelf on the other side of the basement, suddenly ran back to the furnace.

"Did you find it?"

"Combination lock! I don't know why, I didn't even look…" He touched the lock gingerly. It was not hot, as he had expected, but cool to the touch. It was not a combination lock. But there was something even more surprising. "There's no keyhole!" Cooper almost shouted.

Keiter ripped off a string of expletives that Cooper had never before heard combined in such an original or imaginative manner.

"Mr. Keiter!" he said, impressed.

Another string of expletives.

Cooper still had the lock in his hand. Except for the lack of key hole or combination dial, it was a perfectly ordinary padlock, the sort you buy to hold a shed door closed: grey, steel, heavy, a formidable little upside-down U rising and falling back into a solid little metal box. Cooper felt some raised surface beneath his fingers on the back side of the lock. "There's something written on it. Let me see…" The writing was on the side of the lock towards the furnace, so Cooper had to flip the lock upside down to look at it. He could not flip it all the way around, however, because the projecting metal bracket that held the lock prevented it. Cooper knelt on the floor and looked up at the letters. They were partially obscured by shadows.

"What does it say? What does it say?" said Keiter. "It's the password. You need to say the password and it opens. That's the kind of lock it is."

"Really?" said Cooper. "I didn't know that they made–"

"Read the lock. Read the lock!" Keiter hollered. "I'm burning up in here."

"It says—boy, this is hard to read with the light above. It's all in shadow—it says, 'Abandon hops…'" He paused.

"'Abandon hops?' What the hell kind of stupid saying is that? Jesus Christ."

"Maybe it's a temperance motto. My great-grandmother, according to my mom, used to be a campaigner for temperance in the 1910s. It was a big issue back then…"

"The lock is advising me to give up the demon rum?" A remarkable yet pithy string of expletives followed this remark. "I'm on fire in here. My flesh is burning. I've got to get out." He ran at the barred door, all eleven inches of him, and crashed into it with a bang. He bounced back and began to yowl. His face and hands were burned red where he had struck, and blisters began appearing on the skin. He continued to scream, and Cooper recognized the kind of sound he had heard from time to time in his house next door.

Cooper turned his face away. "Yikes," he said. He was still on one knee by the lock, and he looked at it again. "There's more. 'Abandon hops all ye who enter bere.' I guess that's misspelled. He means 'beer.' Then it makes sense. 'Abandon hops all ye who enter beer.'"

"What do you mean it makes sense?" howled Keiter. "This is some kind of Mormon lock? You mean it's telling us this furnace isn't licensed?"

"I don't know if it's saying that, exactly," said Cooper, starting to get annoyed that Keiter was yelling at him even though he was trying to help. "Maybe you can still get wine or spritzers or something like that. I don't know if just because they don't serve beer…"

"Maybe it means you don't get beer made with hops; you just get barley beer? What about that? Aaaaah!" howled Keiter. He bashed his head against the bar in front of him. The furnace echoed with an enthusiastic Bong.

"Really, Mr. Keiter, if you're going to be sarcastic," said Cooper. "I'm trying to help out here. I realize you may be a little warm, but I don't think you should blame me. I didn't put you in there."

"Well, I didn't put me in here either," snarked Keiter, sulky now, no longer shouting. "It's just that I'm a little uncomfortable!" he said, speaking the first words in a conversational tone but hollering the last.

"I'm going to leave if you yell at me again," said Cooper. "I don't have to put up with that, Mr. Keiter. It's not neighborly. It isn't nice. I hurt my foot, you know."

Keiter again held forth for nearly a minute in curses so that Cooper was again dazzled by his scope, reach, and command of the English language. It made him think better of the school system. He could tell that Keiter was cursing in a general way and not at him, and he took this as a good faith attempt to be more cooperative.

"That's better," said Cooper. "Now tell me this. I can't get you out because of this lock, but maybe I can help. I happen to have a beer right here," he said.

"What good will that do?" wailed Keiter.

"Well, it's refreshing," said Cooper. "I just took it from the refrigerator a few minutes ago. I could try to pour it through the bars…"

"I thought I had to abandon hops."

"We need a Scottish gruit. They don't use hops in those. I think he's got Fraoch Heather Ale," suggested Cooper helpfully. "That's a gruit style." Going back to the refrigerator to check. "Oh, a Kvasir, that'll work."

Keiter produced another quick deft skein of expletives.

Cooper returned to the furnace. He was annoyed with Keiter again. Using his shirt, he opened the twist off cap, dipped his finger in the beer and flicked a little at Keiter. The drops turned to steam before they reached him.

"Ow! It scalds me. Stop it! Stop!" Keiter yowled.

Cooper stopped. "Sorry." He took a swig of the beer himself. 'Listen Keiter," said Cooper. "With all your whining, we're getting off the main point, viz., how do you happen to be in there? I just said goodbye to the EMT upstairs who thinks that you're–" Cooper was not sure what word would be polite "–kaput."

"Bull," said Keiter.

"Obviously. You're right here talking to me," said Cooper.

"How could I be dead if I'm right here talking to you?"

Cooper noticed the redundancy but refrained from commenting on it. "It's funny that you're only eleven inches tall, though," he said, pulling up the rocking chair and massaging his foot. He began to rock meditatively back and forth. "And that you're being burned in a fiery furnace."

"What's so funny about that?" said Keiter, taking offense.

"Nothing, nothing," said Cooper, still rocking. "Not a thing. I just happened to notice it."

"I don't think you're very sensitive."

"It's true." Cooper was not sensitive and had struggled from youth with this. He was able to pick up currents of approbation and disapprobation but never deployed them correctly. "I always seem to say the wrong thing to the right person—or maybe it's the right thing, but to the wrong person. I remember…" and he began to tell a story about what his white neighbors said about black men, and how he had mentioned what they said to a black man at a church picnic, and how the black man had pasted him on the side of the head with a bowl of potato salad.

"I don't care about that!" shrieked Keiter. "I'm dying!"

"Oh, stop exaggerating," said Cooper. "You interrupt too much. No wonder no one wants to talk to you."

"Plenty of people want to talk to me."

"Name one."

Keiter opened his mouth, but closed it again. Stymied.

"See. Now maybe if you were more polite and thought less about yourself and more about others…"

"That good-looking woman you were hitting on all night wanted to talk to me."

"She wasn't interested in you. And I wasn't hitting on her all night."

"Was too. Arg!" yelled Keiter as a new burst of flame took him by surprise. More cursing followed.

Though burning to know what Thisbe had said to Keiter, Cooper thought it better to change the subject. "What I'm wondering is, how can you be full grown and dead upstairs, but only eleven inches tall and living in the furnace," said Cooper.

There was no answer to this.

"Why did you climb in there?" asked Cooper.

This set Keiter thinking. "I didn't climb in."

"However you got in there." Academic fussiness made Cooper impatient.

"I was sitting on the chair talking to Scratch and Gormley…"

"Yes."

"…and then I was down here in the furnace."

Cooper waited. "Yes, I know that," he said. "The question is, what happened betwixt and between those times? Talking upstairs, yes. In furnace down here, check. And between?"

"You say you saw me up there?"

"Yes."

"And I wasn't breathing?"

"No. The EMT whacked you all up and down. Pressed you here there and everywhere. Poked and prodded. No response."

"Cooper."

"Yes?"

"Am I dead?"

"That is what they say about you."

"Who?"

"I told you. The EMT. The Emergency Medical Technician. He ought to know. It's what they do."

"So I'm dead. I'm really dead."

He sounded so sad that Cooper tried to cheer him up. "Oh, you're not *that* dead."

"No, I am."

"Well, maybe just a little." For Keiter truly did not seem to be as dead as he might have. He did not seem as dead as Cooper might have expected, for example.

"Cooper, I'm dead. I'm really dead. I'm speaking to you from the world of the dead. Holy frijoles, I've kicked the bucket. I've died."

Cooper saw what he meant.

He made several promises to Keiter which he did not keep track of because he realized that, what with the girl and walking the first Mrs. Rulen home and coming back and cleaning up and Keiter dying and the EMT and the police and then chatting with Keiter in the furnace, he had stayed hours longer than he had planned. "Yes, yes, I promise I'll visit you again," he told Keiter and ran up the stairs. It was after one o'clock, he had to be downtown in seven hours for his interview, and he had left his presentation in a state of incoherence.

"Thanks very much," he said to Scratch as he came up the stairs. His host was sitting at the kitchen table having a glass of milk. Gormley was not there.

"Do you really want to know how he does it?" Scratch asked.

"No," said Cooper, not quite understanding what they were talking about. "I've got an interview tomorrow."

"There," said Scratch. He pointed to a thin black spiral bound notebook. It looked familiar.

"What is it?" Cooper said. Then he realized that Scratch had shown it to him earlier.

"That's how he does it." Scratch reached over and handed the notebook to Cooper. Cooper took it absently and was on his way to the back door. "What took you so long down there?" Scratch asked pleasantly.

Cooper was not sure how Scratch would feel about the whole Keiter thing, so he said, "Oh, nothing." It was a betrayal of sorts, but he really had to get back home. He could talk to Scratch after his interview. "I've got to go," Cooper said. "Thank you very much. I had a nice time." Then he remembered dead Keiter and said, "That is I– what I mean is– well, thank you for dinner. I suppose it isn't always this dramatic." But he felt something more formal was called for, so he stopped, turned back, and held out his hand. Scratch's hand was cold and dry when he shook it. "Well, goodbye."

"Bye-bye," said Scratch insouciantly, unwilling to enter into or insensitive to the nature of the occasion.

"Oh. There is one more thing," said Cooper, smelling beer rising from his shoes and remembering.

"Mm hm?"

He told Scratch, "I accidentally dropped a bottle down there. The beer spilled. Some broken glass. I didn't have a rag." It seemed unpardonably rude when he said it, but he had been absorbed by Keiter. "Sorry about that," he added.

Scratch gave him a look that he could not interpret. Cooper felt small. "No trouble, no trouble," said Scratch.

But Cooper could tell he was a little annoyed. He crossed the lawn and walked into his own house.

Chapter Eight

The Little Black Book of Death

It was one of those frustrating nights where sleep was the most important thing he could do and was also impossible. He needed to be up by six to prepare for his interview, and it was past one. But instead of sleeping, he rolled around in his bed. His mind was racing—his interview, the disembodied telephone voice of Thournier, lovely Thisbe of the BMW with her green eyes. And then there was the death of Keiter. He had always thought of death as something more final-ish than Keiter's. On the other hand, he could not imagine the world after his own death. He could only imagine the world with him still hiding in it—as if, dead, he could still somehow see the world, like Tom Sawyer watching his own funeral. But if death meant anything, it meant the world without him, a world in which his consciousness was not sleeping or hidden, but impossible, blasted, obliterated, not there. But if that were true, what about Keiter's ghost in Scratch's basement?

And then there was Gormley. He touched Keiter and Keiter was gone. Scratch told him that Gormley was Death earlier in the evening. The whole thing was ridiculous, living next to the Devil and being visited by Death. He was beginning to resent these silly men and their pretensions to grandiose mythological titles. If Scratch wanted to run a little church, why didn't he tell everyone to call him Father or Reverend or Rabbi or Grand Imperial Poobah? Why did he settle on Devil? And if Gormley wanted to play at being a Goth, why didn't he just get a skull tattoo and call himself Killer? Buy a Harley-Davidson, the official motorcycle of the male midlife crisis.

He remembered having some trouble with his hot water heater around the time Scratch moved in. Did the dead haunt other major household appliances?

Cooper was so wound up that he turned on the light and got out of bed. He went downstairs and set out the breakfast things, ironed his clothes, and sat down for some Ovaltine at the kitchen table. A small black coil notebook he was unfamiliar with was sitting on the table. He recognized it as the book Scratch had pointed out to him before he left. Apparently he had brought it home.

He flipped it open and leafed through it. It appeared to contain nothing but names, places, and dates. For instance, on one of the first pages:

October 15, 20__ in Moose Jaw, Saskatchewan:
Gottlieb, Nick	847 Rundell St.	03:40
Coluccio, Fred	East Ave & Oxford	04:31
Burleson, Paul J.	Pizza Hut, Julius St.	05:55
Kimmler, Sonia	Mercy Hospital 402	06:41

He flipped pages until he found our city and flipped some more until he found the previous day's date. There was a long list of names. He noticed that there were subheadings for the boroughs and found his. And then he almost fell off the kitchen chair. He saw "Keiter, George," and the name of his street. The time in the book said 10:49, which was about the time that Keiter rolled off his chair. In fact, 10:49 may well have been the exact time Keiter died.

There was a bang on the window next to him and a skeletal face appeared. Cooper was sitting in a daze thinking about the book, and the noise and sudden face made him jump so that he banged his knees on the underside of the table and his chair fell out from under him. His Ovaltine went spilling across the table and the glass shattered on floor. He tripped a little on the chair as he tried to catch himself, his foot landing in a puddle of Ovaltine. It slid out from under him. He landed heavily on his buttocks, splashing Ovaltine and stabbing his left nether cheek with a shard of broken glass.

"Awooo!" he howled.

He was quivering with pain and adrenaline as the back door opened. It was Gormley. He was more disheveled than ever and could be smelled from across the room. He was also laughing with noisy good humor.

"Urf! Urf! Urf! The look on your face when your butt hit the floor! Now that's funny! You should have seen it! Oh my God!" He was pointing at Cooper and laughing like a schoolboy at the guillotining of the French teacher. "Urf urf urf!"

Cooper checked the clock. It was three in the morning. "Gormley, what do you want?" His backside was dripping with Ovaltine and blood. Cooper noticed that he was wearing only a torn white Tshirt and polka dotted boxer shorts and felt that this was not an outfit to inspire respect.

"Oh my God!" Gormley laughed, sitting down heavily at the table across from Cooper. He had left the door open, and the light had brought in a large moth. "Glass in your ass! Hey, that's pretty good." He liked it so much he repeated it. "Glass in your ass. Urf. Urf. Urf."

Cooper closed the exterior door and then swept out of the room with as much haughty dignity as he could manage, which, under the circumstances, wasn't much. As he turned his back on Gormley, his guest laughed even louder. "Hey, it looks like you got a problem back there. Had a little accident, eh? Urf."

Cooper listened to Gormley's guffaws as he changed, washed, and bandaged himself upstairs. The cut was not deep. Gormley was still chuckling to himself when Cooper returned twenty minutes later. He had helped himself to a beer but had not bothered to clean up any of the broken glass or spilled milk. His beer was not opened.

"You got a opener?" he said. "Urf urf."

"What are you doing here?" Cooper asked, in some pique. "Why are you sneaking around backyards banging on windows at three *ante meridien*?"

"Opener," he said.

"No. No you can't have an opener." There was a magnetic bottle opener on the refrigerator, and Cooper handed it to Gormley, for he was by nature helpful. "Now what do you want?"

"Thanks," Gormley said, opening the bottle and taking a long swig. He belched noisily. It occurred to Cooper that Gormley was drunk.

"Besides more drink, of which I think you've already had enough already of, what are you doing here?" Somehow the grammar had gotten away from Cooper, but he felt he had covered the main points.

"I've never seen anyone fall like that. You should be in a movie. Urf urf." He belched again. "Oom."

"What do you want?"

"Oh. Notebook."

"Notebook?"

"Thought I left it at home. When we couldn't find it there, Scratch said he remembered you looking at it. Thought maybe it was here."

"No," Cooper lied. "I don't remember any notebook."

"Black one. Lots of names and dates and places inside. Need it for work." He took another long drink. "Got any peanuts?"

"No," Cooper said, reaching in the cupboard to get some. It was not until he was pouring the peanuts into a bowl that he remembered that the notebook was sitting on the kitchen table.

Gormley spotted it at the same time. "Hey," he said. "There it is."

"There's what?"

"My notebook. It's right on the table."

"You brought it in with you."

"I did?"

"Yes, you must have. It wasn't there before."

"Really? Son of a bitch. So I did."

Cooper handed him the bowl of peanuts.

"Thanks. You got another beer?" He snorted. "Of course you do. I just saw it in your refrigerator."

"What's the notebook about?" Cooper asked.

"It's my day book," he said. "It tells me what to do next. In my job."

"What is your job?"

"I'm Death."

The fact that it was now past three in the morning may have had something to do with it, but given what Cooper had already seen in the notebook, combined with Keiter and the furnace, he was inclined to believe Gormley. So instead of laughing, he said, "How does it work?"

Gormley showed him the book. It contained all the names of all the people in the world and the places and times of the eventual demise of each. He showed Cooper what he had already seen: Keiter's name. "See that little checkmark?" he said. "Appears when it happens." When he asked Gormley about old man Hight, who had been part of Cooper's now-defunct lawsuit, Gormley showed him Hight's name as well. Of course anyone who read a newspaper could have gotten that, but then Gormley showed him the names of other dead persons of Cooper's acquaintance. The already-dead had the little checkmark beside their names. Those still living did not.

It was at this moment that Cooper suddenly found that he could no longer listen to Gormley. He was deafened by The Idea. He didn't know where it came from, but he knew that he had it and that all he needed was this notebook and a little time to put his thoughts together. It may be because he was not an original or clever person so was unused to the experience, but the sudden realization of what he had at his fingertips almost bowled Cooper over. He wanted to scream and sing and shout. He realized that he needed to calm down. He needed to get Gormley talking about how the notebook worked. Because at the time, he still had not figured out exactly how he would use it.

They moved into the living room and Gormley plopped down on the couch. His legs were long and thin, and beneath his shorts his knobby knees were tufted with hair. He had retrieved another beer and pulled ferociously at the cap. He held it sideways and then upside down. The cap suddenly gave way with a small fart, and a quarter of the contents of the bottle coughed out onto his lap.

"This is great!" Cooper said. He was now beside himself with excitement. He ran back to the kitchen where he kept paper towels. "I can't believe it. This is really great!" He ran back and threw them at his visitor. "You should come into business with us!" Cooper called and then was confused for a second when he realized he himself was no longer in business. At least, not until tomorrow, he told himself.

Gormley was drying his legs with the paper towels. "What the hell is the trick?" he yelled. "Where did you get this sofa? The Salvation Army?" The sofa was a firm green vinyl and not one of Cooper's more luxurious pieces—a relic of his grandmother's that he had had since university. Gormley spread out along the length of it, putting his muddy boots up on one armrest, his head on the other. He took a long swig of beer.

"Do you have a scythe?" Cooper asked. "I thought you had a scythe."

Gormley belched loudly. "That's the first stupid question everyone asks me," he said. He took another drink. "Do you think this is the Middle Ages? People would look at me as if I was some kind of nut. What I do have," he began to dig in the pockets of his shorts, "is a credit card!" He pulled his wallet out with a flourish, and a plastic strip card holder unfolded. At the bottom was indeed a golden credit card. Then he lost interest. "Shoes, $72," he mumbled into his bottle in imitation of an old television commercial. "Taking out laughing boy—priceless."

"You use that to kill– to make people die?"

Gormley dropped his wallet on the floor and snorted. He looked at the beer bottle on his rounded stomach. "I can use anything!" he shouted, looking at Cooper now. He went back to staring at the beer bottle. "I used a big sledgehammer on that fellow who did the cartoon voices. I dropped a safe on a banker last month. Sometimes I throw rocks or dog shit."

"You kill people with dog shit?" Cooper asked. He was amazed. This was going to be great.

"No, you idiot. How they get killed, they get killed. I don't have anything to do with that. I'm just the efficient cause. I put the finishing touch on. I give the final okay to their dying. How they get to that stage, when I get to take them—that's their business."

Cooper started to ask another question. Gormley interrupted.

"Look, do you think I've got that kind of time? I don't care how they die. There's over six billion people on this crumby ball of dirt. You think I go over to Mrs. Throckmorton's house twice a week to see that she's properly failing? I'm going to go to Colombia to make sure some low level gang type gets an axe to the side of the head so he can linger for a month before I do my thing? I'm not the lingering type, you know. I've got to go to India twice a day, I've got to check the Arctic and the Antarctic, I've got whites, blacks, pinks, reds, greens. I've got commies, Newfies, okies, murderers, rapists, papists, not mentions doggies, kitties, birdies, pigs, frogs mice, plants, spiders, roaches, beetles, and those little bugs that sit on ponds and go weedie weedie weedie over the water. I've got writers, fighters, botanists, lepidopterists, existentialists, experientialists, monks, skunks, drunks, sociologists, owners of tanning salons, rock concert promoters. Game show hosts. The French. I'm busy. Get me another beer."

Cooper hurried to the kitchen for another beer. This was going to be great! he thought in a kind of mantra. He was still not sure exactly how he would turn the situation to his advantage, but he was sure that it could be done. He returned with the beer, this time popping the cap himself. Gormley was still talking.

"People don't understand at all. I'm only the ticket taker. You line up for the train yourself. I'm just the gateway. You get yourself in position and I come and take you. I'm not consulted. No one tells me anything. I've just got this beeper." He pulled it out of his pocket. "If it goes off, I call in. Toll free number, or expense it if I have to pay. The dispatcher says, 'Lyons, 26 Rue Saint-Sulpice, six year-old, fallen off balcony,' or he says, 'Gander, 26 Saint Joseph Street, sixty-two year-old, terminal illness throat cancer.' And off I go to Miquelon or Newfoundland. You line up for the train yourself. I'm not God. I don't know what goes on or how it works after that."

Cooper was taken aback. "You mean there is a God?" That was something he hadn't considered. What if there was a God? It might change things.

"How the hell should I know?" Gormley yelled. "I just told you, I got a beeper. I call in when it goes off. Does the line worker talk to the president at General Motors? Nobody tells me nothing. I don't even get a cell phone. I'm just run off my feet twenty-four hours a day, seven days a week. I work for a living. Sometimes when I'm too busy I have Don Cherry help out." He finished another beer. "You got any more of this crap?"

"But if you're so busy…" Cooper said.

"Union break," said Gormley. "Causes overpopulation, but what can you do? You don't want to unplug the wrong guy. Get me a beer."

Cooper was a happy man. Gormley was drunk asleep on the couch. While he slept, Cooper studied the black notebook. It was amazing how thin it was, considering it contained billions of names and addresses and dates. It could fit into the breast pocket of your shirt with hardly a bulge; but when you flipped through, there seemed to be endless pages. Probably it was some sort of magic, he thought. Who knew?

He was also impressed by the research that had gone into the book. They only take a census every ten years, and in less civilized places less often. Who had all this information? Was it correct? Could he trust it? Statistics worked backwards in time. The notebook seemed to work forwards. He had never thought of Death as a single person before, much less an ugly twerp who drank himself into stupefaction on a few Blue Lights. What if Gormley was a compulsive liar with a thanatos complex?

He sat in the hammock chair across from the couch and looked at Gormley sleeping. His T shirt was rumpled and the decal faded. *Pardy-hardy!* it said in dull silver sparkles. Gormley's unattractive furry navel peeked through the gap between his belt and shirt. Cooper had always thought of death as an impersonal natural force, a little like gravity only more intermittent. He recalled having read something about the great scientists believing in God again. He wished vaguely that he knew more about medicine. What happened when you died, anyway? He had never thought about it. Your heart stopped, your lungs stopped, your brain stopped. How did they stop? If you destroyed them, they stopped. You could shoot someone, or stab them, or a hippopotamus could run them down. But who turned off the organs? You would think it was something scientists should be looking into.

Gormley snorted and rubbed his face. Then he began to snore again. One of his muddy feet slid off the couch and thudded on the floor.

Cooper had to believe. He had the notebook. He had seen Keiter's corpse, spoken to his ghost, read his name. Incredible! He wondered if he could contact their research department directly. He looked for a publisher or a printing house, but couldn't find one. There was no watermark on the paper, either.

He flipped through the pages to see the names for our city. He almost ripped them out, but then became worried that no one would die. Something like that would be sure to cause problems in the long run. He took the notebook and slunk upstairs.

It was almost five o'clock when he sat down at his computer. The alarm clock was going to go off in less than an hour. He flipped through the book and noted down a series of names. Could he trust them? There was no choice. He was going to go into a job interview with nothing but a half-cocked theory about an equation that might be impossible to develop. But he knew what he had to do. It was one of those golden moments of inspiration where Cooper felt as if he would never die, where years of confusion and aimless wandering suddenly fall away, the chest expands, the back straightens, the wind column from the diaphragm opens up and sends oxygenated blood skipping through the veins with the same *joie de vivre* a lobbyist with a big bank account skips around Parliament. At moments like this, even a humble man feels the way Michelangelo must have felt defacing church ceilings with pictures of nudists. It took only a little bit of time to get the wording right. When Cooper was finished, he felt satisfied. This was a presentation that would win him a director's job.

The important thing was that he not give the notebook back. Gormley would get into trouble with whomever Death answers to, but it couldn't be helped. Cooper needed the notebook. He found a pile of old magazines—*Harvard Business Review, Contingencies, The Actuary, Journal of Applied Statistics* and *Video Game Monthly*—and hid the notebook among them. Then he crept downstairs.

Gormley was still asleep on the sofa, snoring lightly. One foot sat on the floor as it had when Cooper left. A bulge in the front of his shorts showed that he had a hard-on. The pig, thought Cooper. He was about to drop a lamp on Gormley's solar plexus to waken him when the alarm clock went off upstairs. Leaving Gormley to whatever revolting dreams Death may dream, he ran up to turn off the alarm, to shave, shower and begin his journey back to the lucrative and honorable world of human commerce.

Chapter Nine

The Society for Equitable Assurances on Lives and Survivorships

A receptionist, long of leg and lithe of arm, showed Cooper into a handsome conference room named Eden, it being thought witty to give meeting rooms such names. On the table sat the tri-cornered speakerphone whereby Cooper had almost undone himself earlier in the week. Someone better at reading people than Cooper might have seen that around the table sat the usual collection of bozos and bumpkins one becomes used to in business: the professional meeting-goer, happy and relaxed because for him, the meeting was the purpose of his day; the career sycophant, eyes glued on the highest ranking member in the room, fawning like Gollum over the ring of power; the frustrated female middle manager, charming and clever to her management but giving hell to all subordinates. Not one of them had given a second's thought to how the company actually worked—how money, the making of which was the purpose of the corporation, actually left the hands of customers and came into the building to spend time among them. Cooper, however, had been raised to view all people as distinct and unique individuals and saw only a collection of total strangers about whom he knew nothing, yet whom he had to please. Not unreasonably, he was nervous.

And then a penny dropped and the gumball rolled into Cooper's brain. The attractive and frustrated female middle manager—her hair pulled into a severe knot, her face harsh as a hatchet under the fluorescent lights, her large intelligent eyes brittle and hard— was the charming loose-haired, round-faced, green-eyed woman he had met the night before at Scratch's house. Although he had had much to think of since he had last seen her, her face hung importantly in his thoughts, associated, after two brief meetings, with exalted feelings of admiration and longing. He caught her eye. She did not seem surprised to see him.

"Hello, Thisbe," he said, trying her name out for the first time. It was wine on his tongue. "I didn't realize you'd be here," he added pleasantly. He wondered whether she had been one of the voices on the telephone the other day.

"Hello, Cooper," she said.

He was not sure what he had expected, but he realized two things when he heard her speak. First, her voice was much lower than at the party the night before. This probably meant nothing. The second thing was that she was not just one of the voices on the telephone: she was the awful Thournier. He felt a little cheered. Thournier had clearly been his enemy. But the woman at the party liked him. Things were going his way.

Thisbe appeared nervous. She was writing in a notebook with an ordinary orange pencil, and she snapped it in two as she wrote. She stood up to get another one, then sat down and checked around in a large folder, then stood up again, then noticed that she had another pencil beside her. Cooper's spirits rose. Could it be that her professional disagreements with him were fighting with her high personal regard? He could think of no other way to explain her nervousness. She was in the position of power. He had given her directions, met her at a party, even spoken to her about religion—this last being a topic no one broached except with good friends. He began to feel confident.

There were some introductions and shaking of hands and plenty of forced smiling. Questions were asked of him and he answered them with a relaxed ease, even fearlessness. He was so comfortable that he actually missed a question from a small hairy-eyebrowed man because he was looking over at Thisbe, trying to catch her eye, wondering what had her so off-kilter. Had she heard about Keiter? There couldn't have been an obituary so soon. Perhaps Scratch had sent her an email or phoned her? Thisbe had seemed so composed last night, but today seemed rattled and distracted, asking questions but not listening to the answers, jumping in her chair if anyone came into the room, looking around, fiddling with her pencil, her notebook, a cell phone.

Cooper's presentation consisted of three slides: a title; a list of new inputs into actuarial data from sources not dreamed of when the first tables were created in the 1600s (he had come up with over fifty of these and squeezed them into four columns in a small font); and the names of three people from Gormley's book, presented with the dates of their deaths.

"I've got a working prototype that I've built on my own," he explained. "These are all within the month. They're all local, so you can check my work just by reading the obituaries. Now, now—" he said, attempting to cut off the objections that were rising all around the room, "These are not people I know, not people I have had business dealings or, to my memory at least, any contact with. These people are not in old age homes. If they have terminal diseases, I don't know about them. These are the names of people I pulled off the small group I've been tracking in my computer on my prototype of– what did– who was it?– Sridhar, right?"

Sridhar seemed surprised to be called on, but nodded.

"Sridhar called it, my Equation of Almost Infinite Complexity. I thought it would be better to show you rather than try to convince…"

But by now the objections were fast and furious and the whole room in a hubbub. Thisbe attempted to skewer Cooper again and again. He kept almost falling for the bait, but saved himself by pointing to the names on the screen behind him. "I can't get into all the complexities of all the modules. It's something I've been playing with on and off for years. Judge me by the results."

It had come to the point where he would have been happy to leave a copy of the presentation and escape in one piece. It was Thisbe who spotted the flaw.

"Cooper, this is all very well, but you were supposed to come here, not with sample data from your prototype, but a high-level project plan indicating what more you need to finish it. You don't seem to have done what you committed to."

Cooper decided that, charming green-eyed and fine-figured or not, the gal was pushing it. He put on a business-disappointed face he had learned from Ferdie Meisenthal and, sounding aggrieved and hurt just as the hated Ferdie might have, said, "Now Thisbe, I understand that you asked me for a project plan. But you also gave me only one night to complete it. Besides, project management isn't what I'm offering here. Oh, I can do project management, but that's not the most important thing. What I'm offering, as I think I've stated, is something more interesting and, I think, more valuable. You've seen the presentation. Three names. I got them out of my prototype. Exact dates of death. I think that…"

He chatted on, repeating and amplifying points he had already made. More questions and more answers. Thisbe left for a while and returned. He was introduced to more people and walked to more offices. With one man, he completely lost his train of thought and had to stop and ask what the question had been. He had not slept and was losing his concentration. At another point, he became confused when he realized that, the night before, he had told Thisbe that her name, Thournier, worked well in dirty limericks. Had he really said that to her? She stood preoccupied, looking out a window and moving a hand as if in mental argument with someone unseen.

Cooper had a half hour for lunch, then back to the conference room with Thisbe and several people he had met that morning. A handsome well-dressed man Cooper had not seen before entered the room quietly and sat in a corner. Cooper stumbled through more conversation, poked and prodded and punched by all concerned, none of their questions making much sense or, as far as Cooper could see, having much to do with anything that would make him a good hire or not. But such, he reflected philosophically, was the way of interviews. He had read in a magazine that old-time psychoanalysts used to ask their patients what they saw in pictures of blobs, and could diagnose them by listening to the answers. Today was like that—the interviewee acting as a Rorschach blot to the psychological problems of the interviewers. He felt that, all things considered, they liked him. True to the principles of tolerance that were his creed, he at no time thought of them as just the usual sort of morons one found in any office. On the contrary, he did his best to like them. He was looking forward to being able to pay his bills again.

The new man in the corner said nothing, and did nothing, but it was obvious that everyone was trying to impress him. They kept looking over at him after they spoke, like dogs wondering whether or not the master had a cookie to reward their effort. One man held forth for fully three minutes in a stream of actuarial hogswollop that Cooper could not follow. It turned out he didn't need to because there was no question at the end of it. Two others got into an argument about best practices for project management and dominated the conversation for ten minutes before being asked to "take it off-line."

Finally, the interviews ended. Cooper was never introduced to the powerful man but did get a chance to shake his hand on the way out. "I've heard good things," said the man, pleasing Cooper to no end, although he was a little surprised that good things could have been heard already. He made a point of saying goodbye to Thisbe, who had actually left the interviews and was sitting alone in an empty cubicle near the door. "Thanks very much," said Cooper. "It was nice to see you again. I was sorry I missed you at the end of Scratch's party."

She was smiling, and it dazzled Cooper. "I think it's very interesting that you can predict the exact date of someone's death."

"Yes," he said. He wanted her to love him for him, not just for his talent—especially since it was a talent that he was not entirely sure that he possessed. On the other hand, if she thought he was great for all the wrong reasons, that was also pretty good. "Yes, it's something I've been thinking about for years—since university, really," he lied.

"Where did you go to university?" she said suddenly.

He told her.

"So did I. What year did you graduate?"

He told her.

"Isn't that something? We were there at the same time."

Cooper was delighted that they had something in common. "Hey," he said, "Do you want to get some coffee?" Then he thought and cringed—perhaps it was inappropriate to ask her for coffee since he was arguably still in a job interview.

But Thisbe didn't appear to notice. It was not quite half past three, and she smiled and said, "Sure."

It was turning into a great day.

They went to a bagel bar in the underground mall. Cooper did his best to be charming. Feeling effusive, he ordered a submarine sandwich with one of the premium toppings that add to the cost. Thisbe had water.

Cooper asked her after friends and acquaintances of his and she asked him after friends and acquaintances of hers. "Do you know what happened after you left Scratch's party?" he asked suddenly, while at the exact same time she said,

"I'm wondering if this is where old Marxists come to work."

He looked at her with puzzlement. "Old Marxists?"

"Scratch's party?"

"I'm not sure– oh. Oh. Oh, hello, did you used to be with the Marxist-Leninists too?"

Thisbe nodded. She had thought that he might be ashamed or defensive. Instead, he was open and cheerful, as if she were speaking about a fraternity or sports team he had once belonged to.

"I think I remember you," he said. "Didn't you used to go out with that big hairy fellow, the one with the beard down to his chest? He always wore the army uniform, right, the Fidel Castro look… Whatever happened to him?"

She did not know what to make of this. "He's fine," she said. "What about you? How do you justify working for such an ex-ploitive enterprise as an insurance company? Were you a spy all along? Did you never believe in the rights of workers?" The old rhetoric of the Marxists returned to her, and she said, "When they take control, they won't be kind to the ones who betrayed them."

"Hey, that's pretty good. We used to talk that way, didn't we? I never really got the hang of it, to tell you the truth. I mostly joined because a woman invited me. I wonder if you know her. Her name was Gloria Klammerer but she called herself something else, Ethel, Esther Rosenkrantz, something like that?"

"Ethel Rosenberg."

"Yes, some woman who had died in a revolution or something. I never understood why a girl named Gloria Klammerer would take the name Ethel Rosenberg. It was like Bob Smith decided he needed a change and so he became John Doe. It was like Mr. Rulen getting divorced and then marrying… Anyway, she was nice when she invited me. Mostly all I did was stand around at a few speeches, bring some beer and pizza, staple some signs to walls and light poles. I didn't really know what was going on. Are you still with them, then?"

"I was never with them," she said, with some indignation. "I just dated one."

"And what happened to your old boyfriend, the fellow with the beard, old Fidel? Still going with him? What was his name, anyway, I can't recall…"

"Fidel," she said. "He had it changed. It used to be Bob."

"Bob. Yes, I can see that. Bob Castro. Not a good name for a revolutionary."

"His last name was Teitelbaum."

"Fidel Teitelbaum?"

"No, Bob Teitelbaum. When he changed his first name to Fidel, he changed his second name to Freedom."

"Fidel Freedom?"

"Yes."

He took a bite of his sandwich. He lit up for a second. "It's too bad you didn't marry him. You could be Thisbe Freedom. You know, the way the American blacks talk. 'This Be Freedom.' Get it?"

Her brief time with Fidel had coincided with the period of her darkest cynicism, where she had almost decided nothing mattered, just before she first met Julius. "It didn't work out," she said.

"It usually doesn't." He was disappointed that she did not think his joke worldly and clever.

He paused for a minute, waiting for her to say, "This time it's going to be different," and fall into his arms.

After that didn't happen, she said, "He shaved his beard and changed his name back."

"He did? Fidel Tittlebum?"

"Teitelbaum. He's in the cabinet now. At Queen's Park."

Cooper was impressed. He did not follow politics at all. "I didn't know the communists had formed a government."

"Well," said Thisbe.

"Sorry, I mean a minority government," said Cooper, recognizing his mistake.

But that wasn't it either. "Actually, he became a Conservative."

"Did he?" said Cooper. Such distinctions were too fine. "Still, a cabinet minister. That's something," he said. "Isn't it?"

"Yes, it is," said Thisbe, almost bewildered. "But what about you? How did you become a Marxist?" she asked. There was a hint of accusation in her tone.

Cooper did not pick up on it. "Me? Oh, I was in actuarial school then. I got through it. Now I'm here. I ended up falling out with the Marxists. To tell you the truth, they were pretty pissy with me. Didn't seem to understand that a fellow's got to eat. Your boyfriend was one of the worst if you want to know the truth."

Thisbe's part in the drama—her love affair and falling out with Fidel, the slapstick jealousies and rivalries of the Marxists, their endless arguments over orthodoxies now too subtle for recall, her own contempt and manipulations—these things came to her mind, but were pushed from it by some mechanism stronger even than conscience. What she remembered of the Marxists was a story she had given to Abby Bruler and Abby had reported: the particular betrayal of Cooper. "You're the one who tried to break the strike! You were working for– who was it– the agricultural conglomerate–"

"That's right. It was a slaughterhouse, actually. I guess you could call it an agricultural conglomerate. Anyway, your boyfriend–"

"He's not my boyfriend."

"Well I'm glad to hear it. Because he was pretty snarky, let me tell you." And he did tell her. To pay for actuarial school, Cooper had worked in public relations for the slaughterhouse that used to be at Lakeshore and Leslie. He wrote press releases about the cleanliness of the plant and hid the illegal aliens working there from the government inspectors looking for them. "You know," he explained, "the main reason you have to pay the illegal aliens so little money is that it costs so much to hide them."

Around that same time, because of the shapely Gloria Klammerer AKA Ethel Rosenberg, he fell in with the Marxists. Every night after work he tramped around the city hanging posters that said "Make the Rich Pay." Neither the Marxists nor the slaughterhouse knew about his involvement with the other, not because Cooper was secretive, but simply because the subject never came up. This double life might have gone on indefinitely, but that was the summer the slaughterhouse workers went on strike. Cooper explained to the press that working conditions had never been better and that no pay raises nor extended benefits were possible "due to the extremely competitive market conditions currently existing." It was a slow news day, so Cooper was on television at six o'clock as an industry spokesman. But that same night, while the news stations ran soundbytes from the slaughterhouse press conference and the union response, Cooper and several other Marxists were arrested for breaking the windows at a number of meat-packing plants in town. An enterprising young journalist—Abby, in fact, given the scoop by Thisbe and her infuriated boyfriend Fidel—recognized Cooper and scurried to slaughterhouse management and Marxist leaders for quotes. Cooper found himself both fired from his job and shunned by the Marxists. Fortunately, he was near the end of his education, and the unemployment money was enough to pay the bills while he got his certification.

"I remember," said Thisbe.

"You do?"

"I helped break the story about you. I told my girlfriend, and she wrote it up for the *Varsity*, then sent the story to the AP, and called the newspapers and television stations."

"You did?" Cooper blinked. It seemed that Thisbe had been following his career for a great many years with considerable interest. She must really like him.

He realized that the conversation had stopped for a second and returned to an old topic: "I don't know if I ever told you what happened at Scratch's that night…"

But Thisbe's cell phone went off, and she answered it. "Yes. Yes, that's true. No. Sure. Sure, I'll be right there. Downstairs. I'm on my way. Yes."

"What do you think of my chances?" Cooper asked as they were leaving.

She looked almost surprised. "Dean liked you," she said.

A warm glow washed over Cooper. The powerful man had heard good things about him. Dean liked him. It was obvious that Thisbe was crazy about him. She was surprised he was even asking. He was in.

He shook her hand warmly. "I'm really looking forward to it," he said. Everything was going so well. This woman was the best thing that had happened to him for years.

"Okay," said Thisbe, her smile lifting him in its glowing light.

Chapter Ten

The Job

And so Cooper got the job. He had wowed the total strangers with his imagination and verve. He discovered that the powerful man was Dean Darwin, who had had a heart attack or something and was convalescing as president of the division, and who had invited Cooper to come directly to him if he saw "any obstacles in his way, any obstacles at all." Best of all, it was obvious that Thisbe was attracted to him. She had followed him out to have coffee, for God's sake.

The only thing he was nervous about was Gormley's notebook. It had seemed so clear on the night Keiter died, but who knew if he could trust it? He worried that he was involved in some kind of fairy tale story about djinnis and wishes coming true. There was always some kind of limit to the power, like it worked only to cause trouble, or without warning the djinni decided to stop rooting for the home team.

He took comfort that he had not sold the foolproof accuracy of his prediction—he had sold the concept of achieving predictability. After all, the equation was of almost infinite complexity. They wouldn't expect him to get it right every time. They were hiring someone to develop the equation, someone with broad and sweeping ideas and a new approach. Even if Gormley's book was all wrong, Cooper would be running a project to re-create the actuarial tables. At least, he hoped that was what he was getting into.

As it turned out, there was no cause for worry. Before he had even gotten home from the interview, there was a message on his home voice mail. He phoned his realtor and canceled her contract, and took the For Sale sign off his lawn and threw it in his garage. He had a beer with his lunch and spent the afternoon studying the notebook. He found a large number of deaths in the same place about six weeks out and wrote them down. Then he wrote down a single name for every day of the month. It wouldn't hurt to be prepared. He created a spreadsheet and plugged in some future names, made up some graphs showing the people in a housing complex and their "projected" death dates. The key, he felt, was to make his spreadsheet look as if it had been fed by some other, more complex program.

A few days passed. He received an offer letter for a better salary than he had expected. He wrote to Mr. Akkakumarbalapragada with the details and included a copy of the letter, asking for more time and proposed a payment plan that would catch him up over the next nine months. The fact that Thisbe was interested in him made his bright future even shinier.

His street burned with the red and orange leaves signaling the trees' annual going-out-of-business this-week-only clearance sale. He pottered about the yard with a rake and spoke to Scratch, who had been retrieving his mail. They passed the time of day and commented on the weather. Cooper said that, thanks to Scratch's tip, he had gotten a job. "I owe you one," Cooper said.

"Yes. Yes, I suppose you do," said Scratch. "But we can worry about that later. Have you heard about robberies in this neighborhood?"

Cooper had not. In fact, so many of the houses had alarm systems that it was a particularly safe neighborhood.

"Do you have an alarm system, Cooper?" Scratch asked.

Cooper did not. It surprised him that Scratch, usually so perspicacious, had fallen prey to the conventional suburban paranoia about personal property. Cooper, taking the actuary's view that a certain percentage of houses will be broken into, understood that he lived in a neighborhood where that percentage was low enough that no precaution beyond door locks was required, and that the topic was not worth discussing beyond that. He began to explain some of this to Scratch when he was interrupted.

Gormley had come out of the house wearing only his work boots and red jockey shorts, his thin chest all concave and goose-pimply in the cool November air, hairless except for small disturbing curlicues around the pink nipples. Cooper did not know where to look. He and Scratch watched as Gormley attempted a clumsy series of leaping pirouettes that seemed to be patterned on Fred Astaire, then sashayed along the side of the house, right over left, left over right, right over left, left over right, all the while hollering, "I could have spread my wings and done a thousand things…" in a high tenor that resembled the sound of an oboe after it has been kicked in the larynx by a camel. Then Gormley was around the back of the house and disappeared up the deck. "How all at once my heart took flight. I! on! ly! know when he–" Gormley screamed, the final word of the phrase cut off, apparently as he closed the sliding glass door behind him.

"I see," said Cooper.

"Yes," said Scratch. Although neither exactly remembered what they had been talking about. "He's not doing too well," Scratch admitted.

"I see," said Cooper.

"Lost his job."

"Ah."

"You know how that can be."

"Yes. Yes I do," agreed Cooper.

Cooper had a few days of anxiety over whether or not his having the notebook would cause some cosmic rupture. Gormley, after all, had indicated that he ran about inflicting death on the populace, and Cooper had no idea how to go about it. He waited for news stories about overpopulation or miracle cures, but none came. He checked the newspapers. There were the usual obituaries. A famous movie star turned up dead in his hotel room. A terrorist blew up a shopping mall, killing thirty-three people. These things cheered Cooper up.

He needn't have worried. The first three names—the ones he had given in his interview—turned up dead before all the hiring paperwork had been completed, and he was able to get a small raise even before he started work. By the time his first day arrived, he was already something of a celebrity. A woman named June, with strong white teeth and comely shape, sat beside him at lunch and listened to him with an interest that would have flattered Pope John Paul II (whose death Cooper also took credit for in a flight of actuarial enthusiasm).

Dean stopped by and asked whether he was happy working for Thisbe or whether he would prefer some other arrangement. Cooper, much infatuated with his new boss's loveliness and her obvious interest in him, said he was happy.

Dean was also concerned that there was too much work to do, and was of the opinion that Cooper should have a team of mathematicians, actuaries, statisticians, and a secretary working with him. This frightened Cooper and he must have shown it because Dean immediately corrected himself: "Did I say, 'with you'? I mean, of course, for you!"

This was in fact a complication Cooper had foreseen, but had not expected so early. He hemmed.

Dean insisted.

Cooper hawed.

Dean pushed.

Finally Cooper hit on the right note: "I'm still working on certain methodological issues," he said grandly. "Until I'm happy with the approach, it would be wasteful to bring someone else in."

Dean regarded him. "Cooper—perfectionism can be a terrible disease. But I respect your position. I'm very interested, and I want you to come straight to me when you need something. But I'm willing to leave things alone for now. For a short time."

So Cooper worked alone on the equation of almost infinite complexity. Gormley's book was one hundred percent accurate. Since he already had all the answers, his main activity was making up questions. He cobbled together mathematical models from old actuarial software, from complex Excel macros that had been used for management reports in his last company, from a whitepaper that included a VisualBasic program for estimating meter read usage for a photocopier company. He relabeled the columns with various realistic sounding headers: "years of school," "cigarettes smoked (est.)," "butter or margarine?" and was not displeased with the results. He found several excellent chat rooms: one in which serious physicists traded formulae and commented on one another's work; another in which nihilistic undergraduate statisticians showed correlations between the number of times their roommates used the word "like" or "man" in a sentence and the number of beer bottles found on the floor, or mapped IQ charts to hair color, or compared university major to the number of white shirts turned pink by unadvisedly washing them with a red-colored shirt in warm water. There was also a study that correlated pizza toppings to bubbles of flatulence per fart, but the math was flawed, and Cooper had to spend some hours correcting the formula before he could use it.

Cooper found help from more prosaic sources: old textbooks, problem sets, analyses he had done in the past for other jobs, other places. He came up with more fanciful titles to place over the numbers—"Juice Versus Water," "Untied Shoelace Styles," "Contact Lens/Cell Phone Combinations With Carpal Tunnel for Left-Handed or non-Handed." (This last to indicate that the fanciful calculations also applied to subjects whose writing hand was unknown.) He grabbed rows of numbers from the Human Life Database, from the Max Planck institute in Rostock, from UC Berkeley's Department of Demography, and the *Institut national d'études démographiques* in Paris. He found hockey and Olympic statistics, replaced the athletes' names with the names from Gormley's book and changed the column headings to things like "Cups of Coffee per Week," "Height/Weight Ratio," "Museum Visits, Lifetime," "Years subscribed to Local Newspaper," "Birth Weight," "Shoes Owned (Pairs), per Day," "Shoes Owned (Pairs), per Year," "Shoes Owned (Pairs), Lifetime." There were categories for sex, hygiene, eating, urination and defecation, incidences of absence from school and work, and golf scores. He began an email correspondence with an old physics classmate at CERN to get some equations from the Standard Model, which he had heard explained the building blocks not only of matter and motion but also biology. He created a giant database that fed a series of linked spreadsheets, pushed their results into statistical process control engines, pulled them out and pushed them into other engines, and threw all the numbers together into a great clumps, spun them sideways and spit them out again. Finally, he pushed the numbers back into another database and pulled them out of it. The answers had nothing to do with Gormley's book, but that didn't matter. He used a final series of equations to force the numbers into the answers he already had, mathematically erasing all that had come before. He labeled these quadrate equations "Heuristic."

He found an excellent website where a funeral director (who believed "Humor Cures Grief") posted the favorite comic strips of the people he buried. Cooper enjoyed the funeral director's site, which was full of nifty flash animations, including one that showed the compressed lifecycle of a coffin, from the cutting down of a mighty pine in the Canadian north, its free-floating travel downriver, its transfer from river to truck and from truck to factory, scenes of the factory, a quick shot of the coffin inventory in a warehouse, the coffin in a store, the coffin in a church with a candle on it, the coffin sliding down a slurry and into the flaming jaws of a crematorium. The whole movie lasted less than forty seconds. It inspired Cooper to relabel the "Short-Handed Goals" column of NHL statistics he had been using as "Pounds of Meat and Meat Products Consumed per Week" to "Jokes Per Day." The numbers, however, appeared too low, so he multiplied the numbers by pi and then divided each row by a random factor between 1.200 and 1.299.

Along the way, Dean made good on his threat, and Cooper picked up two employees. Vishwas was from Hyderabad, tall, thin, and elegant, with piercing black eyes and thick black hair, immaculate suits and a perfect moustache. Sridhar, the mathematician from Cooper's first interview, was from Goa, short, round, and much paler than Vishwas, with glaucomatous eyes that bulged from their sockets. He had a habit of shaking his head back and forth at a forty-five degree angle while listening. When asked what it meant, he said, "It means, 'I agree, but I don't like it,' " and then laughed. Cooper was never sure if Sridhar was kidding him or not.

He gave Vishwas the task of linking the computer programs together. He liked Sridhar better because of his ugliness and gave him a marketing database of all the people who had visited groups of websites and assigned him the task of matching the names with lists of deaths to see if any correlation could be uncovered. This technical work was difficult but involved no lying since it involved only data and inputs, and none of the outputs.

The Indians were wickedly intelligent and terrified Cooper. His goal was to keep them on tasks far away from the answers he provided Thisbe and Dean. But they were too smart for Cooper to keep them on make-work projects forever. He did not know what he would do with them when they began to look into the content of his work.

Chapter Eleven

In Which Thisbe Learns of a Minor Detail

It was Friday afternoon, and Abby Bruler sat in the lobby of the Ernst and Young tower, watching the handsome men go by in their dark suits and trenchcoats. When she was younger she had liked pretty men, boyish athletic types, swimmers. Now that she was almost thirty, she felt that on the whole she preferred older men with graying hair, vice presidential men who had large expense accounts and larger bank accounts, men who could take care of a girl. She worked for a newspaper in a decrepit old building where her companions were bitter underpaid journalism majors too ugly to make it in television but too lucid to make it as university professors. Abby envied Thisbe her glamorous downtown address, the shopping, these handsome wealthy men in their suits. The newspapers had gone casual even before universities. The sight of a rumpled golf shirt that couldn't quite cover a hairy forty-seven year-old beer belly acted on Abby's constitution in the way the sight of her mother might affect a university girl having the base of her spine tattooed during spring break.

Thisbe came from the elevator, slimmer, thought Abby, than she really had any right to be. When they had spoken, she was full of Dean and a new employee who, Abby gathered, had been hired against Thisbe's wishes. Abby did not know from the new employee, but she was fascinated by Thisbe's obsession with Dean. Abby had been married twice and had no interest in either of her ex-husbands, except insofar as they continued to deposit their portion of her monthly upkeep into her bank account. When Thisbe had taken up with Dean years ago, she had known intuitively that such an intense in-love had to be a sublimation. Now that the ghost of this passion had returned, Abby looked forward to watching Thisbe. She felt that Dean was a great spider, Thisbe a fly, and she, the entomologist. Yet she was more good-hearted than her self-characterizations made out.

"Don't look now, but there he is," hissed Thisbe.

Abby looked for Dean, but did not see him. "Where?" she asked.

"Hello, Cooper," Thisbe said.

"Hello. Abby! How are you?" said Cooper.

Abby looked at him with non-recognition.

"Cooper Smith Cooper. Banff. Remember?" He held out his hand.

Abby's look of non-recognition changed to a look of distaste. "Hello, Cooper," she said with a cold smile.

"Well, it's good to see you again," said Cooper, catching the smile but missing the cold.

"You two know each other?" said Thisbe.

"Yes, of course," said Cooper.

"Slightly," sneered Abby at the same time.

Cooper was gotten rid of, and Meghan Evans appeared. They repaired to a pub. All the talk was about Dean, what did it mean, had he come solely to seek Thisbe out, what was he like now, did he pay especial attention to Thisbe, how were things going? Meghan Evans had found a new drink and made them all have one, then another. Thisbe became excited and giddy. The romantic and professional complexities and confusions of her life faded away as the wine and companionship and memory blended together to recreate the time when she had been loved and the world lay open before her like a flower to deflower. It was only when they had eaten and drunk and shopped and laughed and were all going their separate ways that Thisbe remembered about Cooper.

"How did you know him?" she asked Abby.

Abby was getting into her taxi. She said, "Don't you remember? He's the one the police took away. On the ski trip."

Thisbe knocked on the window. "Abby, what for? What happened?"

The taxi rolled forward, moving away from the curb, looking for an opportunity to break into traffic. Abby rolled down the window. "Oh, they released him. I suppose they just asked him a few questions and let him go."

"Why? What did they want him for?"

But the cab slid into the street. Abby's elegant hand waved back from the window. "I'll call you," she said.

Chapter Twelve

Other Job Seekers

As months go, it had been a springtime of a November for Cooper. After a long glacial winter, tiny green shoots had begun to appear in his bank account, with moist warm breezes forecasting future growth. Dean had stopped by personally to say that he was impressed. Cooper had solved several particularly nasty quadratic equations from an old textbook and baked them into the equation, and found a series of trigonometric calculations that he thought would impress Sridhar and Vishwas when they began looking carefully at his math—a time he knew was coming. As the sun began to shine with the peculiar golden light characteristic of late autumn, he felt effusive and merry, and he remembered his obligation to Mr. Keiter. He took a bottle of Fraoch Heather from his refrigerator and some paper-wrapped straws he had collected from fast food restaurants. Then he went next door to pay a visit.

Scratch let him in. It seemed rude to ask to see Keiter right away, so Cooper attempted a bit of small talk with his host. He asked a question that had recently occurred to him. "This whole bit about you running a church when you're the Devil. Doesn't it imply— and I don't mean to be offensive here—but doesn't running a church imply a sort of disingenuousness on your part?"

Scratch smiled. "How do you mean?" he said pleasantly.

"Well," said Cooper. "I suppose I mean, because the Devil, after all, is supposed to be a somewhat... somewhat..." he stared around, struggling to find a precise word. "Somewhat naughty," he said, giving up the struggle.

Scratch looked hurt. "It's an old stereotype…" he began in a voice of deep general grievance.

Cooper became terribly embarrassed. "Oh, I'm sorry, I wasn't thinking, I didn't mean to characterize…"

"No, no," Scratch interrupted. "No, it's a fair question. I mean, you wouldn't ask it of a negro or a Chinaman or a Jew, but I know that many people still have their prejudices. And, to tell the truth, there were some times when…"

"No, I apologize, it was terribly insensitive…"

"…it seemed to make a very great difference how we acted and what we did…"

"I truly did not mean to offend. It popped out without my thinking, stupid of me."

"Well," said Scratch.

He might have gone on to say more, but Cooper, having committed such a terrible blunder, could think of nothing but to get away. "I'll just go downstairs and see how Mr. Keiter is doing," he said.

"Make yourself at home," said Scratch. "I was going to say—"

"Yes?" said Cooper, stopping at the kitchen door. The devil is not much mentioned in Catholic churches nowadays, and aside from a few references—a movie here, a tv show there—Cooper had little positive knowledge about devils.

"I was going to say that I used to feel it was my responsibility to get people to go to hell."

"Yes?"

"And, to that end, I sometimes tricked people into doing things not quite according to the rules."

"Yes," said Cooper, recognizing this line of thinking. "That's what my dictionary said about you."

"All right," said Scratch. "But that definition is out of date."

"How so?"

"I don't do that sort of thing anymore."

"You don't?"

"No. Do you think I do?"

Cooper thought. "I haven't seen you do anything like that," he admitted.

"Right," said Scratch. "Because I don't. I just go around trying to help people all day."

"You do?"

"Yes, I do."

"Isn't that interesting."

"But, as you know, old prejudices die hard."

"Yes, yes." Cooper shook his head with the correct mass-produced sadness prejudices require.

"It's hard to change people's perceptions."

"So true."

They stood nodding their heads, deploring the inability of people to be more tolerant and open. Then Cooper said, "What was it like?"

Scratch looked at him. "What was what like?"

"You know. Being naughty. All the time." It sounded sexy.

Scratch smiled a mild, self-deprecating smile. "I wasn't naughty all the time," he said. "I was making other people be naughty. I didn't have much time to myself, to tell the truth. No time to get into trouble."

"Ah." Cooper was disappointed.

"Rather a busy life. I thought it was my job to tempt people to hell."

"Yes, you mentioned that." Scratch was becoming a bit of a bore. "How did you figure out you didn't need to anymore?" Cooper added, feeling his previous remark had been a little cold.

"It turns out that I'm unnecessary. People are perfectly capable of getting to hell without any help from me."

"Ah."

"You know what tipped me off? I got a toothache. Knocked me up for the whole day. I got four souls that night. No work, just four souls. I was delighted at first of course–"

"Four souls, no work," said Cooper.

"Exactly. Everything was going my way. As Gormley would say, 'A bright golden haze on the meadow.'" For Gormley was at that moment upstairs bellowing something from *Oklahoma*.

"But it wasn't?"

"Of course not. Don't you see? I got four souls with no work. Unknown to me. How could I be necessary if they could show up on their own?"

"Good point."

"You bet. I got suspicious. So I tried an experiment. I went to Rochester for a while. Went on the Kodak tour, had the garbage plate at Nick Tahoe's, shopped at Wegman's, drank the slurpy beer those Americans make. Really did the town. A nice time. When I came back, I looked at the board."

"And?" The board, Cooper gathered, was some kind of tracking device for customers. Cooper had seen one at the rental car companies when he traveled on business.

"And it had made no difference. Inventories up, work-in-process humming along. So I ignored a few dispatch calls. Just here and there. Nothing major, not a big rebellion or anything–"

"Of course not," Cooper interrupted, eager to show that he was not so small-minded as to associate the devil with rebellion.

"–just a little late there, stuck in the bathroom on Wednesday, forgot my keys on Friday afternoon, went home sick the following Monday. Nothing you could point at. But I knew. Again I checked the board. New stock being delivered every day. WIP unproblematic. Not a damn problem if you'll pardon the expression."

"But what if you had prepared the way? Your earlier work had given them bad habits, and that was what brought them in?"

"What do you mean?"

"1996, you whisper, 'Steal the gum,' in little Johnny's ear. 1997, he steals the gum. 2014, he is hit by a bus and appears in your demesne. If 'demesne' is the word I want, that is."

Scratch appeared to consider this. "Interesting theory," he said at last. "I'll have to think about it." He thought about it. "You know, I really think..."

"Yes?"

"...that you could just use the word 'domain'. Same word, but less pretentious." Then he shook his head. "Anyways," he said. "You know what I did?"

"What?" Cooper was a little miffed that Scratch had not given his idea more consideration.

"I just walked out. I said, 'The hell with this,' and off I went. I rented an apartment in Scarborough for a bit. I looked at my strengths and weaknesses. Opened my little storefront church. I made a down payment and then moved in over here. Since then I've tried to do good. I've done good. There's only one problem..."

"Isn't that interesting?" said Cooper, who had found an uncomfortable wetness on his stomach and realized that the condensation on the cold beer in his jacket pocket had soaked through to his shirt.

"I know. I know. You've got to get downstairs to see your little friends," said Scratch, waving Cooper down the stairs.

Keiter was indeed in the furnace and had a good number of questions about the upcoming municipal election. Cooper was apolitical.

"Why would you pay attention to those people? All they do is lie to you."

"Because they spend huge amounts of your money on themselves and their friends as soon as you're not paying attention?"

Which Cooper had to admit was a point.

They chatted. Cooper had brought a straw with him this time, and Keiter was able to put away a fair amount of beer for an eleven-inch man who had to stand on his toes to drink. Scratch came down and said hello, took a head of lettuce from the refrigerator, and headed back up the stairs.

"I don't trust that man," said Keiter.

"Why not?"

"Things aren't as they seem," said Keiter. "It's not all boomps-a-daisy down here if you catch my drift."

"Do you think he's going out of business?" Cooper's lawsuit was over just such a company, where, in the miserable final months, he had been paid in worthless stock until arriving one day to find the doors locked.

His suggestion appeared to make Keiter angry. "Cooper, he deals in dead souls. It's recession-proof. Like coffins or pornography or selling diet books to fat Americans. Of course he's not going out of business."

"That should come as a relief to you then."

"But word is he's looking for a replacement."

"He wants to sell the business?"

Keiter winked. "Keep this on the down-low," he said, "but there was an ad in the newspaper. I want your help on my résumé."

"Baskerville Old Face," said Cooper without hesitation.

There was a clomping on the stairs, and Gormley was there.

"Did you know that Keiter here," Cooper began, but Keiter poked him with the straw and made frantic signals for Cooper to be quiet.

Gormley looked at the two men without interest. He took a beer from the refrigerator and handed it to Cooper.

"No thanks," said Cooper, taking it.

"It's for me," said Gormley, as if speaking to a particularly stupid child.

"Ah," said Cooper, turning the cap and handing over the opened bottle. Gormley clomped back up the stairs.

"Why don't you want to talk with Gormley?" said Cooper.

Keiter hissed, "He's heir apparent for the job."

"Ah." This made some sense. "Scratch was saying Gormley was unemployed."

"Probably what put the idea into his head."

"But are you sure you want the job? He runs a church and helps people is what—"

But there was a burst of flame, a shriek, and the furnace was empty.

Cooper peered into the dark furnace, then went to the refrigerator and helped himself to one of Scratch's beers. He wondered what Keiter was doing right now. He assumed it was really Keiter in there, but it was odd that he was only eleven inches tall. He seemed more used to his environment than on that first day. Cooper had just read a fantasy novel—the *Hearth on the Heath Septology* book eight, *The Hart's Heart*—in which a ghost was described as a left over bit of a person, not a real thing but an after-image, like when you stare at a dot for five minutes and then see the dot wherever you look. Was Keiter like that? Would he fade away? Cooper thought that the afterlife was supposed to be more permanent but couldn't really remember. The priest at his church emphasized social justice. The religious education classes he had taken through grade six consisted of advice that mostly amounted to being nice to people, combined with coloring rainbows. About the Four Last Things—death, judgment, heaven, and hell—barely a word had been spoken. It all raised a good many questions.

There was shouting upstairs: a male voice, neither Scratch nor Gormley. The front door slammed as Cooper ascended the staircase. Cooper found himself alone with Scratch in the kitchen.

"I had another guest over. He left," said Scratch.

"Ah." Cooper swigged his beer. "What was all the shouting?"

"Some unpleasantness over a contract."

"Your renovations? Tradesmen can be hard to deal with."

"Not exactly," said Scratch. "My caller was looking for a book. Fortunately, I do not have it." And he gave Cooper a Look.

It seemed impolite not to acknowledge this, so Cooper thanked Scratch. "It really helped me get my job."

"Unfortunately, it lost Gormley his."

"Ooh," said Cooper. Was Scratch asking for the notebook back? "Well," dithered Cooper. After all the searching, he would have to give up the notebook and start again from the beginning? "It's just that the notebook really–" But a howl from somewhere inside the house cut him off. Relieved by the interruption, Cooper asked, "Is that Keiter again?"

"It's not the furnace," sighed Scratch.

The howl came again. Unlike the shrieks from the basement, this one seemed inhuman. It continued for a long loop-the-loop, wavered, dove, and then landed with at least eleven fingernails on a blackboard, making Cooper's ears wince. The horrible noise continued, until Cooper realized that it was in fact resolving itself into a song. "Pigs and ducks and geese gonna scurry," came the loud ululation.

"I can't do a thing with him," said Scratch, defeated. "I'd like to retire, Cooper, but what can I do? He needs work."

This confirmed Keiter's rumor. "Retire? Are you ready to do that?"

"I thought I was. But it's Gormley. Ever since he lost his job, he's been in a bad way. He can't support himself."

"The dashboard's genuwine leather," shrieked Gormley from upstairs, sounding like a cat with its foot caught in the stirrup of a horse galloping through a cactus orchard.

"We'll see, Cooper. He's got a lead on a job. If you think about it, he was a little in your line of work. It seems he's made a connection or two. The church ladies. We'll see what comes of it."

Cooper felt his sunken spirits puff up with this unexpected reprieve. Scratch had brought out a small plate of cheese and crackers, and Cooper took some. "Nick," he said, happy to change the subject, "What will happen to Keiter?"

"To whom?" Scratch asked.

"The man I visited down there. Keiter. He was at your party a few weeks ago."

"In the furnace, you mean?"

"Yes. It seems like he was interested in a job."

"A job. Is he unhappy?"

"Um. I suppose he is. He doesn't seem to like it much."

"He who would be happy all the time, must change all the time."

Cooper took a second to absorb this. "He who would–" He shook himself, trying to stay on point. "I was wondering if you could help him. You know, finding a job."

Scratch said, "What happens there isn't really up to me."

"Not up to you? I read about you. It said that you had some executive decision-making abilities anent the fellows who move in."

Scratch appeared somewhat embarrassed by this. "Well, yes and no. People oversimplify. I have 'executive decision-making' just like any other middle manager does. I have a certain discretion, I suppose, but the strategy and real authority is layers and layers above me."

"You mean?"

"Yes, of course."

"Oh." Cooper thought about this. "What can you say about Him?" He said it meaning to imply that the Him had an upper case H.

"I don't really know Him well, of course," Scratch began. He seemed to weigh his words, and Cooper recognized a corporate political aspect to Scratch's character he had not noticed before. "I think He's got a vision, a way He thinks things should go, which isn't really how they usually do go. He finds this frustrating, but doesn't always have a way to correct it. I think there are problems delegating authority, for instance. Issues around control and execution. In a nutshell, I'd have to say I don't agree with everything He does." He smiled. "Of course, I don't have to."

As he lay in bed that night, Cooper mulled over his conversation with Scratch. It was his way to believe everyone and suspect no one of lying. On the other hand, Scratch and Gormley were so far out of his usual way of thinking that even while he believed they were who they said they were, he also did not believe it. He recognized this dual-mindedness even as his head sunk into his pillow in sleep, and before he could decide what he really believed, he sank into a dream of the timeless rolling ocean.

Chapter Thirteen

New Colleagues

Cooper went to mass on Sunday and returned home to see a now familiar and explicable sight: cars filling Scratch's driveway and lined up on the street down to Keiter's house and over across to Mrs. Mazur's. Scratch's Sunday service was in full swing. He craned his neck and was rewarded: surely that was Thisbe's BMW over by Avonwick. It occurred to him that he should really visit Scratch's service sometime—he had, after all, been invited. He made hot chocolate and was looking out the kitchen window toward Scratch's house when there was a buzzing from his doorbell. He walked over, expecting to see one of Scratch's congregation, perhaps someone come to the wrong house, or Scratch needing to borrow some sugar or tea bags. Perhaps Thisbe herself, making a social call. He opened the door with a smile on his face.

"*Coop*er!" It was the first Mrs. Rulen. The smell of perfume, even mixed with the chill fresh air and autumn dead leaf smell, overwhelmed him. She wore a leopard coat and a miniskirt. For a woman with children in their twenties, she pulled off the outfit surprisingly well. "Cooper, have you forgotten about my idea?"

He had no clue what she was talking about. "I've been awfully busy, Mrs. Rulen," he began.

"Yes, I *heard* that you started a new job. Really it's all for the best, I suppose," she said, brushing past him and into his house. "Although *I* was *al*ways on *your* side Cooper, I think you should get *every*thing you have coming from those bastards," she said, her heartfelt profanity contrasting with her usual affectation.

He wanted to protest that he had work to do and put her off with vague promises. But she saw his laptop on the kitchen table ("Oh what a *cute* little computer!"), and when she touched the mouse and it became obvious that he had been playing video games ("That looks *just* like the inside of an *air*plane, doesn't it? And what a cute little map."), he felt he had no excuse not to help her.

She talked to him about her calendar reform, and about amortizations, and leases, and prorations, and he dutifully got out a spreadsheet and made some calculations for her. "But Mrs. Rulen," he protested, "As far as I know, most leasing companies already use a thirty day month and a 360 day year. So they aren't dealing with different sized months anyway." As they spoke, however, he was forced to admit that her idea would simplify the work of anyone troubled by geometric progressions in calendar-based math. The flaw in Mrs. Rulen's idea was that it was less likely to be adopted than pigs were to strap themselves into F-15s to strafe King Kong on the Empire State Building during a colossal flood of New York City while an asteroid the size of the moon was blown apart by American oil riggers.

While he worked, she accidentally touched his shoulders and arms and back. He breathed deeply of her perfume. She stretched and played with her hair. She put a foot on a chair, showing a high-heeled shoe and almost all of her leg, which, as he had already noticed, was rather well-turned. It occurred to him that his infatuation with Thisbe had ruined his appetite for sexual congress with this aging but available and attractive nut. He resented Thisbe for this. But the thought of her also filled him with pleasure and made Mrs. Rulen's unsubtle seductions uninteresting in comparison.

"Mm hm, mm hm," said Mrs. Rulen. He noticed that he had left his notebook out and that she was looking at it.

"Oh, I– uh," he said, reaching for it.

"Oh *no*, excuse me," said Mrs. Rulen. "I'm so rude. I don't know *what* I was thinking, picking up your address book like that and looking all through it. I'm just *terrible*." She put the notebook on the table.

"Don't mention it," said a relieved Cooper.

After an hour of work and blandishments, he sent the spreadsheet examples to her email address and pleaded another engagement, implying, this being Sunday, a long-standing family commitment. He put on his coat, walked out with Mrs. Rulen, and got into his car. Thisbe's BMW was no longer among the few cars left in front of Scratch's house. He drove to Tim Horton's, ate a tasty doughnut, and read about the Leafs' losing streak in the newspaper.

The next day he was back at work. Thisbe passed his office door after lunch, and he hailed her. Though she stopped, she was tight-lipped and unhappy. He tried to cheer her up with actuarial jokes: the one about the half child per couple ("Which half, the top or the bottom?") and the one about living to the age of 108 (0.000,000,005 people do it—the joke he tried to make was that somewhere on your hand or toe there is a hangnail that represents 0.000,000,005 percent of your body, which will live to be 108 while the rest of you dies). As jokes go, these were not top drawer.

She said, "Why don't you meet me upstairs in forty minutes."

Inside Cooper's brain, a whole gymnasium of happiness-causing endorphins began to polka. Thisbe was inviting him to a private conversation, to share some confidence, to engage in hanky panky in a broom closet. "Sure," he said, doing his best to sound businesslike over the clarinets and accordions whooping it up in his brain. "What's up?"

"An interview. There's a candidate coming. I think you should interview him." She gave him a look he could not interpret.

No private conversation, no confidences, no hanky panky. The endorphins, stopped before the barrel could even be properly rolled out, put on their jackets and departed for the St. Andrew subway.

Thisbe absently opened the notebook on Cooper's desk. "What's this?" she asked.

"Just um–" With some upset, Cooper realized that he had left Gormley's notebook out and that Thisbe was leafing through it. "–some addresses," he said, remembering the first Mrs. Rulen.

"That's interesting. Some of these names here look like the names you gave…" She stopped. "Oh no. I see. There's the address, isn't it? Anyway, come at one o'clock."

Cooper said, "Who's the new candidate?"

Thisbe laughed.

Cooper was confused. Her laugh was not one of those heartfelt fond ones that a heroine in romantic comedy laughs when she has decided that the dweeby-yet-truly-good man is The One For Her, which was the sort of laugh Cooper was hoping for. This was more an unpleasant cackle. But what did it signify? Cooper thought: Perhaps she has just gotten the actuarial joke about living to 108.

"I think you've met him," she said.

Less than an hour later, Cooper took a notebook and made his way up the stairs to Thisbe's office. Dean was there. She seemed nervous. Cooper wondered whom both he and Thisbe knew. Scratch? Fidel Teitelbaum Freedom? Neither seemed likely.

"Cooper!" said Dean, rising to shake Cooper's hand. "Congratulations. 'Another one bites the dust,'" he sang. He held a combination histogram scatter plot graph that, Cooper gathered, tracked Cooper's success rate against the standard actuarial tables. "I must say, Thisbe and I have been very pleased Cooper, very pleased…"

Thisbe looked anything but pleased. In fact, she looked as if she were about to throw up.

Cooper admitted that it was going better than he had expected.

"Don't be so modest. You're on to something. This is going to revolutionize our entire industry. We'll be pulling away from everybody once we get this thing scalable. Right now, you realize, it's too small. Just you and the predictions you can produce. What we really need is a bigger pilot. We need hundreds and hundreds of predictions. Now, uh– uh– uh–" he raised a hand to keep Cooper from interjecting, "I know you want it to be perfect. I understand. But Cooper, this thing is too big. That's why we're moving it out. Moving it out and up. I want to put you with someone I think can really really help…" he looked at his watch and at his phone. "Now this isn't in stone yet. I need your impressions. I need Thisbe's impressions. I have my own ideas, but it's not for me to say. At least not yet." He looked at Cooper, an odd look, which lasted only a second. Then he was gone.

Dean's strange look, combined with Thisbe's strange look, comforted Cooper. Quoting the ancient wisdom of Mr. Heptameter, teacher and seer of his grade four class, he said to himself: "If you don't get along with Sally, it may be your fault or Sally's. But if you don't get along with Sally and Susie, then the fault is probably with you." As it turned out, Sally and Susie were both still serving time in the Kingston penitentiary, but Mr Heptameter's point was generally applicable. If Cooper was seeing strange looks from everybody, he must be looking for strange looks where none were looked.

He sat musing over these weighty philosophical speculations when he received a complete surprise. Gormley, wearing a plaid jacket and tweed pants over his work boots, with a bolo tie around a rumpled turtleneck, walked into Thisbe's office and said: "Hi." Dean followed him in.

"Hello," said Cooper.

"Cooper, this is Gormley. He's interested in working with us on the Equation of Almost Infinite Complexity."

"Surprise!" said Gormley, teeth akimbo.

Cooper and Thisbe took Gormley to Thisbe's office for the interview. Thisbe sat at her desk and listened absently, sometimes fading out altogether to examine her computer screen while Cooper sat at a small table with Gormley and asked him questions. To Cooper's mind, the interview did not go well. Gormley smelled of beer. He hinted mysteriously that he knew quite a bit about life actuarial but was unable to name the firm for which he had worked previously. "Family business," was all he would say. When Cooper tried to engage him in usual actuarial chat—equations, methods, famous errors and successes, smoothing strategies—Gormley would do nothing but chuckle and say, "Oh ho ho. You'll learn," and smile smugly. Cooper was a sympathetic interviewer, believing that his job was to give a candidate—any candidate, even one as goofy as his next door neighbor—a chance to put his best foot forward. But Gormley resisted all efforts. At one point he appeared to throw his pen on the floor and then seemed to become stuck while reaching for it. When Cooper asked what was wrong and leaned forward to help, Gormley shushed him impatiently, and Cooper realized that he was looking at Thisbe's legs under her desk. He could not get over the feeling, however, that Thisbe was rather impressed by Gormley.

Dean appeared in the doorway. "Well," he said.

Cooper saw that Dean made Thisbe nervous. He felt sympathetic, knowing that his own relationship with Dean was solid and easy. Some people, he knew, could not rub elbows with executives, and apparently this Thisbe was one of them. He took it upon himself to summarize: "We've been having a nice chat."

"And?" said Dean.

Thisbe appeared tongue-tied, so Cooper pronounced the usual office gobbledygook for her: "I think Thisbe and I want to get together, compile our notes, make sure we know what we've heard…"

"Six figures," said Gormley. "I think that's obvious." His plaid jacket seemed to smile in agreement.

"Gormley has plenty of confidence," Cooper said. He was shocked by Gormley's presumption. Still, it was a habit of long-standing with him to make interactions go smoothly even if they were none of his business. And so he said, "Gormley has plenty of confidence," as if this might be just the virtue they were looking for.

"Hey, wait a minute," said Gormley. "You've got my notebook." He pointed at the small black notebook Cooper had open on the table.

Cooper stopped, stunned.

Dean, who had turned away and was focusing on Thisbe, was suddenly alert. "What's that?" said Dean. "What did you say, Gormley?"

Cooper felt his face and ears heating and realized that his blushing would be perfectly visible to everyone. He slowly raised the hand that held the black notebook. "This is mine," he said.

"No it isn't. I had one just like it. That's my notebook."

"I don't think so," said Cooper.

Cooper had taken some precautions about Gormley's notebook. When he had first been hired, he had purchased several similar books at Grand & Toy as decoys, and carried one everywhere. Once, several weeks ago, he had taken the wrong notebook to a meeting and instead of writing down what was being said found himself staring at pages and pages of the names of the soon-to-be departed. The purchased notebooks were of course not quite the same as the one he had taken from Gormley, but looked similar enough. There was no particular reason why he should have grabbed the wrong notebook today. There was no particular reason Gormley might not have been fooled by a Grand & Toy notebook.

"Cooper, do you have Gormley's notebook?" Dean asked.

Cooper held the notebook up. He had not blundered: the notebook was one of the Grand & Toy ones, black and spiral-bound, about the same size as Gormley's, but perfectly ordinary. He handed it to Gormley. The front cover fell open to reveal the store logo and a page showing Cooper's name, phone number, and email address.

Gormley riffled through some pages. There were only notes and jottings in Cooper's handwriting.

"I had one just like it. In my last job," Gormley said.

"But that's not it?" Dean asked. He seemed disappointed.

"No. This isn't it," said Gormley.

Cooper held out his hand to take the book from Gormley. He felt as though his face and ears were on fire, but no one mentioned it.

When Dean left and Gormley was finally packed off, Thisbe said, "Well, what did you think?"

Cautious Cooper looked at her, wondering what she wanted him to say. "I don't think he's the perfect candidate," he said.

"Would you like to work with him?"

Cooper did not want to betray Gormley, so he said, "I'm not sure that it would work so well," instead of the more direct "No."

"He's revolting," said Thisbe.

Cooper felt a wash of happiness. Not only was the threat of Gormley receding, but Thisbe was favoring him with unprofessional confidences. "I know what you mean," he said, still unwilling to speak ill of a neighbor applying for a job. "I thought you would be partial to a friend of Scratch's," Cooper said.

Thisbe frowned.

"By the way," Cooper said, "You remember that last time we met at Scratch's party? Did I ever tell you what happened afterward? In the basement?"

"Hm?" said Thisbe. But she was caught up with something on her computer and no longer paying attention.

He left Thisbe's office and got in the elevator. The door began to close when a thin plaid arm appeared through the narrowing crack. The elevator door closed on it and bounced open. "Hey! Hey, Cooper," said Gormley.

They stood together in the elevator, each regarding the other. Then Gormley smiled, a crooked smile with teeth that pointed in several directions. "I'm your new boss," said Gormley.

"You are?" said Cooper, goggling a little.

"Yep," said Gormley nodding. "I'm your boss."

"How?" said Cooper. He had intended to ask a more coherent question but felt a little strangled. The elevator chime bonged and the doors opened at Cooper's floor. Gormley got out with him.

"Dean. Guess the big guy wants me," said Gormley, smug as a vegetarian reading about children dying of *E. coli*. "So. Where do you sit?" he asked.

They walked through a flock of cubicles and ended up at Cooper's windowless office. "Right here," he said.

"Good. So I know where to find you. Dean's probably going to give me the office next to his."

Cooper said something proper and bland: about looking forward to hearing about his plans for the department and the initiatives he and Dean were planning.

Gormley appeared shocked, but recovered nicely. "Ah. Yes. My initiatives," he said. "Very deep, far-reaching. Profound. More than I could explain right now," Gormley said, nodding thoughtfully. "Yes. My initiatives. Dean was very interested in my ideas." He paused. "I'll probably be getting the office next to Dean's," he added, by way of elaboration.

Later that day. "Mr. Cooper, Mr. Cooper," came an Indian voice: Vishwas.

"Yes?"

"I am sorry sir, but we have been waiting for you since afternoon at two. Are you coming to the meeting?"

Cooper remembered. The Indians were to show him something today. "Is Sridhar still there?"

"All present and accounted for, sir," said Vishwas.

He took Cooper to the conference room. He was thirty minutes late for the meeting. Sridhar was waiting for him. There were two laptop computers on the table. Vishwas began. "It was very difficult to get my arms around all the permutation and combinations. So I needed to move the data."

Although Cooper had given Sridhar the task of tying the disparate spreadsheets and databases together, Vishwas, it appeared, had become impatient and created a single giant database, simplifying the ridiculous hodgepodge of linked sources Cooper had instructed Sridhar to build. "Much more clearer, much more," said Vishwas, his intense eyes glowing with satisfaction beneath dark brows. "We can work very much faster now."

Cooper looked at the display. There were the names on the left, a column for date of death, and, stretching off to the right, column after column of all the data they had collected on everybody.

"This does look clear, Vishwas," said Cooper, his heart sinking. Since all the equations were at their root fraudulent, clarity was one thing he had been hoping to avoid. The array of different databases and spreadsheets and linking programs he had Sridhar working on would, he thought, ensure this. He clicked to the right of the horizontal scrollbar and watched the screen jump to the right, new columns replacing the old. He noticed that Vishwas had not only achieved completeness, he had even paid attention to small details of presentation: the names and death dates stayed visible on the left as the columns of data on the right flew past.

The columns were grouped as they had been in the data sources Cooper had cobbled together, from the simple "Smoking," "Childhood Disease," "Athletic Clubs/Participation," "Shopping Habits" to the obscure: "Heuristic Lifestyle Factor: Digestive System" or "Cultural Inclination Algorithm: Blue Series." Some of the more fancifully named columns were hiding places for Cooper's quadrate equations—the hidden adjustment factors he used to square the program's death dates with the answers that Gormley's book provided.

I need to stop this right here, thought Cooper. He saw exactly how to do it. "Vish," said Cooper, "What happened to the work that I actually asked you to do?"

But Vishwas, instead of collapsing as Cooper had expected, merely shook his head impatiently. "All done, all done. It is all here." He took the mouse and began flying through the columns. "See here... here, here... and here. All done. All correct. Built in now. Very clear. All together."

It was true. Vishwas had completed the work Cooper set for him. Cooper had a spasm of panic. What would happen when they started looking into his quadrate equations? A couple of them were perhaps justifiable, allowing for the fact that they were based on no data other than the need to shoehorn the right answer into the equation. These could be explained by talking vaguely about estimated values based on the previous columns, a kind of intuition about statistical relationships that every statistician who works with large sets of disparate numbers comes to develop. But others were the simplest kind of math trick, erasing everything that had come before and substituting the right answer, the sort of thing that Engineering Science majors from Waterloo did to win beers from the frosh. What would Vishwas and Sridhar say when they discovered Cooper's bamboozlements?

Cooper was trapped. If Vishwas could bring all his databases together in a couple of months, there was no way he could keep them away from his cheap math tricks. He would have to admit everything. He would have to get them to promise secrecy. Could he trust them? How could he tell? What if they blackmailed him? He did not know what to do. Would it be better to bring them in early, or wait until they had finally worked out for themselves that everything was faked? His ears began to glow.

While Cooper was thinking, help came from an unexpected quarter. "This cannot work. This will not work," said Sridhar. "You need to denormalize all the data. This will not work. You cannot do it this way."

"This works. It works, I tell you. This is going to work. The data is fine. I have denormalized where I needed to. This is the view, the tables are not the view."

"I need to see these tables. What about all my work?" whined Sridhar, addressing Cooper for the first time. "I have put all the disparate sources together." This was not exactly true. Cooper had noted, with some pleasure, that Sridhar's progress reports generally showed little progress—instead, they listed a great many activities that were designed to create the illusion of great effort and later be used as an excuse to push due dates out. Now Sridhar attacked Vishwas again. "Where are your import programs? How are we going to re-import all this data when it changes? I have structured everything so that we can go out to the sources. Are you using the source or have you imported? What about when the source changes? How will you know? You have done everything wrong. This is no good. No good at all."

Sridhar's attack was mean-spirited, self-serving, and destructive. Cooper liked it. It was as if the baby boomers, after a lifetime of careless destructions of all the good and lovely things of the world, finally admitted that Elvis Presley was only someone whom they had pretended to like because he annoyed their fathers.

Vishwas looked to Cooper for help while Sridhar continued his harangue. Cooper gave him a shrug, meaning, 'See what happens when we don't do what we're told.' But Vishwas, knowing he was right, refused to be bullied.

"It is good. This is all right. Since last month, I have put it all together. Now we no longer need to pass the data. Here is what we need." He went to a white board and began drawing boxes and arrows connecting them. Some of the boxes represented tables in his database, some were from the sources Sridhar was responsible for, some sources Cooper had found, others new sources that Vishwas had uncovered of his own initiative.

"But those will break the equations," Cooper interrupted.

"No. No, I have not hooked them in yet. They are columns we can start using when we determine the relationships and transformations."

The two Indians continued to argue, drawing more boxes and more lines, Sridhar drawing new data sources, Vishwas drawing the lines that showed how they would all fit together. They kept using computer jargon like "Pub-Sub," "SOA," (pronounced "Sew-Ah") "Replication," "Services Bus," "Hadoop," or "Hub-and-spoke." Cooper, who knew a lot about statistics and a little about computers, could not quite follow. He was pleased when Sridhar seemed to be winning and sorry when Vishwas had answers. After some time, the Indians began to speak in their own language and dropped English altogether, although the English acronyms still peppered their dialogue.

Finally Cooper stood and interrupted them. "It's obvious that you two have been working at cross purposes," he said. "I have another meeting to go to. I'd like you to work this out and have some kind of recovery plan for me early next week." It was not the strongest response, but he was not getting anywhere listening to his subordinates argue. At least he had bought time to think of something. He left with a show of distaste.

Surprisingly, having Gormley for a colleague made little difference. Or maybe it wasn't surprising. Cooper spent his days developing equations and stringing them together. He began to create more realistic strings of numbers, so that instead of simply inserting a factor that forced everything to equal the number Gormley's book predicted, he created small interventions in several places where, with a handful of factors, he could force the final answer to any result he chose. He began to push some of the made up numbers out of the equations and tried to use more of the real data they had collected. It would all be different when he was finally forced to use the unified database that Vishwas had created, but at least he knew where his interventions would be required. He could stay a step ahead of Vishwas and Sridhar.

Gormley, who did not seem to have much ambition, did not get the office next to Dean's. He took the open office next to Cooper's and stared off into space. He was more fraudulent even than Cooper. He came in late, left early, took long lunches, and when he was in the office, wandered from cubicle to cubicle, asking people their names and what they were doing. As it turned out, his office was near an IT project putting in a new financial system.

"So you guys know a lot about accounting and money and stuff?" Gormley asked.

Yes, that was more or less true.

"Do you think that if the calendar were simplified, we could save billions of dollars?"

Gormley moved an electric pencil sharpener into his office and sharpened three boxes of pencils. Cooper overheard Gormley on the phone in an animated discussion with someone at the cable company about whether or not he had streamed all those movies. "Besides, most of them had no plot at all," Gormley complained. Another time, Gormley was speaking with an airline.

"Are you going on a trip?" Cooper asked.

Gormley looked at him for a second. "Oh," he said. "No, I just like to call a few wrong numbers every day. It helps pass the time."

"Do you want to see the predictions?" Cooper asked.

But Gormley didn't. "I'm sure they're fine. Say, Cooper. How do you spend your time around here?"

"Well," said Cooper, not quite knowing how much to admit. "I work on equations to predict times of death."

"Really," said Gormley. "That's what you do?"

Cooper said it was. He tried a question himself: "What is it you do?" he asked Gormley.

"Oh," and Gormley became self-effacing. "A little of this, a little of that. My dad wanted me to get a job. I had one for a while but I got laid off. Jerks. Anyway, I'm here now."

It hadn't occurred to Cooper before that Gormley had a father. Even as this registered, it was crowded from Cooper's mind by his next question: "What does Dean want you to do?"

"Oh. Yes," said Gormley. "I've got a Big Thing I'm planning. It's really too much to go into just now." He nodded at the jar of sharpened pencils on his desk. There were two dozen of them. He made a little humming grunting noise as he nodded, 'Mm? Mm?', as if the pencils explained exactly how big the plans were and further indicated the difficulty of going into a Big Thing just now. "Say. Cooper," he added. "Can you help me with this?"

"Sure," said Cooper, watching Gormley fumble in a file drawer. This was exciting. He would see what Gormley was working on.

Gormley pulled out a bottle of beer. "I have a blister. It hurts when I open them."

Cooper took the bottle and opened it. "There's a refrigerator in the kitchen on this floor, it's near the elevator," Cooper began helpfully, when Thisbe came in.

"What are you doing here?" she asked Cooper.

Cooper, looking guilty, hastily put the beer bottle on Gormley's desk.

Gormley said, "Yes, this is where I sit now. I think Dean wanted me to have the office next to his, but he's got to throw some people out first to make room." He lowered his voice confidentially. "None of the offices was big enough." He took a swig of beer. "They'll have to renovate."

Cooper looked back at Thisbe, relieved that Gormley had made clear the beer was his.

Gormley continued. "I guess since you'll both be reporting to me we should set up some kind of team meeting. Oh, and Cooper, would you excuse us for a minute? I need to discuss something with Thisbe." He gave Thisbe a strange look, one eyebrow raised and his lips pursed, so that, if his teeth hadn't been pointing in many directions at once and his hair so greasy, it might have been mistaken for what old songs refer to as a "come-hither gleam."

Cooper left the office, closing the door behind him. He went thoughtfully back to his office next door.

He had just sat down and pushed some quadrate formulae into a column called "St. Michael's Choir School, 1937–46," when he heard Thisbe shout next door. He stepped out of his office to see what was the matter when Thisbe came bursting through Gormley's door and stormed right into him. They collided, Thisbe almost fell, and Cooper caught her in his arms to hold her up. "Excuse me," she said. She freed herself and stomped off into the sea of cubicles.

"Don't give in to fear," Gormley called after her as she disappeared.

Cooper looked at him.

"She fears her passion," Gormley said, by way of explanation. He took a drink from his beer bottle, looked at Cooper, and belched. Cooper recoiled from the toxic fumes. Gormley returned to his office and closed the door in Cooper's face.

Cooper, seating himself back in front of Vishwas's unified database, reflected that getting in a tangle with a girl like Thisbe was not a bad thing for a weekday afternoon.

Chapter Fourteen

Thisbe Does Not Fear Her Passion

Despite Gormley's allegation to the contrary, Thisbe did not fear her passion. She wallowed in it. Suspecting Cooper, disgusted by Gormley, and an emotional mess over Dean, it was all she could do to get through a day without screaming. She demanded an appointment with Dean. He was out of town on business. She tried to get him the day he came back, but he was at a doctor's appointment. Meghan Evans bumped into Julius alone at a movie, and he said, "She's so wound up she doesn't have any idea what she's doing." Meghan told him that Thisbe had phoned her three times that week and nothing she said made any sense.

Thisbe did not know what to expect, but she was atremble with anticipations. Dean, she knew, was somehow being used by Cooper. Gormley—repulsive, uncivilized, vile—was part of it. That was obvious when Gormley stupidly accused Cooper of having his notebook. Then she caught them drinking together on the job. The two were in cahoots. The notebook was their list of targets. She had seen enough to know that much.

She thought it was interesting that Cooper continued to act as Dean's subordinate. Cooper had an easy way about him, a plausible, I'm-just-here-to-help attitude that was quite different from the surly tough presentation she expected from a gangster. On the other hand, what did she really know about gangsters?

All the movies that men liked were all about a certain crude type that carried guns and smoked and (if played by a big star) knew exactly what to do in the face of a storm of punches and bullets, or (if played by a minor actor) were killed if anyone in the general vicinity tossed a butter knife. Gormley was the sort of gangster she felt she understood. But Cooper was the dangerous one. She thought of the notebook she had seen on his desk: a list of names addresses, and dates of deaths, and checkmarks. After she had seen it, she had returned to her own office—the names she had seen matched names that Cooper had predicted.

Finally she had her appointment with Dean. "Thisbe," he said. "Close the door."

She did.

The door was a heavy windowless blonde oak. Dean's office was triple the usual size, a long rectangle with a large oaken desk at one end and a matching credenza behind. Barrister bookshelves lined the walls. Instead of the usual fluorescent lamps set into the ceiling, suspended halogen lights beamed into frosted glass tiles, diffusing a bright but warmer light through the room. A green banker's lamp stood on Dean's desk. The desk itself was covered with printed reports and spreadsheets. One wall was covered with windows that looked down to the quad far below and the looming black tower to the west.

Now that she was alone with Dean, the sexual element in their relationship began to work on her. She pushed it away. "Dean, what is going on? Gormley is totally unfit for any kind of role here. What are they doing to you?"

Dean was sitting on the edge of his desk. He looked— infuriatingly—amused. "They're not doing anything just yet," he said. "But I do think they're on to something."

"I knew it!" said Thisbe. "They're blackmailing you. What are they doing? Can't we call in the police? Dean, this isn't a movie, this is real. What are they on to?"

"That's a very good question. I wish I knew the answer to it. You see the results that Cooper is getting?"

"Yes."

"How much help do you think his staff provides? Sridhar and that other one?"

"I don't know. But I'd be surprised if they're any use to him at all."

"You don't think he needs them?"

"No, he doesn't need them. They're setting up computer programs as far as I can tell. Collecting data. I don't think they have anything to do with Cooper's kill rate."

"You don't believe Cooper is completely honest."

"I think he's having people killed. Or he knows someone who's having people killed. It amounts to the same thing. Is it insurance money? Cooper told me something crazy the other day—a drinking buddy of his whom everyone thinks is dead but who lives in a neighbor's basement. This is life insurance fraud, isn't it? What are they doing to you?" She had wanted to be strong and businesslike and felt she was not carrying her end off properly. "What are we going to do?" she asked, pushing her emotions down. "It's not like he borrowed the scissors from the Fates."

"It sounds like he's using Death's notebook," said Dean.

"Yes, exactly that, like he has Death's notebook," said Thisbe, though she thought her simile of the Fates more learned and interesting than Dean's. "Or maybe his scythe."

"That seems unlikely. His record is?"

"His record? Oh. Oh, I don't know." These details were beside the point, Thisbe felt, and they exasperated her. "Fifteen for fifteen?"

"You're quite out of date, actually. He's got over fifty kills. No errors."

"Fifty kills?"

"Fifty-three, I think."

"That just proves my point! The whole thing stinks. And one other thing. Do you remember–" and she mentioned one of the names Cooper had provided.

"Should I?"

"No. No," said Thisbe, angry at herself for presenting her information this way but unable to focus with Dean so near. "No, but he was one of the people whose death Cooper predicted."

"And?"

"And he died, on schedule, just like the others."

"Thisbe, is there a point here?"

"I'm sorry. I'm sorry. It's just–" she felt herself on the verge of weeping and fought to hold her composure. "I read his name in the paper. He killed himself."

"So?"

"So? Don't you see?"

"No. We all know that a certain percentage of the population will choose suicide. What's special about this one?"

Thisbe was taken aback. She stuttered. "Oh. I suppose– well– all right. It's just suspicious. That's all. When there's a suicide and someone knows ahead of time, isn't that suspicious?"

"You think Cooper killed this man?"

"What do you think? Don't you think the police would find that interesting? Suicide my foot. 'He's going to kill himself a week Thursday.' That sounds like first degree murder to me. Dean, what is he doing to you?"

Dean considered. He said, "Let's talk about Gormley."

Thisbe colored. "Dean, I know you like him, but I don't think…"

"I know. I know. Don't worry about that. He's here for a reason."

"He is? What is it? He's awful."

"Yes, he is," said Dean complacently.

"Then why is he here?"

"I have another job for myself in mind. Something better than this. Gormley knows the people who control it."

"He does?" Thisbe would never have guessed Gormley knew anybody. "Dean, he's a fraud."

"He has information."

"He does?" It seemed unlikely.

"Yes," said Dean. "He does." He seemed amused.

"Do you think he's working with Cooper?" she asked.

"They're in the same department," said Dean.

"What do you think he's doing?"

"I have no idea," said Dean.

This stopped Thisbe. "Then why did you hire him? What on earth is he doing here if you don't know what he's doing?"

"He has information."

Thisbe began to understand. "They *are* blackmailing you. Oh Dean, what are we going to do? Should we just call the police? It can't be that bad. You're not married. There's nothing you can't do. They can pick up Gormley and Cooper at the same time. I wish you could tell me what it's all about—" But she saw Dean was shaking his head and thought that he meant that he could not tell her. "I understand. Is it something personal, something about the company, something professional? I wish— no, but I understand, it's probably better that I don't know, is that it? But Dean, this man Cooper is— is— he's like Death, Dean. People die all around him. You don't want to play games with him." While she was talking, she paced the floor with excitement. She noticed that Dean was nowhere to be seen and then realized that he was right beside her. He wrapped her in hot embrace. She said quietly, "Listen. I'm right, aren't I? This is exactly what's going on. He's—"

But Dean's mouth was on hers, and they did not speak again for some time.

Chapter Fifteen

Cooper is Investigated

The two Indians stood in the door of Cooper's office. Did Cooper have time to speak to them?

It had been nearly two weeks since Sridhar and Vishwas had had their argument over Vishwas's new unified database. Cooper's hope was that he could keep the two Indians at each other's throats. They would use their energy to attack each other, and neither would find Cooper's fraud. In the meantime he would come up with a plan to get rid of them. To this end, he had put them off several times already, usually by scowling and claiming another meeting. Now, it seemed, they had caught up to him.

Cooper had been doing nothing—working on another of the *Moscow Puzzles*, in fact "Magic Squares." He checked his watch. It was quarter past ten. He thought of remembering suddenly that he was required at a ten o'clock meeting and almost stood up. He felt a sinking inside. He exhaled a long sigh and sat back. It was time to eat the liver and onions. "Come in," he said.

The two Indians shut the door behind them.

"We have come to an agreement," said Vishwas.

"Good," said Cooper miserably.

"I think we are going to use my database."

"Does Sridhar agree with this?" asked Cooper sharply.

Sridhar nodded.

"And your objections have been satisfied?"

"There are no more objections," said Sridhar, shaking his head in that up-down and back-forth way he had.

"No objections," said Vishwas.

"All right then," said Cooper.

"What we are wanting to know," said Vishwas, "is how you arrived at certain conclusions."

"Yes?"

"For instance, there are some equations that we do not understand."

"Yes," said Cooper. He remembered a negotiation course he had taken that stressed the importance of body language. He decided to cross his arms to indicate that he was closed off.

"For instance, we have found that here," he pulled out a paper and handed it to Cooper. It showed rows of numbers with tiny labels above each one. "We do not see how you derived the haitch eff ell." He pointed at one column.

"The what?" said Cooper, who was having a hard time reading the tiny numbers.

"This," said Vishwas. "Haitch eff ell."

"Oh, HFL," said Cooper.

"Yes," said Vishwas.

Cooper looked to Sridhar for help. "I'm not sure what this— where this particular–"

"This is too much detail, too much detail," said Sridhar. "This is Heuristic Lifestyle Factors. We have found some columns that contain long deep equations that we do not follow. They are used to derive dates, but we do not know why they are there. There does not seem to be a rationale."

Cooper squirmed in his chair. Vishwas glared at him from baleful eyes beneath dark brows. Sridhar watched with interest. "Oh. Ah. Yes. That. Hm," said Cooper, feeling he was not being as articulate as he wanted to be. "Right. Good. Yes." Fearing he was repeating himself, he added, "Quite." Changing tack, he decided to contextualize: "HFL."

"Yes," said Vishwas. He leaned forward. "It looks as though this equation erases everything that comes before it and simply hard codes the date." "Hard code" being computer slang for typing a specific value (in this case, the date of death) into the program instead of using the program to derive it.

Cooper looked from Sridhar to Vishwas and from Vishwas to Sridhar. Had he not been feeling so guilty, he might have seen what to do. As it was, he felt his face beginning to heat up again. Once he noticed this, he became more self-conscious and could think only of how guilty he must look.

"They are different every time. But where they come from— we could not find it in your spreadsheets." Sridhar was almost defensive.

Cooper was so surprised at the note of apology in Sridhar's voice that his funk fell away, and he looked at his antagonists. He said, "As I recall, there are several equations that go into the Heuristic Factors—that is, that a different equation may be called depending on the context…"

"Yes, yes," said Vishwas. "That is what we have seen."

Cooper felt he had it. He held up an imperious hand to indicate he was not to be interrupted, though he had in fact paused. "…and that the equations are varied depending on several things, several triggers are available to modify the equations that are used in the HFL column…" Again he paused, hoping for the Indians to speak, to give him something to work with. When they did not, he continued. "I believe I can get you some of the source equations…"

"Yes, yes," said Vishwas impatiently, "but we have the equations already here. They are all in my database. That is the transformation that this column works. But what we are not understanding is, that here there is only one equation in each column–" indicating most of the data, "but that in this haitch eff ell there are many equations, and we cannot see the pattern for why you have to pick one over the other, nor why sometimes the equation even seems to overwrite what came before it, as if a hard coding but–"

Cooper believed at this point that he had been made to look utterly a fool in front of his two subordinates. They were greater mathematicians than he. They were harder working and more perceptive. They had opened the bottle and smelled the snake oil, and now they were playing with him, waiting for him to admit that he was simply entering dates based on nothing, that he had no Equation of Almost Infinite Complexity, that it was all a swindle. He slouched.

"But–" and for the first time ever, Vishwas broke into a broad smile, "But it works! My God, eh, I don't understand why these equations vary here, but I see the dates you have, and we have seen the hit list, and my God, every time we see that you were right again. Oh my God, but this is the part that we are most needing your help with because why you are doing what you do in this column is the one that…"

It took Cooper some time to realize that Vishwas was not calling him a fraud. In fact, he was being complimented. They thought he was a genius. What could it mean?

"…and we think it will be in the future better practice to create several columns to capture what you have grouped here if you are agreeing…"

Cooper could not follow. He got through the next twenty minutes by agreeing to anything the Indians said. They were excited and full of plans. They wanted to work on his quadrate columns, planning to break them apart according to the kind of equation he had used to jam in the right answer. When they left, Cooper sat at his desk. He felt like a taxpayer selected for an audit, who, expecting to be bankrupted and imprisoned for a lifetime of petty skullduggeries, was instead given a beefy refund and a token for the

King streetcar. He was glad that he had not blabbed a confession. He laughed. Some day, he would have to figure out why the Indians didn't turn him in.

Thisbe left Dean's office that day with no more information than she had when she came in. Her head was swimming. It had happened. Dean, who had made her complete and then torn her apart, was hers again. She walked as if in a daze. She realized that she had not learned why he was letting Gormley stay. But then, what did that matter? The passion of years past burned hotter than ever. She felt weak. She sat down to her desk but could not concentrate. She got up and wandered about the office.

She found Cooper in his office. Feeling good, she decided to attack him. "How do you like your new partner?" she asked.

Cooper seemed embarrassed by her question. "All right," he said, though it was not clear that he thought so. Finally he said, "I didn't know Mr. Scratch meant here when he said Gormley had a line on a job."

Thisbe was not sure what to make of this. She said, "So you knew Gormley was coming here?"

This sounded like blame, and Cooper hastened to stop it. "No! I only knew he was looking for work."

"And here he is."

"He is that," said Cooper.

Thisbe was not sure what to make of the situation. What was Cooper's relationship to Gormley? The two were connected some-how, but Cooper didn't like it. She smiled and said, "I'm sure Dean had his reasons."

"I suppose," said Cooper, unconvinced. "Still, I don't feel like I've traded up if you know what I mean."

This phony bland reaction infuriated Thisbe. Cooper, whatever he was up to, did not want Gormley around. Or was that just an act? She remembered that she had seen them talking together at the party. They were next-door neighbors. There could be anything between them. She wanted to confront him, to ask him what he was up to and tell him to leave Dean alone, that she knew all about him. But she controlled herself and said, to draw him out, "I don't even know what Gormley's job here is."

Cooper blinked. He said, "Pardon me?"

"Gormley's job. Do you know what it is?"

"No."

"No idea?"

"No, not really. I thought maybe he was hired on to help me, but he doesn't seem to know much about what I do, and I haven't heard."

This Cooper was a deep one, she thought. Look how blasé he can be. She decided to push him. She told him what Dean had told her: "He's here because he has *information*."

"Ah," Cooper said. "I see."

"Do you Cooper? Do you?" said Thisbe, glaring at him.

Cooper considered this. "No," he admitted.

Thisbe watched. She could see that she had thrown him off a little bit. "I don't know how you would know," she said with calculated insincerity. "But I was hoping you could guess."

"I could guess," repeated Cooper stupidly.

Thisbe watched and said nothing.

"I see." Cooper appeared unthinking. Then he asked, "Do you remember I told you a man died the night of the party?"

"Yes," she said, slowly and clearly, like a poker player when a second ace is dealt to her hand. She was getting somewhere. Cooper was about to crack. "Your neighbor."

"Yes. Well, you remember I saw him later, and he was–"

But Cooper was interrupted by Thisbe's cell phone. It was Julius, warning her about a snowstorm.

"I don't have time for that right now," she told him. If she had seen his number on the phone, she would not have taken the call.

"Sure. All right, I'll avoid the Gardiner. Traffic's always bad in the snow. I made a salad before I left this morning. Yes."

By the time she was off her phone, however, Cooper was on his. Then, to her delight, Dean phoned her. She left Cooper's office to find a more private place to speak to him. But this was a miscalculation. It was just after five o'clock, and people were everywhere, chatting and finding coats and walking about. She found an empty conference room, but Dean only had a question about a report and some few lovers' words. By the time she got back to Cooper's office, his door was closed, and he was gone.

She cursed herself in the parking lot. How had she missed her opportunity with Cooper? He had been ready to confess. Still, Dean's every word melted her. It had been a glorious intoxicating day. She wished she would have gotten Dean to tell her exactly what Cooper was doing, how he was doing it. She supposed he had threatened to have Dean killed. Or kidnapped and stuffed into someone's basement until a ransom was paid? It wouldn't do to be on the wrong side of one of Cooper's predictions. She would see Dean through it. He could not have come back into her life just to be snuffed out by this mild-mannered thugee.

Her mind was so full of Dean and Cooper that it was not until she sat down in her car and put the key in the ignition that she remembered Julius. It was happening again. Years before she had walked out on Julius without a thought because Dean took over her life. Was she going to do that to Julius again, and for the same reason? And then, as they had for the past several weeks, thoughts of Dean filled her mind and pushed any thought of Julius away.

She did not go home right away. Instead, she sat in her car and opened her glove compartment and her purse. In her purse were an address and a name. In her glove compartment was her Perly's map book. She found the address in the guide, planned her route, and eased the BMW out into the snowy rush hour.

It was an hour later that she turned west on St. Clair, sliding in the snow, and found the address she was looking for: St. Ann's Villa. The massive old house had begun its career as the ostentatious home of a millionaire, experienced a conversion and become a convent to an order of nuns, and now given up the cloister to serve the poor as an old age home. Thisbe was a little surprised. But there was the address she had written down, spelled out in big letters under the sign. She had expected a sleazy bar, or a little Italian restaurant. Inside, she gave a name to the officious receptionist: "Briar Chuba, please." It was one of the names she had seen in Cooper's book: a strange name, one she was grateful for, the sort of name you didn't forget. Briar Chuba was supposed to die at three in the morning tonight. Thisbe had come to warn him.

The receptionist sent Thisbe down a hallway and into another wing, and she took a wrong turn and had to ask a nurse's aide for directions. She found herself in a long corridor that resembled a hospital, lined with doors, each holding two or three beds. Medical carts stood outside some of the rooms, and IV tubes. Harsh fluorescent lights shone down with unforgiving clinical precision.

"Can I help you?" A young black woman in a lab coat was standing in front of Thisbe.

She gave the name she had come to see: "Briar Chuba."

"Are you family?" She had an islands accent, and pronounced the last word with three syllables: "fam-i-ly."

Thisbe had not thought how to answer this question. "No, no," she said. "A friend."

"That is good."

The woman led her to one of the rooms. An ancient man lay in the bed with an octopus of intravenous tubes taking fluids in and out of his body. One of the tubes went into his nose but did not appear to be doing anything. Thisbe pointed to it.

"Oxygen."

"Oh." Thisbe paused. "You know, I'm looking for Briar Chuba," she said, expecting to be led away to a doctor. Was he perhaps only an orderly? Someone who wiped up vomit and excrement from the hospital floors and in his spare time supplied Benzedrine to the black hand? This might be tawdry in the extreme.

"Yes, he looks very different, I'm sure," said the black woman in her warm accent: "dif-fer-ent." "And how are you doing tonight?" she fairly yelled into the sick man's ear. There was no response. "He has not been conscious for some days," she explained to Thisbe. "It is good that you came. No one has been to see him since he was brought here."

"Does Briar work with you?" Thisbe asked.

"Does he– ? No, no. I understand that he retired maybe some years ago."

"And where is he?"

"Where is who?"

"Briar Chuba."

The woman looked at Thisbe. "You see him." She pointed to the ancient man before whose bed they stood.

"Oh. Oh, I'm so sorry." Thisbe's mind was racing. "Yes," she said, trying to recover. "I'm so sorry, I—you're right, he looks so different. I didn't expect–" This was ridiculous. "What happened to him?" Thisbe asked, shoving her embarrassment aside.

The woman peered at Thisbe with a glimmer of interest. Then she seemed to decide Thisbe's reactions were not her business, and the interest ended. When she spoke, she was sympathetic but professional. "Oh, nothing happened to him. He is old and sick with a hundred things. He has the lung cancer. Bad, very bad. No chance, no chance this time. The cancer was so far advanced, you see. Smoker, oh yes, smoker. He will not be with us long. They thought him gone last week. Then he fought it off. Then last night was bad. Very bad night. Now I do not think he has anything left to fight. The next bad night will take him away. Maybe tomorrow, maybe next week."

"Maybe tonight?" asked Thisbe.

This made the woman glance at Thisbe, but her quiet sympathetic affect remained. "Yes, yes, maybe tonight at that. I'll let you say goodbye now." She touched Thisbe's hand and was gone.

Chapter Sixteen

Legal

There were few people who could make Cooper forget Thisbe, but one of them had called when she left to talk to Dean: Goohan. What he had said knocked Cooper for a loop. The lawsuit had settled and the stock—the proceeds realized by the suit—was legally Cooper's.

"Can this be true? Am I a millionaire?" blurted Cooper. He then felt that characteristic embarrassment that accompanied any display of eagerness on his part.

"Not yet," said Goohan.

"But I have the 60,000 shares?"

"You do. Free and clear."

Cooper remembered something from a previous conversation with Goohan. "You've got the releases?"

"I have the releases."

Cooper was a-tingle with excitement. "I haven't checked the paper. What are they worth? Can I resign tomorrow?"

"Ah," said Goohan, and Cooper realized the bad news portion of the conversation had arrived. "You should probably look at the newspaper, Cooper. Or go online. There is a bit of disappointment there."

Cooper was impatient. "What do you mean? How much is the stock worth?"

"Cooper, when the corporation went to blazes, everything was taken. The good news is that you have the stock. The bad news is there's nothing else to have."

"What is it worth?" Cooper insisted.

Goohan banged into the phone, and it took Cooper a second to realize he was hitting buttons on his computer. Then Goohan cursed and banged some more buttons. Cooper grew impatient. The lawyer banged away. There was a great crash as Goohan dropped the telephone, then more cursing. Cooper—who had shut his computer down for the night—started it up again. He could look the information up himself faster than his lawyer. The initialization was maddeningly slow. He had just gotten onto the network when Goohan came back on the line. "Approximately– the market is closed, yes, all right– ah– approximately $4.87. Rounded up."

This was not what Cooper had expected. "What are they rounded down?"

"$4.86. That's why you get to keep them. The people counter-suing you gave it up. It wasn't worth paying a lawyer to get them back."

"Lawyers can be expensive."

"It's all about value. Anyway, there was a fair amount of financial and scientific humbuggery in the corporation leading up to its untimely crash. I was able to convince the people who wanted the shares that there is a legal theory which says the owner of a company is liable for fraud committed by the company's agents."

It took Cooper a few seconds to absorb this. He restated, slowly, "So I own the shares free and clear only because the owner of the shares might have to pay back all the debt the company racked up?"

"Exactly!" said Goohan with enthusiasm.

"Meaning, any debts still out there may become my debts."

"You've got it." Goohan was genuinely pleased. "Just so."

"So this may be an empiric victory."

"Yes. Also Pyrrhic."

"I have the shares, but they're worth nothing."

"They're worth $4.87."

"Rounded up."

"Yes, perhaps I'm being optimistic. Though $4.86 is a little pessimistic."

"And I may be liable for millions in debts the company has not paid."

"True, true. Still, that's only a theoretical liability. The shares are an actual asset."

"Goohan, it will cost me $10 to cover the brokerage fees if I try to sell the shares."

Goohan agreed that this was probable. "Still, it's always better to have theoretical liabilities and actual assets rather than the reverse."

"Even if the asset is only $4.86?"

"Well, it's a little more than $4.86. But there is something else," Goohan said.

"What is that?" asked Cooper hopefully. His superstitious faith in the power of lawyers was beginning to work its magic. Goohan would not call him for no reason. But then the reason appeared to him in depressing clarity. He said, "Is this about your fee for obtaining the releases? So that I can be liable for any debts the corporation incurred, as if I don't have enough of my–"

"Cooper, Cooper," said Goohan, interrupting. "Please. Don't worry about my fee."

Cooper was stunned into silence.

Goohan continued. "The reason I'm calling is to tell you this. Everyone thinks the corporation has no assets. But that's not true. There is one patent outstanding. A patent pending, you may be familiar with the phrase. Just keep that under your hat for now. We've got the releases, and a friend at CIPO is reviewing the case.

There's nothing with it still pending, but we've seen movement before when an approval comes through."

"Movement?"

"You have 60,000 shares. They're worth less than a thousandth of a penny each. Let's say this patent generates some buzz. As it may do. We'll see."

"How much buzz?"

"We'll see."

Cooper had no idea what the CIPO was. Still, it was comforting to know he had a friend there. Or was the friend Goohan's?

Cooper stood at Victoria Park in a line seven rows deep for forty minutes waiting for his bus. The poured concrete bus bays were covered but open on both ends, and wind gusts whipped through them, bringing ice pellets to stab at the faces of the commuters. Outside, the wind howled and the driving snow flashed like meteorites under the orange halogen streetlamps.

"They say mother Earth gettin' warmer," said a black man standing behind Cooper. He talked like the American blacks on television. He paused, but no one answered. He said, "I like to see some of that shit."

There were titters and mutters of approval. Someone else made a funny remark about snow shoveling. No one looked around. The commuters stood with eyes facing front, as if turning would increase the stinging wind. They shifted weight from foot to foot or stomped their boots. Despite the long delays, the storm made them happy.

Cooper was disappointed that he had not had time to finish his conversation with Thisbe. How could she not know what Gormley's job was? He wasn't doing anything as far as Cooper could tell. Did he want Cooper's notebook? But why didn't he ask for it? None of it made sense. And just when he had Thisbe to himself, telephones interrupted everything.

The thought of the telephones pleased him. Goohan wouldn't phone if there were nothing. A patent was pending. If it was granted, the stock might pop. If it went to ten cents a share, Cooper would have $6,000. That was something. At a dollar a share, it would be an annual salary. Perhaps it wouldn't matter if he had a job soon. But this time he would keep working until the money from the shares was safe in his bank account. Now that he had begun to pay Akkakumarbalapragada he didn't need trouble. If things went well, he wouldn't need to take the bus anymore.

After the long wait, five buses arrived at the same time to jeers and moans. Cooper, shuffling forward with careful ruthlessness, was able to moosh himself past two high school girls and a little old lady to get through the rear doors of the third bus. He stood balanced over the steps, holding on to a pole to keep from falling out. The doors closed with a loud sigh and the bus rolled out into the snow.

Gormley had information, Thisbe said. Was Gormley going to expose him? That was the only explanation Cooper could come up with. But if that were true, why had no one confronted him? Dean had been out of town for a few days, but he was back now. It didn't make any sense. They weren't keeping Gormley for his work ethic. What else had Thisbe said? She mentioned an obituary. She was short with her boyfriend on the phone. That was a good thing. He wondered what they were paying Gormley.

The bus lost a good number of people at Eglinton and more at Lawrence, and Cooper was able to find a seat for the last few minutes of his commute. He got off at Ivordale and turned his face to the wind. His left boot had a leak in it, and he felt his foot getting colder as the snow entered and melted into his sock. Wind tunnels in the apartment buildings created small hurricanes that blinded him and sent cold fingers of air shivering beneath his jacket. The ploughs had not yet gotten to the sidewalks, and he trudged through the drifts. His nose was running and there was a long wet streak on the glove where he wiped his nostrils.

When he got home, he found Scratch, head covered in a Russian fur cap, shoveling his driveway. Cooper grabbed a shovel and plunged in beside his neighbor. He pointed to a mound of balled up snow. "What do you think of the chances of one of these in hell?" He meant it in a friendly way, but Scratch did not appear to find it funny. Cooper had noticed that dentists did not laugh at dentist jokes either.

But then Scratch smiled. "Well, Gormley's landed on his feet after all, hasn't he?" he said. "I hear he's working with you."

Cooper admitted that Gormley was now coming to work. He did not know what else to say. He wondered what Gormley was saying to Scratch.

Scratch asked how Gormley was doing. He said this in a casual but careful way, as if he were interested but realized that Cooper might not feel at liberty to speak, or as if he cared too much about the answer and wanted to pretend he did not.

"He's just started," said Cooper. It sounded almost like a negative, so to soften it, he added, "He's feeling his way, I think." Then he remembered Gormley's attempts on Thisbe's legs, the double *entendre* made him blush.

There was no time to follow up on this, however, because a long blue and white police car slowed and stopped in front of Scratch's driveway. The snowflakes twinkled as they fell lightly through the yellow beams of the headlights. Then the big sedan growled, the headlights turned onto Cooper and Scratch, and the car was in the driveway.

"Is this where the break-in was?" asked the emerging policeman. Cooper began to say No, but Scratch said, "Yes."

It was Sergeant Maconochie, who had come on the night of Keiter's death. The three went into Scratch's house. Cooper was dealt with quickly. He lived next door. He had seen nothing, heard nothing, and knew nothing. The policeman fixed him with a stare, to intimidate or commit his features to memory. Then he turned to Scratch, the victim of the crime.

No, nothing was taken, Scratch said. No, nothing broken either. Yes, a big mess, many things tossed around the house, files and file boxes. No, Scratch had no idea who it might be. No, no enemies he could think of. He hadn't been in a fight since many years before you were born, tss tss. Looking for? He did not really know, anything he could say would be pure speculation.

But Scratch gave Cooper a wink when he said this, and Cooper, with his peculiar combination of density and insight, understood in a flash that whoever had broken in was looking for the notebook.

Cooper began to sweat and felt himself blushing. He stood up, hoping that the other two would be too absorbed in their discussion to notice.

The conversation immediately stopped. "Where are you going?" said Maconochie.

"If you're through with me," Cooper began, allowing the sentence to trail off.

"Where were you on the night of the break-in?" asked Maconochie.

"At home," said Cooper. "As I said."

Maconochie regarded him. Cooper felt his face cooling. He had nothing to fear. He had not done anything wrong. There was no reason for Maconochie to suspect him. "I see that the cut on your face has healed," said the policeman.

Cooper could not remember the cut, but he thanked Maconochie for noticing.

Scratch was telling the policeman that Yes, there were religious services at his house, and Maconochie was asking who came to the services. Cooper went to get his boots and returned to make his goodbye when they were interrupted by a horrible shriek from the basement.

"The mechanicals," Scratch explained.

But Maconochie was not so easily put off. "Where did that come from?"

"From the furnace," said Scratch.

"I would like to have a look if I may," said Maconochie, who without waiting for a reply—indeed, without waiting to finish his request—was on his way downstairs.

Scratch followed Maconochie down the staircase. This, thought Cooper, was going to be interesting. He followed, wondering what Maconochie would say when he met Keiter. Scratch noticed Cooper following and made a sign to him not to come, but Cooper, curious rather than prudent, pretended not to understand.

The empty basement and monstrous pale green furnace were just as they had been. Cooper watched Maconochie's face: what would he think when he saw Keiter in there? But the policeman remained impassive.

"You should think about getting this replaced," he said, implying that the police force did not approve. "I need to investigate further," he said, but this meant only that he walked around the basement.

Cooper made his way to the basement floor. If Keiter had been there, the shriek signaled his departure, not his coming. The furnace was empty and dark.

Maconochie spent little time in the basement, where, after all, there was little to see. "Call me if you think of anything else," Maconochie stated, handing both Cooper and Scratch his card. Then he was out into the snow, and soon the big police car was backing out and disappearing down the street.

"What was that all about?" Cooper asked.

"A little break-in. Nothing taken. No harm done."

"Why did you call the police?"

Here Scratch smiled. "I didn't." They had returned to the kitchen, and Scratch was pouring out a fresh pot of tea.

"Who did?"

"A neighbor."

"Ah. So someone saw it?"

"The police were quite efficient. Gormley and I were both out. Someone saw a man climb through a side window and disappear, and he called the police."

"Who made the report?"

"Mr. Rulen. Across the street." It was clear as he said this that the usually placid Scratch was annoyed by this interference.

"I'm sure he meant well." Cooper, who did not like people to be angry, changed the subject. "How does Gormley like his new job?"

"Oh, he's doing much better. Out of the house, drinking is way down, no more naked scenes."

Cooper was relieved that Scratch was pleased. If things were going well with Gormley, perhaps the loss of the notebook was not so bad. So Cooper returned to the subject: "You mentioned he may have lost his old job because he lost his notebook."

Scratch looked down at his teacup. He looked up at the fake tiffany lamp above the kitchen table. "That's the reason he was given," said Scratch. "It's not necessarily a bad thing. We can see only so little of the future that it's foolish to predict too much. You try something, and maybe it's for the best. You just do your best by your lights. No one's been killed, after all."

Cooper was comforted by this wise saying, hearing in it a description of his own precarious work situation and a formula for peace of mind even in the midst of brilliant Indians examining fraudulent equations.

Scratch, however, was still thinking of the notebook. "It's a good thing you had the book," he said. "I wouldn't have liked someone else to steal it."

"I didn't steal it," said Cooper. "You gave it to me."

Scratch thought about this as he sipped his tea. "Yes, I suppose I did. Clever of me."

Cooper did not know how to interpret this remark. He asked, "Do you know who's trying to steal it?"

"Yes."

"Who?"

"Oh, a lot of people want it," Scratch began. But the doorbell was playing its cheery tune, and Scratch excused himself to answer.

"Who was it?" said Cooper, following Scratch to the door.

"I expect it's Gormley," said Scratch.

"Gormley?" Why was Gormley going in and out of windows? Hadn't Scratch just said that he was doing better because of his job? Why would Gormley break in to steal the notebook, when Scratch knew that Cooper had it?

Scratch opened the door. It was Gormley, and Cooper realized that Scratch had understood Cooper to ask a question about who was at the door, not who had committed the break-in.

"Forgot my key," said Gormley. "Kept us waiting long enough."

And then another surprise that put Cooper's earlier questions right out of his mind: Gormley was followed by the first Mrs. Rulen.

"I heard *all* about the break-in," she said. "Cooper! Hel*lo*. She wore tight jeans, a form-fitting pink ski jacket and high leather boots and carried the ensemble off rather well, Cooper thought. He felt a spasm of jealousy: what was she doing with Gormley? But then Gormley belched, and Cooper was comforted. "Thirty-*one* day month, Cooper," she said, winking at him.

Cooper, who had been wearing his boots and coat for some time, said he had to go. Gormley and the first Mrs. Rulen made their way to the kitchen. Cooper was left with Scratch.

"Good luck that no one was in the furnace when Maconochie went down to look," said Cooper.

"Yes indeed," said Scratch.

"What would you have done if he had met Keiter?"

"I really didn't want to move again," said Scratch. "I've got all the plans to change the house done."

"I didn't know you were renovating," said Cooper. "I like what you've done so far."

"Yes," said Scratch. "The kitchen is nice."

Since the dreary Sears-furnished kitchen was the exact room that Cooper thought was not nice, and since Scratch did not seem to be joking, Cooper was not sure how to understand this. So he said, "Why would you have to move?"

"The police can become so unpleasant. Especially when there are deaths on the premises."

Cooper went out into the freezing night air. He was pleased that Scratch was not after him about the notebook. It seemed that in keeping it he was doing Scratch a favor. It was not until he had a cup of hot chocolate and was working through the *Moscow Puzzles* ("Geometry with Matches") with a fresh pencil and graph paper that he remembered that Scratch had used the plural, "deaths on the premises." Keiter and—?

Chapter Seventeen

Thisbe and Julius

"I'm writing a letter to the schoolboard," Julius said by way of greeting when Thisbe came in. "Have you ever read this?" He held up a large old book.

"No," said Thisbe. The sight of Julius made her tired.

"It's by Dickens, a so-called 'classic.' Listen to this sentence: ' "I shall do the same," said Mr. Chester, restoring some errant faggots to their places in the grate with the toe of his boot.' "

Thisbe was taking her coat off. She said, "What are you talking about?"

"Can you believe he gets away with stuff like that in this day and age?"

"Stuff like what?" She went to the kitchenette. "You know, it wouldn't kill you to have dinner started," she said.

"You never know. If I accidentally hit an artery while chopping carrots, that's exactly what it might do. 'Safety first,' that's my motto. But—getting back to the important issues of our times. 'Restoring some errant faggots to their places with the toe of his boot'? That's what they did to them in those days. And to think Dickens was considered a reformer. Makes your skin crawl."

He walked to the kitchen. Thisbe was in fact slicing carrots with a butcher knife.

"At any rate, how is young Thiz? Advent upon us, Christmas fa la la-ing merriness all about. What does old Itch have to say?

How about Dean? Money coming in in wheelbarrows now that the nabob of narcissism has placed his proboscis to the grindstone, I expect." He dropped it. "Well, Thiz," he said, "Are you all right these days? Are they reorganizing you or something? Or is it that new fellow, Scratch's neighbor, the one you think is causing trouble? You don't seem quite–"

He gave it up. Thisbe continued with the dinner. She did not say anything, and Julius began to set the table in silence. "Thiz," Julius said, but stopped. There was an Advent wreath on the table—his purchase, Thisbe had done nothing around the apartment for weeks—and Julius lit two candles. "I think the pink one for week three, don't you?" he asked, but she only mumbled a reply.

"Thisbe, you've been like this for weeks now. What's going on? Do we need to talk about it?"

Thisbe looked up. "I'm sorry. Were you saying something?" she said.

"I said, you're about as much fun as a lemur in a straightjacket listening to Tom Jones covering an endless loop of Lindsey Lohan songs played by a pops orchestra when you're stuck in rush hour and you have to go to the bathroom in the middle of a snowstorm in an unheated car during an earthquake when you're late for work. And waiting at a red light."

Thisbe said, "Why is the lemur in a straightjacket? Now be quiet. I have to think."

They ate in silence for a time. Then Julius said, "When are you leaving me?"

This exasperated her. "I don't know," said Thisbe, shrugging the question off with impatience.

"But soon?"

She flashed anger. "Are you looking for promises?"

"You're not the most stable personality."

"Because I can't give you any."

Julius blew out the candles. "What is it you have to think about?" he asked.

This calmed her. "Right now, I'm thinking about Cooper. Julius, why does he pretend to know when people are going to die?"

"Do you think he really has an equation?"

"I don't see how he could. There are these two Indian mathematicians who work with him, but he doesn't let them touch anything that leads to the results. No. No, I'm sure he doesn't. He makes up the ridiculous spreadsheets, clouds them with buzzwords—Bayesian credibility formula, deterministic solvency margin provisioning, Lorenz attractor, Redding theory of immunization, Gaussian copula function—all a lot of hooey."

"But he does give you spreadsheets to back up his predictions?"

"Yes."

"And have you had the other actuaries look at them?"

"Yes."

"And?"

"And– you know how they all are."

"No. I don't, actually."

"They're a club. They're all statisticians and mathematicians, and I'm just the girl manager. They look at his work, they cluck and tittle-tattle a bit, but they don't really tell you anything. They say things like, 'That's an interesting use of the Bornhuetter-Ferguson method,' in a tone meant to imply they don't think much of it, but they never come out and say it doesn't make any sense."

"They must be jealous of Cooper. After all, if he's right, their entire world is second rate and needs to be taken over by his methods."

"Yes… But they don't hate him, they see him as a fraud who's making a little stir and will be gone soon. Cooper backed away from his first, 'I can predict everyone's death,' in favor of a more limited, 'We can personalize the tables a little more.' I think the other actuaries don't really disagree with that—the more you know about someone, the better you can assess risk—and don't particularly see him as a threat. I talked to one old guy who's playing out the string until retirement, and his take on Cooper was, 'He's just marketing.' "

"But what about his predictions? If he's always right, that must be a threat."

Thisbe thought about this. "I don't know. It may be that they don't know he's always right. Dean calls it Cooper's 'kill rate.' I don't know if that's been publicized."

"What is he now?"

"Oh, it's outrageous. Something like fifty for fifty. He's never been wrong, and this is about people dying. He says, 'John Doe of 23 Carriage House Lane will die on October 22,' and then on October 22, John Doe dies. Every time. Fifty times in a row."

"That's impressive."

"It's impossible. Unless he's got something to do with it."

"But are all these people criminals or connected in some way? Is there any evidence?"

"Dean was looking into that. He had a forensics team looking for patterns across Cooper's subjects."

"Uh huh." The name of Thisbe's boss and former lover introduced a chill in the conversation.

Thisbe noticed this, but pushed on. "And they didn't find anything. No patterns, no connections. A few people had this in common, a few had that in common, but no thread. No real connection. They weren't all gamblers, or people with debts."

"Hm." He cleared off some plates and returned with coffee.

"I went to see one of them tonight."

"One of whom?"

"One of Cooper's victims."

"At the morgue?"

"No. He's going to die tonight."

"Who?"

"Oh, I don't know. Weird name. Briar. Briar Chuba. I guess he's Polish. I went to the address to see him. To warn him, maybe, or talk to him."

"Is that how he gives you the names?"

"Right, an address, the name, date and time of death."

"He gives you the time?"

"Yes."

"Isn't that a little strange? How could anyone predict the time? Down to the minute?"

"Down to the minute. The notes said 'Briar Chuba,' gave me the address, and said tonight, three am. Three eighteen, I think it said."

"So. What did you find?"

Thisbe told him. "Anyone could have predicted his death. In fact, I talked to a nurse who did just that."

"So is that all he does? He goes to all the old age homes and finds out who's really old and sick?"

"I don't think you'd go fifty for fifty doing that."

"So what do you think?"

"He's got to be mixed up in it. He's got to be doing something to them."

"I've got it. He's sprinkling two populations together to throw you off. Gamblers and old sick people."

"We thought of that, but no. The forensics team. The connections they found were all pointless: there were five Rotarians, twelve Unitarians, four stamp collectors, forty-nine people who watched Hockey Night in Canada every Saturday. They said it looked like a random sample. I actually gave the statistics to one of the actuaries, and he said the same thing."

"Using his Bornhuetter-Ferguson slide rule, no doubt."

"No doubt. And Julius?"

"Yes?"

"I suppose I am leaving you."

"Yes."

"Yes. Sorry about that."

"All right."

"You don't want to make a scene about it?"

He looked at her. "Should I? Do you want me to?"

"I just thought you might want to."

"Would it do any good?"

Thisbe thought. "I don't suppose it would."

"It usually doesn't."

"Americans make scenes. At least on television."

"Spaniards too. You sound like you're encouraging me."

"No. I don't want you to if you don't want to."

"I think I won't then."

When they were getting ready for bed that night, Julius said, "Do you want me to move out, or are you leaving?"

Thisbe was running water in the bathroom and did not hear him at first. He came into the bathroom.

"Do you think you'll be moving out, or should I do that?"

"Oh," said Thisbe. "Well. I expect I'll move out."

Chapter Eighteen

Thisbe and Dean

Thisbe lay on her back in Dean's bed. Dean lived in a stylish condominium overlooking the lake so that she could not even hear the Gardiner Expressway and the trains on the other side of the building. You could imagine that you were alone with the Great Lake and the calling seagulls wheeling above it, not tied into the noisy rushing clanging world on the other side with its freight in souls and money and goods across the festering city. Above the pale curtains bars of light hit the ceiling, and in the play of light and shadow there she saw a ship, and she was transported to her bedroom in her parents' old home. She dozed, and would not have been surprised if her mother had walked in and told her that she would be late for her violin lesson. She woke again and asked herself: Why is it that, all the time I lived there, I never once knew that I was happy? Then the tears in her eyes rolled down the sides of her face and into her ears and she had to sit up. Without thinking what she meant by it, she said to herself: My situation is precarious.

Dean was in the shower. Everything in his condo was perfect. The furniture was modern and sleek, a thoroughgoing anti-traditional aesthetic, with pale maple and burnished steel, strangely shaped halogen lamps hanging from the ceiling, a rolltop desk cut in modern lines, a mahogany floor made with an inlaid geometric pattern in the center of the room, long closets full of the expensive and understated clothing that Dean the executive wore. The only thing in the room that indicated any eccentricity or personality, besides the perfection of a certain style, was a giant sign bolted onto the wall that said "Leibniz's" in steel letters two and half feet high. "The name of a coffee shop in Quebec City, as well as the father of differential calculus," Dean had explained. "I took it when they went out of business."

A strange electronic signal went off somewhere in the apartment, and it took Thisbe a second to realize that it was a telephone. The signal stopped, there was a silence, and then a voice:

"Agent Gormley checking in," came the high wheedling voice, now transformed, perhaps, into an attempt to sound like Sean Connery in *Thunderball*. "The report is that ooperCay as-hay ethay ook-bay. ormleyGay–" there was a muttering of Gormley interrupting himself: "Hey. That doesn't mean I'm gay." He continued in his *Thunderball* voice. "atchScray. acationVay omingcay upay. Eh?" The sound of a snorting giggle. "acationVay. omingCay upay." More snorts and giggling. "Cupcake. upcakeCay. OrmleyGay igningsay offay." Giggling. "Urf. Also, the police were by again to alktay about the eak-inbray. Urf. Guess what? Urf urf urf." Gormley's chortling caught in his throat, and he began to cough and snort. "Ooh. Hoo. They were asking about ooperCay!" he blurted when he finally had control of his airways again. "Urf urf urf." The bathroom door opened as Gormley began to sing, his voice not unlike a gnu channeling Robert Goulet while choking on an anchovy after a particularly wild night at the Morrisey: "I'm so glad we had this time together. Just to have a laugh or sing a–"

And then Dean was in the next room with the telephone. "Gormley!" shouted Dean. He was in a red rage, something Thisbe had never witnessed before. "Stop that! Shut up! Gormley! Gormley!" It was obvious that, on the other end of the line, Gormley was concentrating on his singing and not listening. "God damn you, shut up!"

"Hullo?" came Gormley's voice. For Dean had still not turned off the speaker phone.

"Stop that idiotic singing. Never do that to me again. Never."

"Hullo? Is this Dean?" said Gormley. It was evident he had not heard Dean's outburst while singing into the phone.

"Gormley," said Dean, and Thisbe could hear him both from his office in the next room and the speaker. "This is the vacation year then?"

"This is it. He talked about it yesterday. This is the year."

"One day?"

"One day off. And this is the big one. He plans to go to the top. He wants out of the business. Frankly, he doesn't do any work at all. He's turned into a no-fun Freddie, and he doesn't want me home all the time. He's trying to get me to do all these things—"

"Gormley. Gormley. We've taken care of all that. You've got a job now. You are a valued director of a leading firm. He can't say anything against that, can he? I've taken care of all that." This explained patiently, as if said many times before.

This time Gormley's reply was unheard: Dean had flipped off the speakerphone. Thisbe was so amazed that she forgot that she had been crying. Gormley was phoning Dean, and Dean was talking to him. Dean so angry he couldn't control himself. She had never heard that before. Dean was all about control. She had thought that Cooper had brought Gormley in, and somehow they had pushed Dean to make the hire. Now it appeared that Dean and Gormley were in some kind of conspiracy together. What had Gormley said? 'Agent Gormley'? A big vacation coming up. 'The big one.' That sounded like a murder. Had they mentioned Cooper?

Thisbe shook herself and rolled out of bed. She was jumping to conclusions. Who cared about Gormley's silly phone calls? She was with Dean again. This thought overwhelmed her, and all thoughts about work, Gormley, Cooper, murders and deaths went from her mind. She was with Dean again. Dean loved her.

Well, not quite. He had not said that. But he was not the sentimental type. The important thing was that they were together again. She would have to get her things from her old apartment (at the moment, she did not even remember that she shared it with Julius). She wondered when Dean would ask her to move in.

He appeared, feet bare but otherwise beautifully dressed in jeans and an expensive T shirt, casual but powerful at the same time. His hair was wet from his shower, but also perfect. "You're still here?" he said, but smiling.

Thisbe did not know what to say. Was he throwing her out? Or was that a joke, and he assumed that they were so close he could say such things to be funny?

Without waiting for a reply, he went back into his office and listened to other messages on his voice mail. Thisbe found her clothes and purse. She slipped into the bathroom and closed the door. She dressed quickly and looked in the mirror. There were circles under her eyes and her hair flew about with static electricity. She did her best with the makeup she had, brushed her teeth and put some water on her hair. She had decided that, after all, his smile meant that they were close and he was kidding.

Dean was at the bathroom door. "Oh," he said, finding it locked. She heard him walk away. There were small bottles of some drug on the counter: Sectral. It sounded familiar, but she could not think why. It struck her as surprising that Dean should have a medical problem. He was too perfect. She recalled a comic strip she had read years before, where Charlie Brown notices that the little red-haired girl nibbles her pencil. "She's human!" says Charlie Brown, and this discovery fills him with joy. Thisbe smiled and then stopped herself. She was becoming silly.

When she opened the door, Dean had put his shoes on and was lying on the bed. She walked over to him. He seemed to be asleep. Thisbe was surprised. Why would he lie down when he was just getting dressed? She gave him a shake. "Hey," she said. "Sleeping beauty."

His eyes opened. "Ah."

"I didn't take that long in the bathroom, did I?"

He sat up slowly.

"Is something wrong?" Could he really be ill, Thisbe wondered. He looked pale. She wanted to reach her hand out and touch his face, his head, his hair. She controlled the impulse, feeling it might not be welcome. Dean did not like to show weakness, she told herself. Her hand was fluttering nervously, and she moved it to her throat.

Dean stood up. "What's wrong is that I left my shaving things in the bathroom when you're visiting," he said. He went to the sink and turned on the water. Thisbe caught sight of herself in the bedroom mirror and noticed that she was as pale as Dean. It was the lamps, she decided—they were modern and efficient, but played hell with your coloring.

It was ridiculous how her mind was wandering, like a schoolgirl. She was determined to focus. She sat on the bed beside the bathroom door, erect and alert. "Dean," she said, "what's going on with you and Gormley?"

Dean stopped for the briefest instant, and Thisbe could not tell if it was just something in the shaving or if the question bothered him. "Yes, you brought this up before," he said, but with his mouth still so as not to cut himself with the razor. He stopped shaving and said, "You should find out everything you can about Cooper."

"What?"

"Just as I said. Cooper. Find out more about him." He began shaving again.

"I know. I'm trying to, but…"

"That's all," he said, lips frozen as he shaved.

"Dean," she began.

He stopped and regarded her with his half-shaved face. "I'd like you to go now," he said.

"Dean!"

"Please leave. Please leave now." He closed the bathroom door.

"Dean," she said. She went to the bathroom door, but it was locked. She thought, This is ridiculous, absurd, he's acting like a seven year-old. "Dean!" she called, knocking on the door.

While she was knocking, he opened it, surprising her so that she was swinging her arm when suddenly Dean was there. He caught her wrist in a strong grip. "I said, please leave." He shoved her wrist away, and she stumbled back towards the bed. By the time she had righted herself, he was into his office and closing that door behind him.

"Dean!"

No answer came from the closed door. Thisbe stood for a few seconds, not sure what to do. A great choking sob wracked her, and she grabbed her things and fled.

Chapter Nineteen

Tourism

The elevator dropped rapidly down, and Dean's stomach hopped inside him. After what seemed like a long descent, the elevator stopped, and a bell rang to indicate that he had at last reached the bottom. Dean removed Gormley's skeleton key from the elevator's control panel and shoved it into his pocket. He stepped out of the elevator and into hell.

It was not what he expected. There were no black devils flying about on bat-wings and sticking pitchforks into the backsides of naked sinners. There were no flames, no unpleasant heat. There were no monstrosities, no din, no stygian blackness. In fact, Dean stepped out into what appeared to be the underground mall beneath the TD Centre office tower in which he worked.

"Wrong place?" he asked of no one, stepping out.

"That depends," said a tall, aristocratic man with a hawk nose, "on where you wanted to go." The man wore a red smock over a crisply tailored grey suit and a red cap that said "Ask Me" in neat white letters. Beneath the cap his pate was balding, but his hair touched the collar of his elegant white shirt. A carnation was just visible in his boutonnière, peeking out from behind the smock.

"I am your tour guide Pierre," said the aristocrat. "Welcome to hell." He held out his hand to shake, but Dean did not take it.

"So this is the right place," said Dean.

"That depends," repeated Tourguide Pierre, with a whiff of not unbecoming arrogance, "on which place you consider wrong. This is my colleague, Tourguide Joe." A jowly man with large droopy ears and a small rosebud mouth appeared. His suit was covered with the same smock. In contrast to Tourguide Pierre's trim dash, he was frumpy and ill-defined. Dangling from his suit jacket sleeves on either side was a woollen string with mittens attached.

Tourguide Joe began a mumbling announcement, speaking with the excitement and verve of an airline stewardess announcing for the twelfth time that day that the cushion you are seated on may be used as a flotation device: "Welcome to your new home. I'm with Hades's Happy Home Helpers, an accredited body whose task is to ensure that new guests learn where things are, what's what, who's who, and what can be done about that."

Tourguide Pierre slapped him on the back of the head and Tourguide Joe stopped talking. Tourguide Pierre said to Dean: "I suppose you have expectations, ideas, preconceptions and prejudices?" He paused for only a second. "Leave them," he commanded.

The two guides walked into the underground mall, Dean following. Tourguide Joe began his drone, swallowing his words when he spoke, his drooping jowls wobbling like the backside of a cow in a bikini. "Over the next three hours, we'll take a brief tour, show you some of your housing options, and show you the provincial parliament where decisions are made. If at any time you have any questions, just ask. Remember, there are no stupid questions."

"There are, however, stupid people," said Tourguide Pierre, examining his fingernails. He looked up. "Many of them."

"Most of them," agreed Dean.

"Shall we begin," Tourguide Joe began, a non-question delivered in the same stewardess mumble, with no attention paid to either his own words or his audience. He turned and began a tour of the underground mall. "On your right, Tim Horton's. The subways are a little way through that arch. St. Andrew's south will curve and take you north up Yonge Street, or you can get on going north to go up University. There are three-hundred and eighty-five specialty shops in the underground, fifty-seven eating establishments, plus hair salons, banks, obviously, and when the weather is poor, you can walk underground from Union Station all the way to Elm Street, north of Dundas…"

Dean followed, looking all about. Hell was no different from the quotidian Earth he had just left. The corridors and shops of the underground mall seemed to have the same people, all shuffling or striding about as their mood dictated, the same little wind-up human beings Dean excelled in every way in the world above. After a long march through the underground mall and a lot of mumbling by Tourguide Joe, Dean asked. "Where are the punishments?" He had expected tortures, angst, weeping, wailing, and gnashing of teeth, a worm that dieth not and a fire that is not extinguished. "I thought there would be punishments."

"Please," said Tourguide Pierre, as if Dean were embarrassingly crass. To emphasize his displeasure, he slapped Tourguide Joe on the back of the head.

"But I wanted to see Marilyn Monroe being ignored. I wanted to see Jimi Hendrix playing banjo for a choir in an old age home. I wanted to see my high school geography teacher having pencils stuck into his backside by unsympathetic adolescents. I wanted to see Pierre Trudeau with a job as a tour guide in an underground shopping– oops!"

"Nope," mumbled Tourguide Joe. His Ask Me! hat had fallen to the ground, and his ears flapped like sails.

"Shut up," Tourguide Pierre said to his partner, fetching him another whack across the back of the head. "We're not here for your entertainment," Tourguide Pierre said to Dean.

"We're hospitality professionals," Tourguide Joe mumbled.

Tourguide Pierre slapped him on the back of the head again.

Dean said, "This will be easy." Tourguide Pierre looked at him but appeared to consider the comment beneath his notice.

They wandered about for some time, Tourguide Joe pointing out the sights, Tourguide Pierre aloof and superior. They saw Roger's Centre, the CN Tower, the Hummingbird ("I thought that was called something different now"), then took the subway and headed north, getting out to see Yorkville, the ROM with its goofy new tumbling dice, the university buildings, Queen's Park.

"So this is Hell," said Dean.

A passing man in a Grateful Dead t-shirt turned and said, "If you think the Montego Bay tourist traps are Jamaica."

Dean thought that there might be something in this, but his guides swept him on. Hell was in every way like our city, a polyglot mixture of souls jostling past each other without rest, each weighed down under its own solitude and sorrow, each grasping towards some future ambition that turned out to be nothing more than a horizon, a shadow receding away no matter how quickly or cleverly it was pursued. Or, as Dean said at the time, "It's crap."

He had stayed longer than he intended, and when they stopped at the YMCA and Tourguide Joe began handing out vouchers for dinner and the first night's lodging, Dean headed for the subway.

"Where do you think you're going?" snarled Tourguide Pierre, his Ask Me! hat bobbing menacingly on his combover, his lapel flower leering beneath his red smock.

"Back to the world of the living," said Dean.

Tourguide Pierre laughed: an ugly sound. "You're going to the Y with the rest of the guests." He reached out and grabbed Dean by the shoulder.

For a split second Dean had an inkling of what it must be like to stand in a room of second class business functionaries and discover that, instead of being the executive in charge of their small bitter fates, you were just another loser in a cubicle. He shrugged at the hand on his shoulder.

But Tourguide Pierre had already let go. He stared at his hand as if it had been burned. The two looked at each other, Tourguide Pierre shocked, Dean amused. "You're– You're–" he sputtered.

"Yes," said Dean. "I'm alive." He added, with conscious cruelty, "Unlike you."

"What are you doing here?"

Dean, feeling much himself, flagged a passing limousine. It screeched to a halt, and Dean opened the door. "Today, just looking around." He sat down in the car and rolled down the window. "I'm going to be your new boss."

The limousine slid away towards the TD Centre and the elevator that would take Dean back to the world of the living.

"Fiddle faddle," said Tourguide Pierre.

Later that afternoon. Gormley was flopped in a leather chair in Dean's big office, legs splayed like a careless teenager drinking beer, which was in fact what he was doing. Gormley held the skeleton key in his hand. Dean was saying, "You remember, you weren't doing well unemployed. Your drinking was getting out of hand." He did not look up as he spoke but wrote with a silver pen on some papers on his desk.

"Everyone wants to take away the one thing I like to do. My one hobby." He held up his bottle. "You don't happen to have another one of these handy, do you?"

"No, Gormley. And I wish you'd stop smuggling them up to your office."

"I never smuggle beer up to my office."

For the first time, Dean looked at Gormley. He had a slight smile on his face: amused. "Then why is your wastepaper basket full of empties at night?"

Gormley jumped as if he had sat on a bee. He looked around Dean's office as if searching for a clue. Then, for just an instant, a sly smile crinkled his face and his crooked teeth showed. He became passionate. "The cleaning staff!" he yelled. "They fill the garbage with their old bottles after we've all gone home. They're trying to frame me. They're jealous. They think if they get me fired, they'll get my office! After we've all gone home, they stay up here boozing it up, and they bring up midgets and a trampoline, and if you come back after hours, you'll find some of them out front trying to sell meth to minors, and–" Gormley looked as though some unpleasant thought had suddenly occurred to him "–and–and Internet porn! They're fiends for the stuff. I don't know how they got into my computer. I must have left it on by mistake one night, but they download everything. It's horrible, and it takes up my entire hard drive. I had to look at every single picture just to find out what it was because I was worried about deleting something valuable to the corporation because–"

Dean had been waving his hand through much of this to tell Gormley to stop. Finally he said, "Gormley. Gormley. Shut up." Dean looked at his computer and pressed some keys. "Right. All right. Gormley, none of that matters. You do need to stop saying rude things to the young women. Some of them might cause trouble." He raised a hand to stop Gormley, who was trying to interrupt with more excuses. "But none of that matters."

"I don't think I should have to come to work every day," Gormley whined.

Dean said, "Done. Call IT and have them set you up with a laptop. You have to log on in the morning. Then you can be home to keep an eye on him. That might work well."

"I don't want to keep an eye on him."

"Gormley. Gormley, it's just for a short time. You said yourself the vacation is coming. That's our chance, isn't it? That's what we're working for."

Gormley mumbled something: truculent.

"This is our chance. Every fifty years."

"Every fifty years," said Gormley.

"That's right. You don't want to have to find another job, do you?"

Mumbling. This time a negative.

"So we must be attentive." Dean pointed to the skeleton key. "I've visited. I spent a few hours walking around, took a tour. I think it will do. There are some things I'll need to change, of course, but I think the job will do nicely for me. If I'm going to end up there, I'm going to end up in charge. That's where you come in. When he leaves, he leaves someone in charge."

"Girls like it when you use the word 'Power,' " said Gormley, half to himself.

"All right. Power." He waited until Gormley stopped staring off into space and focused again. Then he continued. "But I think we can make things difficult for you here. I think you would not like everyone to know what I know about you, for one thing. An ad in a newspaper, shall we say..."

"Why do you think I wouldn't like that? Chicks love that kind of thing. Imagine if you told everyone what my job was? Think of the chicks!" It was obvious that Gormley was doing just that, for his eyes glazed over, and he squirmed lasciviously in his seat, thin legs writhing. "I'm a middle manager," Gormley said complacently, imagining the effect such a statement would have on the chicks.

"Because your father wouldn't like it," snapped Dean.

Gormley suddenly sat bolt upright like a debauched private in the Queen's Own Rifles called to attention by his sergeant.

"He's loosened up a little, but I don't think he wants open out-and-out publicity yet."

Gormley drooped into his usual liquidlike slouch, defeated. "He doesn't leave anyone in charge."

"He– he– ?" Dean was taken aback.

"He doesn't leave anyone in charge," said Gormley in the whiny know-it-all way that gets so many future software engineers beaten up at the age of eleven, "because there's nothing to be in charge *of*."

"But– but–"

"It's when he comes *back*."

"Ah."

"The question is…"

"The question is?"

"*Whom* comes back."

"Who."

"That's what I said."

"You said Whom."

"Whom comes back. That's the question."

"Who comes back."

"Yeah."

"And who does come back?"

"That's the point."

"What is?"

"Who comes back."

"And who does?"

"He doesn't want to."

"Yes."

"And so–"

"Yes?"

"I think you can switch."

"You do."

"That's the plan."

"The plan is that when it's time to come back, he doesn't return, and I take his place."

"Yeah."

"And this will work?"

"Guaranteed."

"What is your guarantee?"

"I don't know."

"You don't know if this will work. Gormley, you're being paid handsomely…"

"It'll work."

"It will."

"Ya." This last word truncated, "yeah" in the sense of "I have no idea, but I'm not going to tell you that."

"You're sure."

"Ya." Same business.

"How can you be sure? Have you done it before?"

"Ya."

"Really?" There was real interest in Dean's voice. "You mean he's not the original? He's the second?"

"Ya."

"Who was the first? When did it happen? You have to tell me about this. This is what I need to know. How did the switch occur last time?"

"I don't know."

"But there was a switch?"

"Ya."

"Who was the first one?"

"Him."

"Who?"

"Him."

"You mean Scratch?"

"Ya."

"So he's the first one?"

"Ya."

"So there was no switch."

"Ya."

"Gormley. Why did you say there was one?"

"I didn't."

"Yes you did. You just said it a minute ago."

"Oh."

"So you don't know if it will work."

"Ya."

"But you think it will."

"Ya."

"Gormley, I don't have time for this."

"Okay." Now on the defensive.

"You're being well paid."

"Okay."

"So stop complaining."

"Okay."

"And prepare the switch."

"Okay." A pause.

"Gormley, my date is coming up. Soon."

"What is the date?"

Dean slumped. "I don't know. The contract language is vague. 'On or about, not before' language. Time is short." He pulled himself up, all vulnerability gone, replaced by his usual imperial persona. "You told me you couldn't change it, so we came up with this plan. It needs to work."

Gormley sat up straight. His jaw dropped open. "I don't have the book."

"Yes, you explained that to me."

"But we know who has it."

"Cooper."

"Yes."

"We can change the dates. That is, we might be able to."

Dean started in his chair. He stood up. "I thought that you said we couldn't change them."

"I couldn't when it was my book. That's always true. There are rules and laws about that. Very unpleasant laws. Unpleasant and unsympathetic persons come. Persons one would not wish to meet." He shuddered, then brightened. "But it's not my book anymore, is it?" Gormley smiled like an evil child in a horror movie, his teeth dangerous.

"So the rules don't apply to you. Are you telling me we can change the book?"

"It's tricky. There are rules about it."

"You said that."

"The one who owns it can't change anything."

"But you don't own it anymore."

"Right."

"So we can go right downstairs and take it from Cooper and change it."

"Ha. That's what you think."

"Why doesn't that work?"

"Because if you took it like that, you'd be the owner, wouldn't you?"

"How does the book know that?"

"It knows."

Dean looked at Gormley. Dean was not a trustful man, nor was Gormley trustworthy. Though it surprised him, Dean found that he trusted Gormley in this matter. "So I can't just take it from Cooper by force."

"No. Wouldn't work."

"Can I steal it?"

"Of course you can steal it."

"Yes, yes, but if I did, could I update it?"

Gormley considered this. "Maybe."

"What if I borrowed it. If he let me look at it?"

"That's more likely."

"What other scenarios are there? Stealing it is a last resort. Owning it is no good. Asking to borrow it is best. Anything else?"

But Gormley had moved on. "You were going to get me a better office."

"Gormley, we were talking about the book."

"And a parking space."

"The book, anything more on the book?"

"I want a secretary too."

Dean's cell phone rang. This pleased Dean, who often used distractions to reset negotiations. "Yes?"

It was Thisbe. Dean cut her off. "I'm in a meeting. Follow Cooper. Find out how he does it. That's got to be your priority. I'll talk to you later." He hung up and turned to Gormley. "How about this. I've given you a salary and made you a director. Scratch feels he no longer has to worry about you. I've made a succession plan in which you are named. I don't know what more I can do for you." This was said in Dean's negotiating voice, in that tone that indicates a final offer had been made.

"Okay," said Gormley. It was to Gormley's credit, Dean felt, that he crumpled up nicely when threatened. "But you need to be nice to me, or I won't help you."

"Gormley," said Dean. He knew that his threats were hollow. Upon his death, which was rapidly approaching, Scratch would become the owner of his soul, according to the contract he had signed so many years ago. He adopted a reasonable tone. "Gormley, I'd simply like you to follow through on your end of the bargain."

"Oh. Okay."

"If my date is coming up, then I need to be in place before the vacation ends."

"Okay."

"Or, I need access to the notebook in whatever way lets me change my date."

"Okay."

"And you're going to get me one or the other of those things."

"Yeah."

"Because if you don't, you won't have a job here."

"I won't?"

"And you won't have a job anywhere else either."

"Oh. Yeah."

"So we understand each other?"

"I need a beer," said Gormley.

"No you don't! You need to– God damn it, Gormley, you–" And for the second time in a few days, Dean felt himself quivering with rage, furious that he had to depend on someone else, more furious that the someone else was Gormley. Prone to long slow hatreds, he was not a man who lost his temper easily, and he felt his body giving off heat, felt adrenaline rushing, and he jumped out of his chair to diffuse the wave of energy that coursed through him. And then he felt the blood begin to push inside his temples and his chest, and it seemed that he could feel his heart bloating inside him, and he knew that another fainting spell was coming on him.

He leaned heavily on his desk, supporting himself with closed fists. The energy rocketing through him a second before vanished away and he felt weak. "Gormley," he said. If he had not been so distracted by the pain in his core, he would have known how to interpret Gormley's look. For it was as if the two men had switched places: Gormley suddenly cool and professional, an expert watching something he had seen many times before. But Dean saw only that Gormley regarded him with attention and interest. "Gormley, there's one more thing I need you to do."

Gormley, like a doctor observing a patient, said nothing.

"I need a pill. Where are my pills?" Dean noticed that he could not feel his feet or legs. He looked at his fists on the desk. They were blue. He tried to move and fell back. The chair was right beneath him, and he appeared merely to sit down heavily.

"Gormley," he said again. "My pills."

"I don't have them," Gormley whined.

"We know who has it," said Dean, delirious. "I need the date." He felt the anger rising in him and tried to push it away. He gasped, feeling a need for more air as if he had just been running at mountain altitudes. "Get it," he croaked. "I need the date. I need–" His blue hands fumbled at the drawer where his heart medication was kept.

"Why don't you ask Cooper? He's Mister Big Fat Equation."

But Dean had slumped head down on his desk and passed out.

Gormley stood up and peered over the desk to get a better look at Dean. He had the retired practitioner's interest in how things were being done nowadays. Dean certainly looked poorly. All the color was gone from his face, except for a few ugly reddish blotches here and there. His eyes were partly open, but no iris could be seen through the cracks. All in all, thought Gormley, not a bad job.

But he was disappointed. Dean let out a long sighing breath, then gasped, then began to breathe deeply and slowly. It was not death. It was something less. Gormley gave Dean a poke. "Hey," he said, "Wakey wakey."

Dean did not move.

"Hey." This time he shoved Dean. But Dean did not move. Gormley put his hands on either side of Dean's head and lifted it off the desktop. "Yoo hoo," he sang, but Dean did not wake up. While holding Dean's head, he noticed, from his new angle, an official looking paper with the word "Gormley" on it. He reached for the paper, forgetting that he was holding Dean's head up. The head fell, whacking against the solid desktop with a dark thud. "Oh. Sorry," said Gormley to Dean, but Dean seemed to be still asleep. Gormley retrieved the paper and read it with interest. He folded it and put it in his breast pocket.

He stood up and walked to the door, but then thought better of it. He went back to Dean, still collapsed on his desk. He pushed Dean over to one side and pulled at his pants pocket. The wallet came out easily. Gormley looked at the pretty colored paper in the billfold and selected a twenty dollar bill and two fives. He dropped the wallet on the desk and was about to leave, but again stopped and went back to Dean. He took the heavy men's watch from Dean's left arm and put it on his own bony wrist.

"Dean said not to be disturbed," he told Gloria as he shut the office door behind him. The watch settled against his drooping hand like an oversize bracelet.

He walked to the elevator and found Sridhar and Vishwas there, arguing in a language he did not understand. "The only good injun," Gormley said, "is a dead injun. Urf urf."

"Mr. Gormley," said Vishwas, nodding his head from side to side. "I am going out to lunch. Sridhar is going to stay and work. Would you like to come?"

"Urf urf," said Gormley. "Urf."

"I am not sure I understand," said Vishwas.

"No," said Gormley. He looked at Sridhar. His face was puffy, his eyes heavily ringed, his chin and upper lip pasted with ill-shaven black hairs as unkempt in appearance as Gormley's teeth. "Whoosh," said Gormley, "You look like someone shat in a blender."

Chapter Twenty

Sridhar

Cooper was wrong about Sridhar. Sridhar did not work hard. He allowed Vishwas to work hard. Sridhar listened well, sized up the situation, and figured out what needed to be done. He talked it through with Vishwas to ensure that they were doing the right work. Sridhar was himself a combination of such rapid intelligence and sheer brass that he was able to do very little but still know enough and speak well enough that other people's work often appeared to be his personal contribution. He kept aloof from his coworkers, and sat with Vishwas just long enough to learn what was necessary to interpret Vishwas to the world. The interpretations, scrupulously truthful, contained just a hint that he, Sridhar, had been the impetus behind the work. Cooper was entirely taken in. He had revised his early impression that Sridhar did less than Vishwas and now believed that Vishwas worked under Sridhar's direction and in fact that Sridhar was kind to include the simple math-minded Vishwas in the credit for the prodigious tables of probability that the two Indians offered.

Sridhar had come a long way from Goa. Or, since that western coast of India is better known for surfing Catholics than Hindu mystics, perhaps his attitude was only to be expected. The seventh son of a pious Hindu railway engineer, clever Sridhar had taken all the money his father and elder brothers could scrape together to get a first rate education in Canada. He had been unable to resist certain women with whom he lived at University College. When a gossipy Brahmin named Roohi went back to Goa, knowledge of Sridhar's sexual life returned as well and destroyed his father's hope of arranging a marriage into the best families for his brilliant son. Sridhar had not felt how much this had hurt his father. He continued to sleep with the interchangeable women always available at a university and immersed himself in physics, algebra, calculus, and statistics. His plan was simple. White men ran everything. He would follow their paths and join in their culture of success. He had seen enough of them to know that the most successful were not the ones who worked the hardest.

His job at Seals was a logical step. It was a reputable firm. He needed an industry, and insurance, recession-proof, money-oriented, well-connected to government, was as good a choice as any. He would learn what he could and save his money. If he lived frugally, and he did—three roommates, no lunches, no telephone—he would, with moderate loans, be able to afford the Wharton school in two years. As a boy, he had waited on the long-legged ladies in the hotels of Goa. When he returned, he would go as a guest to those hotels, where he would sleep with the daughters of the ladies who had once sent him for bottles of Perrier water and cups of sherbet.

His experience with Cooper, however, had shaken him. While he had thought to leave the religious world of India behind, it seemed that as science waxed greater it converged into mysticism. He had studied enough to know that the physicists, no less than the holy men whom his father admired, believed that the world around us was all an illusion. They believed in subscopic particles that were essentially unknowable. According to the physicists, there could be no such thing as a foot or a leg, a table, a chair, a dollar, a woman. If he had wanted the obscurantism of these physicists, he would never have needed to leave India.

But in fleeing physics for business, he now found himself again confronted with the mystical. This white man Cooper was creating a mathematics that revealed the threshold between life and death. It was now obvious beyond any doubt that Cooper was the greatest mathematician ever, for he had not missed a prediction since Sridhar had come to work for him. There was some intuition Cooper had about these things, some artistry. For Cooper could not say, and not even Vishwas could figure out, how he determined what to do in the columns-of-many-equations, the Heuristic Lifestyle Factors column where Cooper hid his quadrate formulae. Sridhar saw Cooper, seemingly at random, forcing long streams of numbers into an unexpected date. Somehow he knew. Like Michelangelo taking risks with his chisels and his block of marble, Cooper always got it right.

The deeper Sridhar looked into the data, the more he found monstrous correspondences. He had learned as a boy that, for example, the Fibonacci numbers—numbers derived from a mathematical series in which each new number is the sum of the previous two numbers, 1, 1, 2, 3, 5, 8, 13, 21, etc.—were visible in the phyllotaxes of many plants, in the spirals of daisies and pineapples, in seashells, in the family trees of rabbits, cows, and bees. But now he had discovered pages of data used in the calculation of death replicated pages of forty year-old hockey statistics. When he first found this he thought that he must be wrong, or the numbers must represent some specialized stub tables created solely for hockey players. This was not the case: the hockey statistics corresponded to a many different columns of data, but none of them related to hockey.

If Cooper had switched some of the rows about, the correspondence would not have been obvious. But he had not, and their presence appalled Sridhar. Why had Cooper arranged the columns just so? Sridhar looked further, examining long strings of Cooper's data. He discovered a hundred such duplications: flu shots and prescription medications and light switches that were used in Cooper's calculations of death dates corresponded to published sales data for real estate in Scarborough. Rows and rows of data anyone could download from the Toronto Stock Exchange websites matched perfectly to rows and rows of vegetables and meats eaten, television programs watched and miles carried, crawled, walked, bicycled, driven, and wheelchaired in the calculus of death. Sometimes it was just a handful of numbers, but at other times, a thousand rows spread out across dozens of columns matched some completely unrelated data. Sridhar began to look for more correspondences, and, looking, found them. There were complex shadows and echoes, where a group of numbers in Cooper's calculations equaled some totally unrelated set of statistics multiplied by 3, or divided by 2, or where they equaled the square or square root or the inverse or the natural log. All the famous mathematical theorems and proofs were found in Cooper's work. It was as if, at the border of life and death, all the numbers and mathematics that had ever been thought of by man converged.

Sridhar confided his discoveries to Vishwas. Vishwas, sitting in his cubicle surrounded by the statues of three gods and colored pictures of fractals, was unsurprised. He came from the priestly caste, and his Brahminism taught him that this was exactly what one should expect to find. "Are we not taught that all is one?" he asked, dark eyes shining. "And if the world is one, why should it be a surprise to discover that seemingly different things show, on deeper investigation, the same qualities and patterns?" And he continued, happy in his work.

But for Sridhar, who believed he had shucked off useless and ancient superstitions, Cooper's numbers were a pointed stick in the eye. Who could explain why these rows of numbers were the same? What hidden structure of the universe did these equivalencies reveal? It was absurd, yet the matches could not be denied.

And these numbers, when combined as Cooper combined them, uncovered the moment of death for living human beings.

At night, Sridhar sat in front of his computer staring at the matching rows of numbers, his mind reeling as if he were drunk. It was impossible to see such things and still believe that the world was untouched by the hand of any god. But if that were true, then for what had he left his home and the gods of his father and his father's fathers?

Chapter Twenty-One

The Ice Storm

Pressured by Dean to find out more about Cooper, Thisbe kept at her detective work. When Cooper went for lunch, she snuck into his office and managed to get on his laptop. His files were about what she suspected: spreadsheet workbooks with page after page of formulae, as well as some specialized statistics and mathematics software; names and ages, voter roles, marketing data, credit reports, enrollment lists; database software; programming languages and compilers; video games. There was nothing that would prove anything in particular about him. She remembered that Seals had dismissed someone recently for having pornography on their machine, so she did a quick search for picture files on Cooper's machine: *.gif, *.jpg, *.png. Maybe she could get rid of him that way. What she found was a complete surprise.

There was a picture of her. It was old, a younger, focused Thisbe playing her violin in Walter Hall. The picture was familiar, and she realized it had been in the university yearbook. Where had Cooper gotten it? More to the point, why did he have it? She knew people who would pull up a picture of a coworker to show friends or family. But Cooper lived alone. Why would he have a picture of her?

She remembered a scene in a gangster movie where the hit man is shown photographs of his mark. Perhaps Cooper was planning to have her killed too. She shuddered and looked around. One of the accounting team was talking in the cubicle outside Cooper's office. She wished Dean would let her call the police. Cooper must certainly be threatening him somehow—why else would Dean be so warm and then suddenly so cold? Thisbe thought: It would not do to be caught here.

She did a screencapture of her photograph beside Cooper's email. She wanted a record of this. She worked in a panic, nervous that at any moment Cooper might return, and it took her three tries to get her password right. She did not yet know what she would do with it. She did not believe the police would arrest a man for having a picture of a coworker. She had just gotten her email to a compose window and was attaching the file when the unthinkable happened: Cooper walked in the door.

"Thisbe! What a nice surprise," he said. He was carrying a bag from the deli in the underground mall. "Looks nasty outside," he said.

Thisbe could not speak. "Uh– Erg– Uh– Um," she said. She was hammering the Send button with her cursor, but the email would not go. It wallowed on the screen like a hippopotamus in a particularly comfortable mud hole. "God!" she said out loud.

It was an error to let herself become so heated. Cooper had sat down on the other side of his desk where he could not see the computer screen. Now, hearing Thisbe curse and being of a helpful disposition, he stood up. "Anything I can do?" he asked, coming around to his usual position.

Thisbe half closed the laptop so Cooper could not see the screen. "I apologize for this," she said, obviously flustered and embarrassed. "I accidentally sent an email that is not for you. It concerns things outside the scope of your duties here. I had to go on to your machine to delete it," she said. Her voice shook as she spoke.

"Oh," said Cooper. He went back to the visitor's chair and sat down again. "Well, carry on," he said affably. He opened his lunch bag. "Would you like a pickle?"

Thisbe was still on tenterhooks with Dean. He called her; she went and spent the night. And while he had not thrown her out so brutally again, she felt that she was being used. Where was her self-respect? She was a convenience to him.

And then she turned her mind from these thoughts and said to herself that they were both under terrific strain, that this Cooper business was scary and awful and dangerous, and that she and Dean and everything would come out right once Cooper and his blackmail and his hitmen were taken care of.

She spent the afternoon in her office and did not come out until it was well past the hour Cooper had usually left. She had to admit that he was a cool one. He had caught her red-handed with nothing to say, and instead of pressing his advantage he had sat down and eaten his lunch as if there was nothing at all to find. She was ashamed of her own performance. She should have called him out right there. In her imagination she saw herself saying, "You're a liar and a gangster, and I'm going to see that justice is done." It was infuriating to think she had been such a wreck and Cooper so casual. He has nothing to fear. That's what he was saying. He thought she couldn't touch him.

Over the past two weeks, Thisbe had traveled to more of Cooper's projected death addresses, and in each case found nothing incriminating. She had had some vague idea that she would meet someone that she could speak with, warn, ask questions of; someone who would know about Cooper, whom she would take to the police and save; someone who would explain exactly what lay at the heart of Cooper's grisly mystery. But besides Briar Chuba, she had discovered three hospitals, two more old age homes, and a burned-out house in the Jane-Finch corridor that she was not brave enough to enter, and that, she read in the papers, was the site of a drug gang shootout on the night Cooper called for deaths there.

This time, it would be different. She had cased the neighborhood over the weekend. Two deaths were predicted for tonight in a big rambling house on Stephen Frank, above Hogg's Hollow between Avenue Road and Yonge Street.

It was close to eight o'clock when she pulled her car out of the parking garage and onto University. The weather could not make up its mind if it was to snow or rain, and fat icy snowflakes pelted her windshield and froze. She made her way cautiously uptown, fishtailing crazily once around the Queen's Park circle, sliding out into the St. Clair intersection at a red light and being honked at by taxis as she tried to back out of traffic. She turned on the radio to a general report of an ice storm and learned that the police were asking everyone to stay in. This was followed by a long list of events that had been canceled because of the weather. Many cars were off the road, and there had been a huge accident on the Gardiner Expressway: a tractor-trailer had been unable to brake on the raised highway and rear-ended an entire herd of stopped cars. Emergency vehicles, the radio intoned, were in the area. "If you are unlucky enough to be on the roads tonight, avoid the Gardiner—we've just had a listener call in on a cell phone, and cars have been stuck behind the accident for over two hours."

Thisbe smiled smugly at the thought that she was not on the Gardiner tonight, her usual route to Scratch's house. Then she was struck by a memory that almost bowled her over. Cooper's weekly report had said that someone was supposed to die on the Gardiner Expressway this evening. How did he know such things? And then she realized that it was a coincidence: they had planned to kill someone by sabotaging his car. To Cooper's mob, the deadly ice was just a lucky fluke to disguise their deed.

She eased through the streets. After St. Clair the traffic thinned considerably, and by Lawrence she was alone on the icy road. Most people, it seemed, had heeded the warning not to travel. She remembered the huge hill up Hogg's Hollow and was glad that the easiest route to her destination kept her on Avenue Road and did not require her to take Yonge Street. The slush was still falling in large grey splats across her windshield. Even with the wipers on high, visibility was poor. She came to an intersection she did not recognize and could not tell where she was: ice covered the street signs. Not knowing what else to do, she pulled out into the empty intersection and continued on her way. She became aware of an increasing pop pop popping sound. It took her some blocks to realize that it was the small branches of trees, made heavy and brittle by the ice, were cracking under their own weight and dropping to the sidewalk and street below.

Her cell phone rang and, without taking her eyes off the road, she answered with the speakerphone switch. It was Julius.

"Where are you?" he asked.

She told him: in the car, driving.

"Stuck in traffic, eh?"

This was more convenient than making up her own lie, so she agreed. Any work-related overtime, even around Cooper's strange predictions, was interpreted by Julius as time spent with Dean and caused new strain and anxiety.

Julius was saying, "This global warming is the best thing for Canada. We're going to be a country of new year-round luxury resorts. I'm investing in beachfront property on Hudson Bay right now."

"Icy. Gotta go," said Thisbe. She hung up.

There was a loud bang behind her, and Thisbe jumped in her seat. She thought that perhaps someone had hit her, so she slammed on the brakes. Her car made a long slow slide to a stop. She looked all around. There was no car behind her, or indeed anywhere near her. Obscured through the slushy rear window, which even the defroster could not clear, she saw what had made the noise. On the sidewalk beside the road, a large black-clad man, impossibly stretched, lay quivering on the ground.

She put her car in park and stepped outside. The heavy icy rain stung her as it hit. Behind her, transformed because now she could see it, was a large ice-covered tree limb, longer than her car and thicker around the bottom than her thigh. She could see the jagged end where the branch had broken. All around, she heard the sound of the ice storm and the sound of twigs breaking and falling: pop pop pop. The trees, the lamp posts, the telephone wires, the fences and gates all looked as though they were encased in shining silvery glass. The city was desolate and weird and beautiful.

She returned to her car and continued to drive. It suddenly became more difficult to see, and she flipped her windshield wipers to a different setting before she realized that the streetlights had gone out. She continued along the road, driving for two blocks with high beams on before deciding that, because the falling ice picked them up and reflected them back at her, they were worse than the regular headlamps.

Pop. Pop. Pop. At last she came to the street she was looking for. All the lights were out. The house loomed large and dark before her. She pulled into the driveway, cracking a long thin fallen tree limb beneath her tires. It was already 9:30—it had taken her considerably longer to make her way over the icy streets than she had expected. Still, she had some time. According to Cooper, there would be two deaths: Irene Davillo and Colleen Ehrens, at this address, at 10:34 this night. She left the car engine running, just in case, and went to the unlit house. She slipped and almost fell. Besides several larger branches, the entire driveway was covered with tiny iced-over twigs. It now seemed to be raining nothing but ice, and the wind blew it like frozen glass shards against her cheeks and face. The car lights lit her way, and she jumped onto the dry front porch. The rain was insistent, ping-pinging against the porch roof above her.

She rang the dark doorbell. No sound. She stood for a few seconds, uncertain what to do. Then she thought, Of course, the blackout. There was an old-fashioned brass knocker. She gave three loud raps and waited, looking around her. There was a For Sale sign on the lawn, she hadn't noticed that before. Pop pop pop.

No one came. She wished that she could hear better, but the sound of the ice falling and the wind in the trees was insistent. There could be someone inside. She knocked again. Although she was partially sheltered on the porch, the wind gusted around her. She waited, blowing into her hands and stepping back and forth. She checked her watch. It was 9:41. No one was home. She walked and slid back to her car and climbed in, shivering. She turned the heat up high. She brushed at her hair with a thin hand and found ice chips in it. The side and rear windows were covered over and almost opaque, and she turned the defrosters on, trying to melt the ice. The rear windows were so iced over that she was unable to lower them. The right front window still worked and sank into the door, leaving a smooth silver sheet in place. She slapped it with an open hand and had the satisfaction of seeing it shatter outwards.

Could the presence of a bystander prevent the murders from occurring? Julius would call this the Heisenberg principle. Beneath this thought crowded the question she was trying not to think: would they shoot if she were in the line of fire? She had never asked whether Cooper knew the date of her death.

She turned off the headlights and sat with only the parking lights on, the windshield wipers flipping back and forth intermittently to prevent their freezing to the car. Where was everybody? The tension of the drive and the thought of an impending murder made her tense, but the lateness of the hour and the tedium of the wait made her doze. She slouched down in the driver's seat. Her eyes closed. All around her was the sound of ice pelleting down, of the wind and the cracking of trees.

She awakened suddenly to the sound of a horn beeping and lights shining behind her. In front of her windshield, a black opening was rising upwards, and she rubbed her eyes before realizing that she was looking at a garage door opening. She was confused and it took her some seconds to remember where she was. Her head was aching with sleep and her eyes were so heavy that it hurt to keep them open. Her sluggish mind registered the fact that she was in her car, that she had parked in the wrong place, that the rightful owner of the parking place was behind her, that she had to back up and let her in. She put her car in reverse and waited, her foot on the brake. The car behind her backed up, the glare of its headlights receding and then turning to one side. She noticed that a light was on in the garage and remembered the blackout. Power had been restored. She heard the pop of falling twigs and the crack of a small stick against her car. She began to ease down the driveway, and pulled back into the street so that she was opposite the car that had awakened her, the two cars facing each other on either side of the driveway she had just vacated.

The other car was a recent model Honda, a small car—an Accord, she thought sleepily, that's what it is. Inside the car were two people, women by the shape of the heads silhouetted through the windshield. Only at that moment did she remember why she was there. She checked the clock: it was 10:34. With a flash of panic she reached for the gearshift and slammed her car into Park.

Before she could move again, a huge breaking sound split the air above her like a thunderclap. The Honda began to move forward. As she watched, a gigantic branch, as thick around as a large tree itself, fell from the sky and crushed the roof of the little Honda. Where there had been two heads in the windshield, there was now nothing. The fingers of the great branch spread out in all directions, covering the street and slapping the fenders of her own vehicle across the driveway. She jumped in her seat and cried out, but it was all too late. The smaller branches that hung onto the great one that had fallen quivered and shook, and many of them cracked— pop pop pop—and fell off with the impact.

Thisbe opened the door of her car and tried to get out, but something prevented her. She tried again. She tried a third time, cursing and panicking, but could not get up. "Oh!" she cried. She realized that her seatbelt was still fastened. She undid it and stepped out onto the boulevard. She had some traction on the icy grass, but as soon as she tried to cross the driveway she put her feet on a group of sticks that slid out from under her and she fell, hard, on her elbow and hip. She got up, slipping and cursing, and shuffled to where the car lay beneath the branch. Though the limb itself, huge and black, was covered over by the same silver coat that the small twigs beneath her feet were, a thick jagged end, nearly two feet in diameter, had no ice upon it. Its unglossy surface seemed exotic in the weird world of light and shadow and glimmering ice: the pale broken wood that, seconds before, had been attached to the mighty oak tree soaring high above the street. The bough had pounded the entire roof of the car flat and rolled so that nothing was visible of the two women who had been inside except—on the driver's side, sticking out from beneath a great black knot on the side of the tree—a single left hand. Elegant, bony, with long pale fingers and well-sculpted nails, a simple silver band on the middle finger. Thisbe stared at the hand for some time, oblivious to the wind and nettlesome ice. There was a black sleeve above the delicate wrist. Thisbe reached out her own hand to give comfort or hope to the woman inside. The hand was limp and cold to touch, like a trick hand on Hallowe'en. The fingers were wet with icy flecks. She thought of the witch in the *Wizard of Oz*, her feet sticking out from under the house that had fallen on her. She noticed that she was crying and wiped at her face. It was covered with rain and ice and tears. Her elbow hurt. The wind howled, and a new threatening crack sounded loud above her. Tiny twigs fell on her shoulders and at her feet. Pop pop pop. She shook herself and walked quickly back to her own car and tumbled into the driver's seat. She took out her cell phone and pressed 911.

It was a long time before she made it home that night. The police were very good, which surprised Thisbe, who usually looked at them with suspicion. Particularly one named Maconochie, who brought her Tim Horton's coffee and sat with her in the front seat of his car while the ambulances came and the firemen and the huge branch was moved off and the grisly business of pulling the victims from the car went on.

"One more time: you did not know them, but you were here because a man named Cooper at your company predicted this?" He looked at her and at his notes and then at her as he spoke.

Thisbe was embarrassed at her appearance: her hair a windblown tangle, her eyes puffed with lack of sleep and recent tears, her face scored by the wind, her nose red from blowing and weeping and the cold. Even upset and tired and frozen and warmed by coffee and Sergeant Maconochie's car, she felt that she oughtn't to have spoken so unguardedly, but there was nothing for it. She said, "That's right."

"And Cooper knew this because, and then I have you said, 'that's the million dollar question.' Is that right?"

"Oh, I don't know. I don't know."

Chapter Twenty-Two

After the Storm

Many roads and buildings were closed the next day, and the buses did not run. Cooper—who lived farther out in the suburbs than Thisbe—spent the day working from home. So few people made it downtown that a spirit of holiday took over the office, and the few people at work spent the day chatting, drinking coffee, puttering about their cubicles. Thisbe took the opportunity to call her friends, and by the end of the day had told the story of her adventure to Abby, to Meghan, to Julius and to Dean. It was not until two days after the ice storm and the deaths she had witnessed that she was able to corner Cooper in his office, close the door behind her, and say, "Cooper, what the hell is going on?"

Cooper was both delighted and terrified. He longed for Thisbe's full attention, and apparently he had it. He was a little nervous about what he might have done to get it. "I'm eating my lunch," he said, his mouth full of a ham and cheese sandwich.

Thisbe strode around his desk and looked at his screen. It showed a colorful map with a grid and small flashing icons that resembled tanks, planes, soldiers. "You're playing video games," she said. "But I don't even care about that. What's going on? How did you know about Ehrens and Davillo?"

"Just taking a little break. About whom?" Cooper had no idea what she was talking about.

"Ehrens and Davillo. I was there. They died. They died exactly when you said they would. They were killed because of a total fluke, yet you knew it would happen. You knew the exact time. How could you know?"

"Equations. It's all just equations," Cooper said.

"Damn it, stop lying. You're in here playing video games. Gormley does nothing. And yet you give me a spreadsheet with two names on it, two women coming back from one of the few concerts that wasn't canceled because of the storm, and the only reason they were killed was because I prevented them from getting into their garage, so they had to wait under a tree while I backed out, but before they could move this huge branch and Cooper– Cooper–" Her voice faltered with emotion.

Cooper, touched, tried to stand and put his arm around her, but she rebuffed his clumsy gesture and continued, her voice now under control. "Cooper, I want to know what is going on. There was no one on Earth who could have predicted those deaths. No one could have guessed the combination of concert not canceled, decision to car pool—see, usually they go in separate cars, I heard that from someone, God, I was there all night answering questions— because of the ice storm, and then, all because of my being in the driveway they park on the street for—let's say five minutes at most—five minutes, and at four minutes and fifty-eight seconds the ice build up on the top of this two hundred year old tree becomes so heavy that a wind gust—the wind gusting, how did you predict that? A wind gust of ninety kilometers an hour brings a thousand pound branch down on their car. And you have an equation that predicted that? Bullshit. Show it to me. Show me."

"All right, all right," said Cooper. "But first, I don't play video games 'all day.' " When she didn't respond to this, he decided to let it go. He pushed some buttons on his computer. "It was all in the spreadsheets I gave you and Dean…" he said, clicking his mouse and bringing up a document. "This spreadsheet is just an abstract. It doesn't of course have the entire body of calculations, as you know, Excel only allows sixty-five thousand, five-hundred, and thirty-six rows, plus you only get two-hundred and fifty-six columns…"

"Cooper. Cooper, I know about your fake spreadsheets. No one can make heads or tails of them. I know I can't. Now the hell with that. No spreadsheet picked out those two women. I thought you were working for some hit squad or something, but I don't know what to think. Those women were killed by a fluke. Bad luck, wrong place, wrong time, one second either way and they're still alive. Instead, they're dead. You knew it. You didn't cause it, I don't believe. That's what I used to think. But I saw the branch. No one had sawed it or cut it or anything. So if you didn't cause it, and it was a random event, how did you predict it?"

"Well, I think we had already discussed, this is an equation of almost infinite complexity we're dealing with. It's always possible to be right without knowing why you're right. For instance, in Italy, they thought that the disease we know as malaria was caused by just that, *mal aria*, that is, bad air. They had no idea that the transmission of microorganisms by mosquito bite was the real cause. They were, as Italians so often are, completely wrong. But. They drained the swamps to clean the air. And of course draining the swamps destroyed the mosquito habitat. Consequently, they were successful in ending the malarial epidemics. Completely wrong, but also completely right. So technology may be ahead of our ability to explain the Why, and I think…"

"Cooper," said Thisbe. "Cooper. You and I know that's not what happened. You didn't hit upon an equation based on Internet buying habits and credit limits and demographic information, plug it into some huge equation that takes the weather and wind and probability of ice storm in Toronto into account, mix it up with some module that estimates heuristics—God, I'm even starting to talk like you—and cha-ching! out pops Tuesday night at 10:34, two friends die at the same address at the same time. I don't believe it. What you're doing is impossible. I don't know how you're doing it, but it ain't arithmetic."

Cooper began again in his calm, I'm-an-actuary-and-you're-not voice.

"Cooper. Cooper. Shut up. I'm not looking for your usual line of bullshit. You can talk about malaria and modules and almost infinite complexity forever. That's not what happened here. I don't believe it." She softened. "Listen. I won't blow you in if that's what you're worried about. You don't report to me anymore, you're Gormley's problem, and Dean's, not mine. I just need to know. What are you doing?"

"Well…" Cooper had a decision to make. Should he tell Thisbe what he was doing, or continue to snow everyone with his clever tricks? He knew that it was dangerous to tell. She might be lying when she said that she would not 'blow him in'. She would think he was crazy. Not only that, Gormley was looking for the notebook. If others found out, they would want it too. If Cooper lost the notebook, he would lose his job. If he lost his job, Ravi Akkakumarbalapragada, so easy to deal with now that Cooper was again paying his mortgage, might again show the iron fist Cooper's income had so recently shoveled into the velvet glove. Cooper would lose his house.

If he didn't tell, Thisbe couldn't prove anything. He was providing the service they paid him to provide. He gave them names and dates with some supporting detail in the form of calculations. It was hard to see why they would fire him—that is, as long as he was able to convince them that he was necessary to the stream of names and places and dates they wanted.

Cooper knew all the reasons to say nothing. But he also knew that this was Thisbe. She was beautiful and he loved her. They had met as if by destiny. If he had not predicted the deaths, equally unpredictable were the workings of love. What were the chances, after all, of meeting a beautiful stranger of an evening lost in your neighborhood? It might take ten thousand days (27.38 years, taking leap years into account) for such good luck to happen. Cooper, for instance, estimated that he had ridden the bus about three hundred times a year for the previous fifteen years. During that time—4,500 bus rides—he had traveled with, say, 82,500 other people. And weren't not a single one was close to good lookin' like Thisbe was good lookin'. Layer onto that improbability the fact that she was lost and stopped to ask for directions when he met her. Perhaps twice in all his years of walking home from the bus someone had asked him for directions—that was 2/4,500, or 0.000444. And further imagine that you discover the next day that she works for the company you will soon be working for. In a city of 3,000,000, say 10,000 employees work for a large insurance company, or 1/300. That yields a probability of 1/675,000.

Cooper had already calculated these probabilities. He had not even bothered to factor in the fact that Thisbe became his boss (given the hierarchical structure of the office, another 1,000 to 1?), nor that she showed, to Cooper's mind at least, signs of someone who found him desirable and attractive (this was too embarrassing to put a probability to. Past performance was not an indicator of future results, but it sure indicated the probability was not high). And then add: they shared a friend and met at a party by chance. Compared to this, the deaths of two women beneath an unlucky falling tree were inevitable. After all, everyone has to die. Predictions of death are ultimately obvious. What could not be predicted was love.

Cooper made his decision. He said, "I don't want to tell you here. But I'll tell you. Let's go…"

Thisbe's eyes grew wide. She had prodded Cooper, and he was calling her bluff. He was going to kill her. She wondered if she should scream for help. But he hadn't done anything to her yet, and she couldn't prove anything. This was her chance.

Sridhar walked past as they waited for the elevator. He was mumbling to himself, and his shirt tail was sticking out. Cooper called over to him, but Sridhar looked at Cooper and shivered. Then he turned and walked quickly in the other direction.

"Working too hard," Cooper explained to Thisbe.

Thisbe saw in Cooper's assistant the mirror of her own fear. She said to herself: so Sridhar knows about Cooper too. It did not make her feel safer.

They were in the endless underground mall that stretched itself beneath the country's mightiest banking towers. Cooper had not done anything to Thisbe on the elevator. In fact, he had spoken irrelevantly about actuarial school and some man living in Scratch's basement.

"Gormley?"

No, a man she had met at Scratch's party.

Thisbe was too upset to follow. In action movies, when an ordinary man off the street suddenly finds himself embroiled in a murder plot, he rises to the occasion, avoids being shot a dozen times, punches out some evil goons, and ends by outwitting the mobsters who want to do him in. Thisbe did not feel able to punch Cooper out, and, far from outwitting him, she was even finding it difficult to concentrate on what he was saying. For it is a fact not much explored by the action movie industry that ordinary people, faced with mortal peril for which they are totally unprepared, find that adrenalin secretions, flight instinct, and sheer terror are unconducive to clever ruses and sudden effective violence. She took a deep breath. Calm, calm, she told herself. Two blue policemen walked past. Nothing to be afraid of here, she told herself.

Cooper ordered a yogurt smoothie. They sat at a table in the food court. Thisbe kept looking around, expecting that at any minute two large men in pin-striped suits would come to take her for a ride. She thought of all the time she and Dean had wasted in the years of their not being together. She thought of Cooper, who seemed kindly disposed, and she wondered if she should beg for her life. She had always liked Cooper, she told herself. She thought that he liked her. Was it really necessary that she be killed? Was she such a danger? She hoped she would not make a fool of herself. The bottom of her stomach felt queasy.

The policemen walked past again, this time seeming to take an interest. Thisbe recognized one of them—Sergeant Maconochie, with whom she had spent two hours just a couple of nights ago. She gave him a smile and a wave. Cooper looked up, frowning at the interruption, then continued. The sergeant smiled at Thisbe and continued past. Cooper was babbling on about the basement at Scratch's house, the furnace, a notebook—the notebook he had with him. Whatever he was talking about, he was not telling the story particularly well, forgetting bits and rushing back to catch them up, including the keeling over of Keiter, Gormley's thanatopic nickname, the unsurprise of Gormley and Scratch, the furnace, his subsequent conversations with Keiter. The notebook was the only part she understood: this was his hitman's scorecard, where he kept the names and dates and times of people he was planning to murder.

"Cooper, I don't understand. What are you talking about?" she finally said. She felt safe in the mall and was pleased that Cooper had looked up and frowned when he saw the police. If he was planning to kill her, he couldn't get away with it here.

He was picking at his smoothie and did not answer right away. His hesitation began to rekindle her nervousness. It did not do to have someone like Cooper pay too much attention to you. When he began to speak again, she gradually came to realize that he was not telling her anything that she had expected. And then, before she could take it all in, the two policemen were standing beside their table, one on each side of Cooper.

"Hello, Sergeant Maconochie," said Thisbe brightly.

But he ignored her. "Cooper Smith Cooper?" said Maconochie.

"Yes?" said Cooper pleasantly.

"We would like to ask you a few questions."

"Sure," said Cooper. "This is about the break-in? Have a seat."

"I am afraid you do not understand. You will need to come with us."

"Really? I wonder why," said Cooper.

But Maconochie ignored him and spoke to Thisbe: "Do you know this man?"

"Yes," said Thisbe, taken aback. "Yes, we work together. That is, we work at the same– Seals–" she trailed off, wondering what it mattered.

"And this is Cooper Smith Cooper?"

"Yes," said Thisbe. "But–"

"Thank you, ma'am," said Maconochie. "Mr. Cooper?"

"I'd better go with them," Cooper explained to Thisbe.

"Yes. Yes, I can see that."

"Would you just mention– upstairs– if anyone looks for me."

"Oh. Oh, yes, sure."

The officers were leading him away. "I don't suppose I'll be back this afternoon," Cooper was saying over his shoulder.

Maconochie nodded his head in agreement.

Thisbe was amazed. She said to herself: Have I really just been saved? She tried to remember what Cooper had been saying but could not. She looked down at the table. There was his yogurt smoothie and his pen and his notebook. He had mentioned the notebook. She looked up. It was just possible to see Maconochie's hat disappearing around a corner. She picked up Cooper's things and flew to the elevator shaft and up.

Dean wasn't in his office, and Thisbe was burning with the news. Would Dean be displeased? He had not wanted the police. Thisbe decided she didn't care. Cooper would be locked up for good, and

Dean would be kind all the time now. She walked to Gormley's office, but he was out. She called Abby Bruler and found her at the newspaper. After a few breathless minutes, Abby began to get the story right. "Cooper? So this guy who is predicting the deaths has the tree sawed–"

But she did not have the story right. Thisbe said, "No, that's the thing. I was there. There were no marks on the tree. And even if he would've cut it, the chances that those ladies were just underneath the branch at that–"

Abby began to understand. "But what is his motivation? Why does it matter to him?"

Thisbe was impatient with this line of questioning. "He picks all kinds of people. I don't know how he does it. But he's in with the mob. The police– apparently he's involved in some break-in. I'm so relieved. I thought he had taken me out to kill me." She was shaking.

"There must be a motive," said Abby.

Abby worked at a newspaper, a place where anyone looking for a story finds it, whether it is there or not.

Chapter Twenty-Three

After Cooper's Arrest

The police were pleasant. It was not about the break-in at Scratch's at all. It was about the ladies who had been crushed by the falling tree limb. Cooper, always eager to please, answered their questions fully. Yes, he had predicted the deaths. No, he didn't think that strange. As an actuary, it was his job. Life insurance companies always have an interest in the deaths of everyone. It was all about managing the risk of insuring a life for money.

"Isn't it strange that you were able to predict these deaths to the date?"

Yes, that was strange, he said with pardonable pride. It was a new thing he was working on. The project was called the Equation of Almost Infinite Complexity. He and his team took a huge number of statistics about the subjects, and...

Though things went well, Cooper was not able to return to work that afternoon. At one point Maconochie took a phone call. Cooper was on the verge of deciding to become impatient, perhaps by tapping his foot rapidly or glancing at the clock, when Maconochie said, "Really. No signs of tampering. No saw marks." He eyed Cooper. "Explosives?" Cooper, sensing a break in the case, began to listen. Maconochie paused. "So it appears as if nothing was done to the branch." He looked at Cooper, who smiled helpfully back. When he hung up the phone, he ignored Cooper and became absorbed in the computer screen on his desk.

"Anything else, then?" asked Cooper brightly.

"Are you still here?" asked Maconochie, looking away from his screen for just an instant.

Cooper thought about pointing out that this was not a polite way to speak to a concerned citizen who had come to the station at the request of the police, but Maconochie abruptly turned away to answer a ringing telephone. It can't be easy being a policeman, Cooper reflected, and the scolding died before it was uttered. Cooper pulled on his coat.

"Abby who from where?" Maconochie was saying.

Since he had been dismissed and no one was paying attention to him, Cooper left, taking time to shut the door quietly behind him.

There were three messages on Cooper's phone from Dean, but it was already six o'clock, so he felt justified in not returning them. The next day, he was sent to Legal, which occupied two posh floors that Cooper had never before seen. He spent over an hour with an affable young lawyer who asked him all about his encounter with the police in the pleasantest way possible and then pronounced, "Cooper, this is a bloody huge problem you've caused. You've really screwed up. If I had my way, you'd be fired already. That was my recommendation."

Cooper, who had been relaxing in a comfortable leather chair, was stunned. The lawyer had turned away and was now looking at some papers on his desk. Cooper, loathe to disturb the serpentine legal mind at its work, sat in quiet expectation. When the lawyer did not look up after nearly two minutes, Cooper ventured a question. "Is there anything else?"

The lawyer looked up and appeared to have difficulty focusing on Cooper. He looked back down at his papers. Without looking up again, he said, "No. Get out."

Cooper sat for several more seconds, considering how best to respond. Then he stood up as quietly as he could and went to the door.

The lawyer did not look up.

"Thanks then," said Cooper.

The lawyer did not look up. "Out," he said.

Cooper left.

Dean said, "I should never have to answer any questions about my group that I did not create. This mustn't happen again, Cooper."

Cooper apologized.

"No one talks to the police without a lawyer, Cooper. It's not done." As if it were an etiquette breach. But Dean was also reassuring. "I won't say that you haven't put me in an embarrassing position. It can't happen again. I had to pull quite a few strings and pull them hard. But dammit, Cooper, you're the only thing interesting going on here. I need you to keep your nose clean."

It was not good to be called in by your president and hollered at, but Cooper felt that, in the big picture, things were going well. Dean, it seemed, had gone to bat for Cooper, had protected him inside the company. It spoke well of their relationship, he felt.

"Cooper," said Dean, "You are aware that some people think you are involved in the deaths you predict."

Cooper was not aware. "Really? Who?"

"Cooper, why do you think you were taken in by the police?"

"They had some– oh!"

"Yes."

"So that's what that was about?"

"Yes."

"I don't have any idea what causes the deaths. I just look at the numbers. And the police thought– ha!" Cooper was amused.

"I wish you would tell me how you do it," said Dean.

Cooper had decided to tell Thisbe. Now Dean was asking. He looked at Dean. He made his decision. "The mathematical model is really staggering," he began.

Cooper began with his usual blather about math, and Dean had just begun to interrupt him with some kind of challenge: "Cooper. Cooper. You're not telling me the truth. Because I know what the truth is." But before Cooper could respond to this, there was a knock on the office door, and then it banged open. Julius stepped in.

"What do you want?" asked Dean, while at the same time Cooper said,

"The man from the party." The name was on the tip of his tongue, but he couldn't quite get it.

"You don't have an appointment," said Dean.

Cooper thought Dean rather rude. He made to leave.

Dean looked up. "Stay, would you, Cooper? This won't take long, I'm sure. What can I do for you, er– Julius, is it?" said Dean. "Sit right down over there, Cooper," said Dean, pointing to a chair at a small table beside the floor-to-ceiling windows. He turned his full attention to Cooper for a moment more. "Cooper, I don't mind saying, I was terrified I was going to lose you. Stay away from the police. I want you here, where I can keep an eye on you." He turned to Julius.

"Hello, Dean," said Julius. He closed the door and walked to Dean's desk.

Cooper took a seat at the table. Dean did not want to lose him. That was a good thing. It was a little awkward being in the room while Dean and Julius had their meeting, and he looked at the papers on the table in front of him. He did not even notice he was reading them until his own name caught his eye, and he saw that he was being mentioned in a letter from the American government: the NSA. Who were they? The letter said that they were interested in what he had "found." Cooper asked himself why a foreign government was interested in something he had found, and at the same second he answered himself: they knew. Dean knew. Dean knew and was writing to powerful people to tell them. How could they know? He realized that he had just told his secret to Thisbe, and Dean already knew about it. She had betrayed him.

He was just on the point of realizing that Dean could not already have an inbound letter if Thisbe had been his betrayer—there had not been time—when his thoughts were interrupted. Julius had begun to shout at Dean. His turn of phrase was such that Cooper was reminded of the night he had first found Keiter in the furnace, employing as Julius did the same pithy yet astonishing grasp of the vernacular, creating new and imaginative yet biologically dubious combinations. The whole time Dean sat in the modernist leather armchair behind his desk, never fidgeting, never moving, looking with seriousness into the middle distance over Julius's right shoulder.

The issue, Cooper gathered, was that Julius loved Thisbe but Dean was taking Thisbe away. Dean had taken Thisbe away from Julius before. Thisbe belonged with Julius, not with Dean. Thisbe thought she loved Dean, but really she loved Julius. Julius had picked up the pieces of Thisbe's heart the last time Dean had broken them. Dean was not going to do this again.

This surprised Cooper, who was convinced that Thisbe was rather attracted to him. Just this morning he had been thinking that he might ask her for a date next week, or maybe in two weeks. He was confused. It was hard to believe that anything Julius was saying could possibly be about the same Thisbe. He became a little indignant. Thisbe shouldn't have played with his emotions like that, leading him on as she had. It wasn't right. How could she have had two boyfriends the entire time he had known her?

Julius, meanwhile, had moved from verbal to physical expressions of distaste for Dean. To emphasize a particularly telling point, he picked up a pen-holder from Dean's desk and threw it across the office. The pen-holder was a solid little piece of marble with a metal pen cap mounted on it, and it knocked into the lamp on the table at which Cooper sat. The lamp fell with a loud bang against the large window behind Cooper. The window did not break.

"Hey!" said Cooper, rescuing the lamp.

The men ignored him. Dean began to give back to Julius, with considerably more restraint, but in kind: Thisbe had always loved Dean, she had known that Julius was a poor secondrater and went to him only when Dean had no use for her. Dean could take anything he wanted away from Julius. Julius had best watch himself if he didn't want to be crushed underfoot. It would not do to be Dean's enemy. Were he wise, he would watch what he said.

There was more passionate conversation, most of it unpleasant. At one point Cooper began to stand up and leave, but Dean snapped, "Sit down, Cooper," so he did. Julius pounded the desk. Dean pounded the desk. Julius cursed. Dean cursed back. It was like a hockey game.

Cooper's interest was piqued when sex with Thisbe was mentioned as he hoped one day to have first hand knowledge of this topic. Julius alluded to Dean's chronic issues with erectile dysfunction. Dean countered that this had never been an issue for him and queried whether it might not be psychological projection on the part of Julius. No, Julius was sure that the problem lay with Dean and that Thisbe had confirmed this upon several occasions. Dean found this interesting since when he had last enjoyed an act of sexual congress with Thisbe, she had mentioned his name favorably and inquired with some eagerness whether more might be forthcoming. Julius mentioned, somewhat irrelevantly, that much had changed in the world in the last seven years. Dean noted the fact, but, in an effort to bring the conversation up to date, explained that he had been speaking about the previous seven days, not seven years. Much table banging, shortness of breath and healthy pink glow about the cheeks, noses, and ears of both.

Julius began to glow with the joy of victory. "Thisbe has cancer," he said. "She's had a mastectomy. You'd know that if you had gotten close to her."

But apparently Julius had overreached because Dean smiled right back. "I know that that's not true. Perhaps you don't."

It appeared the two men wanted to fight. Neither was particularly large. Julius was a little huskier, taller and had the greater reach. Dean, though smaller, was trim and quick. Julius had passion going for him; on the other hand, Dean had a cool head and calculating mind. It was impossible to predict the outcome of the upcoming mêlée. Cooper wondered whether or not Dean would expect him to enter the fracas on the side of the Society for Equitable Assurances on Lives and Survivorships as a matter of corporate loyalty.

As it turned out, the battle was inconclusive. The desk remained between the two men, and though fists were clenched and a little shadow boxing occurred, no punches were thrown that could have landed. Both men were breathing hard.

"Cooper. Cooper!" barked Dean.

"Sir?"

"Please step outside for just a minute. Stand beside the door, please, I'll call you."

Cooper was torn between the desire to watch the gruesome scene and the desire to escape.

"Outside. I'll be fine," said Dean.

Julius stood staring at Dean.

"Out," said Dean. "But stay by the door."

"Yes, sir," said Cooper, leaving. He went outside and closed the door behind him. Through it, he could only just hear the sound of the two men in quiet intense conversation. Then came a loud crash. Cooper wondered what he should do. He knocked timidly at the door.

"Wait!" came Dean's peremptory holler.

There came the sound of more conversation, and the sound of men—or a man—walking about behind the closed door. Cooper wondered if Dean had killed Julius.

"Cooper!" came Dean's voice. Though it seemed a long time, Cooper checked his watch and found that less than ten minutes had passed. The door opened, and Dean let Cooper in.

Julius was standing at the table where Cooper had been sitting. The lamp that had been sitting on the table was smashed on the floor. Dean marched back to his desk, saying to Julius, "Are you leaving, or do I call security to have you thrown you out?"

Julius appeared for a second defeated: his shoulders slumped, his head dropped. But he almost immediately recovered and stood erect again. He brought a proper sneer to his face and said in fine style, "I've been thrown out of better places than this." He strode to the door, shoulders squared beneath his rumpled sports jacket. "You've been warned."

"Warned about what?" Dean barked, but Julius was through the door. "Cooper!" Dean barked again, but corrected himself and spoke in measured tone. "Cooper, I apologize for the scene you had to witness. I did not seek it, but I do apologize that you had to sit through it. Would you just follow this man out and make sure he leaves? You can call security if you like."

"Is there anything–" Cooper began.

"Get him out of here," Dean commanded, with quiet impatience.

So Cooper followed Julius out. The noise in Dean's office had not been unnoticed. People stared as they walked past, and heads popped out of cubicles to see them. Cooper wondered whether only the desk banging and raised voices had carried, or the gawkers had overheard complete phrases and accusations.

The elevators were frolicking about in some other place, and Cooper and Julius stood together waiting and being goggled at. "Hello," said Julius and waved. "Hello to you too there." A man with a large head and crewcut leaned around a corner to peek at them. "Dean tried to rape me," said Julius, projecting his voice like an actor in a high school play. "Sexual harassment." They stood quietly. "Fortunately, he was castrated by the Commonwealth of Kentucky in 2012," Julius called. "He came to Toronto because he's still wanted in British Columbia and Alberta on child pornography charges." Cooper was glowing pink with embarrassment. A group of people appeared in the corridor, evidently not wanting to miss the show. Julius did not disappoint. "He's also wanted in the Faroe Islands. They take the sexual corruption of sheep very seriously there. Terrible problem." He held up an official-looking identification card. "InterPol," said Julius. "Working with the RCMP. Best leave him alone." He added, in a confidential stage whisper, "The health inspector is very concerned. He picked up something horrible from the sheep." There was some tittering and whispering from the cubicles. "Contagious," Julius declaimed. "Very contagious."

The elevator came at last. Cooper and Julius got on, watched by, it seemed, the entire floor. Julius shouted something about Dean sodomizing raccoons as the elevator doors closed.

Several other people got on the elevator during their long passage to the bottom, but, to Cooper's relief, Julius said nothing, and no one paid any attention to them. The scene upstairs had not yet filtered to any of the floors below.

"Are you really with InterPol?" Cooper asked. But Julius only smiled.

The elevator doors opened on the ground floor, and Cooper and Julius stepped out. "Well," said Cooper. It was dark outside, and the rush hour traffic was already lined up on King, red and yellow lights shining on either side of the street. Cooper held out his hand.

Julius had his hands stuffed in his pockets and did not take Cooper's. "Women are bitches, Cooper," said Julius.

"I'm sorry you feel that way," said Cooper.

Julius gave him a look and then moved off into the crowd. Cooper waited for the elevator, feeling he had defended Thisbe's honor appropriately.

Cooper had much to think about. Besides his arrest and his run-in with the lawyer, he had been shocked at the things Dean and Julius had said about Thisbe. He had reserved a sentimental and romantic space for her in his mind that was, for the most part, as yet untainted with the cruder sort of sexual fantasy. Now it appeared that, all the time he had been dreaming of holding Thisbe's hand while walking in the park, she had been trying out the newly expanded revised and updated with all new material edition of the *Kama Sutra* with both her boss and her boyfriend. Something like that might put things in a different light.

Yet it didn't. Cooper shook himself, shrugging off his worse instincts in favor of his better. Thisbe was still Thisbe. If she had been foolish, if she had spent her time and her body on men who would never love her as he did, so what? Picking up the formula of a prayer he had learned long ago as a boy, he said to himself that it was not his place to question, but to love. This thought pleased him, and he repeated it: Not to question, but to love. He returned to his office and his equations.

The events of the past twenty-four hours had thrown Cooper off his routine, so it was not until late in the day that he returned from his talk with Dean to discover that he did not have his notebook. It was neither in his briefcase nor his desk drawer, the two places he kept it. A childish joke came into his memory: "I looked in the desk for my notebook, and there it was—gone!" He felt a sudden panic. Where could it be? He took everything out of his briefcase. He took everything out of his drawer. When he did not find the notebook, he took everything out of all his drawers. Convinced from a small boy that the right way to find something was to examine everything available carefully, he took everything out of his file cabinet. When his desk was stacked with three foot high piles of paper and there was still no notebook, he remembered that he had been in the mall food court with Thisbe, and he rushed to the elevators.

The yogurt man remembered him, but did not remember the notebook. The Mr. Submarine man was from the islands and did not want to speak to him: "Me no wan no trouble wit no police, mahn. I see no notebook." The Chinese food man and the Harvey's man were from Asia and did not speak much English, and they said only, "Don't know. Didn't see. No. No." With heavy heart, he tried the steakhouse, Tim Horton's, and Yankee Candle. But neither the butcher, the baker, nor the candlestick maker remembered him nor Thisbe nor the notebook. "You should eat more doughnuts," said a saucy counter girl, the stud beside her thin black eyebrow glinting. Cooper bought a dozen Timbits, but this did not have the desired effect of causing the counter girl to produce his notebook.

He returned up the elevator to look for Thisbe, but in her office he found only her coat. He was distracted and nervous and upset. He took a Post-It note and wrote, "Need you, call me," signed it "Cooper," and hurried off, leaving the note on her desk. He walked about her floor in vain.

The elevator bonged, the doors slid open, and Thisbe found herself looking right at Cooper, standing distracted and breathing heavily.

"Thisbe!"

She almost panicked. Her hand went out to look for the Close Door button, but Cooper already had his hand over the door to hold it open.

"I've been looking for you," he said.

Thisbe jumped across the threshold of the elevator. If he was going to kill her, he would have to do it in the open. She wasn't going to make it easy for him by allowing him to get into an elevator with her.

"Cooper! I thought you– that is– I," she blurted. She had not spoken to Dean since Cooper's return, nor had she spoken to legal. Someone had told her that Cooper and her boyfriend had been in a scene, but the accounts had been so ridiculous she could not believe what she heard. "Raccoons?" she had asked, unable to take it in. She had thought that Cooper was in jail. What could this mean? she asked herself, knowing exactly what it meant: He's come back to murder me. She saw his return like the return of the unstoppable maniac in a horror movie, who is run over by a truck, burned with fire and left in the swamp while alligators baste his left leg in hollandaise sauce, but who nonetheless appears carrying his sporty fuel-efficient chainsaw in the next scene.

"Do you have my notebook?" Cooper said, perhaps a little louder than necessary.

She blurted: "I didn't think you were coming back."

This stopped Cooper short. No, he was back. What gave her that idea?

"Someone said you were– were resigning," she stuttered. "And I was at your office, and I saw all your files. It looked like you were moving out and– oh."

"Exactly," he said.

"You've been subpoenaed."

"What?"

"The police. They want your files. Is that it?"

"Thisbe, I'm looking for my notebook. Do you have it?"

"The police want your notebook?"

"No. The notebook I had when we were at the food court yesterday. Small, black, coil bound? Do you know where it is? You didn't by chance pick it up, did you?"

Thisbe thought. "No. No, I don't think so," she said. She said this because she did not remember, and because her years in business had taught Thisbe that questions lead to action items, and action items are time-consuming and lead to no result. To take an action item, especially from a subordinate in a hallway conversation, was not a mistake she was likely to make.

Cooper cursed.

"Why? What's so important about the notebook?" she said.

This recalled Cooper to himself. "Nothing," he said.

"Is that why all your files are out?"

"No," said Cooper, but this was sheer perversity, and Thisbe saw through it.

"You know what? I may have picked it up at that. Come on," she said. For she saw that he was not thinking of murder and felt—absurdly—grateful to him for this.

They went to Thisbe's office but could not find his notebook. "That's odd," said Thisbe. "I thought maybe I did take it. I picked it up yesterday—you left it on the table when the police came. I'm sure I picked it up."

"What did you do with it?"

"I don't remember. But I had it, I know I did."

"Perhaps you took it home? Or left it in your car?"

"Maybe." Thisbe was guarded. Was he trying to get her down into the parking lot to kill her there? "Why is it so important?" She had arranged things so that she was sitting next to the door and Cooper sat across from her, with her desk between them. "What's this? Oh," she said, seeing his note. She picked it up, looked at it—

"Need you, call me. Cooper"—and put it in her pocket. Cooper did not seem to be in a dangerous mood. In any case, it seemed he was not the actual killer. She allowed herself to relax a little, and Cooper, sitting in her desk chair, began to talk.

Chapter Twenty-Four

Cooper Tells Thisbe

And that was how Cooper returned at last to the explanation of the Equation of Almost Infinite Complexity. He spoke at some length about what he had learned in the past several months. He told her about Gormley touching Keiter and Keiter's death, about meeting Keiter in the furnace, about Gormley explaining the notebook to him late that night. He told her about his predictions and how they always came true. To save his job, he also lied and told her that they were close to uncovering the math behind the answer key he already had. The real brain behind the Equation of Almost Infinite Complexity, he explained, was Death's notebook.

Thisbe listened with care for a long time. Then she spoke: "And you used that notebook to get a job?" There was an excitement in her voice that he could not place.

"Sure. I needed a job."

"It seems so– so– unimaginative."

"Well, I never claimed to be imaginative. The point is, in what I do, no–"

Thisbe interrupted. She seemed beside herself. "You said this to me before, in the food court."

"Yes, in what I do, no one has a different approach. It's really all just–"

"I heard you, but I didn't believe you. You got Death's notebook, and you used it to get–"

"A job, yes. I needed one. As I was saying, all I really do is a lot of math. Old people die sooner than young people, men sooner than women, you know, and the insurance rates—the actuarial tables—are based on that. It's a real breakthrough when someone designs a mathematical model that allows us to increase accuracy out at the seventh decimal place. It would be really original if you were able to create a new identifiable category that had predictive value. You know, if you could show that teenaged self-selected Beach Boys fans born west of Kenora had a life expectancy six weeks shorter than teenaged females who go to Catholic schools. Something like that. Or if you could find an application for some fact that we can't apply yet. For instance, there's some evidence that there are more deaths on a full moon than a half moon, but it's hard to find a way to translate that into Thisbe's premium every month."

"I don't have life insurance."

"Yes, well, maybe you should. But the point was, I needed a job, I had to be original to get attention, and it's not easy being original in this business. I made up some stuff, but it was all a lie and would have been seen through. And then Scratch hands me this Godsend, this beautiful notebook of Gormley's, and Gormley comes by and explains how it works."

"Why did they give it to you?"

Here Cooper stopped. "That's a good question." He thought. "I think Scratch was worried about it being stolen."

"So he gave it to you?"

It had not occurred to Cooper before that this was strange, but it occurred to him now. "Yes, he seemed to know that someone would be looking for it…"

"So he gave it to you? How did he know you wouldn't be robbed?"

Cooper did not know. "There was a break-in at his house where nothing was stolen, just papers and files thrown about. I don't know how he knew that that was going to happen."

But Thisbe was back to her earlier topic. "Cooper, I can't believe that you would find something as unbelievable and profound and important as this book and think of nothing except turning it into a job. We don't even pay you that much."

"You don't? Well–" said Cooper. Though not embarrassed by fraud and lying, he was embarrassed to be thought of as someone who was not well-paid. "I needed a job," he repeated. "I help Seals make money. But what did you mean when you said," here he hesitated, "ah– that you don't pay me that much money? How much should I be paid?" For Cooper found it difficult to talk about or negotiate for money.

Thisbe put that aside and asked a hundred questions. Had it been the notebook all along? Was that man in the furnace then truly a man in the furnace, could it have been a hologram? Was Scratch able to do all kinds of magical things? Were the screams from the furnace really the anguish of the damned? Had Gormley really touched Keiter, and then Keiter was dead? Cooper gave her such answers as he could. She was continually frustrated with him for his lack of imagination and insight, but everything he said fit the facts she knew. He had seemed so much more a math dweeb than a sinister hit man, and now she knew why. She was delighted with the turn things were taking. The world seemed full of surprise, of mysteries and wonders. It occurred to her that she had used to think of the world that way all the time, but that at some point she had stopped thinking that way. The change bore looking into.

She was coming down off adrenaline and terror and back to the ordinary world of thought and feeling. A warm glowing relief flowed through her body. Cooper was not planning to do her in. She felt muscles from the back of her neck to her shoulder blades

loosening and realized that they had been twisted tight ever since—
since when? Since Dean had returned, the night of the party at
which she met Cooper. She felt embarrassed at having suspected
him of being a murderer for all these months. He was in fact
only an administrator of a phenomenon that had been going on
since Adam and Eve. He sat across from her, almost-but-not-quite
handsome, intelligent, diffident, vague. He was a dope. Imagine
having something as amazing as a listing of all deaths for all people
and using it to get a job as a nerd.

She decided that she was angry with him. What she had been
through over the past weeks! He was talking about something—
salary structures, was he really talking about salary structures?—
and looking at her with sincere brown eyes, eyes that until today
she had assumed were shielding dark ulterior motives. She smiled
at the thought. No dark ulterior motives in this one, she said to
herself. She had lived with Julius and Dean for too long: one
dissipated and too clever by half and the other relentless, ambitious
and driven. In her entire life of achievement, art, and love, she had
never before dealt with someone like Cooper. He was so simple.
He was so ordinary. She laughed.

He looked at her. "What is it?"

"Nothing," she said, smiling. He was a complete idiot. She
laughed again. She decided that, after all, she liked him.

Cooper continued to talk, amused by her amusement.

"You know, Cooper, that we don't actually make the money in
insurance."

He looked at her. "We don't?"

"The money is all in the investments. Insurance companies take
in huge amounts of money in premiums and invest it. That's
why we have more money than banks. The payouts, the customer
accounts—efficiencies there are trivial. A percent here, a percent
there. All the money comes from the capital."

Cooper knew that. "I knew that," he said.

"So that, while it would be better to pay out less and know more so we can price more accurately, you're impacting only the tiny intake valve or the tiny output valve. The ocean in between is the investment of funds, and nothing you do actually affects that."

Cooper knew that. "I knew that," he said. He resented this. Actuaries were important. "Optimizing intakes and outgoes is important."

"Yes. Just not as important as the investment operations."

"But prerequisite to them."

"Well, yes."

Cooper saw why Thisbe had brought this up. "Are you saying I shouldn't get a raise?"

Thisbe was feeling almost giddy now that she was talking to a fool instead of a killer. She laughed. "You'll have to talk to Dean about it," she said, "but I think you're priceless," forgetting for the moment to be managerial. And then she did something that surprised both of them. She leaned forward and gave him a kiss.

It was an impulsive gesture, a quick peck on the mouth. She immediately sat back and returned to her usual businesslike manner. But she was smiling, and her big eyes were bright and alive.

Cooper sat for a moment, hardly able to believe how wonderful his day had become. The delight of Thisbe's regard was almost overwhelming. He did not want the moment to end.

It ended. "What was that?" While Cooper had been in transports of love, Gormley had transported himself into the office. "Are you two guys sleeping together?"

"No," said Cooper.

"No," said Thisbe, to Cooper's disappointment. Although when he thought about it later, he recognized it was probably too much to hope for her to have added, "But I'd really like to. I think it would be fun."

Gormley peered at Cooper. Then he peered at Thisbe. Thisbe looked amused. Cooper could not help smiling because Thisbe was smiling. Gormley leaned in close, and Cooper caught a whiff of peanut butter and stale beer when Gormley said, "Are you sure?"

"Gormley, this is my office," said Thisbe.

Cooper, who had not felt that he could speak since it was not his office, was grateful for Thisbe's factual remark.

But Gormley was not. "I have an office too. And it's nicer than this one." He paused and peered again. "You're sure you two aren't doing it?"

"Gormley," said Cooper. But he was not unhappy because Thisbe let go a laugh, light, easy, and happy, and laughing, she sparkled.

"Because let me tell you one thing, Cooper," said Gormley leaning down into Cooper's face, and now the beer and peanut butter was overwhelming.

"Yes?" said Cooper, when Gormley elected to continue breathing on him instead of telling him one thing. There was peanut butter in the saliva stuck to Gormley's left canine. Cooper had a childish thought: were Gormley's teeth all in different directions because the peanut butter glued them that way?

"Remember this: I saw her first."

"Gormley, this is inappropriate," said Thisbe, so that Gormley was forced to turn and face her. Cooper breathed the pure air gratefully. "I will not be questioned about my personal life by you. There is nothing to admit or deny here. You have seen nothing inappropriate or beyond the bounds of any propriety. You saw a moment of enthusiasm around something Cooper and I were discussing, well within the bounds of civilized adult behavior. Now, as Cooper and I were in a meeting that does not concern you, I'll ask you to leave my office."

"Humph," said Gormley. He did not make a sound that might reasonably be interpreted by a novelist with the spelling "humph," a snort or a cough or clearing of the throat. He said, with admirable elocution, the actual word: Humph.

"Cooper, I believe we were done. You too are dismissed."

Cooper was crestfallen, having hoped his private interview with Thisbe would last longer. But he saw, when she looked at him, an expression in her eye that the sort of novelist who uses the word "humph" refers to as a "twinkle."

"I can't believe you're sleeping with her," said Gormley, looking at Cooper. "I saw her first."

"You're done. Please go," said Thisbe.

Gormley's remark appeared to have put an end to Thisbe's twinkling. Still, Cooper could hardly bring himself to leave.

"There– ah– is one more thing," he ventured.

"What is it?" said Thisbe, training her large lovely but decidedly now non-twinkling eye on Cooper.

"We were discussing the loss of my–"

"Yes?"

"Of my–" Cooper did not want to say "notebook" in front of Gormley.

"–virginity?" asked Gormley, peering again.

"No!" said Cooper.

"Your what?" said Thisbe. "Is this about the raise?" There were signs of amusement on her lips, and they raised Cooper's hopes.

But there was still the problem of saying "notebook" in front of Gormley. "Ah– um–"

"I'll bet you banged the snot out of her, didn't you?" asked Gormley. "What did you do, lose something while you were in there?" He began to laugh. "Urf urf. Lose something while you were in there," he mumbled. "Urf urf urf urf."

"Gormley, you are way out of line. Get out," snapped imperious Thisbe, all twinkles and relations clearly packed up and gone, return date unknown.

"I'll send you an email," said Cooper, standing.

"Good," said Thisbe.

As they turned and began to walk out, Gormley said, "Did you really boink her? I can't believe you did that without me."

"Well I hardly would have done it with you," Cooper said.

"Oh! I'm sorry Cooper," called Thisbe. "Your notebook!"

Chapter Twenty-Five

Abby and Julius

At the newspaper, the result of Abby's investigations was a 4,000 word story linking a local actuary to the mysterious deaths of two women. The actuary was involved in an ugly lawsuit that had been going on for years. The lawsuit had destroyed an entire corporation. One of the dead women was a government regulator who, at the time of her death, was investigating the ruined company. Police had arrested the suspect. For Abby was one of the better reporters on the paper, the rarer sort who walked about with her eyes open and asked questions.

Abby's editor cut the story back until it was 600 words and completely incoherent. He ran it on page seven of the B section where he had an awkwardly shaped spot to fill between an advertisement for Viagra and a photograph of an eight year-old pole vaulter. He disliked Abby, who, alone of his staff, seemed unable to understand that a journalist's job was to call experts to get their opinions on the press releases that flooded the newspaper every day. He had seen no press release about any actuary or lawsuit. He sighed. If the story was worth anything, they would already know about it.

Above the Viagra ad, he ran a large article about an American reality show that was supposed to pick new celebrities, complete with color photographs of a girl singer with surgically improved breasts, nose, lips, and buttocks. The art department airbrushed the picture to improve the girl's looks. The story had color, pizzazz, zest, human interest, passion, excitement, realism. It had been written by the only reporter he trusted: AP.

Julius sat in front of the television. For once, he was not watching it. Instead, he was staring at the painting that hung above it. It was a winter scene from Barry's Bay that showed the ice pushing out of cracks in the black Canadian Shield rock, a stand of naked sugar maples huddling next to it. He liked the scene, which, whatever it owed to the Group of Seven and Emily Carr paintings that every Canadian artist must come to terms with, was, in its use of color and light, still peculiar to the painter who had done it. He was pleased with the curve of the largest tree in the stand, which managed to suggest both the power of the winter winds and—strange to say, perhaps, about a tree—a certain femininity. It was not a cruel landscape, but it was indifferent to the sufferings it inflicted, and the trees, bent and twisted by fate, endured uncomplaining. It was not a perfect picture, he thought. The light that caught the rocks and trees seemed to have missed a bit of the ice, although the ice protruded beyond them and therefore should have been illuminated; and a stand of jack pines in the far left background looked more like they had been painted by someone who had spent too much time looking at Tom Thomson's jack pines instead of seeing the trees that might have grown in the world of the picture. These were small but significant flaws. What could be said was that the painting had been done by an artist who had some power. Not a great or mighty artist, but still, an artist and not a sentimentalist or a hack. Julius, who had painted the picture almost twenty years earlier, understood all this.

It would have reflected well on Julius's character to be able to say that those bent and feminine maples, nearly undone by winter but enduring without complaint, captured the feeling of some time or place or person that Julius loved and wanted to pay tribute to: his mother, Thisbe, the defunct empire that had birthed Jane Austen;

or beer, the halls of his university, Tom Thomson, Emily Carr. But this was not the case. The long-suffering and noble trees, if they meant anything outside themselves, stood for Julius—an example, as if anyone needed another, that an artist may do good work without being good himself. For if one understood the trees as an allegory for Julius, the painting turned into something close to self-pity instead of what it was, a winter scene embodying the stoic sad gallantry of anything that would live and die on a pre-Cambrian rock north of 45 degrees latitude.

When Julius was in his twenties, he had had a showing at a well-known gallery. Some people came, and there were reviews in two newspapers that mentioned him by name. Three paintings sold, one at a price considerably higher than Julius had expected. He received a friendly letter from a famous and well-connected artist whose work he admired. Julius wrote a long arrogant reply in which he said many things he could not afterwards remember, as he had written in the flush of success and red wine and mailed it without once reading it over. He did not hear from the famous artist again, and was too proud himself to write a second time.

It was his last significant show. Now if his pictures went any-where, they hung on the walls of trendy fly-by-night Queen Street restaurants, or, more embarrassing, on peg boards during the art days of the Central Reference Library. As he often said, "When you have TV, who needs art?"

Julius did not think of himself as a man who never had the courage to be, who had been seduced by the pleasant things of life and rendered unable to do the work required to become what he might have been. He did not think about these things because he took care not to. Nor did he think, as certain religious do, that whatever paths he might have taken, the task of life was to do his best every day on the path he was on. He did not reject his life, but neither did he accept it. Instead, he had a joke for everything, he had work and sex and television and alcohol to fill his waking hours, he had a girl, and he had a host of distractions. He was busy and, by some lights, successful: he possessed, after all, a fashionable condominium (for Julius was not a man to own a house), a young and beautiful girlfriend (until recently), and a responsible job in government. He was ugly, no great flaw in a successful man, and in good health, a significant benison. Though closer to fifty than to forty, he pretended that nothing permanent had been done. In a spare room, he sometimes painted and filled the condominium with the smell of oils, paint thinner, and turpentine.

The phone rang, and without looking at the caller ID, he put it mechanically to his ear. "Yeah," he grumped. For the working day was ending, and it was Thisbe's time to phone him and tell him that she would not be home.

It was not Thisbe's voice, but another woman: her friend, Abby Bruler.

"She hasn't phoned. I don't know where she is," said Julius.

"I'm not looking for Thisbe. I'm looking for you."

Abby had been trying to get in touch with Julius for two days. She had tried him at work, but had made the mistake of telling his office that she was with the newspaper. They intercepted her call and sent her to the ministry's public relations department, or, as the reporters called it, the DOL: Deny, Obfuscate, Lie. She tried getting through to Julius as a personal call, but repeatedly got his voice mail. She did not know, but she suspected, that he was erasing her messages without listening. For in years past, she had advised Thisbe to leave him, and he knew it.

"What do you want?" said Julius.

"It's not what you think," she said quickly. "It's nothing to do with Thisbe."

"I thought you two were going out tonight."

"No. No, not tonight."

"Then what?" said Julius.

Abby told him about Cooper, about the branch falling, about the dead woman Davillo.

"I know all about it," said Julius, cutting her short. "I used to work with her."

Which Abby knew. In fact, it was the reason she was calling. "Julius, there's something going on here. Do you know that besides the lawsuit, Cooper has been arrested multiple times?"

"No."

"It's true. I know because— because— well, never mind how I know." It was not necessary for Julius to know that about her weekend in Banff nor how she had been humiliated in the hotel lobby when the police took Cooper away. "The fact is, I know. And not only that. I know that your department has the oversight over his suit. And not only that. It so happens that the woman who died—"

"Yes?"

"The woman who died had Cooper's file."

"How do you know that?"

"She's on record at court. You know there've been hearings and motions and all that court nonsense. It's all part of the public record." Abby was not comfortable with things legal, and so tended to deprecate them. "I looked it up. 'Davillo,' right in the court case. You can look it up."

"I can?"

"You think you're funny. My point is, someone is going to inherit Davillo's files. I was hoping that you—"

"Yes, I understand. You were hoping I would inherit the file because then I would leak information to the press. To you in particular."

She heard anger in Julius's voice. "Julius, I'm so sorry that poor woman died. Was she a friend of yours? Did you know her well?"

she asked, thinking: Thisbe liked Julius. Her friend Meghan always liked Julius. She had no idea why.

"Your sudden sensitivity is touching."

Oh dear, thought Abby. "Julius, I'm sorry. I know I'm rushing too fast. I *am* sorry for your loss. I didn't know her, but I do feel for you. How long did you work together?"

"The rest of us are splitting her files. I don't know who's got what. It's a little recent for us to know what to do. I don't know if they've even got a req out for a replacement or if they're just going to write the job down to attrition."

"Julius, this Cooper may be after you next."

Julius snorted. "Why would he be after me?"

"Don't you see what he's doing? People die all around this guy. Lots of people die. He knows exactly when and where. He's connected, Julius. He's connected, and he's dangerous."

"He's a wimp," said Julius, thinking of Cooper's passivity during his fight with Dean. But this was just bravado.

"He was arrested by the police in Banff less than a year ago. The Metro police picked him up yesterday—"

"Maconochie?"

"Yes, Maconochie. How do you know that? Anyway," said Abby, genuinely surprised at what Julius knew but unwilling to stop her own train of thought, "they had to release him because they don't have enough on him. You don't want to mess with this man."

"Your concern touches me. So your point is that if I tell you all about his file, that will make him my friend?"

"Julius. Now you know that's not what I want."

"Because it so happens that I have his file right here on my lap while we're speaking..."

"You do?" Abby could not believe her luck.

"No. I don't. I told you, I don't know who gets what file, and I don't care. I go to work and do my job. I'm not interested in Cooper, and I'm not interested in getting fired for narcing on government business to the papers."

"Julius, listen, I know that we've been–" But he had hung up.

She looked at her dead phone. "That didn't go so well," she said.

Julius stood up and went to his briefcase. He in fact had already been given Cooper's file, had already examined it with considerable interest, bringing the most significant documents home. He had taken it when the police—tipped off by Abby, he now realized—had phoned the ministry. It was what Julius thought of as a liminal file, a file that occupied the no man's land between work and goofing off.

The regulations by which Julius's ministry did its work were ambiguous and required human interpretation. For the lazy and unambitious, liminal files facilitated goofing off with safety, requiring attention only when some lawyer wanted to cause trouble over them. Since the lawyers had not called, Davillo had done what any government employee with twenty years experience would do: nothing. After doing that for two years, she closed the case. A worker like Davillo might have a hundred files on the go at once, all ignored with masterful hand, allowing her to come to work late, drink coffee, and eat doughnuts at her desk through several breaks a day. This saved the ministry millions of dollars in research and court appearances. Taxes were kept low. Everybody was a winner.

But when the lawyers or newspapers fussed, cases like Cooper's had to be sued out in court. Bribes were also a possibility, and, to Julius's surprise, not as uncommon as he had once thought. For Julius, though cynical in attitude and sexual conduct, was in fact scrupulous in matters relating to money. "It's what comes," he said, "of being an atheist. You have to believe in something."

It was odd that Cooper had Davillo killed. She had closed his file. Did the mob not know the case was closed? How did one communicate with such people? Clever in other things, Julius realized that he had no idea how to get in touch with the mob. Should he call Cooper? He thought, What if I were murdered over some stupid file that has nothing to do with me? It would be embarrassing.

Julius went to his computer and found a directory called *publicrelations*, opened several files, then typed a long memo. He picked up the telephone and began dialing numbers, leaving voice mails or having quick conversations: "A rough sketch. It won't come from an official address, but you'll understand when you see it." He began sending emails from different accounts, some to addresses with the names of newspapers, others to addresses inside the government, pasting text from his memo again and again. That done, he logged into his official account and emailed the complete memo to his minister. He followed it up with a long voice mail: "Need to respond… a lot of media interest… Check your email, I've sent a briefing document with talking points… call if you need more… expect phone calls from…"

Chapter Twenty-Six

In Which Thisbe Discovers Something of Interest

Thisbe entered, and, though she was unaware of it, she gave Julius the first happy "Hello" he had had from her since Dean had returned.

"I guess you heard that I was at your office," he said, wondering if that was why she was pleased. He stood up. Was she to be happy with him again? For a split second, he felt an uncharacteristic hope for something more than he had. It was the sort of feeling that leads a man to attempt some noble deed, to fight a battle or take a new job, to write sonnets or buy a new car. To paint. He looked. But Thisbe, already past him and into the kitchen, shone with some other light than his.

"Did you—" He was about to ask an obscene question about her relations with Dean but thought better of it. "You fire someone today?" he asked.

She had disappeared into the kitchen, but now put her head out. "No," she said. "No, why?"

Even a month ago, he thought, she would have said, "That's not what you were going to say.'" She would have caught his hesitation and called him on it. But today she saw nothing. He understood: he was a stranger to her.

So he said, "You seem pleased about something."

She made a friendly grimace, a homey happy easy teasing. Julius, who loved her best when she was happy and scolding, saw again a happiness that was no longer for him. He fell back into his usual seat in front of the television.

"That Cooper is a piece of work," she said. "Do you know what he's done?" Thisbe saw that Julius was out of sorts. It occurred to her that although they lived together, it had been many days—weeks?—since they had had a conversation. She decided that, whether or not their relationship was over, she would continue to be decent. She began to tell Julius about Cooper. He interrupted her.

"I thought you said he was having people killed."

"That's what I thought. But there's no way that branch was cut. Do you know the police picked him up to talk to him about it? But even they had to admit there was no evidence. And, Julius, you should really see him—he's so, so… he's not like anyone I think I've ever known," she said giving up. "He's such a dork," she added, fondly. "I need to catch a shower. I got a call from–" but she became veiled again, as Julius had seen her veiled years ago when she left him for Dean and now again for the past several months. "I got a call to go out on the way over. I need to get going."

"With Abby?"

Thisbe seized on this. "Yes. Abby wanted to get dinner," she said.

Julius took a grim satisfaction in not telling her that he had spoken to Abby, who had said that they were not going out. For the second time in ten minutes she did not notice his mood. He said, "I found out something about Cooper too," but she had already gone into the bathroom and closed the door.

Thisbe had been so upset the night that Ehrens and Davillo died that, although Julius had mentioned that there was a Davillo in his office, she had not heard. And then, since she barely spoke to Julius, and so often left to go to Dean ("or to Cooper?" Julius asked himself for the first time), she had again not paid any attention when he told her that the Davillo, whom she had seen die, was indeed the woman in his office.

Julius had not known Davillo well. She was an unhelpful woman whose goal, as near as Julius could tell, was to give as much trouble as possible to everyone else in order to avoid being assigned work. This was a common and winning strategy in government work. Davillo had four years to go until her fully-funded pension would enable her to flee Canada forever for a Fort Lauderdale condo. And now she was dead.

Thisbe was just out of the shower when the phone rang. Julius had not moved from his post in front of the television, and Thisbe, wearing only her underwear and a big shirt, a towel around her head, answered it. Her bare legs filled Julius with angry lust.

"I'm so glad you called. No, I haven't seen it yet, but I'm sure it's here. I'll look for it. No, I won't forget. We wouldn't want to hold up an equation of almost infinite complexity now, would we?" She laughed. "Oh, yes, I'm sorry. It just came out. I don't think Gormley heard, do– Oh, he did. He mentioned it. What did you tell him? All right. I can say that too. All right. Yes, I'll see you Monday."

"Wait. Who was that?" Julius asked. Thisbe's cheerful chatter was like champagne drunk by an enemy while Julius's throat parched.

"Cooper," said Thisbe. "Something I'm supposed to bring in for him." She continued to bustle about the apartment. She was different tonight. There had been some kind of leap. Ever since Dean had come back, she had been planning to move out, but months had gone by and she had not left. Things were not going well in honeymoonville. Dean was sleeping with her. He was sure of that. Dean did not want to marry her. And though many times she had stayed out all night, it seemed that Dean did not want her to move in. She had been nervous, edgy, easily frustrated and upset. Julius had taken advantage of this to enjoy an angry sexual congress with her on more than one night. Mostly she slept on the couch. Julius liked to watch television late at night, and Thisbe went to bed early, but Julius did not change his habits. He would stay up watching television in the easy chair beside her, keeping her awake with programs in which he had no interest and ignoring her complaints. If she doesn't like it, he would say to himself, then good. He was not going to ask about her tawdry affairs.

Now there had been a breakthrough. She was humming—humming of all things, Mozart, something from an opera. Had Dean proposed? He did not like this. He studied Thisbe's fingers. There was no new ring. He was not going to ask.

Her phone rang, and she spoke as she bustled about. "Yes. Yes, I've found out the whole story. Yes, that's right. You knew that? A notebook. Exactly right. No, I don't know where he keeps it. I have it right here, though, I'm returning it to him Monday. Um. Okay, I can do that. Yes. All right."

She came out of the bedroom dressed up for a night on the town, her long hair a waterfall, her dress grey and black, eyes and lips made up, a delicate scent following her movements like a breeze smiling with flowers. She dropped a black notebook on the counter and disappeared back into the bathroom. He noticed that she had decided on an oversize purse with a shoulder strap—big enough to serve as an overnight bag.

"*Vorrei, e non vorrei…*" she sang.

Julius, agitated by her happiness, stood up and went to the kitchen. He retrieved a beer and opened it. The notebook had fallen open. The page showed a long list of names and dates.

"What is this?"

"It's Cooper's," said Thisbe, still getting ready.

"Well, why are you in here?" asked Julius, turning over a page. What was going on between her and Cooper?

Thisbe stopped singing. She came quickly out to the kitchen. "What did you say?"

"You. You're down right here. Why does Cooper have you in his book?"

"Oh my God."

"Here's the date. What is that, a week from Sunday?"

"Oh my God."

Thisbe suddenly became all of a fluster, rushing back and forth, half completing her ablutions, picking up the book, putting it down somewhere else, going off to do something else, not finding the book ("It's disappeared. It can't just disappear, can it?"), finding the book, putting it down somewhere else, rushing off to do something else. She began at least three phone calls but hung up before she spoke to anyone. She put on her winter coat, then thought better of it and put on her trenchcoat. She had used the toilet, but forgot and went in to use it again, then came out as quickly. She put lipstick over her lipstick.

There was a certain satisfaction in this—Julius had not been pleased to have her walking about the apartment singing arias from *Don Giovanni* for another man—but her utter distraction annoyed him. "What the hell is going on?" he said more than once, but got no coherent answer. Over Julius's objections ("You can't go out like this. You can't think straight, let alone drive straight."), Thisbe left in a rush, holding the notebook, muttering to herself and dialing her cell phone. She came back in to get her car keys and left again.

Julius, distracted now himself, finished the last sip of beer remaining in his bottle. It was tepid and gave no satisfaction. He went to the refrigerator but found only water and orange juice. "Indeed," he said aloud. He wanted a real drink. On the counter beside him was the black coil bound notebook. She had dropped it when she came in to look for her car keys. He lifted the cover.

Dean's name was there too, and on the front page. But more disturbing was a Post-It note that said, "Need you, call me. Cooper."
He peeled the note off and threw it in the trash.

Chapter Twenty-Seven

Two Bars in Toronto

Dean, whose heart did not work terribly well, had nursed his way through two drinks, but still Thisbe had not arrived. He was beautifully dressed, dressed, as Meghan Evans once said to Julius, as though his clothes were an argument, "a way to put everyone else in the wrong." Thisbe's phone was rolling straight to voicemail, and Dean had left two messages for her already. What had happened? How could she be so late? When he had spoken to her earlier in the evening, she had been getting dressed and on her way with the notebook. He left twenty-five dollars on the bar, left another twenty dollars and a message with a hostess, found his coat, and went outside.

It was a Friday night in downtown Toronto, and the street was crowded. It had been hot in the bar, and the freezing weather felt good. Unsure what to do now that Thisbe had stood him up, he allowed the young Vietnamese man in front of the club to park three cars before handing in his valet ticket. He began to feel faint and had time to say to himself, "Not here," before he became so overwhelmed that he could not think at all. He clutched a street lamp for support. His head swam.

For it was a little known fact that Dean suffered from hyper-trophic cardiomyopathy, or, as Meghan Evans said years before with not quite clinical insight, "The heartless son of a bitch." The defect was congenital. The most usual symptom was a tendency toward faintness when excitement—in Dean's case, usually in the form of anger—caused his heart rate to rise. This had been more or less successfully controlled with exercise, diet, and beta blockers. The young heart-stricken Dean (he had been diagnosed after a mild heart attack at the age of eleven) had been terrified of an imminent death, and he learned to find in work of all kinds a true distraction. Whether it was brilliance, fear, or some other agency, Dean delighted his proud mother with a rocketing course of achievement that began in high school. A spell of bad health forced him to relinquish a CFO position at another firm and, after a period of convalescence, led to his becoming the head of the Seals life insurance group twenty-eight years after the first heart attack.

But his attacks had come more frequently of late, and sometimes, as tonight, without warning, without an increased heart rate, without excitement. An ethanol ablation two years before did not significantly shrink his swollen septum, and, despite a septal myectomy a year ago, the outflow tract from ventricle to aorta had narrowed again. Two generalists and three specialists agreed that his near term future was in doubt. Though contemptuous of people who worried about their health, Dean worried about his health. Achievements were no longer enough to keep his mind pure of fear. Five out of five doctors agreed: at this point, a likely result of his condition was sudden death.

"That's quite a symptom," he said to Doctor Number Two.

"Yes," said the doctor. Feeling perhaps that this was not enough, he added, "Yes, it is." Personalizing his message, he added, "Dean."

This conversation failed to comfort Dean. He was particularly nervous about his impending death because, as a young man, he had sold his soul to the devil.

He was only fifteen years old and had just suffered his third heart attack. It happened the morning after the cast party for a high school play, and he lay in bed unable to move. He stared at the ceiling of his bedroom thinking, "This is the last sight I will see," and, "I have never slept with a woman," the thought of women having haunted him for the past several months. He felt the pain in his chest wax and wane and the vertigo that sometimes accompanied his inability to process sufficient quantities of oxygen. Sadness overwhelmed him. He stared at the stippled white ceiling because he could not move his head, closed his eyes to doze only to open them and look at the ceiling again, feeling that the miracle of woman would never be his. He began to weep because he had never had a chance to do anything and life had been constructed so that he had to live in fear since his first heart attack as a child, and now he would die because he had chosen to stay out late with his friends instead of coming home. He wept, but the gasping compromised his oxygen flow, and he lost consciousness for a time.

The morning grew light. His mother, looking in, saw her darling boy sleeping off his first high school party and thought, It is good for him to have pleasure, he works so hard.

The morning wore on. His father, looking in, saw his only son and remembered the time when he too had been young and beautiful and tender and feckless, and he felt the strength in his arms and was pleased to have a son who even now had grown to feel his arms full of strength.

But as Dean's heart bumped and sputtered inside his chest, as he fell in and out of consciousness, he became aware of another presence in the room. He was frightened, and he turned toward the man (he had not opened his eyes, but somehow knew it was a man) in the room with him.

"I can help you," said the man.

Dean opened his eyes to see a short man with a broad stomach sitting in a folding chair beside him. "Are you the doctor?" Dean asked.

The man smiled a kindly smile and said that, no, he was not really a doctor. "People call me Mr. Scratch," he said.

"I need a doctor," said Dean.

No, Scratch said, he did not think so. "You'll be feeling better in no time."

This annoyed Dean, who was holding on to himself tightly waiting for the next attack to wrack his body with pain. But when it came, it was weaker, and he found he could stand it. "Did you give me something?" he asked.

Scratch looked about modestly. "Just a sample."

"When did you do it? I didn't see you."

Scratch ignored his question. "You can speak again, can't you? Doesn't that feel better?"

It did feel better, and Dean said so.

"Would you like to be better all the time?" asked Scratch.

Young as he was, Dean could see that there was more to this question than its surface. "I suppose I would," he said, hedging.

"Ooh—wrong answer," said Scratch. Dean felt the next attack coming on, felt his heart spasming and the room spinning. He was unable to call out, but in his mind he was begging Scratch to forgive him and offering Scratch anything he wanted, only to bring him through the attack.

Dean did not know if he had passed out or not, but Scratch was still sitting there as if nothing had happened when Dean next opened his eyes.

"Now. Would you like to be better all the time?" Scratch asked in a kindly voice.

Dean knew the answer he had to give. He gave it.

"I have certain powers that I can exercise in certain circumstances," Scratch said. "I can do a lot for a boy your age."

Dean felt more frightened of Scratch than of the pain, and he longed for his parents to come to his room, for he had the feeling that if they were there, he would not have to give in to this devil. But—whether through Scratch's agency, or simply because they were busy elsewhere—he was left alone. Terms were discussed. He was given a twenty-four year guarantee, which, at his age, seemed like forever, plus important perquisites like career success in some field, wealth, and the love of women.

"You're really getting the better of me," Scratch said fondly, "but I like you. Let's sign." He pricked Dean's finger with a small black pin, and a tiny spot of blood welled up into a red sphere on the pale fingertip.

"Dean. Dean," came a voice and a whiff of spices.

Have I died and gone to an Indian restaurant? Dean asked himself. His buttocks were freezing. He looked up and found that he was sitting on the icy ground outside the bar at which he was to meet Thisbe. An Indian man was helping him up. "I'm sorry, I–" Dean said.

"I am Sridhar," said the Indian man. "From Seals."

Dean recognized him. "Yes. Thank you, Sridhar."

"You are welcome."

"Well. Thank you. I don't know what happened."

"I saw you slip."

"Yes. I slipped. Can I buy you a drink?"

"That would be great," said Sridhar. He was pleased.

Dean was pleased. He realized that Sridhar worked with Cooper. "I would like to hear all about the great equation," said Dean. Though agitated by Thisbe's lateness, it was not a bad idea to wait for her in the bar. He said to Sridhar, "Do you know we've already begun to deny insurance and personally tailor the premiums based on your data? We've found some correspondences..." But Dean was surprised to see that Sridhar had suddenly become upset. He tried again. "I think your group is doing wonderful work. Really, the only exciting work in actuarial science since the Italians invented the damn thing in the Renaissance."

"Sir?" came a voice: the Vietnamese teenager had brought around Dean's car and was opening the door for him.

"Sridhar?" asked Dean, perfectly willing to let his car wait and buy one of his mathematicians a drink. He was also interested in what Sridhar would say about Cooper.

"I'm sorry. I must go," said Sridhar, and he walked away before Dean could stop him, looking all about him as if he expected someone in the crowd to attack.

"Thank you!" called Dean. "Keep up the good work!" He said to himself: No wonder Thisbe thought Cooper was dangerous. This Indian is terrified of him.

He had the valet hold his car while he checked once more with the hostess, but there had been no one looking for him and no one had called. He went back to his car, undecided. His legs felt unsteady, and his car was before him, so he plopped into the driver's seat. It was snowing. Dean pulled out into traffic on Adelaide. When he hit University, he turned left instead of right and headed north. It was time to do something he should have done months ago.

It was snowing as Julius left the condominium and made his way to the pub. He entered, stomping and shaking himself. Sitting at the bar already was a man he had seen before. Julius hung up his coat and hat and took the stool beside him.

"You're the son of that priest," said Julius. For he thought of Scratch as a religious huckster that Thisbe had fallen in with despite the fact that she should have known better, in the way certain women fall in with a fad diet or exercise program for a season.

Besides meeting at Scratch's party and one or two other times when Julius had accompanied Thisbe or dropped her off, the two had seen each other in the pub before. It was located on St. Clair west of Avenue Road, a quiet ethnic dive that was far enough away from both Queen's Park and the condominium so that Julius— misanthropic and not inclined to networking—would see nei- ther neighbors nor the politicians and bureaucrats with whom he worked. Gormley liked it because in his old job he had once been called there to do in an attractive female accountant. The bar stool on which Gormley now sat was the bar stool on which she had died and was replete with carnal fantasy for him.

"I hate Dean," said Julius.

"I hate Dean too," said Gormley.

Julius was feeling more companionable now that this important point of communion was established. "So what is it you used to do, Gormley? I mean, before you started working for the prince of darkness?"

"I worked for the Prince of Darkness."

"No, I mean before Dean."

"Right."

"You worked for?"

"For the Prince of Darkness."

"Meaning?"

"Scratch. The Prince of Darkness. Old Nick."

"Your dad?"

"That's right."

"Why is he the prince of darkness?"

"I don't know. He's trying to retire."

"Life as a preacher got him down?"

"But he doesn't want to turn the business over to me."

"Really? Why not?" said Julius, though looking at Gormley, slouching in front his beer and rooting about in his ear with a long finger, a gross of reasons immediately leapt to mind. "Seems like he makes pretty good dough."

"He doesn't want me to fall into the trap he fell into. That's what he says."

"So what trap does he want you to fall into? Oh," said Julius, answering his own question. "You mean– life insurance."

"I'm a middle manager," said Gormley with pardonable pride.

"I can see that," said Julius. "What did you do for your dad?"

"I was Death," said Gormley. He removed his finger from his ear and peered at it.

"Every job feels like that sometimes," said Julius.

"I'm not kidding," said Gormley. "I was Death."

Julius smiled. "You mean you were the manifestation of the universal force of entropy, the curse brought to all things by the Original Sin that Adam and Eve committed in the Garden of Eden, the Fate Atropos with her inevitable scissors, the Grim Reaper who takes from each and every one of us the final debt we owe to God, life itself?"

"Yep." Gormley took a drink of beer. "That's me."

"But you don't have that job anymore," said Julius, playing along without interest.

"I got fired. It was so totally unfair."

"Is that so?"

"It was a set up. An inside job. I was framed."

"It sounds bad," said Julius. He was trying to decide whether Gormley was more amusing or repulsive. "Who framed you?"

This stumped Gormley for a second, perhaps because of the amount of beer he had consumed. Then he remembered. "My neighbor. A guy I had done a lot for. Someone who I had taken under my wing, had him over to my house, shown a good time. He drank my beer."

"A bad guy," said Julius.

"Some day I'll have my revenge."

"I wouldn't want to be him when you do."

"I wouldn't want to be him now. Except—" Here Gormley paused.

"Except?"

"Except he's boffing the hottest girl in our office."

"Is he now?"

"I walked right in on them."

"Really?"

"She was by the desk, there they were, him and that Thisbe, with her long hair and those big–"

An involuntary glottal spasm caused Julius to spit his beer onto the bar. He began to cough, and Gormley pounded his back. "Did you say Thisbe?" Julius rasped when he was able to speak again.

"Yeah. She's the best-looking piece– hey, wait a minute. You were her boyfriend, weren't you?"

"I knew her."

"You were her boyfriend. That's how I first met you, isn't it? Boy, I don't know who your girlfriend is now, but I think you're nuts. She is one hot tamale. I just look at her and my toes get toasty."

Julius was interrupting. "So you walked in on Thisbe and your enemy, and they were engaged in the act of coition?"

"The act of what?"

"Coition. Copulation. Sexual intercourse. Doing the nasty. Making the beast with four buttocks."

Gormley looked at him uncomprehendingly. "The best of four buttocks?"

"Beast. The beast with four buttocks. Shakespeare."

"Never heard of him. Friend of yours?" Gormley belched. "Because I don't think she had four buttocks. At least I always assumed..." Gormley reached around behind and put his hand down his pants. "I've only got two," he said, retrieving the hand and looking at it.

Julius was impatient with this. "Screwing, Gormley, screwing. You saw Thisbe in the office?"

"Yeah."

"On the desk?"

"She was kind of by the desk, and he was in the chair in front of her."

Julius's powerful visual imagination, informed by helpful R-rated movies, easily filled in the details of lurid sexual encounter. "Really? And so she and Dean, in Dean's office..."

"Dean? No. Cooper."

"Cooper? Who's Cooper?"

"He's my enemy. Cooper. He's the one who's doing it to her."

"Cooper?" Julius was at sea.

"Cooper."

"You mean the one who's working on that big equation?" But in his mind, he was seeing the note: "Need you, call me. Cooper."

Gormley snorted. "Yeah, right. Big equation. I'll show you a big equation," he said, fumbling with the waistband of his trousers.

"That won't be necessary," said Julius hastily. He took a serviette and absently began to mop the bar where he had discharged his drink. "But I thought—so tell me about this Cooper."

"He's the one got me fired."

"Is he? He's your–"

"My next-door neighbor. The one got me fired. He stole my notebook, then got a job at Seals, then I got a job at Seals, and when I get there, everyone's oohing and ahing like he's got some super math thing, and all it is is it's the notebook he stole from me that's giving him all the answers, and he and that Thisbe even admitted it…"

The beer hit the spot, and conversational Gormley turned out to be not only amusing but informative. Julius stood up suddenly. "Let's go to my place," he said. "There's something I need to get."

Chapter Twenty-Eight

Visiting on Cooper's Street

It was Friday night, and Cooper, late coming home from shopping and dinner alone at Mr. Sub, slid along the unseasonably frozen street. He was thinking about Thisbe saying that she couldn't believe he had used Death's notebook to get a job as an actuary. Maybe she was right. But what else would he do with it? The only other thing he could think of was to sell it to the newspapers. They could get their obituaries written early.

As he walked around the curve by the high school, he could just make out Thisbe's car parked in Scratch's driveway. Thisbe was there. No one visited Scratch on Friday nights—there were no services. Cooper felt a small glow of confidence warm him. Thisbe wasn't really visiting Scratch at all. She had come to see him and was going to Scratch's because she didn't want to admit it.

As he came closer, however, he saw that things were better than he had even suspected. The BMW was in Cooper's driveway. She had come to see him directly. She was not coy or shy. She was waiting for him.

Cooper crossed Wallingford and walked the last block briskly, holding his toes tight inside his boots to prevent himself from slipping on the ice. There had been a thaw and a refreeze, and it was only because he knew someone must have been there that he was able to make out the traces of boot prints in the remaining snow on his icy staircase. Cooper dug his key from his pocket. There was a light on in the living room.

He was having a difficult time getting the door unlocked. When he stopped thinking about the lights and footprints and Thisbe and looked at the door, he realized why. The door was already unlocked. Could he have left it unlocked this morning? He recalled a similar scene in a James Bond movie. Sean Connery finds his hotel room door has been tampered with, and, though Sean is ready for anything with drawn pistol, he discovers instead a fabulous woman taking a shower in his bathroom.

The fantasy had such hold on Cooper that he did not even call out when he entered. Instead, he removed his boots and went straight upstairs to check in the bathroom. Thisbe was not there. It was a moment of disappointment.

"Thisbe," he called. "Thisbe?" He poked his head into his bedroom and office, then went downstairs. Thisbe was not only not naked in his shower, she was not naked anywhere. Still, the light was on. That was an indication that someone had been inside. On the other hand, it was still dark when he left these winter mornings, so he may have left it on himself. He went to the kitchen and checked the back door. The lock had been broken some months ago, and Cooper, newly out of straitened economic circumstance, had not gotten around to fixing it. There were traces of water on the mat he kept in front of the door. He reconstructed the scene: Thisbe had knocked at the front door, found no one home, and so gone around the house to let herself in the back. When he was not home, she had left through the front door, leaving it unlocked. Where had she gone? "Thisbe!" he called, walking back through the house.

He recalled another movie in which a fabulous woman arrives at her lover's house wearing a trenchcoat with only lingerie beneath it. Perhaps she was hiding somewhere, waiting for him to find her. "Thisbe!" He looked in the downstairs bathroom, checked the closets, the basement, and the other rooms. He found a coffee cup in the den, which looked promising. Then he saw the white hairy growths on the surface of the cold cup, indicating that he had forgotten it a week or two before. He went back to the kitchen to rinse it out in the sink and hoped that Thisbe had not seen it.

"Thisbe!" he called. And then he realized. When he was not home, she would of course have gone next door to see Scratch. There was some disappointment in this—no sassy woman in the shower, no trenchcoat hiding panties and camisole—but perhaps, since she had only kissed him for the first time today, he was moving things along too fast. If she had been free and easy as he had overheard Dean and Julius say, she was also, he recalled, a newly religious girl. Cooper left the front door unlocked in case she returned. He took a quick shower. It was not until he was toweling off that he remembered she had promised to return his notebook. Was that the reason she had come? "Here it is. See you Monday"? The disappointment brought a flavor of plastic and submarine sandwich to his tongue. But she had said she would bring it to work on Monday. He said to himself: She came because she wanted to see me. She wants to see me because she is interested in me. Cooper shaved, put on clean clothes, and went next door.

Gormley answered. "What?" he said, breath stinking of stale alcohol. Crooked yellow teeth slouched about his mouth, looking like Stonehenge during its awkward teenage years.

Cooper, who felt it might be rude to ask for Thisbe directly, said that he was wondering whether Scratch was home.

"I guess you don't want to see me. I guess that's one thing for sure. Why would you want to see your friend and colleague Gormley is what I want to know? Of course you wouldn't." He slurred his words as he spoke. Cooper realized: Gormley was sozzled.

"I'm sorry. How are you, Gormley?" Cooper asked. "Are you

enjoying the office?" They walked through the great hall to the kitchen.

"I've just come in with Julius."

"Julius?" said Cooper, surprised. "What's he doing here?"

"Friend of mine," said Gormley, evidently pleased to be able to make this remark. It occurred to Cooper that it was unlikely that Gormley was able to claim many people as friends. "We were just out having a drink."

"So I gather."

The kitchen door opened. "Cooper!" said Scratch. "I thought I recognized your voice. I've just made tea. Or would you like something stronger?"

Cooper was relieved to escape Gormley. He accepted tea and asked whether Thisbe was there.

As a matter of fact, she was. "But she's a little upset with you this evening, Cooper, if you don't mind my saying so."

Cooper was stunned. He asked himself: Why would Thisbe be upset with me? Feeling the question to be a good one, he gave tongue: "Why would Thisbe be upset with me?"

"An excellent question. You mean, besides the fact that she saw her name written in Death's notebook?"

"She what?"

"She saw her name in Death's notebook."

"She what?" This was too different from Cooper's expectations for the evening, and he could not take it in.

When Scratch said the same thing for the third time, Cooper said, "That isn't my fault. I'm not going to kill her."

"She may not see it that way."

This was too much to take. Cooper stood up and then sat down. He took a sip of tea, burned his tongue, realized that it was some urinous herbal girl tea, and put it aside. "What do you mean?" But there was a shriek from downstairs, and Cooper said, "Is she down there?"

"Yes, she is. But I don't advise you going down just now," Scratch said.

"Why not?" said Cooper, opening the door.

Scratch sat down heavily at his kitchen table. "I don't care. Go if you want to then."

It would have been obvious to someone less observant than Cooper that Scratch was depressed. Though anxious to see Thisbe, Cooper felt he could do no less than ask. He sat down. "You're upset about something," he said reluctantly.

"No. No, nothing, nothing at all." He made a poor attempt at a smile, mouth forcing itself into an upturning stripe on a downcast face.

"Something," Cooper said. He took another sip of tea, which was awful. Why did women drink this stuff?

"No. No, you just go on downstairs and see your friends."

Cooper, relieved, stood up. "Well, if you'd prefer not to talk about it–" he began happily.

"It's just that sometimes I get so tired," continued Scratch. "All the efforts, and no end in sight." He looked up.

Cooper resigned himself to the conversation and sat down.

"I wish I could retire," said Scratch.

This was something Cooper understood. "Job getting you down?"

"I'm just tired. Tired of it. I really can't tell you how tired I am."

"You just did."

"That's true."

"But you mean it's tiring."

"Yes."

"Your job."

"Yes."

"Tiresome."

"Exactly."

"Yes," said Cooper. "I know how that can be."

"Do you?"

"Well, no," Cooper admitted, "Not really. I mean, I've never held a job long enough to get that tired of it. As you know, I was unemployed until recently."

"Yes. I remember."

"But unemployment was tiring."

"Good thing you got a job."

"Yes."

"I guess you're happy with it?"

"Yes. Yes I am," said Cooper, thinking of meeting Thisbe, of the brilliant Indians who admired him, of the fact that Thisbe had kissed him. He was so pleased he forgot the tea in front of him was horrible and took a sip. The tea was horrible.

"I helped you get it, didn't I?"

Cooper saw that he had fallen into a trap. "Yes. Yes, you did," he admitted. It was coming. Cooper waited.

It did not come. "What if there was an even better job? Same line of work, but more money. A lot more money. You could have a house like this."

Cooper, who believed Scratch was winding up to ask him for a job, was at sea. "I do have a house like this."

Scratch had to admit that was true. "You know what I mean."

Cooper cut him off. He could make inquiries at Seals if that is what his neighbor wanted, but he was not aware that there was open headcount at this time, and besides...

But Scratch was not looking for a job, he was offering one. "Cooper, wait. Things may not be as they seem to you now. I have another job for you to consider. Other people have plans for your notebook. There are Other Considerations." Scratch's eyes opened wide as he repeated the last two words: "Other Considerations."

"There are?"

"You remember the night you took the notebook–"

"Yes?"

"And then a few days later, there was that robbery attempt?" Cooper remembered.

"Do you know who the burglar was?"

This seemed to be the point. Cooper asked, "The police caught him?"

"No. No, they didn't. But I know who it was."

"You do? Did you call the police?"

"Cooper. No. You know I'm not interested in the police. After all, it's not about doing things because you're forced to do them. People need to do the right thing because it's right, not because a man with a badge is watching them."

Cooper recognized this line of argument, but was not sure of its relevance. "So you didn't call the police." Where was this going?

Gormley had tromped into the room a minute or so before. Now he spoke: "We're going to get baseball bats and break his kneecaps. Wanna come?"

Scratch frowned at Gormley. "No. No, that's one thing we're not going to do."

"The fun stuff is always on the list of things we're not going to do," complained Gormley.

"The list of things anyone does not do is generally longer than the list of things anyone does," said Scratch sympathetically. "Except in the case of the devil."

"Isn't that interesting," said Cooper, hoping to end the conversation quickly and get downstairs.

This did not succeed, for Scratch elaborated. "It's what having an eternal job means. Unlike everyone else, I have to do everything there is. When I've finally done everything that can possibly be done, then time will stop and the world will end."

Cooper, sucked in against his will, pointed out the flaw in this. "But you can't do everything. You can't both be Helen of Troy's husband and not be her husband."

"It worked for Elizabeth Taylor. Six or eight times."

"She wasn't anybody's husband," said the confused Cooper. He continued: "If you do one thing, then you haven't done the other, so that on Thursday at 2 pm, if you go to Pape, then you haven't gone to Greenwood at 2 pm on that particular Thursday. You can never do everything."

Scratch smiled. "Forgive me for saying so, but your assumptions about time and space, Cooper, are a touch middle class," he said. "I'm sure they serve you well in business, I've no wonder that they like you at that job of yours. You're right, of course, about detailed particulars. I'm talking more about the kind of thing. Its moral flavor, if you like. Here's an easier way to think of it. Take the human race, for example."

"And break its kneecaps?" asked Gormley with enthusiasm.

Scratch ignored him. "The race will end when every potential of humanity has been exhausted. Adam gives birth to Cain and Abel. They realize humanity's potential for shepherding and farming, for innocence and murder. The Buddha comes and demonstrates humanity's capacity for mercy. Genghis Khan comes and shows its capacity for cruelty. All destinies must be played out. Every one. A miner in Sudbury has a capacity for science, music, and love. He develops none of these things, for he is brutalized by his job and must work every day of his short life. He has three sons: a scientist, a musician, and a lover. The potential of the father is realized in his children. Just so with the human race. All the destinies that Adam and Eve were capable of must be fulfilled. One man is destined to be the greatest, another the least. One has led a life of purest happiness at all moments. Another has lived a life in which every waking moment was black misery. Between these extremes, every fate must be played out. When the last one is complete, the trump will sound and the human race will have finished itself, complete, and that will be the end."

This was too mystical for Cooper, who did in fact possess middle class assumptions about time and space, which did, truth be told, serve him well in that job of his. "So when every possible food has been deep-fried?"

"For example," said Scratch.

"I saw deep-fried Snickers bars last time I went to Calgary," Cooper mused.

"Some would say, a sign that the end is near."

"I see what you mean," said Cooper, who saw nothing of the kind but did not see what could be gained by arguing. He was gratified because Scratch seemed pleased to be so well understood.

"Speaking of destinies, Cooper," Scratch said. "There's another job I'd like you to consider."

"Another one? Which was the first?"

"The Society for Equitable Assurances on Lives and Survivorships," said Scratch. "As we were discussing."

"Another job," said Cooper. "I like the one I've got."

"Of course, Cooper, of course. This is one that you might think about. As you know, I've been tired of my job. I've been looking for someone to take over the old store."

"I didn't know you ran a store." He lifted the tea cup to his lips, but remembered in time and put it down before drinking.

"I don't."

"Then—?"

"Cooper, I'm just so tired. I'm really looking to retire. My point is, do you know what I might consider if I were you?" Scratch asked.

"No," said Cooper, opening the door to the basement.

"I would consider a succession plan–" But he was cut off by the sound of a scream from the basement.

"I'll think about it," said Cooper, although he was not sure what he was supposed to consider. The thought that Thisbe was upset, perhaps angry with him, and was sitting just a staircase away overwhelmed his patience for a sad old man. "I'll definitely think about it," he said, stepping onto the basement staircase.

"I don't think you heard me," said Scratch, but Cooper had closed the basement door. The cricket behind the stove began to chirp. "Oh shut up," said Scratch.

Chapter Twenty-Nine

A Party at the Fiery Furnace

Julius was there, standing beside the furnace, in the middle of another one of his literary movie reviews: "*Sense and Sensibility II: Sensei and Sensibility*. It's Jane Austen's kung fu book. Imagine the Austen bestseller machine turning its imagination to *Kill Bill*. Three ninja spinsters go visiting in the English countryside, but they are attacked by Vietnamese gangs in Shropshire and forced to do battle with fists of martial fury. Beneath the over-the-top martial arts mayhem beats the burning question: Will they ever stand as high again in Mr. Darcy's regard?"

"I thought Mr. Darcy was *Pride and Prejudice*," said Keiter from the furnace. Cooper could see the dancing orange light of the fire.

"Oh, he is. But he's in this one too. It's sort of like *Marvel Team-Up*, where it was really a Spider-Man book, but he'd have guest stars like the Hulk. In the CBC version Mr. Darcy is played by Chris Rock and Mr. Bingley by Bing Crosby."

"I've just met Bing Crosby," said Keiter. "Today."

"How nice. What's he like?"

"He's a lot nicer than Martin Luther," said Keiter, and Julius blew a raspberry. They both laughed, for they had been swapping humorous anecdotes about the father of intra-Christian religious warfare earlier in the evening.

Thisbe had pulled the rocking chair up to the furnace and was sitting with her back to the stairs. She was saying something that

Cooper could not hear, and he noticed then that she was speaking into her cell phone. Cooper stood and admired her: the long hair cascading down her back, the small but perfectly formed figure, shoulders tapering down to thin waist, curving out to generous hips in the seat of the rocking chair. What was Julius doing here? Cooper felt jealous and angry. Had Thisbe been at the bar with Gormley and Julius?

Even as his anger came, it went from him as he remembered Thisbe's kiss. He felt himself fill with pity and love. Poor Thisbe, who had not waited for the man who was destined to love her. Instead she had wasted herself on these pointless men. Their fates— all of them, everyone everywhere, Scratch and Gormley, Dean and Julius, Keiter, Thisbe, Cooper—were knitted together in an equation of almost infinite complexity. There were so many variables and interlocking formulae that it would take a mathematician who was part god to comprehend it. It was not given to any single person to understand it all. But Cooper had grasped this much: that he and Thisbe were destined for one another. The equation had brought them together. It would not be denied.

Thus Cooper's meditations as he looked down into the basement from the staircase. And while he was lost in these high falutin contemplations, the door behind him swung open suddenly and startled him, so that he hopped down a stair or two, as a huge and terrible cry came forth above him: "A boy who kills cannot love! A boy who kills has no heart! Very smart, Anita, very smart!"

It was Gormley making An Entrance. He brushed past Cooper and stumbled down the stairway. He belched and his breath was like the fermentation of mouldy peanuts.

"It's 'Maria,' " came Keiter's petulant voice from the furnace.

"No. Gormley," Gormley said, and this struck him so funny that he began to laugh: "Urf urf urf. Oh, hi, Thisbe," he added in a softer voice, grinning so that his crooked teeth all seemed to be waving a merry hello. He stumbled as he walked, then looked behind angrily to see what had tripped him. The floor was smooth concrete.

Thisbe continued to speak into her cell phone.

"Hello, Keiter. Hello, Julius," said Cooper, following Gormley down the stairs. He tried to catch Thisbe's eye, but her phone held her attention. "Thisbe?" he ventured, but she did not look up.

Gormley had placed a long thin arm around Thisbe. She had put her phone away, and her shoulders appeared to be shaking.

"I'm all right. I'm all right," Thisbe was saying, but she was weeping.

"Thisbe!" said Cooper.

"It's not good when they know the date," remarked Gormley.

This stung Cooper. "I didn't tell her. I didn't even know," he said. He felt he was being unfairly criticized. "And besides," he added, "Why *don't* you allow hops in your beer?" To show his defiance, he retrieved a bottle from the refrigerator, opened it, placed a straw in it, and held it to Keiter in the furnace.

"About time," grumbled Keiter.

"You're welcome," sulked Cooper.

"What I want to know, old bean" said Julius, now addressing Keiter again, "are the parameters of that furnace. Can you get out for dinner? If you order a pizza, will they deliver? What about Amazon? Do drones bring you books, pots and hosiery?" He turned to Gormley. "In your expert opinion, Gormley. Say Mr. Keiter fancied a fair maid. Could he go on a date? Send flowers to her with whom he is desirous of having a fling? If he's late getting back, does his left foot turn into a pumpkin? A nation wants to know."

There was something other than the usual flapdoodle in Julius's merry blather, but it would be many years before Cooper understood.

Keiter answered Julius: "There's something about a day off for us coming up, but the tour guides never explain anything. First

Sunday after the first new moon after the equinox. Very medieval, the way this place is run. I guess it will be nice to have a day where I don't have to feel like I'm dea–!" He cut himself off by slapping his hands over his mouth, realizing he had been about to say something he did not want Thisbe to hear. His eyes were wide with horror.

"I know you're dead!" Thisbe shouted. Her voice was hoarse. She sniffed noisily. "I will be too. Soon."

"You?" said Keiter hopefully.

Cooper glared at him.

"Excellent," said Keiter, cheering up. He began to comb his hair. "We can hang out."

Thisbe said, "I'm cold." She hung down her head and sobbed.

"Oh, good one, Keiter. Mr. Compassion. And you say I'm insensitive," said Cooper.

"You're just jealous. You've been trying to keep her to yourself. Now she's going to be with me."

"I am not jealous," Cooper lied, looking for Julius's reaction from the corner of his eye. "Besides, she's not going because she wants to. She's going because she has to."

There were some metal folding chairs leaning against the basement wall. Cooper set some of them out in a semi-circle around Thisbe's rocker and the furnace. Julius found a small table and placed Keiter's beer on it with a straw sticking through the furnace grate.

"Thanks!" said Keiter.

Julius moved beside Cooper, leaned in, and said quietly, "Cooper, I need to speak to you."

"All right," said Cooper. He said to himself, Thisbe has told Julius that she loves me. Even if he wasn't going to have Thisbe all to himself, perhaps the evening wasn't going so badly.

"Hey!" yelled Thisbe, swinging a small fist.

"Gormley," said Cooper. For Thisbe was punching Gormley, who had again copped a feel.

"I was just comforting her," Gormley argued with the room at large, standing up and rubbing his arm where Thisbe had socked him.

"I'm fine," said Thisbe. She sounded it. Gormley's lechery had brought her to herself and she was once again under control. "Keiter, I'm not dying just so I can date you."

"Damn!"

"Gormley–" Thisbe continued.

But Gormley was heading upstairs.

"Gormley!" she shouted.

He stopped.

"Come back here."

He returned. Thisbe, when angered, had cowed braver souls than Death.

"I want you to tell us what you know."

Gormley explained. He used to have a job but it was too busy. He had to be everywhere at once. ("That's where we disagree," Cooper said, though this remark was ignored). Gormley continued: Then he lost his notebook and got fired. He wanted to get a job as a singer, but instead he had to go to the insurance office all day because Dean needed him. It was likely that he would take over Dean's job shortly, and then—who could say—he would likely become president of the company. That at least was the plan as it had been explained to him. In the meantime, he was single, and he was looking for a certain special someone. She should be petite and have long hair, make a lot of money—perhaps a middle manager. She should love music and dancing. His own certain special little... He inhaled deeply, apparently winding up for another showtune.

Thisbe said, "That's quite enough of that."

Gormley deflated.

"What we want to know is, what do you know about dying?" said Thisbe. "What about this notebook that tells when everyone is about to die?"

"I'm a good singer," sulked Gormley.

A voice came from the top of the stairs. "*This*be! How nice to see you. Oh and there's *quite* a party. Isn't that something? The door was open so I just let myself in. Oh and there's beer, and here I thought I might be interrupting a religious ceremony." The first Mrs. Rulen waggled a finger at them as she clicked down the stairs on high heels, her perfume filling the air with a heady reminder of sample inserts from women's magazines. "Gormley!" she called. "Oh, hello, Cooper," she sneered, and Cooper realized that he was to be punished for his lack of interest in things calendar-related.

Gormley seemed not to know what to do with his hands, and they fluttered about nervously at the end of his bony wrists.

"Tell her," Julius hissed at Gormley.

"The Muslim year consists of 354 days, twelve lunar months, with no adjustment to the solar calendar. There are about 103 of these Hirji years to every 100 Gregorian years," barked Gormley, like a not-particularly-bright eleven year-old reciting a half-understood poem. "The Jewish calendar is dated from the creation of the world and consists of twelve lunar months, but is adjusted to the solar year by the– by the–"

"Intercalation?" asked Julius, as if guessing.

"–the intercalation of an extra month at seven points in a nine year–"

"Or could it be nineteen year?" asked Julius, as if to no one in particular.

"–nineteen year cycle. The French revolution created a new calendar..."

"Oh *Chest*er!" squealed the first Mrs. Rulen. She wrapped her arm in Gormley's.

"Is it hot in here?" asked Thisbe. "I feel flushed."

She spoke to Julius, but Keiter hollered from the furnace, "Not as hot as it is in here, baby!" He laughed: "Heh."

"Chester?" said Cooper, looking at Gormley.

"That girl just wants at*ten*tion," said the first Mrs. Rulen to Gormley in a stage whisper, looking up on the last word or two to include Keiter in the comment. She frowned at Thisbe.

"She's going to die soon," Keiter announced happily.

The first Mrs. Rulen looked at Gormley, a question in her glance.

"So we hear," Gormley admitted.

"Do a little dance. Make a little love. Get down tonight," sang Keiter from the furnace.

"Keiter," said Cooper. "That's distasteful."

"To you, maybe," said Keiter. He continued the song, "Baby, baby, I'll meet you. Same place, same time."

Gormley had picked up Keiter's song and was singing along, "Do a little dance. Make a little love. Get down tonight."

The first Mrs. Rulen took Gormley's hand. She shimmied, her enhanced breasts moving with almost lifelike realism. She, Gormley, and Keiter sang in untuneful harmony, "Get down, get down, get down, get down, get down tonight, baby…"

The party continued their chatter. Scratch came down with a plate of cookies. The conversation turned to Keiter's small size. Theories were propounded, but Scratch denied them. "I don't know that they're really that small. It's all a matter of perspective, isn't it? He isn't so much small as far away."

"But he's right here. He's drinking beer. Show him how you can drink beer, Keiter," said Julius.

"Cooper, do you have another straw? This one's melted."

Cooper produced a box of straws. "See. I've been thinking of you Keiter."

"Cooper. That's– Well. Thank you." It was obvious that Keiter was touched.

Cooper noticed with some annoyance that Julius had taken Thisbe's hand in his. He replaced Keiter's straw, but brusquely, to show that he was hurt.

"See?" said Julius. "How far away can he be?"

"Perspective is always relative," said Scratch. And he himself grew and grew to an enormous size, so that he filled much of the basement and had to kneel on one knee on the floor, and still he grew so that his back was pressed against the ceiling and one monstrous arm wrapped almost around the entire little group. And then he shrank back down to normal size and was once again sitting on his folding metal chair.

"Ooh."

"Ah."

"That was incredible."

"Scary."

"Do that again."

"Oh, no," said Scratch, looking absently about him.

"It wears out the batteries," said Julius, but looking to Scratch as if more explanation might be forthcoming.

"I didn't know you knew about the furnace," said Cooper to Julius. "Do you come here often?" He was peeved that Julius's hand was still in Thisbe's.

"Just stopping through the woods on a snowy evening," said Julius.

"It's 'by the woods,'" corrected pedantic Keiter.

"You can't buy the woods," said Julius. "The First Nations knew that. As Geronimo said to Booker T. Washington that stormy Yom Kippur of 1917, 'Anyone who kisses his own wife is crazy.'" He patted Thisbe's hand and said, "I'll be back." And Julius ascended the staircase.

"Isn't he *fun*ny?" said the first Mrs. Rulen.

"Why is he going?" asked Gormley.

There was a lull in the conversation. With Julius gone, Cooper was able to take the chair next to Thisbe. It was she who spoke: "Gormley, this is serious." There were tears on her face. "I'm due to– to–" Cooper thought she was going to lose her composure again, but she pushed on. "My name is in the notebook. I only have a week. Can I change it? What can I do? What can you do? Don't play games. If something can be done, I need to know. Pronto."

"Ooh hoo hoo," said Gormley. "Ms. High-and-Mighty needs to know. Pronto. And right after punching perfectly innocent persons who were just trying to lend comfort. And what praytell has Ms. High-and-Mighty ever done for O.F.G.?"

("O.F.G.?" whispered Keiter.

"Our Friend Gormley," murmured Cooper, who had heard this sort of thing before.

"Ah.")

But this sudden attack was too much for Thisbe, who sank down in her chair and put her head down. "I don't feel at all well," she said.

Cooper, still holding her hand, went after Gormley. "Gormley, you don't need to kill Thisbe. I'm the one who's got your book. Tell me. You'll get your book back. Can we save Thisbe? How do we do it? What do you do with the book?"

"Bring it. Bring it here. I'll tell you," said Gormley.

"Now don't go back to that old job," nagged Scratch, "Not when you've just settled in to your new one."

"Cooper," said Thisbe. Her eyes were large and wet and looked to him. While he would not have said that he wanted to see her cry, Thisbe looking to him for succor while her eyes shone with tears was a Great Moment in Cooper's life.

"All right. I'll go right now. I'll be right back." He squeezed Thisbe's hand. "Don't go anywhere," he told her, feeling these words carried an extra freight of meaning. He stood up and re-membered. He said, "You have the notebook. I don't."

"Julius brought it."

"He just left. Where did he go?" Cooper stood up.

"He said he left it in your house," said Thisbe.

Cooper did not remember seeing it. "Gormley? You came with Julius."

Gormley nodded. "Kitchen table," he said. He began to sing: "Got no mansion, got no yacht. Still I'm happy with what I got. I got…"

Cooper pelted up the stairs. Inside, his heart was singing. He and Thisbe had been holding *hands*! Thisbe looked to him for help. He laughed out loud. Gormley knew how to do something with the notebook. Thisbe's doom could be postponed, put off into the indefinite future, which is where doom belonged. "I got the sun in the morning and the moon at night!" he hollered, picking up Gormley's dopey song. He had the most valuable notebook in the history of the world and he was going to trade it for Thisbe's life. He would take that deal any day. It seemed to him that his life would never be any better than it was now.

And he was right.

He was through the dining room and into the great hall when Scratch's door opened. A gust of cold air blew in, and Dean appeared on its wings.

"Oh, hello, Cooper," he said. In his hand, he held the notebook.

Chapter Thirty

Another Visitor

"That's mine. I need it," said Cooper. "Thanks."

But Dean refused. "This doesn't leave my hands," he said. He hung his coat on Erubis's head, walked to the modernist dining room and took a seat at the head of the table. Cooper, hovering, aghast, followed. "You," Dean commanded, "are going to tell me how this thing works."

Cooper stared at him dumbly.

Dean gave a short bark of laughter. "You don't know? Ha!" He opened the book, reading through the list, sliding a finger down the page as he read. A name caught his eye and he stopped for a moment. "Well, well," he said. But it was not what he was looking for, and he continued scanning the book, first one page, then the next.

Cooper took a step towards Dean.

"Nuh-uh-uh," said Dean, head bowed, finger still sliding down the page. He paused and looked at Cooper. "Did you calculate my death date?"

"Not that I recall." This was true. Cooper spent all his time on the math to get the dates right and barely glanced at the names, most of which meant nothing to him. He added, "It's not a good thing to know," echoing Gormley. "What do you mean, 'how this thing works'?" For Cooper did not think of the notebook as something that did any work. It was just a listing, a telephone directory of deaths.

At that moment, Scratch appeared in the room, Gormley clomping beside him. "I thought I heard– Dean. Good you're here. There is some news. It turns out that Cooper and I have reached an agreement about that job you were interested in," said Scratch.

"You have?" asked Dean.

"We have?" asked Cooper. He could not think of what the job was.

"Cooper," said Dean, and he spoke in almost a whisper, intense, hushed, hurried. "Cooper, there are powerful people who want this book. It's the key. The key to power, to wealth, to anything you ever dreamed of. Cooper, don't throw it away. I'm already in touch with some of them, Cooper. We can be partners. You need to help me."

This put Cooper in mind of something. "The NSA. I saw—in your office—the letter from–"

"Exactly Cooper. And they're only one agency. There are governments, businesses, billionaires. Cooper, everyone wants this. If–" But now Dean interrupted himself. "Wait. You've taken a new job? With Scratch? Is this the holiday?" But Dean was glaring, not at Cooper or Scratch, but at Gormley.

Gormley was leaning down and fussing with his boots.

"I haven't said I'll take it yet," said Cooper, not quite sure what was going on. Scratch talked about a job earlier. Why did Dean care? Perhaps it was a better opportunity than Cooper had thought.

"It's practically agreed," said Scratch, looking not at Cooper, but at Dean.

"It is, is it?" said Dean, looking at Gormley.

"My toenail is really screwed up," said Gormley as if Dean had not spoken. He had in fact taken a boot off and was sitting with one leg crossed and holding his foot in his hands. He was peering at his big toe.

Downstairs, there was a howl—Keiter leaving the furnace.

"Dean," Scratch said, "You're not looking well, if I may say so. A little worn out." Scratch smiled and sat down next to Dean. Dean, his attention now back on the book, turned so that he held it away from Scratch. Meanwhile Scratch watched with almost paternal interest. "Not looking well at all."

"I had forgotten that you two knew each other," said Cooper. He had not, really, but Scratch's seeming satisfaction in Dean's illness threw him off.

"In my line, you get to know a lot of people," said Scratch.

"Will you look at my toenail?" Gormley asked the table, contorting himself by pulling his foot up so that the sole was upside down and almost parallel to the floor. "Look."

"Ew," said Cooper with polite disgust.

"Known each other for years," said Dean absently, head down, finger sliding over names.

Scratch laughed in agreement: "Tss, tss, tss. We did some business together."

"What's going on up here?" said Thisbe, appearing through the kitchen door.

She had said that she did not feel well before Cooper had gone in search of the book, and it showed: her skin, usually pink and rosy, had turned yellow. Her eyes had raccoon circles beneath them. She walked slowly, listing to one side.

"Thisbe?" said Cooper. "You need a doctor."

"Yes, I don't feel at all well," she said. "Do you think you could drive me home?"

"Yes! Ah, just one minute," he said, full of joy that Thisbe was asking him for a service that would be a delight to perform. "Dean," he said, "Thisbe's date is in there. She only has a week. We have to help her."

"Thisbe?" Dean said. "What about her?" His head was back down in the notebook. He had flipped to the end and back to the front page. He froze. "Ha! The first page. How did I miss it?"

"Tss tss tss," laughed Scratch.

"They said Thisbe had a week to go," said Cooper. "If you can–"

But Dean shook himself and stood up. "This notebook," he declaimed, "isn't just a record of what will happen. It is more than information."

Thisbe, who did not appear to have heard Dean, was saying, "I got tired of waiting downstairs, Keiter had to go, and then–" But instead of finishing, she sank slowly into a chair by the kitchen door.

"It has the power," Dean announced. He pulled a black Sharpie from his pocket.

Cooper was looking at Dean and wondering if Thisbe understood the dramatic scene in front of her. But when he looked over he saw that she had put her head down on the table. "Thisbe?" She did not respond. "We need to call an ambulance!" said Cooper, alarmed.

"Hey! That's a permanent marker," Gormley cried.

"Don't do it!" shouted Scratch.

But Cooper was watching Thisbe. She sat with her head resting on one arm, her long hair streaming down her back. She seemed to be shivering. Then she went limp and sagged.

"Thisbe!" Cooper said.

She was at the far diagonal from Cooper, he near the kitchen door but toward the front of the house side, she near the archway to the great hall on the backyard side of the table. Cooper made his way to reach Thisbe on the other side, fumbling the while in his pockets for his cell phone to call an ambulance.

Dean and Scratch were both shouting, there was a scuffle, and then Gormley falling backwards over a chair, Scratch pushed back into his chair and Dean standing over the notebook, pen in hand. "There! And there!" he cried, scoring the notebook with great black lines. Gormley began to stir. Dean dropped another chair on him.

Thisbe did not move. She appeared to be asleep. "Thisbe," said Cooper, ignoring the fracas on the other side of the table. She opened her eyes a little, looked at him and said, "Cooper." She smiled at him, a quiet sleepy smile. Cooper touched her hand. Thisbe's eyes opened wide and she said, "You." Her entire body jerked with an involuntary spasm, like a dozing man who dreams that he is falling into water. Cooper felt an almost electric charge leaving Thisbe, flowing through him and dissipating into the air. Her head was down on the table, lying on one cheek, her face turned towards Cooper. Her eyes, which had shut again, slowly opened, staring at nothing. Cooper jumped back.

"Finished! It is finished!" Dean yelled in Scratch's face.

"You shouldn't have done that," Scratch said to Dean.

"The date! Change Thisbe's date. Change the year on it!" Cooper yelled at Dean.

Dean gave Cooper a look he could not interpret—confusion, interest?

"Find Thisbe's name. Change her date. Move it out fifty years! Change it!" He put his hand on Thisbe's shoulder. He pushed at her. She felt heavy and did not respond to his touch.

Scratch glared at Dean. Gormley lay on the floor amid fallen chairs. Dean kicked him, then tipped another chair on him. "It's over," he said, but no longer yelling. He seemed relieved.

Gormley's thin hand appeared on the table. He righted a chair and hauled himself up into it. "Ouch," he said. His nose was bleeding.

Cooper put his hand to Thisbe's mouth. No breath came from it. "Her date!" he cried in anguish. He felt Thisbe's wrist and throat. There was no pulse. Finally he put a hand to her chest, pushing aside the breasts he had hoped one day to caress in the act of love. The heart no longer beat.

Gormley was holding a grey sock to his bloody nose. "That hurt," he said to Dean.

At the other end of the table, a relaxed Dean was slowly flipping through the notebook. He was humming a tune.

Cooper dropped into a chair beside Thisbe. "A week," he said. "The book said she had a week." He looked at Scratch. "The book said a week." He looked at Gormley. "The book said a week." He touched Thisbe's long hair with a tentative hand, something he had never done while she was alive. It was smooth and fine, and a trace of static electricity held it briefly to his fingers when he let it drop. Gaining courage, he pushed a thick swath of it behind her ear. Already the skin was growing cold. Her staring eyes were frightening. His hand fluttered above them as he thought about closing them, but he could not bring himself to touch the long eyelashes, as delicate as the legs of a spider.

There was a banging at the door, followed by the sound of "You are my sunshine, my only sunshine." Cooper, sitting beside Thisbe's corpse, did not even look up.

"I'm ba-ack," sang the first Mrs. Rulen. "Did I miss anything?"

"I got a nosebleed," Gormley answered, still holding the sock to his nose.

Dean looked at the new arrival, at Cooper, at Scratch, at the mortal remains of departed Thisbe, at Gormley. Something on Gormley's upraised arm caught his attention. "Gormley," he said, "that's a nice watch you're wearing."

"Tss, tss, tss," laughed Scratch.

Chapter Thirty-One

Dying Changes a Person

Dying changes a person. The dead do not have the same interests as the living. Rarely, for example, do we see them at parties. They do not do math puzzles, nor do they have friends over to watch movies on Saturday night. They neither pay income taxes nor ask for raises. They do not worry about cancer, and the votes they so often cast in our municipal elections are considered not good for democracy. The question is, why are there so many of them? Why are more and more people dying every day? Where are they, after their brains have been replaced by clay and their faces by grass? What do they do there in those tombs and urns and coffins?

If Thisbe was doing anything under her plot of earth in the Mount Pleasant cemetery, she wasn't telling. The autopsy showed that her heart had stopped as a result of a myxedema coma, a symptom of the hypothyroidism that had been with her since her teenage cancer. No one had seen her since they closed the casket over her at the funeral parlor. The mourners left, the backhoe returned to its garage, the funeral director cashed another check. The next morning, the sun shone down on Thisbe's small granite headstone. It sparkled like the sequins on a Las Vegas showgirl. Four long-stemmed roses woven into a small wreath stood on a green stand in front of it. Cooper had bought the arrangement at the florist. No one visited her at the cemetery, and no one had heard from her since the day she was buried.

No one except Cooper. He was down in Scratch's basement sitting in the rocking chair beside the furnace, reading, as it happened, the fourth book of the Wacker Tally trilogy, *John Johns in the Dungeon of Don Juan,* when Thisbe, nine inches tall and wearing a green dress, appeared at the furnace grate.

Her appearance, with its rush of fire and inevitable sound of screaming, startled Cooper, but he looked up and saw that it was her, that she was small but perfectly formed, that she wore a becoming green dress. He smiled at her and said, "Hello. I've been waiting for you."

"Cooper!" she said. "Then I'm–"

"I'm afraid so."

They both tried to smile bravely at the same time, and each caught it on the other's face, and they laughed. Cooper watched Thisbe's eyes, again bright and wide and intelligent, instead of blank and staring as he had last seen them. And because a death is a fearful thing and because, against all possibility, they had come through it together, they both began to cry, Thisbe first, and when he saw the first great tear roll from her lovely lively eye, Cooper. And when they had eased their hearts with weeping for a short time, Cooper said, "How are you, Thisbe?" and Thisbe said that she was glad he was there at the end of all things.

They sat for a time, and Cooper asked Thisbe how they were treating her, and she said that there wasn't too much to say, but it was hot and uncomfortable, and Cooper told her that he liked her green dress, and she laughed and said that it was the bridesmaid dress she had worn for Abby's first wedding years ago, she had given it to the Salvation Army last year and now here it was, this is what happens to old bridesmaid dresses, and they laughed again.

"Do you remember the first time I met you?" Cooper asked.

"No," said Thisbe. "It was a long time ago."

Cooper saw she meant years before, when they had been at university. "No, not then," he said. "I mean the night of Scratch's party. When you asked me for directions, and we talked about church."

"Yes," she said.

"You said something about– something about a new plan, and you hadn't told anybody yet, something like that."

"Yes," said Thisbe, and Cooper could see that she remembered but he could not tell whether she wanted to talk about it or not.

He asked, "What was your plan?"

"It was– Cooper, I feel like such a fool. It was–"

He saw her hesitation and jumped in: "You don't have to say if you'd rather not." But he wanted her to confide in him.

"No. No, it's all right. I can tell you. I was deciding to get married."

"Married?"

"Just an ordinary life. Marriage. Children. That's what I was deciding."

Cooper looked around the basement. "That doesn't sound like such a strange secret plan."

"I know. But I had never even considered it before. I was always the artistic type, you know. Bohemian. It never occurred to me that I could just marry and have a child and settle down and have a simple life."

"It didn't?" For Cooper, despite his fantasies of easy cash through lawsuits and his intimacy with death in all its parts, had never not imagined settling down and having a simple life.

Thisbe was embarrassed. "It just never occurred to me."

"Oh. I see."

"And then it did, and it was like a revelation, and I thought that that's what I would do."

"Oh." For Cooper was thinking only that Thisbe's decision did not include him. Thisbe's death had left him in a black despair, and her appearance in the furnace had hit him like a physical relief. He had said to himself, I have not lost her, without asking what he meant. Now that she was talking about the possibility of a normal life without him, he felt, of all things, angry. He said, with cold politeness, "I'm sorry it didn't work out for you."

She did not notice his mood. "Yes," she said simply. "And I suppose it never will now."

"I suppose not." And in his relief that she was back, her acceptance that a normal life without him was not for her, and his sympathy for her, his anger left him as quickly as it had come, and he loved her again.

She said, "It all went so fast."

"I hear it does."

"What about you, Cooper? Do you have a plan?"

Cooper's plan had been to woo and wed Thisbe, to turn her away from the men who did not love her, to turn her towards the man who did. He had thought of her every day for months as the goal towards which he worked. He realized that he had even thought about her that way after her death, that he had expected her to appear in the furnace, and that, perhaps not right away, but soon, after many long intimate tête-à-têtes, he would declare his undying love for her and she would confess to the same feeling for him. It was only now, seeing her so small in her green dress inside the furnace, hearing her rich quiet smooth voice, and seeing her large green eyes, that he realized that it would never be. His voice caught a little, and he said, "No. No, no plan."

The office, hearing of Thisbe's death, was grim. Rumors and scuttlebutt flew about. Cooper visited with Vishwas and Sridhar to see how they were getting on. Each had somewhere acquired a staff of junior mathematicians and programmers. He found the two Indians unsettled. Sridhar, usually the more talkative, sat glowering and barely looked at Cooper. Vishwas, handsome, intense, and silent, waited until it became clear that Sridhar was not going to speak. Finally, Vishwas took the burden of communication upon himself. What he said surprised Cooper. He was proud and pleased. "We are close, getting close. Eighty percent done."

It had not occurred to Cooper that the Indians could possibly be "close," whatever that meant, and he did not know what to think of it. Was this a good thing or a bad thing? He was cautious. "The last five percent of any problem takes ninety-five percent of the effort," he said, "so I wouldn't get too excited about eighty percent."

Vishwas, who was smiling, lost his smile. Sridhar continued to glower. He seemed to be holding his breath.

That night, Cooper visited Thisbe again. They talked about what had happened on their last night, how sick she had been, and she said, "Cooper, your book was wrong. Why was the book wrong?"

"It wasn't wrong. Someone changed it." He explained that the date had been overwritten, that it had taken him too long to figure out that such a thing could be done, and they had not had time to change it to something else.

"But who? Who could have changed it?"

"You were there. You saw– no, you were too sick," said Cooper. "Everything happened at once. Dean found the date in the book and started writing. Scratch and Gormley fought for the book, but Dean won. He was changing your date with a marker, and then you– you–" Cooper hesitated. Was he remembering correctly? Something was not right.

"Why didn't you take better care of the notebook?" asked Thisbe in anguish.

This cut Cooper to the heart and he forgot all about Dean. He stuttered: "I– I didn't– You were– I–"

"And now I'm–" Thisbe did not want to say the word any more than Keiter did. "I'm here," she concluded simply. She turned her back to Cooper and walked to the far end of the furnace floor. There was a low fire burning, and the flames went out and reappeared as her feet stepped and then stepped away.

"Thisbe– I'm sorry– I didn't mean– I didn't–"

"Well, thank you Cooper. Thanks a lot," she said over her shoulder.

"I brought… I brought–" said Cooper.

"Goodbye." There was a flash, and the fire in the furnace died, and Cooper was alone in Scratch's basement.

Chapter Thirty-Two

Back to Work

Cooper was unable to sleep that night. He lay in his bed, torn between the desire to be with Thisbe and the necessity of forgetting her. As he rolled over onto his stomach and then back again, as he got up and wandered to the bathroom to get a drink, as he huddled down under the blankets and then kicked them off because they were too warm, he made up his mind first one way and then another, recognizing now the impossibility of the life he had planned with Thisbe and then the impossibility of finding another woman, at one time placing her image in the halls of nostalgia where good things that have passed learn to shine more brightly than they did on earth, at another time looking forward to the conversations they would have, him in Scratch's rocking chair and Thisbe in her furnace, her green dress graceful and her long dark hair like a wave on the sea. It had never occurred to him that he could manipulate the notebook. Never. He was supposed to be an imaginative and risk-taking actuary, but he had proven himself a dolt. His stupidity caused her death. He rolled over and stretched, he got up to urinate and climbed back into bed, he tangled himself in the blankets. The windows were brightening to grey and the first birds of morning were calling before sleep overtook him.

At work. Cooper had not spoken to Dean since the night of Thisbe's death. Gloria told him that Dean had come and gone in the morning before she arrived. He had not been in since and had left no word.

"I'll tell you, Cooper," she said, for she mistook Cooper's habitual deference as recognition of her superior qualities, "that there's nothing on his calendar, but I haven't even heard from him."

"What do you think it means?"

"He hasn't been well," Gloria said mysteriously, but Cooper said, "I know all about that. He's cured."

"How would you know that?" said Gloria, dubious.

Cooper was at first not sure how to answer this. Then he hit on it. "I saw him at church. It sounded like his disease was just crossed out."

"Isn't that something. Do you know what it was?"

Cooper thought. "No. No, I can't say that I do."

Gloria promised to tell Dean that Cooper wanted to speak to him.

Cooper went to his own office and logged into the equation. As he had for months, he went directly to the quadrate columns, but today he felt a crushing fatigue. Thisbe was no longer there. He thought that the math would, as it had his whole life, remove his mind from his troubles, but there was a problem: he no longer had the notebook. He no longer knew in which direction to fix his equations.

He stared at the rows and columns of numbers in front of him for a minute. What could he do? He remembered: he had copied several hundred death dates from the notebook into the Excel workbook where he worked up his quadrate equations. He found the spreadsheet. There would be enough work to keep him busy for a week or two. And—now that he thought about it—at one point he had photocopied several pages of the notebook, so there might be another few hundred names he could enter.

But soon the jig would be up. He would be forced to admit that it was all a fraud, that there was nothing in the equation that really predicted anything, that he was what the older actuaries called him, "just marketing." He would be fired, and Akkakumarbalapragada would take his house away. Perhaps instead of the equation, he considered, he should work on his résumé.

But the equation was open in front of him, and the fascination of the statistics drew him. The future and its unhappiness could wait. He navigated to the rows where he had left off and opened his spreadsheet, intending to wile away the morning with his equations. He was a methodical worker and easily found the bookmarked row: Herman Gottlieb at 57 Avonwick Gate. The date was October 15, 20__. He checked his spreadsheet: October 15, 20__. He looked at the next row, Phillip Desjardins, 87 Rue Guy, February 12, 20__. The date was the same as in his spreadsheet. He checked five more dates. They all matched.

The equation had a row lock function that Cooper had insisted be built in, so that as he corrected each row to the death date provided by Gormley's notebook, he could lock the answer in place and subsequent refinements and tinkering in the hundreds of modules would not affect it. This was something he had been careful about, had prided himself on the foresight that insisted that Vishwas build it. Now he was finding rows that were obviously his final work that had not been locked. This was not a thing he was likely to miss. Had the disruptions of Maconochie and Thisbe made him forget? After all, he had left his notebook behind in the underground mall, and it was only luck that Thisbe had thought to take it up. He must have forgotten to lock his records after he worked through them. Thisbe, after all, was enough to distract... But no, thinking of her was not helpful, and he pushed her from his mind's eye and turned instead to his work.

He found the first row where his spreadsheet did not match the equation and spent an hour on a new trick he had decided to use—changing a simple random number into a function that hung some equations off a strange attractor to drive the correct date. He had thought it might take him a day or two to work this magic, but it was easier than he thought, in part because the answer that the equation provided was only two days removed from the date Cooper had found in the notebook.

He continued to work through the rows. To his surprise, he found another date that was already correct and did not need to be changed. He locked it and went to the next row. This one was also correct. Had he missed some rows? It was a good thing he was going back. The next few rows had wrong dates, and he found the use of the strange attractor difficult. At one point Vishwas messaged him to ask him to exit—the programmers wanted to compile something and needed everyone off the system. Cooper was impatient with this return to the quotidian world of all that is the case, so cluttered and befogged compared to the luminous world of numbers. While there was always an element of difficulty in the passage between the eidetic world and the world of things, his anxiety and depression over Thisbe's death made it harder than before. He got coffee, returned and found a phone message from Maconochie: Would he call ahead and set up a time to see Maconochie at the station at his earliest possible convenience? He called and made the appointment with a secretary. He found himself angry and out of sorts. He returned to the lucid world of his work, creating more convincing fraud with more esoteric math.

A little after noon, Vishwas came by and asked if Cooper had spoken to Sridhar.

"No," said Cooper.

"Perhaps you should come."

So Cooper went with Vishwas to the place the Indians had their cubicles. Sridhar was putting everything in boxes.

"Sridhar, what is this?"

Sridhar did not answer.

"He is leaving," said Vishwas when Sridhar again would not speak.

"Why?"

Vishwas shrugged. Sridhar did not look up.

"Is it for family reasons?" said Cooper.

Sridhar looked at Cooper for the first time, then looked away. It seemed to Cooper that Sridhar felt a physical revulsion for him and felt, in his anger and depression, that Sridhar was right to hate him. Then he told himself that most things in this world were not about Cooper Smith Cooper and that Sridhar no doubt had problems that were larger than working at Seals.

Cooper suggested a few things—a leave of absence, family emergency. There were forms online that Sridhar could fill out. He should not leave like this, it might make things difficult for him later. Nothing worked. Vishwas did not know why Sridhar was leaving. Sridhar would not talk to Cooper. When he did speak, it was to Vishwas, and only in Marathi.

"What does he say?"

"He's leaving to go back to India."

"Why?"

Vishwas asked Sridhar.

Sridhar looked at Cooper and said something in his own language. Vishwas responded. The two began to argue, speaking rapidly and noisily, interrupting each other. The only word Cooper understood were references to himself, as if he were a dog who knew only his own name: "___ ____ ___ Cooper ___ ___ ___", " ___ ___ Cooper___", "___ Cooper ___ ___".

"What is it? What is it?" said Cooper, burning with curiosity.

"He says he's leaving," said Vishwas

"What was all that about me?"

Vishwas said, "It's better that you don't know."

Sridhar would not change his mind. Cooper gave Sridhar's laptop to Vishwas and called security. It would not do to have him destroy the equation because of something he wouldn't give them a chance to rectify. He asked Vishwas, "Do you know his passwords?"

"No."

"Has his latest work been synched to the server?"

"I don't know." He spoke to Sridhar. Cooper could not tell what passed between them, but Vishwas seemed satisfied. "It's all right," he said.

They waited in awkward silence until security came. As they walked Sridhar to the elevator for the last time, Sridhar barked, "You didn't predict Thisbe."

Cooper, surprised to be addressed at all, said, "No. No, we didn't predict Thiz—" Saying this made him unutterably sad, and he choked on her name. Even though he had seen her just last night, the emotion of loss suddenly caught him up.

As he stepped into the elevator, Sridhar glared at Cooper and declaimed, "There is still some mystery!" He said it as if it were a parting curse. As the doors slid closed on him, he began to cackle, a crazed malicious laughter. Then he was gone.

Cooper had no idea what Sridhar was talking about. "Nutty," he said to Vishwas.

Cooper had Vishwas upload the latest copy of the equation and then gave him the rest of the day off. He found himself back at his office. He composed a memo to Dean and Thisbe to explain what had happened. Then he realized that Thisbe would not receive the email and put Gormley in the CC field. He was confused. Why would Sridhar, who had done most of the work, leave? What did Vishwas mean, "It's better that you don't know"? Could Vishwas handle the work alone? Then he recalled that he would not likely continue working on the project now that Dean had his notebook.

He stopped by the police station on Dundas that evening on his way home. "This is just a routine examination, you understand," said Maconochie, who had leapt up when Cooper arrived as if this was anything but routine. "Ms. Thournier has died, and that always raises certain questions."

Cooper told Maconochie what he had seen. He and Thisbe had been together at work that day. She had seemed fine. That evening he had met her at a neighbor's house and discovered her upset. While he and others were in the dining room having a discussion, she had entered, looking very ill. He had suggested an ambulance, but before he could get his cell phone from his pocket, she had collapsed. She was pronounced dead on the scene.

It was both brutal and yet somehow comforting to relive the events of that night, even holding back much of the information about the notebook and Dean's dirty tricks. "There were others present. Are you interviewing them as well?" Cooper asked.

Maconochie admitted only that there might be others in whom the police were interested.

Cooper was annoyed at Maconochie for being so mysterious. To let the police officer know that he resented being called into the office for no reason, he said, "Am I under suspicion?"

"We will be in touch," was Maconochie's reply.

Cooper's unhappiness overflowed its banks, and he said, "You've been suspicious of me from day one. You took me away from Thisbe before for no reason at all. Now you call me in here for no reason again. I'm tired of this. You're wasting my time, Maconochie, and I'm not going to stand for it." The more he spoke, the more he felt he had to say, so that even though he was soon merely repeating himself, he felt as if he was going to get somewhere in his next sentence. He kept talking to find out where he would get and found only repetitions. He stopped in a muddle of angry redundancies.

Maconochie smiled without humor. "The next time I come for you, you will not be going home again."

Chapter Thirty-Three

Black Mass

The next night Cooper sat in the rocking chair between the cold furnace and the cinderblock walls, but Thisbe did not appear. The folding metal chairs were still spread about as they had been the night Thisbe died. Cooper rocked forward and kicked at one. It rasped along the concrete floor and was stopped by the huge dark furnace. He thought of Sridhar and wondered what could have made him so upset. It was just as well. Dean wouldn't need them anymore, and they would all be fired. Cooper yawned and stretched. The basement was damp and chilly, but he dozed. It hurt to think that Thisbe was angry with him. "I will never see her again," he said to himself, and the thought came so hard that, though in his sleep he did not move, he imagined that his arms flew to his head to cover himself against a blow. He sank back into an unrestful slumber.

He woke suddenly, almost falling forward out of his chair. The doorbell was ringing, and he had the sense that it had been ringing on and off for some time. There were voices and the sound of people moving about upstairs. The furnace was still cold and dark. He walked up the stairs in a sleep-befogged depression. The kitchen smelled of coffee and cookies, and Cooper—stupidly, he would later tell himself—walked into the great hall.

It was aglow with candles, and Cooper saw a dozen people he recognized from Scratch's party. They were standing in a circle around a stone table at the front of the great hall. He realized: Scratch was having one of his religious services. Cooper turned around, thinking to sneak out the back door, but Scratch caught his eye and gestured to him to come in.

He found a place behind the first Mrs. Rulen and Gormley, hoping to be inconspicuous. Scratch stepped forward, took him by the elbow, and, to his horror, brought him to a small ambo facing the little congregation. Candles stood on either side of the ambo, and on it a huge book, opened and ready for reading.

"I can't– I don't–" Cooper muttered, not because he was worried about what he would read but because he was embarrassed to be at the front of a religious service.

"Go ahead," said Scratch, smiling. "We have a guest. Mr. Cooper will read our second reading."

There were folding chairs set out around the table, and a couch with a floral print had been pushed up. Everyone except Cooper sat. Cooper looked at the page in front of him.

"A reading from the book of Deuteronomy," he said, just as the readers at his Catholic church did before launching in. "This fiftieth year you shall make sacred by proclaiming liberty in the land for all its inhabitants. It shall be a jubilee for you. Do not make him work as a slave. Rather, let him be like a hired servant or like your tenant, working with you until the jubilee year, when he, together with his children, shall be released from your service and return to his kindred and to the property of his ancestors. He shall nevertheless be released, together with his children, in the jubilee year…"

After his reading, Cooper found a folding chair, his ears bright with embarrassment. He looked up. Without noticing, he had sat between the first and second Mrs. Rulenses.

"That was very nice," said the first Mrs. Rulen in a raspy whisper. She had been annoyed with him on the night Thisbe died but had apparently forgiven him.

Scratch then announced a reading from the Apocalypse of Paul. Cooper was too stuffed with self-consciousness from his own reading to pay much attention, but, because it was something that Scratch would mention much later, he remembered that Scratch read, " 'Yet now on that day on which I rose from the dead, I grant, unto all in torment, refreshment for a day and a night forever…' "

After reading, everyone settled in and Scratch sat in a folding chair to the side of the stone table. He stood. "Well," he said. "Well." He looked at everyone. Cooper, used to this sort of thing from church, almost chucked in an "Amen" in response, but thought better of it. "Are you happy?" Scratch asked.

No one said anything.

"Really," said Scratch. "Are you happy?"

Still no response.

Cooper did not like the way this was going. If Scratch was going to ask questions in the middle of his sermon, it would be difficult to nap through it. A lifetime of Sundays listening to the homilies of Catholic priests had trained some atavistic sleep protection mechanism, the deep flight impulse of the animal mind. The sight of a preacher at an ambo attacked his wakefulness like an antibody bullying a bacterium it has pushed around since they were in grammar school together in 1985. It seemed like it should be against the rules for a homilist to ask questions. No wonder Scratch had such a small congregation.

"You can be happy, you know," Scratch said. "It's possible. But there are two things stopping you."

This was more like it. Positive teaching, the kind that could be napped through without danger. But then the second Mrs. Rulen jumped in and suggested, "Anxiety?"

The first Mrs. Rulen, not be outdone, stated, "Fear."

"Good," said Scratch. "Yes, that is the second thing. Anxiety," here the second Mrs. Rulen's face began to twist into a smile of triumph until Scratch added, "Or fear." The first Mrs. Rulen nodded angrily. "And that is the right thing that prevents our happiness, the human thing. Many of us, however, are not properly capable of fear…"

"I've never been scared of any–" the first Mrs. Rulen was whispering noisily to Gormley.

"…because we have not achieved a high enough level of awareness about our own lives, our own selves," continued Scratch.

The first Mrs. Rulen looked put out.

"And what is it that prevents us from being afraid?"

Cooper was really becoming annoyed. It was one thing to be trapped at a church he didn't belong to and another thing to be forced to pay attention. If this was what visiting Scratch was like, he would rather be at home with math puzzles and a beer.

"God?" asked the second Mrs. Rulen.

But she was so wrong that even mild Scratch looked slightly annoyed. "No," said Scratch. "Not Him." He said it with a special emphasis that may have been a capital letter, or may just have been his annoyance at the second Mrs. Rulen. In any case, the second Mrs. Rulen looked abashed, and the first beamed.

"The word I'm looking for is Addiction."

"Addition?" said Mrs. Mazur in a noisy stage whisper. She was the retired nurse and partially deaf.

"Addiction," said Cooper helpfully over his shoulder, for she sat behind him.

"Edition?"

"Addiction."

"Ammunition," commented Mrs. Mazur to her neighbor, and settled back, pleased.

"Addiction is our desire for things that do not help us. For things that we know are not good for us. It takes many forms— drugs and alcohol, yes, but also sex, television, politics, shopping, work, computers, cars, sports, the Internet, video games— all these things that we prefer to do rather than things that are life-giving, good, healthy. We have times, all of us, when we feel more fully alive, more human, better, and yet we do not seek these things out. Instead we return again and again to the old things, the same thoughts, the same habits, again and again–"

"What's wrong with working?" whispered a severe looking lady whom Cooper did not recognize.

Cooper, feeling that the danger had passed, allowed his eyes to close and his mind to wander. Bits and snatches filtered through sleep's restful sieve, watering the brain without disturbing the roots:

"–an older psychology, which, whatever its limitations as a way of explaining the world, captured, perhaps, with its demons and devils and temptings, something more fundamental in the experience of addiction than our modern inner psychologized–"

"–and this is the fear that truly hangs over us like the sword of–"

"–the only fear, but at least the right thing to be afraid of, the human thing–"

"–our lives, he said, were like a sparrow that flies into the hall from a storm outside–"

"–nor where it goes–"

The voices rang in Cooper's semisomnolent mind and changed their form and shape and their concerns. "–just been so unhappy with my vacuum cleaner–"

"–lazy lazy, I don't know what he–"

The animal mind harbors deep currents unknown to the waking rational mind. No doubt eighteen hundred years ago, when Cooper's chthon-worshipping ancestors were still bunging virgins into bogs as protection money for a good harvest, the fittest ensured their progeny by catnapping during the speeches and ritual sacrifices and awakened, fresh as daisies, just in time for the orgy. They coupled and brought forth children. Meanwhile, the ones who stayed awake for the whole ceremony were too tired to orgy it up properly so did not multiply. Just so did Cooper's inner alarm clock, with the feral dark cunning of a thousand generations of churchgoing, cause his eyes to open when the droning homily stopped.

"Amen," he said loudly, awake, alert, and confident.

But he was seated by himself on a chair in Scratch's dark hall. The ambo had been pushed back into a corner, the stone table was gone, and the rest of the congregation departed. Cooper's feral dark cunning was deficient, perhaps on his paternal grandfather's side, who, Cooper's grandmother said, would sleep through her funeral if she didn't come back to haunt him.

"Hm," said Cooper.

"Awake now?" came Scratch's voice from the kitchen.

"Just about." He stood and stretched.

"You missed most of the service," said Scratch.

Cooper made his way into the kitchen. Scratch was washing dishes at the sink. "I guess so," said Cooper. He sat at the kitchen table. "I must've needed sleep." He felt groggy.

"I know what you mean," said Scratch.

Cooper recognized in this a reversion to the conversation about how tired Scratch was and regretted sitting down. He tried to change the subject. "That was a very nice service. Very much like the mass I go to."

"Yes," said Scratch. "Sometimes I like to go orthodox just to mess with people." He said this with something almost resembling a spark, and Cooper thought it was good that Scratch was off the dreary topic of how much he disliked his job. But Scratch reverted to his old whining. "Frankly, Cooper, I'm ready to retire."

"Isn't that nice," said Cooper. He had been to retirement parties before. Actuaries who retired often went fishing, so he said, "Fishing?"

"But first I need someone to take my place."

"I see," said Cooper.

"There's a term for it, legacy plan, something like that—some business term, you must know it…"

"Oh, yes," said Cooper, nodding. He thought there might be a term for it as well.

"Well, it doesn't matter. The point is, I need someone to take over the business, mind the store, as it were."

"Mm hm."

"Someone I can trust, someone who would like the job, someone–"

Cooper had a thought. "Gormley?" he suggested brightly. There were cookies on a plate. Cooper helped himself.

Scratch frowned. "Yes, I thought of him." It did not appear to be a cheerful thought. "Someone responsible."

"Ah," said Cooper. He had no idea why Scratch would bore him with this, and though Scratch continued to list the attributes of a proper replacement ("Young. New ideas. Hard working. Plenty of brass…"), Cooper interrupted. "Did I miss anything exciting in the mass? I thought the black mass was supposed to be kind of exciting." He thought for a second. "Is that why I fell asleep? You were using marijuana or something, weren't you?" Cooper was pleased. "I was at a black mass," he said, in the way a child might say, "I went on the bumper cars."

"You mean the African-American mass, don't you?" said Scratch.

Cooper looked at him, not understanding.

"Tss tss tss," laughed Scratch.

"Oh," said Cooper. "Actually, that's not really funny."

"I know," said Scratch, abruptly stopping his laughter. "We used to do it up right. The whole bit: stealing the Eucharist consecrated by a Catholic priest, the ritual forni–"

But Cooper was interrupting. "It has to be Catholic, doesn't it? Protestant communion doesn't count, right? The Devil is

Catholic." This pleased Cooper, as if it were one of the proofs of the Catholic church.

"Well, if the Devil *were* Catholic, that would hardly be a recommendation, would it?" asked the non-sectarian Scratch.

Cooper saw what he meant. "But, still, it's the Catholic communion–"

"Yes, yes, that's true. You have to remember that I started the whole thing a long time ago, before there were Protestants. After that, it took on a life of its own."

"You mean you don't sponsor it any more?"

"Oh no. No, I gave it up years and years ago. Didn't like it. Then of course rock stars started doing it, and I was embarrassed I had ever invented the bally thing."

"When did you give it up?"

"Oh, I don't know. Time runs a little differently when you're me, which I realize you aren't. I gave it all up almost as soon as I started it. But you know what happens when you're on to a good thing; people won't let it die. They like a little ceremony, I suppose."

"But you lost interest."

"Yes. I attended a few, did my best—I had a large staff then— we marketed it, made it exciting, brought in the young people. A lot of preparation. Kidnap an infant, steal the host. It was rather impressive when it got rolling. Ritual fornication with a virgin, some of whom were attractive, I don't mind saying. We would kill the baby, of course, sprinkle the blood, desecrate the Eucharist. Very creative team in those days, a good spirit, lots of good ideas. There's no 'I' in team, you know. It was all 'we.' "

Babies? Blood? Was that a joke or some sort of weird devil thing? But all Cooper said was, "There's no 'we' in team either."

The conversation was beginning to lose its drive. "Yes, I suppose you're right," said Scratch, without interest.

"There is 'we' in weasel," said Cooper, trying to bring some life back to their talk. It was around this time that Cooper felt his outlook beginning to change. For the first time in some years, he realized that he would rather chat than do math puzzles or play video games. Scratch was growing on him.

Scratch said, "But now none of it interests me really. I want to stay home. I'm looking forward to spring so that I can grow begonias."

"It's warming up," said Cooper.

"Yes," said Scratch. "The job is just like everything else. There's not a lot to it. I did it one way, I did it another. No difference. Nothing mattered."

"But if that's true, why do you need a successor? You've already admitted that your job doesn't amount to anything."

Scratch sighed. "It's in the by-laws. There has to be someone in the office."

"But you don't do anything. You said yourself that the souls got dispositioned without you. They did it to themselves." Cooper often did not pay much attention to people when they spoke to him, but this fact had been surprising enough that he remembered it.

"That's true. That's why I've petitioned to give it up."

"Petitioned?"

"Yes. There's not really any process in place, as far as I can tell, so I wrote something up in triplicate and sent in two copies."

"So that you could leave the job."

"Yes."

"And did you get any answer?"

"Not exactly. They never know what to do with me. It's part of the problem. But I do have a theory."

"What does 'not exactly' mean?"

Scratch sighed. "It's too complicated to go into."

"Try."

Scratch began a few times before he really got going. But even when he got going, he didn't really get further than saying, "There are many hints that something like this may be possible."

"Something like what?" Cooper was thinking that the petitioning process might be a way to get to Thisbe. He was annoyed that he had listened to Scratch talk about so many things, but now that he was interested, Scratch was inarticulate.

"The idea is that, if I could find my replacement—"

"Dean?" said Cooper.

"Oh, you noticed that, did you?" said Scratch.

Cooper, who had not noticed, said, "Does he want the job?"

Scratch smiled. "He used to want the job. Been after it for years."

"Why don't you just give it to him?"

"Oh, it was all a muddle. He was so defensive around me, sneaking around behind my back, working with Gormley. They thought they were going to steal it, as if they could do it without my noticing. But it's too late. Dean doesn't want it anymore. I think he'll be sorry, frankly." Scratch smiled. "But enough about him. Cooper, I really want you to take the job."

Scratch looked like a man who has long wanted to say something and has said it. Cooper, who was nervous about his position at Seals, was not eager to explore Scratch's offer, but felt he could not afford to turn anything down, just in case. He said, "That's awfully decent of you, Mr. Scratch. Of course, I'm always open to options."

Scratch broke into a wide smile. "Really? How soon can you start?"

"Not right away. I have some things to finish up. I also have some legal matters…" Cooper gestured vaguely, as if the legal matters were a pile of papers somewhere off in the distance and it would take some time to sort through them all.

"Cooper, leave that to us. We can take care of all of that for you. Just say the word, and we'll clear everything up."

Cooper was not prepared for this. "Oh. Well. That's a very attractive offer. Mighty white of you. I still don't think I'm ready to pull the trigger if you know what I mean."

Scratch was leaning forward, concerned, empathetic. Another adjective came to Cooper's mind: hungry. But Scratch leaned back in his chair and said, "I understand, Cooper. You'll want to think it over. The job will be open a little while longer. Sleep on it and let me know tomorrow."

"Why did Dean want the job?" asked Cooper.

"There were some terms in his contract– oops!" said Scratch. "I forgot. Until you join, I'm not at liberty to discuss his contract with you."

"Dean's contract?" asked Cooper. "You mean for the insurance company, with Gormley?"

"No. Not that contract. That's not really a contract, actually. It's more a gentleman's agreement if that's not too strong a word."

" 'Agreement'?"

"No, 'gentleman.' "

"Then what contract are you talking about?"

Scratch sighed. "I always tell the truth, Cooper. You know that."

Cooper felt constrained to remark, "That's not what they say about you."

Scratch sighed again. "Yes, I know, I haven't been perfect in the past. But I've tried to change. I have changed. I–"

"Please don't think I'm saying what *I* think," Cooper interrupted. "I said, 'they say.' *I* don't say that about you."

"Thank you, Cooper," said Scratch. "Anyway, Dean's contract is with me. Since you're under consideration for the job, I think I can mention a few things. It's a personal service sort of contract. You've probably heard about them. I used to do them quite a lot, and they were written up."

"You mean like Wayne Gretzky's?" For when Cooper was a small boy, he had first heard of personal services contracts when the hockey player signed one with Peter Pocklington in Edmonton.

"Ah– actually, yes, very much like Wayne Gretzky's," said Scratch, and Cooper could see more was in that than Scratch was willing to discuss. "Dean signed one with me."

"He's your insurance agent then?" This was not interesting.

"No. No, I suppose I'm his agent. I can't get into the particulars—non-disclosure agreements, lawyers, you know—but, not to put too fine a point on it, our contract deeds his soul over to me at his death in return for my performing some few little services for him over the years."

"Oh." Cooper, who rarely read books that did not have the words "Star" with "Trek" or "Wars" in the title, had no context for this. "And?"

Scratch seemed disappointed that Cooper was not more impressed with this information, so Cooper tried to look more impressed. Gratified, Scratch continued. "Now that he's scratched his name out of the book—you remember, last Friday night, he took the book and–"

"Is that what he was doing?"

"That's what he was doing."

"He scratched his name out?"

"I saw him do it."

"I thought–"

"Yes?"

"–that he also– well, never mind, you were saying."

"He scratched his name out, so now he won't die."

"Ah."

"Don't you see?"

"Yes. Lucky him."

"Yes, but there's the matter of our contract."

"There is?"

"Cooper, I get his soul when he dies."

"Right."

"But he's scratched his name out of the book."

"Check."

"Well, that means he won't die."

"Yes."

"Which—stay with me here—means my contract with him is no good."

"It's still good." Cooper was not following Scratch's meaning. He pointed out that a contract was always a contract and you could always sue if someone didn't keep up their end. Goohan had taught him that much.

"Yes, all right, I suppose it's still good, but Dean was supposed to die at some point or other, and now he won't, and that means I don't get his soul."

Cooper finally got it. "Oooh," he said.

"Ooh indeed. Here I am giving all kinds of nice little perquisites to Dean. He's got to live up to his end of the bargain and die."

"I suppose," admitted Cooper. "But, devil's advocate and all, when you signed the deal, you knew that Dean wanted not to die."

"Well, of course. That's how I got him to sign it in the first place."

"But at the time, he fully intended to die. He entered into the contract in good faith. In a manner of speaking."

"He thought he wouldn't have a choice."

"Right."

"What's your point?"

"You might have a hard time in court with this one is all I'm trying to say," Cooper concluded.

He checked the basement for Thisbe again before he left, but the furnace remained cold and dark.

Chapter Thirty-Four

The Zombie Love Drug

He did not see Dean or Gormley at work the next day. Sridhar's cube was empty. He spoke to Vishwas, who believed Sridhar was gone for good. "Well, I guess we'll just carry on for now," said Cooper. It was a depressing prospect. He thought that perhaps he should call Scratch after all and accept his job offer.

Goohan called. There was news. Cooper should come before lunch. Cooper got to his office a little past noon.

Sitting in an outer office, reading old copies of *Sports Illustrated* and *The Remnant*, Cooper listened to Goohan from his inner office. "The bitch! There's no way in hell I'm paying her phone bill. It's all to that schnook she left me for, why would I pay?" or, "Terrible game, terrible. Worst call I've seen in years. The ref's a Jew from Montreal, what do you expect? No offense, Irving," or, "No, no, you call the student loan people and tell them I've cut you off completely. Completely. And to make it look good, I need to borrow your car for a week or two..." It comforted Cooper that his attorney's life was worse than his own.

He sat with the balls of his feet on the floor and his long thighs spread so far apart that the chairs on either side of him were inaccessible. He wore the clothes of a gangster in a rap video. His mother sat one chair away from him, proper and erect in a checkered coat and an old-fashioned lady's hat.

Goohan did not have a receptionist, and he came out from time to time to see who was in the waiting area.

"Cooper!" said Goohan.

"Sir?" said Cooper.

They went into Goohan's office. "Listen, there's good news and bad news. I guess you saw the patent was granted."

"Good."

"And as I predicted, it has generated considerable buzz."

"Good."

"It turns out that the drug in aid of male sexual potency does not in fact aid male sexual potency."

"Bad."

"Except in an indirect way."

"Better."

"Which is to say, it does not directly make the detumescent tumescent."

"Bad."

"But it may make the deceased to be—"

"Ceased?"

"Quickened, I suppose. To come alive again."

"The deceased?"

"Yes. They come back to life."

"If they take this drug."

"Yes."

"Do they take it before or after they die? Because if it's after, I see a flaw…"

"As a matter of fact," began Goohan, and he spent some time explaining the failure of the pharmacists to create a new sex drug for men, their backbiting and betrayals, their corrupt attorneys and the corrupt board, the false claims and the gross looting of funds. "But amid all the jiggery-pokery, there was a very interesting clinical result that was never followed up."

"Which was?"

"They accidentally injected a dead lab mouse with it."

"And the mouse became stimulated?"

"The mouse woke up."

"Stimulated or not?"

"Not."

"Oh," said Cooper, disappointed.

"Cooper, you're being dense. If the mouse is alive, he can go get some other product to put the judge back in his gavel."

"By prescription."

"Yes, of course by prescription. We can't have people eating that stuff like it was candy. Anyway, my point is that you're sitting on shares in a company that has the patent to the greatest drug ever created. The drug that cures the ultimate symptom."

"Death?"

"Death."

"Death."

"Death."

Goohan tried to explain. "You see Cooper, it turns out that death is as much a process as life. The wall between the two, once thought to be absolute (*ab*, meaning 'away from,' and solute, meaning 'soluble'), turns out to be soluble after all. Porous. When we die—"

"Wait. Wait," said Cooper. "We have to die? As in you and me?"

"Well, yes, eventually."

"You mean, for this drug to work?"

"Cooper, I meant by example. Let's use that woman you murdered as an example."

"Which woman?"

"Which woman? Why? How many women have you murdered? The one you called me about from the police station. The one with the log fell on her head and boom, she is no more. That woman. Which woman. Don't say that in front of a jury. Jesus." Goohan laughed, an ugly wheezing sound. "Anyway, as I was saying. For a woman like that, this doesn't work. The body has to be intact. Cardiac arrest. Cancer. Suffocation. The corpse has to be in good shape."

"And so?" Cooper felt the head lice of hope stir on his scalp.

Like many people who had never been in a lab, Goohan loved science. "Apoptosis is the process by which mitochondria kill off damaged cells. Keeps the body working by getting rid of the bad stuff. The problem with death is, all the cells get a little damaged. Apoptosis recognizes that everything is damaged, and the mitochondria leave home to join Al-Qaeda, strapping nail bombs to themselves and blowing up everything in there. It's why heart attack victims, for example, often stabilize in the hospital and then crash and die. Scientists have known this for years, but stopping the cellular death march has proven too much. It's a complex process, cell-membranes breaking down, oxidation, inflammation. They've had a little success with induced hypothermia, for instance, but they don't know why it works. The people who worked with you seem to have figured it out."

"So if we give this drug—"

"Yes…"

"To a dead person,"

"Yes…"

"That dead person is cured of death?"

"Yes."

"Permanently?"

"No. Just for that time."

"Well, isn't that a problem? I mean if you were killed because you had a heart failure, you'd wake up with a heart ready to fail."

"True."

"Or if you had cancer, you'd wake up with cancer."

"True."

"So the drug isn't that hot."

"I'd say it's pretty hot. Many deaths, as I understand it, are caused by poor timing or incorrect intervention. So for instance, a heart attack that need not be fatal is fatal because it was not treated in time. A hemorrhage results in bleeding to death because no plasma is available. This drug does a series of things—cools the body way down and somehow interferes with the destructive tendencies of the mitochondria, lets them know everything is— hey, do you work for an insurance company?"

"Yes."

"Well, I don't know. I don't know."

"What don't you know?"

"Whether it will be a good or a bad thing for you. If no one dies, you don't have to pay out. You just collect."

"A very good thing."

"But on the other hand, if I'm not going to die, would I buy insurance?"

"Ooh, I see."

"But on the other hand," (though Cooper noticed that Goohan gestured with the hand that previously had been the "no one dies" option) "if someone dies, is pronounced dead, you have to pay out anyway. Then he uses your drug to come back to life…"

"We'd have to pay twice, once when he dies the first time and again when he dies the second time. That would be terrible!" said Cooper.

"No, that would be terrific! Think of the lawsuits!" If people were cartoon characters and could have dollar signs for eyeballs, Goohan would have had dollar signs for eyeballs. "Think of it… Legally dead. Perhaps for hours. Then, back to life. Death certificate. You could take the death certificate down to the insurance office yourself. Ready to collect. Then: everyone would sue everybody. Hundreds of thousands of dollars." With increasing emphasis: "Millions. Billions! Thirty-three percent contingency fees! Well," and it was clear Goohan was pulling himself out of a

Love's Young Dream with regret. "Have you looked at your shares today?"

Cooper, forthright and true, said: "No."

"I thought not. Your step was missing a certain springy lightness."

"It was?" Cooper mentioned that he was not aware that his step was seasonal or wanting with regard to illumination.

"But it is. Because: guess how much your stock is worth today?"

Something in Goohan's voice made it sound like a good thing was coming next, so Cooper said, "More than $4.87? One hundred dollars?"

Goohan whistled.

"Cooper. Your shares are worth– let me check the web–" Goohan, chin up and looking under the bottoms of his reading glasses down at the keyboard, began to hunt and peck for some buttons: tap... tap tap tap... tap... tap tap. He let out a string of curses. Then tap tap tap, then a huge bang as his tapping pushed the keyboard into a stack of books that were on a corner of the desk and knocked them overboard, then more curses, then more tapping, then more curses.

Cooper grew impatient. Goohan's voice indicated that the shares were worth more than his first guess, so he guessed again, largely because he was growing bored. "Six thousand dollars."

Goohan, still tapping, cursed. He pushed the keyboard away. "Well, I looked it up this morning. Cooper, your shares are worth three million dollars plus."

"Plus what?"

Goohan was nonplussed. "Well, plus more."

"A lot more?"

"I don't know. It depends on the exact price."

"What is it?"

"I don't know. Let me try to find it again." Head tilted up. Eyes looking down. Tap tap. Tap tap tap.

Cooper's brain fizzed like a just-opened can of ginger ale. He didn't hear what Goohan said next. Then Goohan said again, "Do you want to sell the shares or keep them?"

"I don't know. Sell them. Keep them. I don't know. What would you do?"

"Cooper, I can't advise you in this. You own the shares outright and clear, I can tell you that."

"So I don't have to make a decision today."

That was true.

"The shares will still be there tomorrow."

That was true.

"I'll have to think about it."

That was reasonable.

"I guess the question is, do I want to cash out now or see where the company takes me?"

That was a good summary of the question. As Goohan had so wisely foreseen, Cooper's step did indeed exhibit a certain springy lightness as he left the lawyer's office. He saw Maconochie sitting slouched down in his unmarked sedan and waved cheerily to him. The policeman slouched down and looked the other way.

Cooper, feeling expansive, walked over to the car. "Hello, Maconochie," he called. But the policeman continued to look the other way. "Hey," he hollered. He knocked on the passenger-side window. Finally, Maconochie rolled it down. "Hey, Maconochie, what are you doing here?" Cooper asked. "My lawyer is in this building. Are you– ?" But he stopped talking in response to Maconochie, who was gesturing him to be quiet and looking wildly around. "Oh. Oh, I get it. You're on a stake-out!" said Cooper, looking up and down the street. "Criminal types around here, eh?"

Maconochie appeared to be choking. He was certainly turning red.

"Oh, I get it. Mum's the word. Right." He put a finger to his lips. Then Cooper remembered how unpleasant Maconochie had been the last time he had seen him. "Hey, everyone," he hollered up the street. The law office was in an undistinguished building near Queen Street, and a few passersby turned to look, though not as many as you might think. In the downtowns of great cities, indifference is cultivated more surely than asparagus. "Hey, this is constable Maconochie! He's a cop! Right here, in this brown car! Hey! Copper here! Unmarked ca-ar!"

Through Cooper's yelling, Maconochie had slouched lower and lower in his seat. Now, however, he leapt from the car and came around to Cooper, grabbing him by the jacket.

"Hey," said Cooper.

"Shut your mouth," said Maconochie.

"Watch it," said Cooper. "I hope I blew your cover. I hope whoever you're watching knows exactly who and where you are. You bully," he added as Maconochie let go of his jacket.

Maconochie was back around the car and into the driver's seat. The window on Cooper's side slid down, and Maconochie leaned over towards him. "Idiot," said the policeman.

"Maybe you shouldn't go around threatening people," said Cooper, leaning into the police car to avoid passing traffic.

"You are worth a lot to me, Cooper. I need you. Take good care of yourself."

"What does that mean?" Cooper asked, for Maconochie did not seem sincerely concerned about his welfare. But the window had slid up.

Cooper adjusted his jacket in a manner designed to convey disdain and walked towards the subway.

Chapter Thirty-Five

Another Death

At the office was a message from Gloria. Dean had returned. Did three o'clock work? At three, Cooper rode the elevator to the president's office.

Cooper walked straight up to Dean and stood across the desk from him. "You bastard," said Cooper. "You killed Thisbe." He felt, for the first time in years, the strength in his hands, in his shoulders, his neck, his thighs. He would take Dean and shake him. He would throw the blighter through the office wall.

Dean, who had been smiling, frowned. "No, I didn't," he said.

"She had a week. Then you had the book, you wrote in it, and she was dead."

"That's not true. I wrote in it for me, not for her."

"You didn't write for you. Thisbe died, not you."

"I didn't write anything about Thisbe. Just me."

The fight went out of Cooper. He remembered Scratch had told him this was what Dean had done. He began, "But then why did Thisbe–?" but gave it up. "So you won't die?"

"Cooper," said Dean, his voice choked with emotion, "I lived in fear all my life. And now I no longer do. I'm free. Cooper, I'm free."

"What about Thisbe?" said Cooper.

"Cooper, I don't know. I'm sorry if you liked her. I liked her myself. I should be the one beating on you. You never played it straight with me. Things might have gone a lot…" He was talking himself into anger, but he suddenly relaxed. He became, of all things, easy, even friendly. "But I don't care. I'm free now. You were part of it. In fact, I never would have been able to get to the notebook without you."

"Why didn't Scratch and Gormley just let you do it?" Cooper sat in one of the chairs across from Dean's desk.

"Their code. They never let anyone do such things. No one until you." Dean smiled at Cooper as if at a movie star.

"No one until me?"

"Right. They took a shine to you. But I knew Gormley had experimented before. You may have noticed, he's rather… corruptible, let's say. I had an inkling from him that something like it might be done. I also knew that Scratch wanted to retire, and I thought that maybe I could take his job when it was my time to go. But I think I'm more pleased with the way things worked out."

"What are you going to do now?"

The notebook was on Dean's desk, and he ran a finger lovingly over the spiral binding. "I'm making my own deals now. I've been in touch with some Americans. As you may or may not know, they claim jurisdiction over everything and everybody, including the Moon, outer space, the Queen, et cetera. They have secret places where they deal with extraterrestrial life and undersea creatures, spies from other countries and other planets. They are unconscionably gullible. Some Americans believe that the Jews run everything. Others say the Jesuits. Their major parties insist that all presidential candidates become thirty-third degree Masons. Anyway, I've been in touch with them for some time regarding your notebook. They would like to extend their reach to Heaven and Hell, claiming jurisdiction over the dead as well as the living."

"To do what?"

"Oh, same as the Americans always do. Meddle. Involve themselves pointlessly with sovereign governments. Control and manipulate people. Kill off national leaders that they don't like and replace them with tractable puppets, then kill off the puppets and replace them with national leaders. Keep the world safe for Hollywood movies, rap music, Mobil, Exxon, and Coca-Cola." Dean leaned back in his chair. "But enough about me. First, there is some bad news for you, I'm afraid. I've resigned here, and that has implications regarding your project." He looked at Cooper. "Perhaps that will be a relief for you. Without the notebook…"

Cooper jumped in. "Actually, we're close to not needing the notebook. Vishwas and I were looking at the equation just yesterday. It looks as though our program now agrees with the notebook about four out of five times."

"Really?" Dean was impressed.

"Yes. And if we could just keep the notebook as something to test against, I think we could complete–"

But Dean was shaking his head. "No, no no. That phase is all over. I've resigned and they're canceling the project. You're not an American citizen yourself, are you?"

"No," said Cooper.

"Ah. Well, it was just a thought. At any rate, the Equation of Almost Infinite Complexity project is canceled. You and Vishwas and Sridhar all the rest are done. You can–"

"Sridhar already left," interrupted Cooper.

"He has? Oh, yes, I think I saw an email. Why?"

"I don't know."

"Interesting. Well, I daresay he knows his own business. Anyway, Cooper, it's no longer my place to run things here, but I'll put in a recommendation that they keep you on if you like. I imagine you'd be best in the general actuary pool, you know that work, you can join the bunch that reports to– that used to report to Thisbe. Or, if you have your eye on something else, let me know, I don't think Gormley would ignore all my–"

"Gormley?"

"Yes. He's taking over for me."

Cooper suddenly regretted that he had joined the employee stock purchase program. "No. No, I don't think I could do that."

"But you'll need a job, *non*? Do you have something lined up?"

"As a matter of fact–"

"Oh, of course! I'm sorry, I was forgetting. Scratch said you're taking over for him. Congratulations on that. Have you had the tour down there? Gormley was able to get me in. What a screwed up place, I don't wish that job– what I mean is–"

Cooper listened with interest. This was indeed a new Dean: indecisive, even considerate of others' feelings. So this is what happened when driven people lost their drive. Cooper finally took up the conversation. "I don't know that I want to take Scratch's job."

This surprised Dean. "Ah. So you would like to stay here? Cooper, I don't know if–"

"No, I don't suppose I need to stay here. Some shares I owned. In a small company. I believe I've just become a rich man." Cooper was surprised that he could say this. Goohan had assured him it was finally true.

"Really? Well, that's terrific Cooper. I'll wish you all the best then." There was a buzz from the telephone on Dean's desk. "Yes, Gloria," he told the phone. "I'll be right out." He stood. Cooper stood with him. "The Americans are here. We're going to have a little demonstration. Would you like to stay and watch? Really, Cooper, I don't know how you kept this book– well, that's all done, I suppose it would be inappropriate." He shook Cooper's hand. "All the best then. Good bye."

Cooper said goodbye to Gloria. There were three men in dark suits and short haircuts, wearing little bluetooth ear pieces, another man Cooper thought he should know, and– "Gormley!"

"In the flesh," said Gormley. Instead of his usual office attire— bolo tie and plaid shirt—he was now dressed in an expensive but understated brown silky T shirt with a dashing brown sports coat and perfectly contrasting slacks.

"Gormley, you've got a new tailor."

"My new executive style. Look, Cooper, I'm sorry I won't be able to keep you on, but I'm branching out to bigger and better things, and…"

"You won't be able to keep me on?" asked Cooper, not knowing whether to be insulted or amused.

"Yes, no superstitious claptrap on my watch. From now on, we're running everything according to scientific principles."

"Dean will see you now," said Gloria, interrupting Gormley.

"Thanks, hon," said Gormley.

"Well, I guess I'll have to find something else to do. Best of luck to you, Gormley," said Cooper, shaking the limp greasy hand of Seals' newest executive.

Gormley and one of the dark-suit men filed past Cooper. A third man, bald and wearing an ill-fitting suit, followed them. "Hello, Cooper," he said. He was looking around nervously, as if for a way out. Though the room was not warm, he appeared to be sweating.

"Mr. Rulen!" said Cooper. "Fancy meeting you here. Are you a spook too, then?" He had always thought Mr. Rulen a bit of a bore, and here he was, involved with American spies.

The men in the dark suits glared at Cooper.

"Cooper," said Mr. Rulen, with some passion. In fact, he seemed to have tears in his eyes. "Cooper, they're going to–" But he was hoarse with emotion and could not get out another word.

"It's nice to see you too," said Cooper, confused that Mr. Rulen should be so emotional. Cooper had not thought that he had made such an impression on his neighbor. "We should have a barbecue some time," he said, feeling that if a man chokes up on meeting you in a public place, the least you can do is give him a hot dog and a beer. "Imagine you a spy!" he said.

"Cooper!" said Mr. Rulen again, with surprising vehemence.

"Oh, right. Must keep it mum. Hush-hush in your business," said Cooper. The thought that he was leaving Seals to cash in his millions made him cheerful.

Gormley said, "Can't keep Dean waiting," and the American agents helped Mr. Rulen—who was so emotional his legs were giving out—through the door into Dean's office.

"Goodbye, Mr. Rulen. Goodbye, Gormley. Goodbye, Gloria," called Cooper, walking down the hallway and slapping the elevator button for the last time.

Cooper was both surprised and gratified that Mr. Rulen had been so happy to see him. He had always thought that no one on the planet would mind if Mr. Rulen died. As sometimes happened, he was more right than he knew.

A few floors later, Cooper cleaned out his desk and downloaded his more interesting files to flash drives. He had some small regret that the greatest work he had done in his life, the Equation of Almost Infinite Complexity, had grown far beyond the point where he could take it with him. Perhaps he could buy some hard drives in the mall? But no. The data was in petabytes, and the equation formulae were a sprawling mass of programs that, uncompiled, would take a week to download. He should have asked Dean for a reference letter. Then he thought, No, that chapter of my life is over. He was a rich man now, and he no longer needed to worry about equations or résumés or references.

To make himself feel better, he went to an Internet finance page and typed in the symbol for his stock. News articles came up. Everyone was interested in the stock's meteoric rise, from governments to grandmas, it seemed. One news article said, "Too good to be true?" and another said, "Regulatory hurdles." Sour grapes for suckers, chortled Cooper. The stock was trading for more than $500 a share. Cooper punched some numbers into his calculator. His net worth, in securities at least, was $31,058,604.32. The feeling of airy lightness returned, and a smile curved his lips. "Yep," he said. He would not be needing the details behind any actuarial equation soon. He laughed, "Heh heh." He had turned out the lights and almost left the office when he remembered, and he had to wait three minutes while his computer booted up again. He cut the picture of Thisbe from his hard drive and pasted it on his memory stick.

Spring was giving every indication of springing. The snow had melted down to hard black piles along the boulevards of Victoria Park, Canada geese made long straggling Vs in the air as they returned for their annual orgy on Lake Simcoe, and the Sunshine girl in the newspaper on the subway floor had changed from her winter yoga pants to her summer Daisy Dukes. In universities across the True North Strong and Free, students ministered to themselves with potato chips and Ritalin as they realized that the George Eliot novels they had ignored all semester could not be read in the twenty-four hours prior to the exam. The first tulips appeared in their smart reds and yellows, seducing the bees with pollen and nectar and then frisking them for the sexual byproducts of their neighbors. Unloved, ugly and full of spite, solitary weeds popped out of every untended cranny, raising their contrary nettles to the air, planning their takeover of the planet, laughing their cruel laughter, urf, urf, urf, and cursing the gardeners who in their turn cursed the weeds. The manager of the Tim Horton's appeared and swept away the sand that had provided traction on the ice. Cooper left his bus and walked. He said to himself: The only thing I am lacking in my life is a certain special someone. That fact did not seem so bad now that he was a millionaire.

When he got home, he threw his coat on the table and laughed out loud. He was worth millions of dollars, and it had not occurred to him once to take a taxi home. It would have cost seventy dollars—maybe a hundred. He laughed again. He should have bought a car! There was a Corvette he had noticed in the newspaper. He decided that he needed to talk with someone. He would go to see Scratch.

There was one beer in the refrigerator, so he took it. Maybe Thisbe would be in the furnace today. The thought of talking to her suddenly made it urgent that he be next door. Ignoring the buzzing of his phone, he stepped outside.

"Hi, Maconochie!" he called to the brown sedan parked three doors down and waved. The silhouette in the driver's seat crouched a little lower.

There was a BMW in Scratch's driveway, and Cooper had a rush of hope that Thisbe had not died; she had driven to Scratch's. He was just around the back of the car when, immediately in front of him, the driver door opened. Though not a superstitious man, he thought for a second that this was Thisbe's ghost, back from the dead. He would put an arm around her again, as he had for those glorious minutes on the night of her death, he would kiss her mouth as she had surprised him with the kiss in her office—and then, in less than the time it takes to tell, it was not Thisbe and Thisbe's car, it was Gormley.

"Gormley! Where did you get this beautiful automobile?"

"Insurance money coming up," Gormley said, teeth relaxing indolently about his mouth.

"Insurance money?" asked Cooper.

But the first Mrs. Rulen was out of the car at the same time on the other side, her hair tousled with wind, and she was saying, "Chester's *such* a kidder." She gave Gormley a Look, as if he had said something he shouldn't. "He's so shy about his big pro*mot*ion. Insurance. Why would we have in*sur*ance?" she told Cooper.

Cooper said Hello to Scratch as the couple disappeared up the stairs, presumably to Gormley's bedroom. Cooper's own parents had not permitted him that kind of hanky and/or panky under their roof.

Chapter Thirty-Six

A Job Offer

"I have got to get out," said Scratch.

"Job got you down?"

"Do you know what they're doing? Cooper, I lost a mouse last month."

"You lost a mouse?" Cooper had not known that Scratch used a computer.

"A mouse. A little furry brown one. He died and was mine. Then– poof!– I look around, and he's gone."

"Gone?"

"Gone. It's not supposed to happen. I mean, what is the point?"

"I think I heard about that," said Cooper.

"You've really got to take over for me, Cooper. I'm losing it. Can you imagine? Dead, then not dead. What is the world coming to?"

"A lot of lawsuits over life insurance, I suppose," said Cooper, thinking of Goohan.

"Oh. Are they insuring rodents nowadays? Isn't that interesting. Anyway, Cooper, my point is, I have to get out. This has never happened to me before. The condition used to be permanent. There was one famous incident, which I'm sure you heard of, but that was a unique situation, and in any case it happened a long time ago. But this– I mean, it was bad enough Dean crossing out his name entirely, but this! A mouse just up and leaves. I can't control a mouse. Cooper, what am I going to do? They used to call me a prince. Now I'm like a– like a–" Words failed him.

"A viscount?" asked Cooper, not quite getting it. "An earl? Marquis?" He pronounced it "mark-wiss."

"Like the doorman. I just let 'em in and let 'em out. It's depressing. Cooper, you have to take over for me. You'll turn it all around."

But Cooper had had enough. He was not prone to giving advice, but felt that the time had come for him to unsheathe his wisdom. "Mr. Scratch," said Cooper. "I don't know if I want to take over for you. It sounds interesting, yet on the other hand you tell me it's not a good job. But whether the job is good or bad, it's your job, and you have to stick with it." This phrase seemed to be the right note, so he struck it again: "Stick with it. Don't give in to despondency and, pardon me for saying so, whining. You want to be strong. As a great warrior once said, 'The coward dies a thousand deaths; the brave man, only five-hundred.' " Here Cooper faltered, realizing that the great warrior he was thinking of was actually a comedian in a Broadway musical. He decided to go back to his winner: "Stick with it," he said. He sat back with the air of a man who has said something that needed to be said.

Scratch appeared to consider this. But then he came back with, "Cooper, I'm not just kidding around. You need to take this job. Is it that you think it's low class? Or you don't like the hoof?"

"It's not that I don't value diversity," Cooper said, stung by this worst of all accusations: the sin of intolerance. "I have the greatest respect for people of the hoof. We're a multicultural society." By which he meant precisely what other people mean when they say these things, *id est*:

1. I am nice.

2. I am personally acquainted with at least two non-whites, e.g. Sridhar and Vishwas.

3. I have no use for my own parents, who, through their own middle class bad taste, were white all their lives.

4. I do not participate in old-fashioned religious confession and expiation rituals and so must throw off the inevitable guilt that accompanies active omnivorous life through pious magic words, for example "diversity" and "multicultural."

But Scratch was a religious professional and knew phony piety when he heard it. "Cooper. You know you don't care about those things, laudable as they may be. What is your reason?"

"I do care," said Cooper, but he added, "I've just been laid off at Seals–"

For an instant, Cooper saw Scratch's wise guru look replaced by desire. He paused.

"You're in need of employment," Scratch began.

"–and I'd like to take some time off."

"You need a job. Remember before, taking time off didn't work out. Remember? You remember how Gormley was when he didn't have anything to do…"

"But he's a big executive now," said Cooper, made nervous by Scratch's enthusiasm. "I saw him today. He has a new tailor. He even has a girlfriend."

"Yes," sighed Scratch. "That's why it's time for me to retire. You should take the job, Cooper, I know they'd all love you."

This was a new angle. Cooper felt the stirrings of interest. "Who would?"

"Them. Everyone. All the people. I confess, and you've seen it: I've gotten stale. Don't have the oomph, the vigor, the lollapalooza. I'm just going through the motions. You'll be new, exciting, dynamic. You'll bring some fun back to the old ballgame."

"Who else would be there?"

"Who else wouldn't be there, more like. Eventually, everyone gets there. Everyone! You'd be their boss. You'd be Number

One. Keiter, Mr. Rulen (poor Mr. Rulen), the second Mrs. Rulen, Davillo, you name it. Your entire high school class will be there eventually. Your first teacher, the one with the short jumpers. The girls from the university."

"The Rulenses?" Cooper said, surprised. "I didn't even know they were sick." But a new thought pushed them out of his mind. "Thisbe?"

"Thisbe! You're right, Thisbe's there right now. Yes, I suppose she'd be there too. And you'll be in charge."

Cooper had the impression that Scratch might be playing with him and had tossed Thisbe's name out as some kind of lure, but he did not like to be suspicious. He did like to think about Thisbe. "Thisbe would be there, wouldn't she?" Cooper said, half to himself.

"She's there now! In the flesh," said Scratch. "That is, in a manner of speaking."

The thought of being reunited with Thisbe spread open in Cooper's mind like the beautiful princess's enchanted kingdom in a pop-up book.

Chapter Thirty-Seven

Journalism

At the newspaper, Abby's editor sat at his desk eating his fifth doughnut of the morning and shaking his head. All three of the other newspapers were running front page stories about this thirty million dollar man who had invented something they were calling "The Zombie Drug" in the *Sun* and "The Ultimate Viagra" in the *Globe & Mail.* "How come you didn't bring me the story?" he yelled at Abby.

Abby, stylish and cool, was not sure if she was going to cry or laugh and held her tongue. She sat at an open cubicle that could be seen from his office and kept her eyes glued on her computer. She had known the story was a good one. Sex, death, corporate fraud, lawsuits, murder, obscene amounts of money, sudden wealth for the undeserving. The editors of the other papers had all recognized it for what it was: pure gold. But Abby—whose stories had been used by the other papers as the basis for their own reporting—was relegated to the Business section, page one of the section yes, but below the fold.

"You have to be better than that," hollered her editor.

She was. At Thisbe's wake, she had convinced Julius that something had to be done about Cooper. "Don't you see? He didn't care about anything. He killed that Davillo, and he killed Thisbe. We need to fight this man. What kind of world is it if people like him are the winners?"

The next day, she visited Goohan and told him, in great and entirely fictitious detail, all about the re-opening of Davillo's file and the pains the ministry was taking to destroy Cooper. "And as you know, Al, when the government wants to take somebody down, they can."

At lunch with Julius the next day, she convinced him to go to the ministry's lawyers. "You need to get that file reopened. You see if Cooper's lawyer hasn't already phoned snooping around. You go ask your legal department if they don't know about this guy. I was in his office yesterday, and the repo man was after his car. Probably a payment for his bill, stolen from someone Cooper's gang murdered. Goohan, an Irish mobster."

Abby was also in touch with Maconochie. "You know Julius is next on his list. I don't care what you say about that branch. It was a little too lucky that a huge tree falls out of the sky on the very woman sitting on his file, on the night he predicted. And now Thisbe, who witnessed that murder, who is also the girlfriend of the government official who inherited the file, turns up dead. And this Cooper was there when she died. And here's something else. He was arrested in Banff just over a year ago." Abby had to suppress a tear when she talked about Thisbe. I'm doing this for her, she said to herself.

She called Seals and discovered that Dean had suddenly stepped down as president. His place, she discovered, had been taken by one of Cooper's henchmen. She did not know that Gormley was one of Cooper's henchmen, of course, but there seemed no other explanation for it. Although an executive of an ancient insurance company, he immediately made himself available for lunch, boasted about his brilliant ideas for the company, and seemed surprised that his shrimp cocktail was not an alcoholic beverage. Besides that, his mouth showed clear evidence of a life of violence. The teeth were terrifying.

"I have to ask," she said, pretending not to notice as Gormley rooted about between his lower lip and his gum for a bit of lettuce that had taken up residence there. "You used to have an employee named Cooper Smith Cooper. Are you aware that—"

She could see that she had hit a nerve. Gormley was immediately on his guard. "We had to let him go. It was all a budget issue. Nothing to do with me."

"But Cooper spoke very highly of you, as a mentor, I got the impression, someone he learned a lot from." Abby was annoyed with herself for this. She should have been more vague.

But like many executives she had interviewed, Gormley was easily flattered. "Yes, well. He got all that Equation of Almost Infinite Complexity from me."

"The equation?"

"The big equation he was working on."

"His predictions, you mean?" Abby had discussed this with Maconochie.

"He couldn't really execute on the idea."

"I heard he did very well," said Abby as sweetly as she could.

Gormley frowned despite her sweetness. "Yeah, but it was my idea. I had it all documented in a certain notebook. There were things Cooper couldn't understand in it, of course. That's one of the reasons Dean brought me on, to explain things to Cooper—and…"

"Where is Dean now?" Again the sweetness.

But again, the frown. "Dean? I don't know. He disappeared."

Abby had to wait a long time before Gormley took the waitress's hint and paid the check. She noticed that he left no tip. It made her wish the old Marxists from her university days were still vandalizing the city. She allowed Gormley to hold her arm while they strolled underground from the Royal York back to the TD Centre. She had no doubt that by now Cooper had killed Dean, with or without

Gormley's help. She thought on the whole it would have been with Gormley. He was obviously not the executive he claimed to be, and it was also clear that he had gained the most out of Dean's disappearance and then fired Cooper.

The only one she hadn't spoken to was Cooper. She had left voice mail after voice mail for him. His phone at Seals was still active, but the HR department confirmed Gormley's statement: he no longer worked there. Of course he didn't, owning stock in the zombie drug. "Sometimes it just takes a while for them to disconnect everything," the helpful HR lady explained. Cooper's cell and home voice mails were both full. She borrowed a car from a friend and drove out to the suburbs to find him.

Chapter Thirty-Eight

Maconochie

There is nothing like the job of a policeman for pursuing a vendetta. Maconochie had personal reasons for antipathy against That Cooper. That Cooper ate lunch with hot Thisbe, who thought and spoke so much about That Cooper that she barely noticed the dashing policeman. Now Thisbe was dead. That Cooper was a source of fascination to arguably hotter Abby, who, Maconochie was well aware, cultivated the dashing policeman only because she was fascinated with That Cooper. Maconochie was of the opinion that the majesty of the law should find something to condemn in That Cooper.

The state of law in any advanced society is such that everyone is guilty of something most of the time: a traffic violation; an error on a tax return; a careless remark that can be interpreted as harassment or hate speech. The American gangster Al Capone was incarcerated, not for his murders, but for defrauding the government of its rightful revenue—in case anyone was confused about where the priorities of government ever and always lie. It is an axiom ever ancient and ever new that if the government wants to get someone, it gets him. Young criminals, learning this in civics classes, have increasingly migrated towards government as toward a truer vocation; such are the benefits of education. Maconochie felt it was time that That Cooper rose to the top of the governmental agenda.

Maconochie's own criminality was of the mildest sort. It is true that he had been among the three officers reprimanded for shooting a stock trader outside a Queen Street bar on the night before the young man's wedding. But there were extenuating circumstances. The stock trader was black. He was young. He had an earring. He was with three friends. He was gesturing and talking, perhaps even shouting. He had a hand in a jacket pocket when the police told him to stop. The police had been told that drugs were being traded in the vicinity. Add those circumstances together, and a shooting seems inevitable. A judge quickly concluded that the young man was almost as much to blame as the police officers. As the dead man was unavailable to speak for himself, the majesty of the law saw fit to suspend the officers for a month and delay their promotions six weeks. One of the thirty-seven gunshot wounds that killed him had penetrated the cell phone that he had been reaching for inside his jacket pocket.

Maconochie had also been accused of selling goods confiscated at Toronto Harbour on eBay. As this accusation was pleaded down to driving without a seatbelt, and he promptly paid the forty dollar fine, it should not be held against him.

There were rumors of large amounts of public monies incorrectly accounted for, and more rumors of these funds finding their way into additions and improvements to the beautiful and spacious houses of unaccountably wealthy police officers. Maconochie's house near Dansville and Mount Pleasant was mentioned. The official report, however, noted that he was something of a handyman. A high school shop teacher was quoted, recalling Maconochie as a student of promise. This endorsement of his skill by an objective third party was seen as confirming evidence that a hard-working man of taste might well improve his home. Further evidence was uncovered: Maconochie subscribed to *House Beautiful* magazine. This was the subject of some good-humored ribbing at his expense but lent credence to his story that his opulent digs were the result of craftsmanship and not graft. Wealthy relatives were adduced who, it was pointed out, might have helped him with the finances. The report was accepted as satisfactory by all but a single journalist, an acknowledged pest. Besides, said journalist was unable to find anyone to comment on the case: apparently Maconochie's innocence could not be spoken against. Ill fortune follows the wicked, and the journalist suffered a series of misfortunes: tickets for traffic and vehicular violations and then a brutal beating suffered in an open parking lot near Dundas and Elizabeth. This last was seen as ironic justice, as the beating occurred within sight of the police headquarters—clear evidence that more police were needed and that denigrating their efforts was not conducive to the common weal. After a brief hospitalization, the journalist, searching for calmer and more innocent environs, moved to Las Vegas.

So it is surprising, but Maconochie was at this time under a cloud. A new regime had come to power on a good government platform, with a new commissioner and a new captain and a new ombudsman. Some of the old guard, as they called themselves, were pushed aside. Maconochie, who had been a sergeant with hopes of promotion to staff, was busted down to corporal. He was willing to take this setback with good grace until more interference was foisted upon him. He found his usual work practices, his common sense approach, suddenly attacked with obscure and bizarre mumbo-jumbo. "Due process," "illegal," "unethical," "just plain wrong" were just some of the murky gobbledygook they used to undermine simple expedients that had proven, time and again, the most efficient ways to do real police work: to turn citizens into suspects and suspects into criminals. Maconochie, the spokesman for a certain faction of the old guard, pointed out that his methods saved literally millions in tax dollars and created respect for and even outright fear of the police force throughout the city. His superiors pretended to be shocked. "This Machiavellianism has no place on the force."

"Always blame the Scotsman," Maconochie retorted. He seemed to have a vague recollection of a newspaper story in which this MacIanvellian character had been drummed out of the force, perhaps in Moncton. Uncharacteristically letting his guard down and saying more than was wise, he blurted, "You wouldn't've busted me if I were a Paki."

They sent Maconochie to sensitivity training, where he learned that it was hard to be a minority and hard to be poor and hard to be a woman and hard to be a homosexual and that these things did not cause anyone to become a criminal. Rather they were to be celebrated like chocolate cupcakes and Stanley Cup victories. The logic was so surprising that he began to suspect that minorities, poor people, women, and homosexuals had a hand in preparing the course material. He was wrong about that. The textbook had been written by a consumptive white man named Ernest F. Horlen, Ph.D. Maconochie dreamed of the day he would run into Ernest F. Horlen, Ph.D. at a traffic stop.

Still, the tailfeather had been plucked from Maconochie's goosestep. He had joined the police force out of true and noble desire to give parking tickets to people he didn't like, to impress women, and to shoot people, and now they were tying his hands with bureaucratic red tape. Like any good employee, he resolved to buckle down and do his best inside the new constraints while resorting to what worked when he could get away with it.

Then he had run into That Cooper. First, on the night the school teacher died: That Cooper had had a cut face and as much as admitted that Thisbe, the first Mrs. Rulen, and Keiter had been involved in some perverted *menage* that had led to Keiter's death. There had been no forensic evidence on the body, but Maconochie had had his suspicions.

Next, the break-in at the neighbor's house. It was obvious that That Cooper had climbed in through a window and then chickened out and run away before he could steal anything.

Then came the magical falling tree limb of doom. Maconochie suspected a small explosive planted on the branch, but whatever That Cooper had used left no trace in the freezing rain.

Fourth, there had been the death of the hot insurance lady. He had seen the autopsy: a sudden crash into a coma and death caused by a history of hypothyroidism. "The sort of symptoms," the coroner explained, "that people often miss: fatigue, feeling cold, dry skin, sleepiness. You take a young woman with a lot on the go, add bad weather and winter time, throw in some stress—*pfft!*" He blew a raspberry, which is the Latin scientific term for "then they die." Maconochie understood that this provided no evidence against That Cooper.

But Maconochie was also open-minded enough to know that guilt and innocence were not the most important thing. There was a bigger picture. Maconochie's career was in reverse. The media were fascinated by That Cooper, and, as everyone knows, the media must be satisfied. Maconochie was also open-minded enough to admit that he felt a good deal of resentment towards That Cooper, this accountant who ran about with beautiful women, had government officials killed with oak trees, and made his money in shady lawsuits.

In That Cooper, Maconochie had found great opportunity. He was the expert, the cop who had been on the beat from the very beginning. Now his case was burning up three newspapers. Because of Cooper, Maconochie had been loaned from Division to the more prestigious Special Ops Detective Services branch, Organized Crime unit. He had escaped away from a Division captain who hated him. Instead of Sergeant, as he still called himself, or Corporal, which was his actual rank, in Special Ops he had the acting rank of Lieutenant. With a little luck and a little blackmail, he might not have to go back to Division. He could already see there would also be more opportunities for skimming the small bonuses that supplemented a policeman's income in times of government austerity. A lieutenant in the new unit told him that they had impounded an entire truck of cocaine just last week. As Maconochie rightly reasoned, the bad guys would go to jail whether the truck had nine hundred kilos or eight-hundred and eighty-two. But that small difference meant an August visit to Banff versus an August visit to the movies for a hard-working public servant risking his life in service to an indifferent public.

Cooper's story was turning Maconochie into a celebrity. Reporters snuck around the official spokesman to ask Maconochie's opinion. Every morning he clipped the articles and pinned them to his cubicle. As he suspected, the higher-ups were keenly interested. His new captain had called him in for a briefing and listened as Maconochie explained his investigation.

The interest of the higher-ups went higher than Maconochie suspected. His entire force was threatened. The latest good government initiative was by that point in its six month and losing steam in the face of bureaucratic inertia. The usual critical editorials were appearing. One journalist devoted several columns to the fact that, despite a flurry of press conferences, trivial reorganizations, and made-for-media non-events (a backhoe filmed dropping a filing cabinet into a dumpster), nothing substantial changed. Maconochie disagreed with this, but the media's version was, as is so often the case, more persuasive than the facts. Another editorial pointed to the influence of organized crime on our nation's institutions. But what created much buzz in police circles was a single column in the *Globe & Mail*: it called for an end to the bumbleshuffle of local police forces and their takeover by the RCMP. Subsequent editorials picked up this theme as An Idea Whose Time Has Come. This threat to local police forces turned old enemies into allies as quickly as a sinking ship might. As Maconochie preened and primped and boasted of his special insight in the dark office of the Special Ops captain, he was suddenly cut off:

"Maconochie, you're only here because you know this Cooper and my guys don't. I need you now, but that doesn't mean I don't know you're a bad cop." The Special Ops captain wore a turban and a steel bracelet. He pointed at Maconochie with a long menacing finger.

Maconochie, fearing more sensitivity training, said nothing.

"The RCMP has their own team on this case. I need you to make this collar. If you don't, if the RCMP gets this Cooper before we do, the whole force will be nationalized. But before that happens, I'll make sure you go down so hard that your suppositories pop out your ears."

When Maconochie left the station that night, his trained eye picked up the RCMP plainclothesman tailing him in a blue sedan. As he drove, he picked up another tail, this one an old Volvo: a reporter. He checked the mirror carefully. The reporter was an old man. He wished Abby would tail him. As he arrived at Queen's Park, he took the large circle around the parliament buildings, turned east on Wellesley, came back north on St. Joseph, circled again and headed west on Harbord. He lost the Volvo in a traffic snarl by Victoria College, and a cyclist cut off the Mountie near Robart's library.

Though more determined than ever to catch Cooper, he had one problem. There was no evidence linking Cooper to any crime. As he drove north along Spadina, Maconochie began to whistle. There was plenty of evidence for everything. The trick was to attach it to the right person.

Chapter Thirty-Nine

Police and Perquisites

"The point is, you shouldn't listen to him," Thisbe was saying. "He's not to be trusted."

They were talking about Scratch, whom Cooper had grown fond of and whom Thisbe claimed was dangerous.

"Do you see much of him down there, then?" Cooper asked.

"No," Thisbe admitted.

"See, I've been talking to him a lot, and I think he's misunderstood. He used to be bad, but he's given all that up. I feel sorry for him."

"Cooper, he's the devil. Do you know what that means?"

"A lot of stereotyping," Cooper pooh-poohed. He rolled the dice and hit a lucky double four that enabled him to close his inner board and blot Thisbe. "Double you," he said.

She conceded the game. "How about another glass of ice water?"

It was over these games of backgammon that Cooper's love for Thisbe transformed from immature infatuation to something that would last the rest of his days. Since she had come to the furnace, he spent more and more of his time in Scratch's house. He did his best to be polite, but he could not hide his disappointment when Keiter showed up in the furnace instead of Thisbe.

It occurred to Cooper that their relationship might not be healthy. He should be getting to know living girls, girls of at least five feet, or even four eleven and three-quarters—but it was nine-inch Thisbe he loved. The fact that she lived in flames was something you got used to. Fire gave her an attractive glow. Cooper would come over, chat with Scratch, run downstairs to check the furnace, and, if it was alight, spend a delightful hour playing backgammon with Thisbe in her green dress. She was, she explained, in Hell.

That was the only thing Cooper didn't like about her. We rarely discuss religion out in the suburbs, and anyone who does—at a block party, say, or a church dinner—finds himself standing alone with his Molson Golden. The only other people Cooper knew who spoke about religion were the black-suited humorless Baptists who sometimes came to his door.

"Cooper, he wants something. Do you know what it is?" Thisbe asked as they set up the board for another game. "He's dangerous."

Cooper, sitting on Scratch's rocking chair in Scratch's basement, felt obliged to defend his host. "He's done nothing but good for me. Got me a job, introduced me to you. Now he's found another job for me…"

"Cooper, he's using you."

"For what?" A light went off in Cooper's mind: Thisbe blamed Scratch for what had happened to her. She didn't know him like Cooper did. He decided to change the subject. "Do you know why you're in there?"

"I don't know. I got some papers once explaining something about it, but the legal jargon was thick and there was no lawyer to interpret for me. I remember the phrase 'strict liability,' which someone told me meant a crime in which intentions were not considered but only the crime itself. Or maybe it meant that intent was assumed. Anyway, it meant that what I did, regardless of why, was bad enough to get me here."

"That sounds awfully legalistic."

"Yes, well, I thought so too, but there's not a lot you can do about it."

"Isn't there an appeal? You should make an appeal." Goohan often spoke about making appeals.

"I've been trying to find that out. People here aren't very helpful. Mostly, they want to torture you anyway, and if you ask for directions to one place, they..."

"They just tell you to get lost."

"No, no, it's worse. They give you long and detailed directions—but to somewhere else entirely."

"You mean they... they...?" Cooper was helpful by nature, and more than once had gone out of his way to make sure a stranger got a tricky turn. He had never imagined anything so diabolical.

"You have to watch it. Once they had me sign some complicated paper that actually meant I was signing up for less room and lower-quality food. But tricks like that are the least of things they do. I mean, it's better than being whipped, for instance."

"They...?" Cooper gulped and nodded. In high school he had seen a poster of a woman with a whip, an advertisement for a film called *Elsa, She Wolf of the SS*. It had haunted his more interesting dreams ever since. He shifted in his chair. "Goodness."

"Double you," Thisbe said. She had just made his five point with two of her blots.

"Damn," Cooper said.

Cooper found Thisbe's religious obsessions annoying. He told her she needed to change her attitude about where she lived. "Impossible," she said. He had been reading a book about guilt, lack of self-esteem, and the secret desire to be punished and wondered if he should bring a psychologist to talk to her. She suggested that Cooper read a book called *Sinners in the Hands of a Mad God*, but he could not find it at the library. It was around this time that he admitted to himself that Thisbe's desire to be punished was interesting to him in ways that other facts were not.

In many ways she made Cooper nervous. Unlike Keiter, she now openly talked about herself as if she were dead. She sat in fire all day, she was religious, she spoke about "sin," a word Cooper had only seen in dessert menus. When he asked what sins she could have committed, she described deeds no worse than what anyone might read in the newspaper any day of the week—less, even, since most of her sins would not make any newspaper. She had had some men at one time or another in her life, and then she spoke about despair and her violin, as if a little depression was something anyone could control. It seemed morbid.

Cooper took to bringing self-help books when he went to see her, books with titles like, *You Can Become Effective, Seven Ways to Heal Yourself,* or *The Thirteenth Step.* These were best-selling books, books that had helped millions of people and were talked about on television, books that were positive and uplifting and wise. The whole key was to adopt a new personality, a new attitude. "Put away the old habits and create new ones. Re-create yourself," Cooper quoted. "You've just got these tapes in your head that you need to change. Get some new tapes…"

But Thisbe was never impressed. "I don't think that's what I need to do at all. It's too late for me to change what I did. I already did it. It's not as if adopting a new attitude would fix anything."

Cooper had her trapped in his inner board behind a six point prime and was ready to start bringing in the outliers. He sighed. Bright as Thisbe was, she seemed unable to grasp the simple concept of useful ways of thinking versus self-limiting ways. She was literal-minded. Things were true or false for her in a black and white way that drove him crazy. He told her, "Your problem is you don't understand how the world is. Take sports. Every time Babe Ruth swings, he thinks he's going to hit the ball. He's wrong. He's going to strike out more often than he hits a homerun. But if he thinks about that, he'll never swing. Even to have a chance to hit a homerun, he has to think he's going to hit one on this swing. Of course he's wrong, but you can't get anywhere with your attitude."

"Babe Ruth is dead, isn't he?" was all she said.

Cooper was annoyed. "Yes, he is. Do you see him often?"

"Once in a while," she admitted.

That night Cooper saw a television show about UFOs and a government conspiracy to hide the knowledge of them. Some of the things they said made him wonder if Thisbe was part of the plot.

He came to the conclusion that she was obsessed with religion, long known to be a source of neurosis. There was no topic that did not lead to it with her. The next day he was telling her about an interesting conversation he had had with Scratch before he came downstairs to see her.

Thisbe did not like Scratch. "He's bad news. You think he's a nice guy, but that's just a cover." She set up the board for another game.

"You used to like him. Besides, I'm sure you're much too hard on him. It's just a job, after all. You can't judge people by what they do for a living."

"It's not a job with him. It's an eternal decision."

"I see," said Cooper, but when he thought about it, he realized he had no idea what Thisbe was talking about.

While his time with Thisbe was intoxicating, his life in the quotidian world was lurching like a drunken frat boy looking for a toilet to stick his head in. Cooper saw the newspaper articles. He took the *Financial Times* and not Abby's newspaper, but the outlook for his stock was clear enough. From a peak of over $500 per share, it had crashed to $85 and was dropping like a Spanish galleon after the Royal Navy used it for target practice. Meanwhile the government regulators, who had not paid a whit of attention to the company since it had been looted by its founders, were swirling about like baby boomers at an erectile dysfunction clinic. Cooper put in an order to sell half the stock at $100, at $90, at $80, which still would have garnered him over $6,000,000, but the broker was unable to execute his trade. The shares had been frozen. Goohan was filing papers to have them released and preparing a lawsuit for the money lost and damages caused by the freeze. But Cooper knew better than to count on lawsuits for his money.

He looked up his old résumés and created a new one based on the work he had done at Seals: "highly tailored actuarial charts with individualized end dates to facilitate prospect rating and customer renewal and viability." Not as pithy as "an equation of nearly infinite complexity", but more professional. He could not remember which font had won him his position at Seals, but decided that Garamond fit his new credentials nicely.

He tried to get in touch with Dean, but his old boss had disappeared completely. Goohan was busy with his motions. He thought that Maconochie, being a policeman, might have some insight. He put on his jacket and walked to the brown car that was now always a few doors from his house.

"Maconochie," he said, rapping on the passenger side window.

Maconochie gestured at him to go away.

"Hey, I have a question for you."

Maconochie gestured again, but as Cooper continued to stand on the boulevard beside the car, he pressed a button and the window rolled down.

"Are those doughnuts from Tim Horton's?" Cooper asked.

Maconochie swore at him. The window began to slide up.

"That wasn't my question! That wasn't my question!"

The window stopped.

"Cooper," said Maconochie, "Is there a blue car parked over behind the stop sign on Avonwick?"

There was.

Maconochie cursed again. "Listen, get lost, eh?" The window began to roll up.

"They know I've seen you," Cooper pointed out.

Which was true. The window stopped. "What?" asked Maconochie.

"It's a legal question," said Cooper. "Have you read the newspapers about this stock thing?"

"No," he lied. The newspaper, with Abby's article, was sitting on the seat beside him. He had underlined parts of the latest story about Cooper in red pen.

But Cooper, who had been raised to be polite and not let his eyes wander, did not notice. He said, "Oh. I just thought you might have."

"Well, I have not. And, for your reference, when a police officer is engaged in the execution of official business relating to the law and therefore the welfare of us all, it is a prosecutable offense to interfere with said officer."

"Eh?" Cooper did not quite follow. "I just thought you might know the answer to some legal troubles."

"Do I look like a lawyer? Get lost."

"Why are you sitting here if you don't want to talk to me?"

"Every time you come over here, the Mounties in the other car laugh at me."

Cooper, who could see the car parked on the next side street over, saw the vague shapes inside shaking with mirth. "I believe you're right," he said.

"So buzz off." The window rolled up.

Cooper knocked on the window one more time. It rolled down a little. "Why are you here then?"

Maconochie swore. "I'm watching for you to commit a crime so I can bring you in."

"Ah," said Cooper. "I thought that was it." He paused. "Well, good luck with that, I guess," he said and went next door to visit with Scratch.

He found renovations going on. The dining room, once done in an austere Scandinavian style, all brushed steel and blonde maple and halogen lamps, had changed. The hardwood floor had been replaced by a layer of brown linoleum, and the modernist furniture had been replaced by an old-fashioned dark brown table and high back chairs with tasteless scarlet and gold upholstery, mid-tier department store furniture with pretensions to the King Arthur's court portrayed in lower budget films circa 1954.

"Are you putting in a new floor?" Cooper asked Scratch.

"Yes. Or rather, that *is* the new floor."

"What was wrong with the old one?"

"Oh, it was a mistake. This was the look we were going for all along."

Since it was too late to help Scratch by telling the truth, Cooper lied: "It's nice."

"Yes, I like it. Gormley thought that if he was going to be a big executive we should have something a little better than we had."

"I can understand that," said Cooper.

"I hope you're coming over here to accept my offer. I don't know if I explained, but I need a decision soon."

"It's kind of you," said Cooper, "But I don't know when I'll know something. All of this lawsuit business that I thought I'd put behind me has started up again."

"Ah," said Scratch. "I guess I never understand all this scratching and clawing for things you don't have. Why not take the sure thing?"

Cooper felt that this was disingenuous and spoke in winged words. "But I thought you were the reason people were like that. That's what I heard. Besides, you want something you can't have too. You want to quit your job." He was not usually perspicacious in arguments that did not involve mathematics, and he sat back, justifiably proud of his speech.

Scratch sighed. "Cooper, you have me there. I admit it. I want a change. Things aren't bad for me. Far from it. But you have to remember, I've been doing the same job for thousands of years. Most people want a change after a week or two years. I don't even notice that."

"Then why the deadline for me?"

"Oh. I thought I told you. The day for me to do the switch is Easter Sunday. Coming right up. If I don't have someone by then, I might not have an opportunity for fifty years."

"Can I tell you in fifty years?"

"Will you live that long? Do you know?"

Cooper, realizing he had never found himself in the book, had to shake his head.

"Just as well. It's not good to know." Scratch had been fussing at the counter and now brought out the tea things. He continued, "Besides, I don't know that I'd stay here if I have to do another fifty year term. Maybe I'll travel."

"Where would you go?"

"Las Vegas. I don't usually go there."

"They call it Sin City."

"Yes, apparently they're able to accomplish quite a lot on their own. Many of the sins are automated, I understand. Coveting your neighbor's wife, for example, has been computerized."

"So you can cut back on the working hours."

"Yes, that's what I put in my reports. Of course, they still expect me to bust hump."

"Doesn't anyone complain that you aren't as active as you used to be?"

"I told you. I get results no matter what I do. I don't need to be active to get the same number of wins every year."

"So you don't really have to work much at all."

"Exactly. I work just to keep a hand in. I think they like that upstairs."

"I can imagine."

"And the pay—did we talk about that? The sky's the limit. You know how they say everyone could use a little more money?"

"I don't know who says that, but I suppose everyone would agree with it."

"Well with this job—"

"Yes?"

"You actually don't need more money. There's more than you can spend."

Cooper could not imagine this. "How can that be? How much do you get paid? Is it in American dollars, or Canadian, or what? Euros?"

"Gold."

"Gold?"

"Gold."

"Gold." This reminded Cooper of an earlier conversation, but he couldn't put his finger on it. "Oh, I get it. It's like the ironic punishments you hear about. You mean, I get gold, but gold isn't legal tender, so I can't spend it, so I get more than I can spend."

"Whoosh!" said Scratch. "You're good Cooper. Hardly anyone gets that."

"But you can sell the gold to a broker."

Scratch made a clucking noise, winked and pointed a finger at Cooper, like a jaunty mafioso pleased with his protégé. "Exactly. You'd be surprised how upset some people are when I pay in gold. I have to explain exactly the same thing. You see, Cooper, I knew you'd be good. You're all over this job, and you haven't even started yet."

"I haven't even accepted yet."

"Well, I wish you would. You know what? I'll give you the bank account numbers for the Isle of Man. You can check how much money is in there."

"Why not Swiss banks?"

"Cooper, Cooper! So behind the times? Swiss banks are out. It's all the Isle of Man now."

"And you're going to give me the account number?"

"And the name of the bank. They have a website. You can use it tonight."

At police headquarters, Maconochie was watching a movie on the captain's computer. It showed Cooper leaning on Maconochie's car and the window going up and down. Though grainy and a little out of focus, it did not reflect well on Maconochie's powers of subtlety and forensic detection. "The Mounties are laughing at us, Maconochie. Laughing at us. Is there any reason I shouldn't send you back to Division today?"

The scene had been filmed by the RCMP plainclothesmen who tailed Maconochie. It was emailed to the captain with the subject line "Nationalize today!" Maconochie was not sure what kind of answer would harbor him from the wrath. "I'm trying to build rapport..." he ventured.

The captain, already red in the face, appeared ready to explode. Maconochie left the office to the sound of roaring.

Chapter Forty

More Journalism

The only one Abby could not get in touch with was Cooper. She had left message after message for him. She had seen the reporting in the other papers, she knew she was on to something. Cooper had been a scoop. But to keep in front, she needed him. She wanted an interview with him before he went to prison. Why wouldn't he call her back? On two or three voice mails, she made clear she was a reporter, but when he hadn't answered those, she said she remembered Banff fondly, and on another mentioned that she was a friend of a lady he had worked with, Thisbe. Finally she left a message saying that it was important that he have the opportunity to tell his own story to the nation. None of the messages had gotten her a call back. She decided to visit him in person.

She chose four o'clock as a time likely to catch him at home. It was the afternoon of Good Friday, and many businesses—though not the newspaper—were closed. She came to Cooper's house in the late afternoon and knocked. No one answered, but she found the door unlocked. Maybe he was in the shower, or doing laundry in the basement, and didn't hear her. She went inside.

"Cooper! Cooper?" she called. There was no answer. She decided to wait and went to the kitchen. Waiting, she decided to look around. Looking around, she found Cooper's computer.

It was on the kitchen table, on, but with the screen black as if turned off. She touched a key. The screen came to life. There was no password protection—though Abby did not know it, Cooper, having left Seals, working exclusively from home, and no longer having Thisbe, Indian mathematicians, or an equation of almost infinite complexity to worry about, had just that morning decided to turn off the password on his machine. Abby found herself looking at some kind of word document: Cooper's résumé. She scanned it over quickly. Were people really using Courier again? But the résumé only confirmed Cooper's cover story: he was an actuary who worked on life insurance tables and had distinguished himself as leader of a large project, blah blah blah. She already knew that he was a convincing liar and had made it past Dean and Thisbe, both of whom had disappeared. She looked at his recently opened documents. There was a reference letter from Dean—obviously something he had blackmailed out of his old boss before doing him in. She opened a browser to email it to herself.

She was surprised to see that the browser opened to some kind of banking page that she had never seen before. She saw what she had done. Instead of opening a new browser, she had brought the focus to something Cooper had been looking at before he left. www.iombank.com—the Isle of Man bank. She hit the login button and found a dialogue asking for a customer number and password. There was a piece of paper with a number scrawled on it next to her, and she typed it in and pressed Enter. She was into Cooper's Isle of Man bank account. There was something important about the Isle of Man banks, she recalled, but what was it?

There was a list of choices along the side. Account information? Maybe. Deposit? No. Withdrawal? Interesting, but no. Preferences, Privacy Policy, Contact Us? No, no, no. Pay bills? No. And then she saw the one she wanted: Transaction register. She hit the link, and she hit the jackpot.

There were transactions going back months and months, for huge dollar amounts. She heard a rustling at the front door. There was a printer on a counter near the table. She hit the print button for the web page and listened in frustration as the inkjet printer whirred and buzzed as it primed itself without beginning to print. The door opened. She heard Cooper's voice. "Hello? Is someone here?"

"Come on. Come on," she whispered to the printer. She thought of closing the browser, but she was worried that if she did not let the printer start, she would lose everything. Finally, the printer grabbed a sheet of paper and began humming.

"Who's here? Dean? Is that you?"

Even in the midst of an almost hysterical impatience for the printer to begin, Abby was able to recognize the importance of Cooper's question. Dean! He's expecting Dean. So Dean is in it with him. Paid off and sent to the Isle of Man? No, that was just the bank account.

Paper was slowly feeding out the front of the printer. She called out, "It's me. Abby! I'm sorry, I let myself in." The page was printed. She hit the X in the upper right corner of the browser, then grabbed the paper and shoved it in her pocket just as Cooper walked into the kitchen.

"Abby! What are you doing here?"

"I'm… I'm… Didn't you get my phone messages?" she stuttered, trying to recover her composure.

Cooper admitted that he had so many messages he hadn't listened to them all. "It hasn't been a good time," he said, thinking of his frozen stock transaction.

"Well, I came to interview you. You're quite in the public eye these days. I'm surprised you don't lock your door. Do you realize you're still in the phonebook?"

Cooper was confused. "I suppose so."

"Cooper, have you checked your voicemail?"

"I suppose so."

"It's full."

"It is?"

As had Thisbe on the day she kissed him, Abby began to get some sense of Cooper the Naïve. Unlike Thisbe, Abby was not charmed. The extreme nervousness she had felt when she thought he might catch her looking at his banking records and his unexpected responses to her questions threw her off. She did not know if she should be the friendly celebrity interviewer, the tough crime reporter, the serious documentary psychologist. What angle did you take with someone so detached? "Cooper, a lot of people are interested in you. What's going on?" She tried to remember what her plan had been when she had come in the door, but could not.

"It's complicated," he said.

This was helpful. She was nervous still but controlling it. She found his coffee machine and a mug and poured herself a cup. "Want some?" she asked.

He nodded.

She decided to be sympathetic and see if he would confide. "I'll bet it's been tough."

"Yes." He began telling her about a job he was interested in, an actuarial position with a good firm. It wouldn't be as interesting as some of the work he had been doing, but on the other hand...

Abby felt that she had underestimated Cooper before. She had always thought of him as a dull sort of fellow, a man who was no more than he seemed: an accountant in a life insurance company. She now believed that he was involved in organized crime, that he was part of a conspiracy that involved murders and disappearances and securities fraud and hundreds of millions of dollars. And yet, as he rambled on about the job he hoped to get, he sounded just like any other thirtysomething schmoe, another underutilized tool in the great capitalist factory, easily melted down and replaced. If it hadn't been for Thisbe, she thought she might try to present Cooper from a Robin Hood angle, downtrodden white collar worker gets his own back from the corporate world of greed. It was probably a stupid angle. Cooper was getting money because some sex drug turned out to be a death drug and his mafia buddies were able to pull strings with a judge to get Cooper the shares. It was hard to make that sound like an allegory of good beating evil.

Abby's greatest fault as a reporter was the fact that she was easily distracted, that she spent too much time thinking and not enough watching. She scolded herself for this now as she realized that she had not heard a word Cooper said in the past three minutes. He was a man with dangerous connections, and she was alone with him. Who knew what he might be planning? She made an effort to focus on his words. He seemed to be talking about interviewing techniques.

"I don't like to share my secrets with someone I'm interviewing," she said.

Cooper said he could see that. Then he said, "Wait, what do you mean?" but at the same time Abby was saying, "Was that a résumé I saw in the printer?" and he said yes it was and that he was interviewing.

"But what about the new drug?"

"Oh, that." He didn't know much about it, only what he had heard, same as everybody. "I did some work there but just on demographics. I'm not a scientist. But when cash was low, they paid me in stock for a while, so I ended up with a pile of shares."

"Which are frozen."

"Yes."

"What do you think of the constructive trust?"

"Oh, yes. What is that?"

Abby did not quite know, but she explained what she had written in the newspaper: this was how the government was attempting to wrest Cooper's shares from him. "The idea is that some collection of people have an interest in the shares that trumps your interest, and they can take them away from you," said Abby, who had listened to the government lawyer with slightly more attention than Cooper listened to Goohan.

"Yes, I thought that I had the shares free and clear. At least, that's what I understood."

"You did own them. The point of a constructive trust is that the award may be invalidated. What do you think of that?" Abby was beginning to feel that instead of interviewing Cooper she was teaching him, and reminded herself again that everything he said was full of manipulations and dark double meaning.

"It doesn't seem fair," said Cooper. "Why did they change their minds?"

"Why do you think they changed their minds?"

"I don't know. Why?"

"Cooper, I don't know either. I thought it would be interesting if you had some thoughts you'd like to share with our readers."

"You mean you're going to write up what I tell you?"

Abby explained that was the basic idea.

But this was a misstep. "Oh in that case, I can't talk to you. Goohan was clear on that. He's often not clear on many things, but he did tell me that I might compromise the case if I spoke to journalists."

And despite Abby's protestations, Cooper was firm. Goohan had told him that he should not say anything to anyone. "I do have one question I'd like to ask before you go," said Cooper.

"Yes?" This was it, Abby thought. Either he would threaten her or he would tell her something, something significant that he wanted reported in the papers despite his lawyer's— no, likely with the collusion of his lawyer. She did not have her notebook or tape recorder ready and reminded herself to remember every word.

"What do you really think of sans serif fonts?"

So Abby left Cooper's house with little more than her printout from his bank website. Still, a story needs to be written, whether one is there or not. She tried a couple of angles but could not get anything going. She remembered that Cooper, before he had known who was there, had asked if she was Dean. Why was he expecting Dean? She was annoyed with herself for not asking him that question. She decided to dig into Cooper's bank account. Once she started to dig, she realized that a whole different angle could be taken on the story, and she called a delighted Maconochie.

Chapter Forty-One

Gardening

The business news was full of Cooper's story. Julius's cabinet minister, interviewed on the *Journal*, was clear: This was a case of greed and profiteering on the backs of ordinary people, and he and the government were simply doing the right thing in preventing this Russian-style kleptocracy that the business interests wanted. The show also featured the head of Canadian operations of a giant American pharmaceutical conglomerate, who, perhaps surprisingly, agreed with the minister. Goohan was there, and he argued against them both: No, it was a case of government regulators overreaching their authority and trying to pull back shares that had been legally granted to his client. Was this a country of laws or a country where only those businesses favored by the government could do business? There was also a spokesman from a consumer affairs watchdog, who said that all this chatter was very well, but what was really going on was that a small independent company had invented something important, and the government regulators were acting on behalf of the Fortune 500 to see that the price was kept low enough for a big multinational to scoop up the little guy.

The CBC moderator then began to ask about the crimes that seemed to follow this company around: first, the lack of financial controls that had resulted in the original consortium losing on their investment, and the prison time and fines that some of them had reaped; the lawsuits and countersuits that had put Cooper in possession of 60,000 shares of worthless company stock; the granting of a patent when everyone thought there was nothing worth pursuing; and finally, the deaths of at least two people, one of the minister's own staff and a young lady who worked with this Cooper. Was there not a history of deceit, greed, and outright criminality here, to say nothing of murder?

"And that is why my ministry is doing everything in its power to slow these transactions down until we get to the bottom of this," said the minister.

Goohan attacked this statement. "No one has even been charged with a crime, yet shareholders are losing the opportunity to profit from their foresight and hard work, and the people of this country—of the world—will die unnecessarily as this new drug is kept off the shelves by a frivolous lawsuit brought by an out-of-control ministry!"

There was no time to go back to the activist, so Cooper's lawyer had the last word.

Julius, slouched in his usual spot in front of the television, was pleased with his minister's performance. The old goat had blundered twice around things he had been particularly briefed not to mention, but that would only be a problem for his re-election—if he lived that long. It had nothing to do with Julius. The minister had done the most important thing: he had made himself the spokesman for the government case against Cooper. If, as Abby and Maconochie suspected, Cooper was somehow linked to organized crime, they could target the minister and not Julius. It had taken time, many phone calls, badgering, the cultivation of Abby Bruler and the television stations, but everything had come out right. Julius would not suffer Davillo's fate—no tree branch squashing his car. It was always a pleasure to see hard work pay off.

Despite the annoying fact that she had no life insurance, Thisbe's death was a triumph for Julius. If she had lived, he would have had nothing from it but the humiliating end to their relationship. Instead, he was receiving a goodly share of sympathy. A coworker had given him an excellent lasagna, and another a chicken pot pie. Abby Bruler–the hottest of Thisbe's friends—was calling him every day to ask about the ministry's secret doings, and he was gratified to see himself quoted (albeit as an "unnamed source") in four newspapers. He had already determined that Abby was available. It seemed likely that she would be available to him with small exertion.

The phone rang: Abby. Julius picked it up. "Julius? Listen, I've just been with Maconochie. I think I've found something important," Abby said.

"Don't talk," said Julius. "This phone may not be secure. Call my cell in five minutes."

What was even more interesting was the next phone call Julius got. At first he did not recognize the ringtone and went to dig his own cell phone from his jacket pocket in the closet. But it was Thisbe's phone ringing—Julius had plugged it in absentmindedly some days ago and forgotten about it. The number on the caller ID was from overseas. Julius pulled the phone from its cradle and clicked it on. A voice said, "Hello?" The sound was familiar, but Julius could not place it.

"Yes? This is Julius. Thisbe isn't here."

"Julius, this is Dean. There's something I'd like you to do."

Chapter Forty-Two

Julius Ascending

"Dean?" said Julius into the phone. "Well. This is turning into a more interesting day than I expected. I think you'll admit, it's actually rather unlikely that I would do anything for you. But say on. What would you have me do?"

Julius had the satisfaction of hearing a frustrated silence on the other end of the line. "Julius, I don't care what you do. I'm calling because I'm not in a position to do anything and you are. What you do with the information will be on your conscience, not mine."

Julius, though fascinated, could not resist saying, "It's interesting to hear you, of all people, use the word conscience."

"Yes, yes, I'm sure it's terribly riveting. Look, Julius, I'm calling because they're going to kill Cooper next."

This was news. "Cooper? You mean your math whiz? The one who stole Gormley's book? Who's going to kill him?"

"It's better that you don't know."

"I don't think so. I think it's better that I do know. Why don't you tell me?"

There was a sigh on the other end of the line. "Julius, I don't have time for games."

"What kind of warning am I giving Cooper if I can't tell him who's trying to get him? What can he do about it even if he knows? Are you trying to help him or just frighten him? What should he look out for?"

Dean seemed to consider this because when he began speaking again, he said, "I don't know. I don't know what he can do about it."

"Who wants to kill him?"

"The people who have Gormley's book now. They're experimenting, testing the limits of date modification. And they'd like to see Cooper disappear for other reasons."

"Which are?"

"Who cares? The first is obvious. He knows a lot, and they don't like that. The second reason is that new company of his, they're not interested in medical technologies like that being made public."

"Why not?"

It was interesting to Julius that Dean, who sounded as if he were in a hurry, continued to answer questions. But Dean had come to his limit. "Julius, they don't want to acquire Death's notebook just to have it rendered obsolete by modern medicine. I don't know if you can help Cooper or not. He was difficult, but I thought I might like to start out this new phase of my life by doing things differently. I don't suppose it makes much difference, but that's all I'm doing. The only number I have for Cooper rolls into a full voicemail. I thought I would tell you so that you might help him. Goodbye." And Dean was gone.

"I wonder," said Julius out loud, "what he thinks he's doing?" It was interesting that Dean phoned him. On the night Thisbe died, he understood that everyone had been arguing over the notebook so that no one noticed that Thisbe was dying until she actually keeled over. Julius snorted. What kind of people were these?

Julius's last beer bottle seemed to have gotten itself empty, and he returned to the kitchen to get another. He wondered if he should move to another apartment but decided against it. If he was going to date Abby, he had no doubt that she would find the bedroom that he had shared with Thisbe an extra stimulant. He would not have been able to say how he knew this, but he was sure that he was right.

Sexual fantasy about Abby and her competition with posthumous Thisbe kept his mind engaged and interfered with leisure to reflect further on Dean's phone call. Julius did, however, ask himself the important questions:

1. Was Dean right that someone was planning to kill Cooper?

2. Would warning Cooper about it do any good?

3. Assuming that the answers to 1 and 2 were Yes, was it worth getting mixed up with Cooper long enough to warn him?

As Abby had pointed out, people close to Cooper had a habit of dying. Now that he had set up his minister as spokesman for the government interest, Dean wanted Julius to involve himself again. In any case, it was unlikely that Dean was telling the truth.

Julius began to contemplate a new path of sexual fantasy. Death was a big turn on for some women, and Julius wondered how much use Cooper had made of his specialty in it. He was a New Age mobster: you'd think Cooper would be able to bed hundreds of university spiritual types, a kind of post-modern séance sort of thing, "Come over, and I'll show you the notebook where I have all the dates of everyone's death," "Am I in there?" "You bet; come and see." It wouldn't take much work at all to make the whole thing irresistible to the right kind of girl. As anyone who'd ever taken a date to a horror movie or an amusement park knew, fear and death were terrific aphrodisiacs.

He found himself rather stimulated when his cell phone went off and interrupted him. He was not in a good state to walk, and he hopped back to the television set to find the phone. "Hello?"

It was Abby phoning back. She had to tell him what she had found out about Cooper. Julius told her that he had found out something interesting about Cooper himself, something she would really want to know.

"What is it? About his bank accounts?"

Bank accounts? "No, nothing like that," said Julius. "Though I'd be interested to hear. No, I've found out something even more grave."

"What is it?"

"You'll have to come over here. There's too much to talk about. Can you come over tonight?"

She could.

Abby arrived looking stunning in tight jeans and a turtleneck sweater. She wore knee-high boots, something that was just then coming into style, for Abby always knew which way the styles were going to go. She smelled good too. Julius asked himself: Did she wear the perfume for me? and smiled.

She was full of her own news. She had discovered that Cooper had made a large withdrawal from an Isle of Man bank account. She had given the number to the police.

"Maconochie?"

"Maconochie. Anyway, what they came back with confirmed everything that we suspected."

"What did we suspect?" Julius asked.

Abby rolled her eyes. She was sitting on the couch in the living room, Julius on the easy chair beside her. "Organized crime," she said. Her lips were moist and her perfume filled Julius's nostrils. "The bank account is a clearing house. Millions of dollars have funneled through it. I don't know how they arrange things like this—I suppose it has to do with passwords–"

"And the fact that they kill you if you mess with anything?" suggested Julius.

"I guess that's it, isn't it? Anyway, there was a big transaction by Cooper—a six hundred thousand dollar withdrawal. There are other interesting people connected to this account."

"How can you tell?" Julius moved to the couch beside Abby.

"It took them a while to find it, but it turns out that this particular account has been under surveillance for some time. The Isle of Man is popular with drug dealers and money launderers because it has strict secrecy laws."

Julius began to run his hand along Abby's leg. "Better than Swiss banks."

"Much better. The Swiss banking thing is over ever since they gave up the accounts of Germans who made money off the Second World War to the Israelis twenty years ago or something, I don't remember when. Anyway, the Isle of Man bank won't tell you anything about anyone, but the RCMP and the FBI have been looking at this account, and– what are you doing?"

Julius in fact now had one hand moving high up inside her thigh and another crisscrossing her chest. His lips were against her throat. "What did the RCMP and the FBI find?" he asked.

"Well," Abby began, trying to collect her thoughts. "That's just it. There have been deposits and withdrawals from Paraguay, from Mexico, from Bolivia, from Amsterdam and Sicily, as well as other places. And at least one, from Colombia, they were able to trace back the IP address. I guess they mask them. I need to understand a little more about that to explain it all properly, but– Julius?"

"Yes?" He had just succeeded in getting the clasp out of the big leather belt she wore and was working on the button of her jeans. Her waist was wonderfully narrow.

"Do you know a lot about how the Internet works?"

"A little," he said, now concentrating on her zipper.

"Men always do," sighed Abby and gave herself over to Julius's attentions.

Chapter Forty-Three

Pearl Beyond Price

It had been a great day for Cooper. Thisbe, in her green dress, had been in the furnace when he went down to visit her. They had some disagreements—Cooper thought Scratch wise and deep, where Thisbe had become suspicious of him—but they had a nice afternoon together, chatting and playing backgammon, Cooper providing Thisbe ice water through a straw as he had once provided beer to Keiter. With Gormley at work and Keiter nowhere to be found, Cooper had Thisbe all to himself, and he was in love.

The basement had been made less comfortable because Scratch's modern Dutch dining room set had replaced the old metal folding chairs that had been there the night Thisbe died. The chairs—each a variation on a theme—were elegant, modern, stylish, and also ghastly uncomfortable to sit in for any amount of time. Nonetheless, Cooper could not help but think Scratch had taken a step down with the comfortable faux-King Arthur dining room he purchased from Walmart.

"I have a surprise for you," Cooper told Thisbe. "You remember you asked me if I had a plan? Well, I do."

Thisbe smiled and waited quietly for him to continue.

Her silence was like an invitation, Cooper thought, and he wondered how she did it. Instead of telling her his plan, he blurted out, "I would like to kiss you."

Thisbe did not laugh, but she did not encourage him either. She said, "Cooper, you can't kiss me. You would have to be dead."

"We would be together."

"It would cost you your life."

The fact that Thisbe was even entertaining the notion of being kissed worked on Cooper like wine. Inside, his heart shouted to his life, "If that's all it costs, let's buy it!"

Thisbe rolled the dice. "Ha," she said. Her blot escaped, and she took Cooper's five point.

"I've come to a decision," Cooper said.

"Something more than the Corvette?" For, using money he had taken from Scratch's account, Cooper had purchased a sportscar. It had been an impulse and a foolish one: the car was noisy, and Cooper was not accustomed to the standard transmission and kept stalling.

"Yes," said Cooper. "I've decided to take over for Scratch." He rolled the dice and pretended not to watch Thisbe.

"You what?"

"I'm taking Scratch's job."

"Cooper, what does that mean?"

"What do you think it means?" Cooper was annoyed. Thisbe did not seem to understand that he had done it so that they could be together.

"Cooper."

Cooper had never discussed Scratch's retirement plans with Thisbe. There had always been something else to talk about. And, he had to admit: she seemed so antipathetic toward Scratch, he did not like to spoil their time together by talking about his next-door neighbor. He began to explain. "He's getting on, Gormley has the big job at Seals, and Scratch is ready to retire. He's asked for his official release, and the main obstacle, he felt, was finding someone to replace him. So we talked, and he's made me a good offer, and

I was thinking about you, you and me, you, me, you know…"
This part of the conversation was getting away from Cooper. He
realized that, while fairly certain he had told Thisbe how he felt
about her, he had never quite heard specifically and in detail how
she felt about him. He was not quite sure how to proceed, but in
any case, Thisbe made it easy.

She fairly shouted, "Cooper!"

Of all the inconvenient times, it was just then that the furnace
flamed, Thisbe screamed, and Cooper was alone in the basement.
He could not tell if she had been delighted or upset. Excited, no
doubt, but excited good or excited bad? The difference might be
important.

He wished she would not scream when the fire came. She had
told him that she was getting more used to the flames, but they
still startled her. Cooper wanted to find Scratch and ask him if he
could cut the flames out, at least for Thisbe. That's what I would
do if I ran that place, he said to himself. This thought pulled him
up short. "I will run that place," he said aloud. His words echoed
in the basement.

He scooted up the staircase. He had the feeling that, if he took
over Scratch's job for a bit, it would not be easy to leave if he
found it uncongenial. This was one thing he wanted to get straight
with Scratch. Could he take the job for a trial period, a kind of
transition period or probation where, if it was working out, he
would go the next step and release Scratch, whereas if he decided
it really wasn't for him, he could shake hands and no harm done,
thanks for your efforts and best of luck in future endeavors, I shall
follow your career with interest.

But he could not find Scratch. The house above was as dark
and empty as the furnace in the basement. Cooper called, "Mr.
Scratch?" No answer. He tried "Nick?" but that went unanswered
as well. He considered whether or not to look upstairs in case

Scratch had gone to bed, but decided against it. He went to the front door to leave, opened it, then thought better of it. He closed the door and went back to the kitchen to leave Scratch a note thanking him for his hospitality.

Maconochie did not usually speak to reporters, and he had never spoken to a beautiful one, so it may not be surprising that he had told Abby Bruler more than was usual. On the other hand, she had provided a considerable amount of information to him as well. Though he discovered Cooper and his predictions through Thisbe on the night of the ice storm, the connection to Julius's government ministry would have eluded him without Abby. And now she had brought him evidence that he would never have thought to look for, evidence that, as far as he could tell, was one hundred percent court-worthy: the printed page of Cooper's Isle of Man bank account, acquired on a social visit to the accused's house, given to the police by a private citizen concerned about criminal activity.

Maconochie had languished for many years waiting for an opportunity like this. Ten years ago, he had been involved in another high profile case, and the entire thing had slipped away because of some technicality in the gathering of evidence—or, as the defense lawyer had put it, the illegal search and seizure of private property by an unlawful out-of-control police administration. The captain had lost his job for that, but the actual blunder had been made by Maconochie. There was a huge amount of cash, drugs, and weapons that they knew were on a houseboat, and when the warrants did not arrive, Maconochie had broken into the boat and gathered the evidence, all of which was duly barred from court proceedings. The defendants then violated the terms of their parole and escaped back to Trinidad. Not only were the police furious, but the Vietnamese gang that particularly wanted the Trinidadians imprisoned were outraged that their tips had been fumbled and began to work exclusively with the RCMP instead of the Metropolitan force. Maconochie, who had found the bust personally profitable if professionally inexpedient, was protected in the end, largely through the lubricious application of cash to various high and low squeaks in the system.

Now Maconochie was the lead on what had become the case that would make the Metropolitan force and push those snooty Mounties back to Nunavut where they belonged. He and Abby were going to make each other's careers with this.

He had the printout of the bank information in his hand, and he had the printouts of the confirming documents that he had been sent by the FBI, the CIA, the RCMP, Scotland Yard, and Interpol. Each of those more famous agencies were sending agents to see him tomorrow morning. He had all the warrants for search and arrest at Cooper's house. He had left a phone message on Abby's cell inviting her to bring a photographer.

It was the bank account that drew everything together. Organized crime wanted the zombie drug. They wanted control of the insurance industry. Cooper was bringing them both in. Somehow there had been a falling out at insurance, but it was clear enough why they wanted it: they would have their own conduit into the banking industry. The Swiss had given up secrecy for their own banks, the American War on Terror and TARP requirements were closing in on the Isle of Man and Caribbean banks. That left casinos and the innovation: insurance. Millions of tiny checks creating a huge pile of fungible undifferentiated cash going into the strongest investment portfolios on earth. Casinos took cash in, tidied it up a bit, and gave it back out. Insurance took cash in and threw a thousand mathematicians at it to make it work. A dollar in a casino was a dollar on a vacation cruise. But a dollar given to the insurance industry was a dollar strapped into the emperor's galley and whipped to row at ramming speed. Those insurance guys were operators.

It seemed obvious, given what Thisbe had told him and her subsequent death, that insurance provided another benefit. Casinos allowed you to bet on almost anything, but one thing was forbidden. This one thing was the cottage industry that organized crime specialized in: murder. In insurance, the entire point of the enterprise was to bet on death. Cooper—who, from what Abby had told him and his own observation, appeared to be nothing more than a mathematically inclined stooge—was the probe. He and his Equation of Almost Infinite Complexity were organized crime's foray into the legitimate insurance industry.

Maconochie gathered up his warrants and went to his car. He was about to make the collar of a lifetime.

Chapter Forty-Four

A Deal is Struck

The cricket's constant chirping drew Cooper's attention with more insistence than even the screams from the basement, and he drew breath and uttered, "He talks more than a damned politician!" But he was not angry. In fact, he was happy for the first time since the night Thisbe had held his hand. His future was no longer in doubt. He had signed all of the papers for his new job, the one about the healthcare, and the one about the insurance, and the one about what to do in case of fire, flood or accidental damage, the one about death and dismemberment, the car allowance, the overtime waiver, and the agreement that all taxes that must needs be withheld would be withheld. He had signed the one agreeing that he knew the risks involved, the one guaranteeing that if he was unable to continue in his chosen field he would repay a portion of the investment made in his training, on a sliding scale, $13,000 if in the first month, $12,000 if in the second, "So that, you see Cooper, it's very much expected that we want to keep you once you start." He signed the one agreeing to corporate travel, the one about the expense account, and the form stating that he had read the code of conduct and ethics and that he would abide by the strictures, guidelines, rules and spirit thereof. He signed so many papers and initialed so many clauses and wrote so many dates that the index finger of his right hand began to ooze blood. "It's like selling your soul," he complained. Scratch and Gormley looked at one another as if he had said something in bad taste, the way people look at each other when statistics unflattering to Jews or Negroes are mentioned at a party. Cooper grew embarrassed. "It's not really like it at all," he said, to be polite. Gormley left the room.

"Only one more to go," said Scratch, but they were interrupted by the doorbell's merry song. "Could you get that?" Scratch called to Gormley, but Gormley's holler came back from down the hallway:

"Get it yourself. I'm giving birth to the biggest log in the world!"

"Did you even *try* the Bran Flakes™?" Scratch yelled back in frustration. He turned to Cooper and said with unfazed politeness, "You'll have to excuse me. Gormley appears to be indisposed," and toddled off to the doorway.

Cooper was sucking on his bleeding finger and the cricket continued his song, which, instead of "cheep cheep cheep" or even "wirra wirra wirra" sounded like, "It's not too late. It's not too late."

There were voices at the door, Scratch talking to whomever his guests were, and Cooper considered slipping down to the basement to see if Thisbe were there. He stood up when he noticed that the cricket had crawled out from his usual hiding place behind the oven and was visible on the stove top: small, grey, with knobby knees and bulging black eyes. Cooper, feeling pleased, looked at the kitchen table for a crumb or a drop of something to feed the bug. There was a dish of scones across the table from Cooper's documents. He leaned forward to reach them, and as he did so, his bleeding finger touched down on the last document he was supposed to sign. It left a small red semi-circle in the signature block, like an upper case letter C. Cooper, retrieving a scone, turned back to the stove to give some to the chirping cricket.

It was not a cricket. It was a tiny, shriveled, impossibly old man, so shrunken and pale he might have been a large grey insect. "Too late, too late," he chirped.

Cooper's cell phone rang. It was Goohan. "Cooper, where are you? You have to get out of town. They're coming to arrest you."

Cooper's answer brought all his intelligence and years of schooling and life experience to bear: "Eh?" But he recovered and asked, "Why are they arresting me?"

"Cooper, haven't you read the papers?"

Cooper admitted to having perused the comics and the hockey news. The Maple Leafs had lost, and he did not approve of the Toronto Raptors, professional basketball being an upstart in the country that had invented it.

"Cooper, the newspaper stories about you. That woman who was killed by the branch had shares in your company. They think they've found a motive for you killing her."

Cooper pointed out that he did not kill her. The ancient cricket-man took a piece of scone from Cooper's hand.

"Yes, you're probably right about that," Goohan said. "For a certain type of judge, however, the fact that you are not guilty is not nearly so important as the fact that the media would like it if you were guilty."

"What type of judge?"

"The type that wants to keep his job. Judges fear only two things: reporters and policemen."

Cooper did not understand the legal system. He asked what he should do.

"Do? Aren't you in your car yet? Get the hell out of there is what you should do. Don't go to America. They'll send you right back. St. Pierre and Miquelon are still owned by the French. If you can get there, they'll never extradite you."

"Too late, too late," mumbled the cricket-man, munching a bit of scone.

What happened next was never entirely clear to Cooper. Abby was there, and Maconochie. Scratch was there. While Cooper said,

"Hello," Maconochie began to say something formal and severe, but he was interrupted by Abby, who cried, "Ooh, a bug!" in some alarm at the same time that Scratch was saying, "Tithonus," and Julius, there for what purpose and for God knew what reason, produced a large shoe and bashed the tiny old man on the stovetop into a flat little mess.

"Toilet paper! I need some God damned toilet paper!" Gormley was yelling down the hallway.

Maconochie held out handcuffs for Cooper, who at first thought the policeman was giving them to him to look at. He tried to take them in his hand while still looking at the poor crushed little bug-man, and only when Maconochie drew back did Cooper look at him and realize that he was being arrested.

Maconochie for a second time began to say the holy ritual words of arrest, and Cooper submitted his wrists to the cuffs, but he was again distracted because Abby—his friend Abby, Thisbe's friend, who had remembered their trip to Banff fondly and who had wanted to know all about him and whom he had given tea in his kitchen—was taking flash photographs of him in his disgrace. Cooper looked at her with incomprehension.

When Cooper was cuffed properly and the little kitchen was full of people, Scratch suddenly began laughing, his pleasant-old-man's or slightly-sinister as the mood took you "Tss tss tss" laugh, and everyone looked at him and Cooper realized that Scratch was holding the sheaf of papers that Cooper had signed, and Abby said, "What's so funny?" and Maconochie—who felt that no one properly appreciated the gravity of the situation—looked on with the resentment of a leading lady being upstaged during her big scene.

"Best of luck to you, Cooper," said Scratch.

"Can I see those papers?" Abby and Maconochie asked at the same time.

Then Cooper found that his own heart was full, and he spoke to Maconochie: "Why are you always arresting people? You won't have any friends at all if you keep this up." He felt that he had been as cooperative as possible with the police, he had always come to see them whenever they asked, and that Maconochie was really verging on rudeness by cuffing him, especially in front of an attractive woman like Abby Bruler, who, he realized with a blinding flash of stupidity, was photographing him because the idea of a man in handcuffs fascinated her sexually. For his libido had noticed her dashing high leather boots.

"No, these are my own private papers," said Scratch.

"They might be evidence," said Maconochie.

"They might be a story," said Abby.

"They might be toilet paper," Julius threw in, because no one was paying attention to him and Gormley was still howling from the bathroom.

At that moment, the furnace in the basement let loose one of its unearthly screeches, so that everyone stopped for an instant.

"I have to get downstairs," said Cooper, for he thought he had detected some timbre of Thisbe in the scream.

"You go where I say," said Maconochie. "What's downstairs? Just that bally furnace?"

"Let's go have a look," said Scratch, which Cooper noticed because Scratch, though he allowed people to go to the basement, had never before invited them.

They marched down the stairs in file, Cooper in front of Maconochie, Scratch behind, Abby and Julius behind them, accompanied by Gormley's voice, alternately cursing and pleading from the bathroom. Scratch was curiously ebullient and was mentioning the locations of the forests that had yielded the structural beams visible in the unfinished ceiling of the basement, the quarries that had yielded the materials for the cinder blocks of the walls and the concrete floor: "It was actually south of Lake Simcoe, if you can believe that, but of course these beams were machined in the late 1920s…" Cooper realized that he had never heard Scratch speak with such irrelevance, and it took him a minute to realize that the change had come about because Cooper had signed the documents.

By that time they were in front of the furnace, and Cooper immediately forgot about Scratch because of who was standing inside.

"Keiter!" Cooper had barely seen his ex-next-door neighbor since Thisbe died and had in fact forgotten that Keiter existed.

"In the flesh," said Keiter.

"Who is that?" said Maconochie.

"Jorge Keiter."

"And what is he doing in there?"

"I don't know. Keiter, what are you doing in there?"

"Just stopped by to visit."

"Come out of there," said Maconochie.

"I can't," said Keiter.

"Why not?"

"I can't open the grate."

"There's a lock," said Cooper, pointing helpfully with manacled hands.

"Who has the key?" Maconochie turned to Scratch.

"I don't actually have the key to that," Scratch said. "I've only lived here for a year."

"How did he get in there?"

But Scratch only shrugged.

"He's the Devil! Get me out of here!" shouted Keiter from the furnace.

"Mr… Mr. Keiter, was it?" asked Abby. "I'm from—" and she gave the name of her newspaper. She spoke in her calm public-television-interviewer voice, the voice of the sympathetic and intellectually interested. "What are you doing in there?" She had a vague recollection of Julius mentioning something like this. "Are you a holograph?" she asked, pleased to have the correct word, the word Julius had used.

It turned out that Abby had struck the right note. Like many school teachers, Keiter had always longed to be involved in documentaries on public television, although he had rather fancied himself the expert, speaking from a desk with an impressive bookshelf behind it, rather than the subject of the documentary, a victim of war, perversions, or the Devil. Still, he would take what he could get, for the interest of a journalist is precious. "I'm not a holograph," said Keiter in the rather large articulate voice he used when describing the ideas of Max Weber to the fourteen year-olds of the Victoria Park Collegiate Institute. "As a matter of fact, I am now a resident of Dis, Hades, or, in the vernacular, Hell."

"And how long have you felt that you are living in hell?" Abby followed up.

"Ever since– ever since–"

"Go on," said Abby. It was clear that Keiter was struggling with some emotion that was keeping back his words.

"Ever since he died," said Cooper. The handcuffs were making him cross.

"Cooper," hissed Keiter.

"Where's Thisbe?" Cooper asked. "What have you done with her?"

"What haven't I done with her," leered Keiter.

"And I brought you beer. And straws!" Cooper said.

"You didn't give me any help with her when I was up there," accused Keiter.

"What are you doing with her? Where is she?" Cooper asked. He attempted to gesture with his hands, but the handcuffs prevented him.

"What's going on?" asked Abby, breaking in, touching Cooper's arm to calm him and holding a hand out to quiet Keiter. "Why not start the story calmly, from the beginning?"

Keiter, who realized that his public television moment was in danger of dissolving into the worst sort of reality show, in which members of the crew are called on just a moment too late to stop the fisticuffs between the principals, addressed Abby. "There's an ugly rumor that I am here because I died several months ago, and that I will be here for quite a while. I categorically deny–"

"Her paper carried your obituary," Cooper, impatient and angry, interrupted.

"–any such old-fashioned metaphysical notion. As Mr Scratch and I were discussing on the night–"

"That you died," said Cooper.

"–the night I took ill, I believe that Hell is an outmoded cruel idea used to inflict psychological compulsions on a credulous mass by an elitist clerisy–"

("Is he making fun of the Mass?" said Maconochie to Julius, for Maconochie was a Catholic of the type that newspapers describe as conservative.

"No, 'credulous' means 'believing,' " said Julius.

"Ah," said Maconochie, mollified.)

The police officer considered. A tiny person inside a flaming furnace was not the sort of thing you saw every day. It seemed worth investigating, especially in the context of murder and screaming and torture and kidnapping and people dying. And, although he did not know the Baltimore catechism like his father did, Maconochie nonetheless knew enough to disapprove of devils using hellfire to heat their homes. At the least, there was a zoning violation.

On the other hand, he was not here to investigate tiny persons padlocked in flaming furnaces, especially chatty ones whom everyone knew and who didn't seem particularly upset. His captain told him not to "screw up the collar," with a clear implication that Maconochie had screwed up so many collars that no one had any idea why he should not screw up this one, but the captain felt it his duty to mention it anyway. If Maconochie brought Cooper in ahead of the RCMP, he would be the savior of the Metro force—in fact, the savior of local police forces across the country. He would be a hero. And he would tell his whole story to Abby, who was so beautiful and smart and built like holy cow.

So Maconochie had just decided to take Cooper to the station and come back to investigate Scratch and his crazy furnace later, when, with a shriek that made his eyes water, the furnace flared, and Thisbe appeared inside.

Chapter Forty-Five

A Contract Fulfilled

She wore a pretty green bridesmaid's dress and stood, lovely and composed as always, her long hair hanging richly past her shoulders, her green eyes wide and gleaming, all of nine inches tall and stuck behind the furnace grate with that other one, Keiter.

"Alive. They're alive." The fog that obscured Maconochie's slow understanding cleared. "An insurance scam." He looked at Julius, whom he had hated ever since he discovered that Julius was romantically entangled with both Thisbe and Abby. It was the sort resentment that drove a man to hand out parking tickets to all and sundry.

"Thisbe!" Cooper called.

"Thisbe!" called Julius, and both Maconochie and Abby looked at Julius with some surprise. For the smartass was moved by the sight of the woman with whom he had spent so many years in non-marital infidelity.

"Hello, Cooper," said Thisbe, and Maconochie's hand twitched involuntarily toward the pocket that usually held his big yellow ticket pad. "Hello, everyone. Julius! Oh, hello, Sergeant Maconochie," said Thisbe, looking about.

Her greeting filled soulful Maconochie with poetry: "Clean out of sight, don't you know that she is, some kind of wonderful, yes she is, yeah, she's," he hummed.

"Keiter. Keiter, what are you doing?" said Thisbe.

His arm was around Thisbe's neck. "Let me out of here," Keiter yelled at the group in the basement. "Or I'll hurt her." Despite his small size, he towered over the smaller woman, and appeared ready to hurt her. "Open that door!" he yelled.

"Keiter. Keiter, stop that," said Cooper. For Thisbe had lost her footing and Keiter was dragging her toward the grate.

"Keiter!" called Thisbe. She was swinging at him, but he caught her hand. "Ouch. That hurts. Keiter, what are you doing? Stop it. Stop! Ow!"

"Keiter!" shouted Cooper.

Thisbe managed to twist away and escape her captor's grasp. She shoved him and he staggered against the inside wall of the furnace. Thisbe ran, pelting along the flat furnace floor.

"This is pathetic," said Abby. "Keiter, leave her alone."

Julius was watching with intensity, as if hungry.

"You can't run," Keiter called after Thisbe, who stood panting against the far wall of the furnace. Indeed, the distance looked too near for safety.

"Where's the key?" Abby demanded of Scratch, then Julius, then Maconochie. "He could hurt her."

But Maconochie stood confused, unable to decide on a protocol for domestic disputes among tiny persons locked inside furnaces.

It was Cooper who acted. He always carried a pen, and, even with hands cuffed together, he was able to reach it in his hip pocket. He pushed a small ballpoint through the bars. Keiter was starting after Thisbe, but Cooper's pen fouled his legs and he fell. Cooper poked at him. A blue line appeared on Keiter's shirt.

"Hey!" Keiter complained.

Cooper poked him again with the pen.

"Ouch!" Keiter yelled.

Now Thisbe was at the barred grate. "Julius," she called, holding out her Barbie doll-sized hand.

"Hi, Thisbe," said Julius cheerfully.

"Thisbe," Cooper croaked, his voice choking with tears, his heart breaking. He held a manacled hand toward hers.

But before he could say anything else, Keiter, with a snarl and growl, was at her again, this time from behind, dragging her away from the grate. "Who's going to get me out of here?" he shouted.

"Keiter," said Cooper. "Leave her alone!"

"What are you going to do— ooh" Keiter called, suddenly cut off as Thisbe flailed against his head with an active fist.

"Stop it!" she commanded Keiter.

Cooper looked around for help. Abby was watching the violence with fascination, perhaps even enjoyment. Julius was fiddling with a cell phone. Scratch appeared lost in a funk and was mouthing the words, "It didn't work," and shaking his head as if the scene in the furnace was not happening. Maconochie was fumbling with something at his pocket.

"You're a policeman. Do something!" Cooper yelled at Maconochie.

"Stop," Maconochie called to the furnace. "Halt!"

Cooper turned away in disgust. He reached forward to jab Keiter with his pen.

"Cut it out," said Keiter.

"We can't get you out of there. We haven't got the key," Cooper said. He turned to Scratch. "You can stop this. Make it stop. You have the power!" But Scratch ignored him, lost in thought and shaking his head as if his best laid plans had failed unaccountably. Julius, instead of phoning for help, was using his phone to take pictures.

Back in the furnace, Keiter had Thisbe in an armlock. "You're hurting me," Thisbe said.

"Shut up and I'll get us out of here," Keiter hissed, but out loud he called, "I'll break her arm!"

Cooper leaned in to jab Keiter with this pen again.

It was at that moment that Maconochie's pistol went off behind him and Cooper felt something tear through his back. At first he did not associate the pain with a bullet, for he felt quite distinctly that he had felt the pain prior to hearing the sound, but he realized that this could not be true. He felt himself falling and flying through the air, tumbling and somersaulting down and down and down, and the pain was left behind him and became only a memory along the length of his back, and he fell and tumbled and spun until he landed with a loud clang, eleven inches tall and wearing, not the jeans and T shirt and windbreaker he had been wearing in Scratch's basement, but instead a cotton shirt with a button-down collar, twill pants and a brown sports jacket that he had worn to a wedding twelve years ago. His hands were free of the handcuffs.

He looked up. Maconochie's face, looming like a harvest moon above him, wore a look of despair and horror. Julius and Abby were watching with keen interest. Julius raised his camera phone to snap a picture of Cooper in his sports jacket. Cooper, in an atavistic reflex of childhood, put on a phony smile and waved. Scratch, behind Julius, pumped his fist in the air, jumped up and down, and shouted, "Boo-yeah! Boo-yeah! Now who's condemned to eternal perdition? Hoo! Hoo! Hoo! Hoo! It's my birthday! It's my birthday!" And he popped his thickened middle-aged Italian-or-Jewish pelvis like a choreographer of dance movies made between 1975 and 1983.

In front of Cooper, no longer doll-sized but large as life, Keiter held Thisbe in hands like claws. "Keiter," said Cooper. "Keiter, turn around." Then he was beside them, pulling Keiter by the shoulders, and, all pain gone from Maconochie's pistol shot, he felt the life in his thighs and in his back and in his arms, and he pulled, and Keiter was spun off Thisbe as easily as if he had been a child.

"Cooper!" said Keiter.

Cooper had only a second to register Thisbe's successful rescue when he felt Keiter's fist slam into his jaw, and he reeled away. Keiter did not press his advantage but instead looked about for Thisbe as she scrambled away. Cooper said, "Get out."

Keiter looked at Cooper, startled, perhaps, by the determination in his words. "That's what I'm trying to do, Cooper, but it's not exactly–" Keiter began, but he did not finish, for he suddenly rushed at Cooper, burying his shoulder in Cooper's chest and driving him backward so that Cooper crashed heavily into the metal wall of the furnace. Winded but not incapacitated, Cooper leaned against the wall for support, but Keiter followed up with a nasty kick that only missed Cooper's groin and instead hit him in the thigh. Cooper pushed off from the wall and tackled Keiter so that they both went sprawling on the floor of the furnace. Cooper was on top, but Keiter had fallen so that Cooper's arm was pinned beneath him, and, unhurt by the fall, Keiter delivered two or three sharp jabs to Cooper's head before Cooper could free his arm to roll away.

Then Thisbe was between them. "Stop this. Stop it!" she said. She was rumpled and her long hair wild and tangled, but she spoke with authority. The two men stopped and climbed to their feet on either side of her, panting.

"He was using you as a hostage," said Cooper.

Keiter walked away towards the grate. "Open up! Get me out!" he yelled to the giants in Scratch's basement.

"That rotten–" began Cooper, taking a step toward Keiter.

Thisbe stopped him. "It's over, Cooper. It doesn't matter. You'll always be sinned against. People sin against each other all the time. You can't count all that, all the bad things that are done. We have to let them go."

Cooper felt he was being scolded. He blinked and said, "I rescued you."

"Yes, thank you. I should have said that before. Thank you, Cooper. I'm happy you did." She smiled at him, her lovely luminous green-eyed smile, showing her neat small teeth, and Cooper had his reward.

"Bravely done, Cooper," said Scratch.

Cooper looked around, and, through the bars on the grate above him, saw his next-door neighbor looming like a giant and peering down at him.

Chapter Forty-Six

Unseasonable Weather

"Am I dead?" Cooper asked.

"Nyah ha!" laughed Keiter, who was standing some way off.

"Not so very dead," said Thisbe gently. Her eyes were shining with tears. Cooper asked himself whether those tears were for him and felt that, whatever he had done, it had been the right thing. But these tender ruminations were interrupted.

"Ha! See how you like it now, you vainglorious son of a bitch, with your condescending beer and straws," yelled Keiter.

"I thought you liked the beer," said Cooper, hurt.

"Go to hell," said Keiter, turning his back on Cooper and Thisbe and walking to the far end of the furnace. From the inside, it was surprisingly far—one hundred feet, Cooper would have guessed, four or six living rooms, though of course it couldn't really have been that big.

Thisbe touched his arm with her delicate hand. It smarted where it had been twisted beneath Keiter in the fight. "You're all right?"

"Yes," said Cooper, and he felt so well that it took him a moment to realize that, since he had just been shot, this might be surprising. "Well," he said. "Here we are."

"Yes," said Thisbe. It occurred to Cooper now that he might kiss her, but again, he was interrupted.

"Cooper. You are under arrest for money laundering and conspiracy, for insurance fraud and kidnapping, for interfering with an officer in the discharge of his duty. You do not want to add resisting arrest and attempting to escape. Come out of there right now."

Cooper began to see what had happened. "You shot me," he said to Maconochie. "I'm dead."

"Line of duty," said Maconochie. "Besides, it was accidental."

"I can't believe you shot me."

"I was trying to end a difficult hostage situation so that I could free the victims of a kidnapping and defeat a conspiracy to commit insurance fraud." Maconochie answered crisply and precisely. It was the sort of statement he had made from the witness box many times.

"Yes, but instead you shot me, you dolt. What do you mean going around and shooting people for?" Though the grammar was not quite right, Cooper felt the content strong.

"You jumped forward at the wrong moment and were hit. I fired my weapon in the legitimate pursuance of my duty and followed all pertinent regulations."

"It wasn't legitimate pursuance, it was depraved bleeding indifference. You shot me. You shouldn't just shoot people. What do you think, having a badge means you can just shoot perfectly innocent citizens any time you feel like removing a lock? I don't see how that follows at all. How about calling a locksmith? 'No, no, I'll just shoot everyone in sight.'" Cooper imitated Maconochie's rather precise way of speaking: "'The bullet will pass through the back of the man in front of me and disable the lock.' I am disappointed in you, Maconochie. Thoroughly. You should be ashamed."

Maconochie was superb. "Many witnesses saw that I was acting to free the victims of a kidnapping and prevent a hostage situation. What I did was perfectly correct. Line of duty. No more need be said. Except," he paused and smiled. "You are under arrest. Come with me, please."

"I most certainly will not come with you after the way you treated me. Why would I go anywhere with someone who shoots me? You might decide to hit me with a baseball bat next."

"You are under arrest. You have to come with me."

"I do not."

"Mr. Cooper, you have already been most regrettably and accidentally shot by a police officer acting in the line of his duty. Do not force me to use force a second time."

"Well, I won't go with you. I think you're dangerous."

"Is this what they call a Mexican standoff?" Abby asked. "Should I write this was a Mexican standoff?" She was filming everybody with her cell phone camera.

"No. No," said Keiter. He had come back from the far side of the furnace. "A Mexican standoff is when I have a gun on you, you have a gun on Scratch, Scratch has a gun on Maconochie, and Maconochie has a gun on Cooper. When everyone has a gun on everyone else and no one can shoot because someone else will shoot him the second he does."

Maconochie looked over his shoulder. "Mr. Scratch is not now in the possession of any firearm."

"Tss, tss, tss," said Scratch.

"He was explaining that this is *not* a Mexican standoff," said Abby reproachfully.

"Oh," said Maconochie, abashed.

"A Pyrrhic victory?" suggested Thisbe from the furnace.

"No, no," said Keiter, who liked to show off. "A Pyrrhic victory refers to Pyrrhus of Epirus, who defeated the Romans at Heraclea and Asculum. The Romans just kept showing up with more men, and Pyrrhus lost most of his army. After the battle, Pyrrhus said that one more victory like that would be the end of him."

"It would be the end of me," suggested Cooper.

"Cooper," said Thisbe gently, "I think it was the end of you."

"Loser," said Keiter.

"You're dead too," snapped Cooper, who was still cross with Keiter.

"But there's no corpse," said Abby. "Shouldn't there be a corpse?"

Cooper stood on tiptoe and tried to see the floor through the grate. Because of the shape of the door and his short Barbie doll size, there was a good bit of the floor that he could not see. Still, his body did not appear to be there. "When Keiter died, there was a corpse. The body was upstairs, and he was here in the furnace."

"You're so smug. You make me puke," said Keiter.

Everyone looked around. "We *habeas* no *corpus*," said Julius.

"*Non habeamus*," Keiter corrected pedantically. "And besides, that's not what it means."

Thisbe stretched her arms. Her dress was torn at the shoulder. "It's nice in here now that you're here," she said to Cooper.

Cooper had a leaping hope that Thisbe meant that wherever he was would be nice. He thought that this, now, was the moment to take her in his arms and kiss her. But before he could, she turned away.

"It's really nice in here," she repeated. As she walked, the green dress flounced around her legs.

Cooper remembered bitterly that Thisbe, like many women, was willing to talk about trivialities. "I don't think this is the time to chat about the weather," he said. "I may be dead."

"No, I mean really. It's usually burning in here. Fire, flames, red hot."

Keiter nodded as if he too had just noticed this remarkable fact. "That's true," he said. "What's going on?"

"This man is under arrest is 'what's going on,' " said Maconochie. "Anyone aiding and/or abetting his escape will be in serious trouble."

"Oh come on," said Abby. "We never helped him."

It began to dawn on Cooper that Abby might not be the friend he had assumed.

Maconochie spoke: "Witness, citizens, for future reference, that this man, Cooper, has refused to come with a duly-appointed officer of the law in a jurisdiction in which he has authority. Now," he raised his pistol, "Everyone stand back." Seeing the raised weapon, everyone did indeed step back. Again Maconochie pulled the trigger. His pistol spit fire, there was a huge sound like a cannon that fairly made the eardrums ring, the lock on the grate spun wildly and the high-pitched sound of the ricochet followed. Everyone ducked.

"Jesus!" yelled Julius. "Don't do that. You'll kill someone else."

"That would not be my fault," said Maconochie, "But the fault of those as did not follow pertinent instructions." He peered at the grate. The lock did not appear to be damaged. He grabbed it and pulled. It was firm. He said, "No dent. And cold. As if I missed."

"Maybe you did miss," suggested Abby.

"Drinking, most likely. Makes the hand shake," Julius said.

"You saw. The lock moved," said annoyed Maconochie.

"Well don't let's try that again," said Julius.

"I need a crowbar," said Maconochie. "Or a long screwdriver."

"If a bullet won't break the lock, I hardly think a screwdriver will do," said Keiter with contempt.

"It's getting foggy," said Thisbe. This was true. Inside the furnace, a grey mist had begun to rise.

"I'm cold," said Keiter.

"Um, the cold would be the reason for the fog," said Cooper unkindly, annoyed with Keiter's mental hebetude. Truth be told, the events of the past hour had shaken Cooper and made him irritable.

"I'm just saying," sulked Keiter.

"Scratch," called Cooper, "What's going on? Am I dead or what?"

In the instant before he had spoken, Cooper had made the positive decision to take Thisbe's hand and kiss her. But as he turned towards Thisbe to put this bold plan into action, his eyes fell on Scratch. It was then Cooper realized that the devil, alone of the party, had not flinched when Maconochie fired his gun. As he watched, an irregular red blotch began to spread on Scratch's bright yellow shirt.

"You're bleeding," said Cooper.

Suddenly, a commanding voice rang out from the top of the stairs. "Everyone stand still. Maconochie, put that weapon down!" The sound of heavy footsteps on the staircase could be heard, but Cooper could not see in that direction.

"Not the Mounties!" groaned Maconochie. "This is Metropolitan jurisdiction," he yelled back. "Where are your teaming agreements?"

The voices on the stairs called back something in reply, but Cooper was not listening. He was watching Scratch, who, alone of the party, was grinning from ear to ear, like a baby boomer musicology professor who has finally had the course "The Classical Symphony: From C.P.E. Bach to Beethoven" removed from the curriculum and replaced it with a cutting-edge graduate seminar on the Craptones' use of the chord B.

"Scratch," said Cooper, "You're happy." It was positively chilly, and the fog was obscuring Cooper's vision.

New people appeared in the basement, their features obscured by the greyness filling the furnace. Scratch began to laugh, "Tss, tss, tss," and his laughing transformed into a kind of quiet happy weeping, "Kss, kss, kss," and he put his hand to his shirt, brought it back with the fingers dark with blood, looked at his hand, and laughed, only this time aloud, "Ha ha-ha ha," and he said, "Alive in the blue and green world above, Ha ha-ha ha!" Scratch, perhaps from happiness or perhaps from loss of blood, dropped to a knee.

Cooper had begun to shiver. Ice crowded the gaps in the grate, and the fog was now so thick he could hardly see through it, and then it was so thick he could see nothing at all, and he huddled in his sports jacket and shook with the freezing cold. He remembered Thisbe and reached out for her warmth. She was no longer beside him. "Thisbe! Thisbe, where are you?" He stepped blindly into the fog but touched no one. He bumped into the freezing side of the furnace, and his hand burned as he hit the ice. The skin tore as he pulled his hand away. Hell had frozen over.

In the grey mist he could hear Scratch laughing, "Ha ha-ha ha!" Scratch called out, "Cooper, we did it!"

Chapter Forty-Seven

Cooper's Life Then

And then Cooper found himself alone in the basement of Scratch's house. He was outside the furnace, sitting on one of the uncomfortable fancy Scandinavian chairs. The basement was empty. The furnace was burning with an orange and purple glow, but no one was inside it. There was no fog, and the temperature in the room was pleasant. He wandered through Scratch's house, where all was exactly as it had been in its newly renovated Kmart style, except that no one else was there.

His first shock came when he went to the front door. It was icy cold to the touch and difficult to open. Cooper saw why: a huge snowstorm had covered the street. The door was iced over, and Cooper had to move a three-foot high snowdrift to get it open. The cold hit him like a wall so that even the water in his eyes seemed to freeze. He hopped down the stairs, his shoes filling with snow, and hopped across Scratch's driveway to his own house.

His second shock came when he turned to go up his own front stair. Instead of Scratch's squashy Cape Cod, so familiar that he never looked at it, he instead discovered that it had turned into a monstrous dark castle. It stood like the palace of the wicked sorcerer in a fairy tale book, with brooding turrets and ramparts, with arrow loops instead of proper windows and an evil black brick instead of sensible vinyl siding. A mighty smokestack rose along the wall nearest Cooper's house, rising several storeys like a power plant's and belching black smoke high into the air.

Cooper gained his front door, yanked it open with numb hands, and slipped into his own house, stomping to clear the snow that coated him up to his thighs. He was so cold that the interior warmth delighted but could not immediately warm him, and he shivered wildly as he slammed the door behind him and kicked off his snow-filled shoes. He went to the window to look at Scratch's house. A massive black wall rose out of high snow drifts and into the heights.

Cooper was in hell.

He explored his house and found it had not changed in any way. His clothes were still in the closets, his laundry in the hamper, dirty dishes still in the sink. There were milk and orange juice in the refrigerator, but he was low on cereal and out of beer. When he looked out the windows, everything was as he had seen it earlier in the day, except for the snow and Scratch's castle. Keiter's old house next door was unchanged as were the houses across the street. The coniferous trees were covered with snow but still kept their needles, and the deciduous trees were not in leaf, but then they had not been in leaf in the world above anyway. Cooper had seen the first tulips earlier in the week, but the snow would have covered them over even if they were out here. It occurred to him that there might be some symbolic meaning in the fact that hell looked exactly like the world he had lived in his whole life, but he couldn't think of what it might be.

It took him some time to learn the limits of his new environs. For one thing, he could not figure out how to translate himself to Scratch's furnace and then back. At certain times he would find himself in the furnace and then would unaccountably be dropped into Hell proper. This was confusing, but there was no user guide, no website with instructions, no customer support line, and no one to tell him what to do or how to do it. He would be in one place, then without warning be in another.

Besides that, the weather was foul. Instead of the heat that had tormented Thisbe and Keiter and was, Cooper understood, traditional, an alarming climate change had occurred. The cold snap was brutal and lasting. Cooper, who had put away his winter things with the coming of Easter, had to dig them out again. It was both strange and comforting that he found them in the exact places he had left them during his life on Earth a few days before.

Perhaps it was the cold weather, but Cooper did not see a single soul. There were no cars on the streets, no one walking past. No one picked up a telephone, although he did mistake Two-Ton Tony's voicemail for a living person and gave it most of his pizza order before the beep cut him off. When Cooper walked outside, the only footprints in the snow were his own. Thisbe and Keiter had vanished. Scratch was nowhere to be found. Cooper stumbled through deserted streets on numb feet and saw no one. He stopped at the mall. The stores were all open—that is, the doors were un-locked and the shelves were stocked with merchandise—but there were no clerks inside.

One afternoon he took a pack of chocolate-covered digestive biscuits and a Coffee Crisp from Loblaw's, leaving two twonies behind. When he returned on subsequent days, the money had not moved. The other stores at the mall were stocked with use-less things: summer clothing, shorts, sandals, T shirts and short-sleeved sport shirts, swimsuits, beach toys, baseball gloves and caps, frisbees, tennis rackets, outdoor furniture and sun umbrellas. He noticed that the drugstore had many ointments for burns but nothing for cold: no heating pads, no hand warmers, no frostbite medication.

For some time, Cooper believed that this meant that everyone had emptied out of hell last summer. Then he recalled a river and a boatman and believed that if the river froze, it might be possible to walk across it and escape once more to the world of the living. Perhaps that was why Hell seemed to be empty. He had walked down to look at the frozen Don when he realized the truth: that the freezing was an effect and not a cause.

He discovered an interesting thing about Scratch's castle. In the world above, Cooper's street held his house, then Scratch's, then the Smythe house, and across the street were their modest partners, numbers 187, 189, and 191. This geography did not seem to be in any way compromised by the fact that Scratch's house was now, from a distance at least, a castle as large as a city block and nearly four or five storeys high. When you walked down the street from Avonwick on Cooper's side, Cooper's house was opposite 187 and the castle opposite 189. The Smythe house was lost behind Scratch's mighty walls. But when you walked up the street from Underhill, the Smythe house was opposite 191, Scratch's castle was opposite 189, and Cooper's house could not be seen. It was also interesting that inside, Scratch's castle remained what it had been in the world above: the renovations were complete, and the interior of the giant castle was as small and linoleumed as Cooper's own modest cape cod. It had, Cooper supposed, something to do with what Scratch had called perspective. He resolved to look up Snell's law of refraction the next time he had an opportunity.

Besides the remarkable fact of Scratch's castle and the continuing cold weather, in every physical respect the neighborhood in which he now lived was the same as the neighborhood he had just left. The two Rulen houses were still there, and the same walk took Cooper to the same mall across the same Victoria Park Avenue. One day he took a trip downtown—he had to walk because the buses weren't running—and he found the same skyscrapers he had left. He went to Seals, where he found his old office. His desk was empty and neat. If the sheer loneliness of his situation were not so pressing, he might have believed that he was still alive. He

toyed with the idea that he might be living in a world created out
of his own memories, the sort of idea that might form the basis
of an episode of the *Twilight Zone*. But his memories were replete
with the people he had known, with his parents, Thisbe, Scratch,
Gormley, Abby, Maconochie, and Goohan, and the city was empty.
Later, when he met the janitor, he realized that here was something
he would neither have remembered nor predicted and gave up the
theory that he lived in a solipsistic world.

On the way home, he stopped at the public library and found a
book called *Hell*. He took it with him. When he got home, frozen
and blowing, he found that it was written in Italian on one side
and English on the other. The book was a disappointment. It was
clear that the fellow who wrote it had never been there and did
not know what he was talking about. It did clear up one mystery.
Cooper concluded that Scratch was Italian and not Jewish.

From time to time he found himself in Scratch's furnace in
the world above. He could not predict when or how he would
be there, nor could he make it happen by any technique. As it
had been on that first foggy night, the furnace was icy cold. He
looked out through the frozen grate onto the same grey cinderblock
basement with its refrigerator and rocking chair and staircase and
the uncomfortable modernist chairs, still standing about as they
had been on the night that Maconochie had shot him. He could
even see the sheaf of legal documents he had signed to take the job.
He could just make out his backgammon board under one of the
chairs. He and Thisbe had never finished their last game.

"Hey!" he called. "Scratch! Hey, Gormley! Hey!"

No one answered. He walked about the icy plain of the furnace
floor to keep warm. At intervals, he called out again but received
no answer. Then he found himself back in his house in hell, cold,
lonely, and lorn.

There was a small fireplace in Cooper's living room. He recalled that Mr. Rulen had kept a nice fireplace and sure enough found a face cord of hardwood in Mr. Rulen's garage. He helped himself, carrying the logs in his arms until he remembered that the Smythes, having children, would of course have a toboggan. He broke into their garage and spent an afternoon dragging sleds of logs from Mr. Rulen's to his own garage.

He was engaged in this activity when he felt the sudden shift that was by then becoming familiar, and he found himself in the furnace. This time, Scratch's basement was not empty.

"Dean!" Dean was sitting in the rocking chair with a large book on his lap. Beside him was a modernist lamp that had once been in a corner of Scratch's dining room. The lamp stand was a lightning bolt zigzag with an anomalous smooth semicircle in the middle. It was made of burnished steel and instead of a single lamp had something like a broom's end of wires with tiny bulbs on them. Dean was unshaven. He wore jeans and a T shirt and did not appear to be terribly clean.

"Cooper. So there you are. Scratch told me I might find you here."

"Here I am," said Cooper.

"You look different."

"I'm cold."

"Yes. Yes, I hadn't realized that it was such a cold place. It was rather nice when I was there. Spring."

"Climate change. We're exporting heat," said Cooper and then picked up the last part. "Wait. You were here?"

"Not there exactly," said Dean. "But I did take the tour."

"Really? See, I had no idea about any of that."

"I was interviewing for Scratch's job. Not interviewing exactly, but– anyway, things worked out the way they worked out." After a pause, Dean added, "I'm not sorry."

"I thought you were going out of town."

"I was. I'm back. I've completed the transaction on your book, you'll be interested to know."

"With the Americans?"

"Surprisingly, no. They were outbid in the end."

"So who got the book?"

"I'm afraid I signed a nondisclosure agreement. But we can play a game. Who has more money than the American government?"

It was unlike Dean to be sloppy, and even more unlike him to play games, at least to play any game that had no immediate benefit for him. He was—and when Cooper thought of it, he realized that it was the right word, which he would never before have applied to Dean—relaxed.

Dean said, "Come on. Guess. If the Americans didn't buy it, who would?"

"China?"

"Good. I thought of them but never made the offer. Guess again."

"Russia?"

Dean snorted. "Of course not. They're being run by the KGB again. There are so many double agents and triple agents and watchdogs watching the agents, you'd never get the deal done without a handful of deaths. It would be an ugly proposition."

"What about the Swiss? They're neutral–"

But Dean cut him off with a snort. "They're neutered, you mean. The weasels who stayed out of the Second World War. I should have set all their dates to yesterday when I had the book. 'Killing everyone in extermination camps? None of my business. Thank you for your bank deposit. Come again.' Business is business, but the Swiss?"

"How about the Arabs? Some sheik…"

"Too unstable. Cooper, I'll give you a hint. You're going down the wrong track. The days of nation-states are over. Hell, the days of states are over. Nowadays you pay your taxes to the states, but the states are in turn subsidiaries of much larger, much wealthier entities who pull the strings…"

The light finally went on. "Walmart? General Electric? Exxon? Amazon? How about the big insurance companies—"

Dean was nodding his head. "Bingo."

"Insurance?"

Dean shook his head. "No, no, and I'm not going to tell you more, but yes, exactly that track. Members of the Fortune 100. More money and more power than they allow any country to have. Of course, if America wanted to get Amazon, they still could, but not for long. It's just a matter of time. And really, let's face it, why would America want to get Amazon? Countries exist only to serve large corporations. God knows the politicians are only too happy to crawl to them. It seemed only fitting to consolidate their power with the Doomsday Book."

"Doomsday Book?"

"Your notebook. Gormley's notebook. Just a little marketing spin I put on it. I had the Americans help broker the deal. They took a percentage, I took a percentage. I paid taxes on my piece, to Canada and the U.S. I'm not the richest man in the world, but I sure don't have to worry about money for as long as I live. And," he smiled, "in my case, that's going to be quite a while."

"I'm happy for you," said Cooper. This was not quite what he meant, however. The truth was that he was happy to have someone to talk to. "But, if you don't mind my saying so, you don't look especially, ah…" he searched for the right word. "Prosperous."

Dean laughed. "Cooper, you don't understand. I don't have to look prosperous. I don't have to do anything. I've put all that behind me. You're looking at the only man who no longer has to fear death. I can do whatever I want. I'm free. Can you imagine what that means?"

Cooper suddenly realized that he could imagine it. "Dean," he said. "I'm afraid I have some bad news for you."

Dean smiled. "No, you don't. There is no more bad news for me. I'm immortal."

"Yes, about that," said Cooper.

"No, no, no," said Dean. "I know what you're thinking. We tried that already. We filmed the whole thing that last day I saw you."

"That last day…?"

"You remember, your last day at Seals. Remember, you met your neighbor, that guinea pig fellow Gormley brought in for the demonstration. Anyway, first we took care of– well, let's put it this way, first we did the simplest demonstration, you know, writing in new dates and times and watching how the subject behaved. Boom, worked like a champ. Then—and this is my point here—then I wrote myself back in. Right in front of them. Wrote my name down, wrote in the date and time, that very day. I gave myself a few minutes—and let me tell you, if you've never seen me sweat, you would have seen me sweat there—we watched the clock, everyone on the cell phone, satellite time. The room was quiet as the Jane-Finch public housing on a Monday morning when it's time to go to work. Not a sound. And the time came—the time went—and here I still am. You can't write a new name in the Doomsday Book."

"Dean," said Cooper, "Was there a cricket chirping upstairs when you came in here?"

Dean was surprised by this, but admitted, "Yes. Yes, there was. What about it?"

"Nothing," said Cooper. "Someone slapped him last I was up there, I was just wondering if he survived."

"Apparently it did."

"Apparently he did," confirmed Cooper.

"Anyway, Cooper, I saw something about you on the news, and I'd never actually been down here, so I thought I would come and see." He stretched and yawned. "You know, I wanted that job once."

"Yes, I remember."

"Oh, of course, that's right, you know all about it. Well. How is it? Do you like it?"

Cooper decided that he had nothing to lose. "No," he said. "No, I don't."

Dean was surprised. "Why not?"

Cooper told him: the loneliness, the cold, the constricted environment.

"But can't you get out? Scratch could get out."

"I can't."

"You probably just haven't figured it out yet."

"There's no user manual."

"No, I suppose not," said Dean, sympathetic.

Upstairs the doorbell rang. Dean ignored it, speaking on about a place his parents had owned when he was young and how frightened he had been that he would die there. His heart, he explained, had always been a problem.

Cooper was thinking. He interrupted: "Dean, would you call my lawyer? See those papers there?" Dean found the papers on one of the chairs. "I need you to get them to Goohan. I don't know when I can get there myself, but I need you to get those papers to my lawyer. And have him come here and visit."

"All right, Cooper. All right," said Dean, picking up the papers. "Hey, this looks familiar. I signed something a lot like these." He ruffled through the pages. "This brings it all back. Of course, I was young, not even sixteen..."

Cooper was not interested. "Aloysius Goohan. He's got a website. You can google it." It was surprising, but, after longing for company, Dean's anecdotes bored him.

"Goohan. Got it. Wow, these forms haven't changed much. There it is. I signed that one. Now this one is a little different—see, I wasn't going to have any special title when I got there..."
Dean spoke of the forms in the way an older alumnus, gone from

school years ago, might speak of student transcripts from a major he once considered. Upstairs, the doorbell rang again. "Well," he said, dropping the papers back on the chair beside him. "I don't know what you hope to accomplish by all that."

"Aloysius Goohan," said Cooper. "Have you seen Scratch?"

The doorbell rang again, but Dean continued to talk about, seemingly, anything that popped into his head. He told Cooper about his mother, whom he had admired, and his father, whom he did not. He talked about lawyers he had known. "A surprising number have contracts similar to mine, though of course they tended not to have any particular disease spurring them on. It's funny how you can always tell..." He paused, musing. Cooper heard the basement door swing open and the sound of light feet on the stairs. "My own lawyer, for instance," Dean began again, but interrupted himself. "Thisbe! I thought you were dead."

Thisbe blurted, "Didn't you hear? Cooper's changed all that. There's been a big holiday declared, and we don't have to go back."

Cooper strained to see but was blocked by the walls of the furnace. He tried to call out, but his voice failed. It was Thisbe's way to be self-possessed, and even as emotion whelmed him he realized that, though she spoke in her usual tone, she was beside herself with excitement—only this would account for her announcing her news without saying a proper hello to Dean.

She appeared to collect herself, for as she came to the bottom of the stairs, she said, "But what are you doing here? I thought you killed me. Has Scratch made you a prisoner?"

"Scratch? No. No, he doesn't have any power over me," said Dean, bursting with his own news.

She was dressed in a simple white cotton shirt and tight blue jeans, and seeing her, Cooper was faint with love. "Cooper!" said Thisbe, seeing him for the first time.

"Hello, Thisbe," he said, discovering that his voice worked again.

"But so small," said Thisbe.

This irritated Cooper, but he forced himself to focus on what was important. "And you. So big," he said. Again he choked with emotion.

"I'm free," she told him.

Again the irritation. "It appears everyone is," said Cooper.

"Cooper, come out of there. Will you come out?"

"No."

"You can't, or you won't?" asked Thisbe, somewhat taken aback. "Cooper, what did Scratch do to you? What have you done?"

Dean picked up Cooper's documents and rifled through the pages. "I think you want this one," he said, holding a sheet of paper out to Thisbe. Cooper could just see: the paper with the red C his blood had made.

Thisbe took the paper and read. "Cooper. Oh, Cooper," she said. "You trusted him. Oh, Cooper."

"What? What does it say?" It occurred to Cooper that he had been rather dazzled by all the documents Scratch had had him sign and that he no longer remembered what any of them said, if indeed he had known. He was unable to control his irritation. "Listen. Take those to Goohan. If there's anything wrong, he'll find it. Take them to my lawyer."

"Cooper, it's Easter Sunday. Do you think he's working today?"

Cooper could not believe this. "It can't be Easter again. A few weeks maybe at most. I came here on Easter."

"It's the same Easter Sunday," said Dean. "It hasn't been a year. Say, Thisbe," he said.

"No!" snapped Thisbe. "That's over. That's all over."

Cooper was becoming more irritated. "Listen. It's not Easter Sunday. Time has passed."

"Nevertheless," said Dean. "You need to loosen up, Cooper. Your notions of time and space belong in the eighteenth century, if you don't mind my saying so," he added.

Cooper, who had heard as much from Scratch, minded but did not say so. They established, with the help of Dean's cell phone, that it was indeed Easter Sunday of the same year that Cooper had signed the documents for Scratch, that in fact it was only a few hours since he had been shot and found himself in the furnace with Thisbe. "Son of a gun," said Cooper. He was beginning to think that perhaps his notions of time and space really did need a once over with the furniture polish.

"Dean," said Cooper. Now that Thisbe was here, Cooper wanted Dean to go away. "You need to go upstairs and look at Scratch's cricket. See if he'll eat a scone."

"A scone?"

"The cricket."

"Why?"

"I think you'll find it interesting."

"You think so."

"I do."

Dean gave Cooper a look: his old look, the look of a busy man who brooks no nonsense. Then he smiled. "All right," he said, jumping up. "Not like I'm going to run short on time." He patted Thisbe's bottom. "I'll be back in a minute."

"Cooper," said Thisbe, as if her heart was breaking. She pulled a chair up to the grate and sat down.

Cooper looked at her: huge and green-eyed and beautiful.

"Cooper, I'm so sorry."

He did not trust his voice, but he was able to say, "I got you out."

"But at what price?"

"Think nothing of it." He tried to smile.

"Cooper," she said. "Cooper," she said again, as if she could not make up her mind to say whatever it was. She said, "It was kind of you."

"I did it–" he began, but could not finish. He tried again. "I did it–" but he could not add, as he wanted, 'for you.'

Thisbe looked at him quizzically, waiting for him to continue. He tried one more time and gave it up. Instead he asked, "Where will you go? What happens next?"

"I don't really know," said Thisbe. "But I've heard that we go on."

"Where?"

"I don't know, exactly. We don't stay here. We don't stay– in this world."

Cooper felt a rush of hope. "You come back, right? The holiday, then the holiday ends, and you come back here." He remembered Scratch's service. "I read this. You have one day, and then–"

Thisbe shook her head. "No. No, I don't think so. Keiter says that we're moving out. I don't know too much about it. But he says that we're all done. We're moving on to the next thing."

"The next thing? What's that?"

Thisbe almost whispered: "I don't know. Keiter says that it's the Last Things for us."

"No," Cooper insisted. "It was in Scratch's book. One day, once a year, in honor of–"

"It's all changed," Thisbe said.

"All right," said Cooper, realizing that he did not want to spend his time arguing with Thisbe. "What are the Last Things?" said Cooper, repeating the odd emphasis she gave to the words. "What do you mean, Last Things?"

"Four last things. Cooper, you should know this. You're Catholic. Keiter told me. Death, Judgment, Heaven, Hell."

"Keiter? You were talking to Keiter?" The thought of this twisted Cooper's bowels. He did not understand at first that this physical pain was jealousy.

Thisbe nodded.

"Thisbe, he's a creep."

"That's likely true."

"But it doesn't matter?"

"Just so. You darken yourself by holding it. It doesn't matter."

Cooper could not speak. Finally he said, "The Four Last Things."

"Cooper, we– everyone I was– we had all died, been judged, and gone to Hell. It was supposed to be permanent."

"No kidding," said Cooper, but Thisbe did not catch the edge in his voice.

"But then came the holiday. And this time, the jubilee. Cooper, think of it. Everyone has been freed. We've all been given another chance."

"Do you think you could make me a hot chocolate?" said Cooper, stomping his feet to keep warm.

Thisbe was so interested in her story that she did not hear him. "Cooper, I think the next thing for us is Judgment."

"You were already judged."

"We're getting a second chance. Perhaps we've atoned. Or perhaps another atoned for us."

She spoke with reverence, and Cooper felt better. It was unlike him to boast, but he had felt things were going badly and he said, "You mean me."

"Oh, I don't think so," said Thisbe matter-of-factly. "I've been reading about it. And I think–"

The irritation flooded over Cooper. "What do you mean, not me?" Cooper interrupted. "Of course it was me. I disrupted everything. Scratch is free, and so all his subjects have a vacation. How can you say–"

But Thisbe was interrupting. "Cooper, Cooper, you were part of it, no doubt. I don't know that it could have happened in the same way without you. But we're only part of a much bigger story…"

Cooper saw that she was trying. He realized that something might yet be saved. "Stay. Stay behind. Stay with me," said Cooper.

He was standing against the grate, and he reached out his tiny hand to Thisbe. "Stay," he whispered.

Thisbe touched his hand with her huge long-nailed fingertip. "Oh, Cooper," she said, and he could see her beautiful green eyes above him and that they were full of tears. "Cooper," she said. "Cooper."

They looked at each other, both overcome by emotion. Cooper forgot for the moment to be cold, so overwhelmed was he by the touch of Thisbe's warm fingertip in his hand and her wet green eyes, as large and deep as the sea.

But the moment passed. Cooper saw that she would not stay, that there was nothing that he could say or do, that her heart might be full, but that she would not do for him what he had done for her.

"So that's it," he said.

"Cooper," said Thisbe.

"I guess that's all," he said.

"Cooper. It's not like that. Don't be brutal."

"On to the next thing then." There were more bitter things he thought to say, but he was interrupted by footsteps on the stairs. It was Dean, moving like a sleepwalker.

"That's not a cricket," he said.

"What are you talking about?" asked Thisbe. Cooper saw with anger, bitterness and perverse satisfaction that she was glad of the interruption.

"It's not a cricket. It's a man."

"Who isn't?" asked Thisbe.

Dean appeared to see her for the first time. "His name is Tithonus. I think he has a broken rib. I put some masking tape around his chest."

Cooper shouted, "Ha! You see? Immortal, are you? Immortal? You think you got the better of me? That's your future, Dean. You're not going to die, but that doesn't mean you're going to stay young. You'll just get older and older, and you won't be able to die. You'll just shrink and shrivel and waste away, and maybe I'll make a space for you behind my stove. Ha ha ha!"

He stopped because Dean had retreated out of sight, back up the staircase. Thisbe was looking at Cooper with new eyes. "Why did you save us if you're going to be horrible?" she said. And then she was gone as well, and Cooper was alone and freezing in the furnace.

"I don't know why I did it either," he shouted to the empty basement. He saw that they had left his paperwork behind. "Hey! Hey!" he shouted. But the door had already closed behind them. "You didn't even have life insurance!"

Chapter Forty-Eight

In Which We Take Leave of Old Friends

And that was the last time Cooper saw Thisbe. Now began his new career as the Prime Minister of Darkness. There was, after all, nothing irregular in Scratch's contract. Goohan advised him not to fight it. The angels came and taught him how to go back and forth between the nether regions and our own world, showed him where the thermostat was, and helped him find a good repairman who could replace it for a reasonable price. The ice receded, and Cooper, all but frostbitten, kept the blast furnaces on night and day to warm the place up.

He crossed the void and the chaos and flew to Earth, searching high and low for Thisbe, but she had disappeared into whatever dreams are dreamt by the forgiven when they find their final sleep. All that was left was her grave in the Mount Pleasant cemetery. Cooper knelt at the small plot and tried to pray, but the words would not come, and the cloudy heavens seemed crisscrossed with tangles of spiders' webs. He took a pinch of earth from her grave and put it to his lips. It was gritty and bitter and tasted of ashes.

He was, it turned out, a personage of some consequence in the world. The United Nations recognized his new regime immediately, delighted that the Americans did not get it. China protested. The World Council of Churches called for understanding and more atheism and used the brief flurry of interest to point out that this was the final proof, as if one more were needed, that there would be no justice until African same-sex couples could marry, experience *in vitro* fertilization, and then abort the scientifically engendered foetus. They called for Cooper to become their leader. The African bishops, known to be conservative, left the council in protest. "They are, after all, primitive and in need of guidance," pronounced the presiding bishop of the council, a formidable lesbian ex-nun from Victoria. She was displeased when it was pointed out that her exact words had been used by Cecil Rhodes over a century earlier.

Other Protestants were pleased that the Devil was, as they had always suspected, a Catholic. University professors signed a petition asking for deeper understanding, respect, and tolerance between good and evil and returned to pursue their eternal goal of pushing all teaching to untenured adjunct faculty and graduate students. Black advocacy groups, insecure as Soviet propagandists in the 1950s, claimed that the Devil had been a black man but white people covered it up. Feminist groups said that it was time a woman got the job and pointed out that a woman's greater sensitivity, attention to domestic detail, and well-documented ability to hate would make for a superior eternal damnation experience. The Civil Liberties Union sued the newspapers for printing anything about Cooper, on the grounds of their deeply held conviction that "free speech" and "freedom of expression" mean "what Civil Liberties Union lawyers like to hear." Two homosexuals who had been briefly popular as fashion advisors on television commented acidly on Cooper's curly hair and poor choice in shoes:

"They look like Instamatic cameras."

"Oh, stop."

"They do. See, and the laces are just like that dopey loop that passed for a handle."

"You know, I think my mom had one of those."

"Well, of *course* she did. There's a picture of you grinning at the science fair with those big pilot glasses and that awful 1980s mullet. That *had* to have been taken with a Kodak Instamatic."

"Oh my God, I thought I threw that picture out!"

"The hair was cute back then."

"God."

"It's a lot cuter than those shoes."

"They do look like Instamatic cameras, don't they?"

"I wonder if you can see up his pantleg when the flash goes off."

"Ew, but who would want to?"

Conservatives, who love the Devil better than God or man, were full of joy because unlike God or man, only the Devil proves them right. Now that a new devil had acceded to the throne of Satan, they spoke through lips made thin by constipation about a new era in which only vigilance, sobriety, and the constant clenching of the sphincter muscle could defeat eternal peril, and in their hearts they smiled with teeth even more crooked than the dreams of Gormley's orthodontist.

Because the first Mrs. Rulen had made Gormley go to an orthodontist in preparation for their wedding. They had spent a large portion of Mr. Rulen's life insurance on their new BMW, but the still greater portion was made available for Gormley's teeth. It was around this time that he got a permanent, so that instead of floppy blond hair that hung like greased wax paper, he now had the springy little curls that had been popular on movie stars when the first Mrs. Rulen had bloomed in youth. "It's as if the wildness in his mouth has been transferred to his hair," his friends on the Seals board commented favorably.

Gormley was married on a sunny May afternoon, and the first Mrs. Rulen became the first Mrs. Gormley. It was a quiet ceremony, enlivened by Gormley's enthusiastic rendition of "Luck Be a Lady Tonight," accompanied by the septuagenarian organist who had programmed her instrument's drum machine to Samba-

Latin especially for the performance. The entire Seals board of directors attended to wish the happy couple well and presented Gormley with a honeymoon trip to Tahiti, whereupon Gormley regaled them with highlights from South Pacific for another thirty minutes.

It turned out that Gormley's previous job as Death was in fact the perfect training for an executive position in a large insurance company. His distinguishing characteristics—lying, stupidity, irresponsibility, greed, laziness, and a sociopathic insensitivity to others—while not what one looks for in a roommate or co-worker, were no handicaps to a corporate executive. In fact, the opposite was true. Gormley instituted three important reforms.

First, he stopped the payment of any protection monies to supernatural agents such as Death, an immediate and ongoing savings direct to the firm's bottom line.

Second, although it was incomplete, he brought the results of the Equation of Almost Infinite Complexity to bear in pricing and risk rating decisions. Several customers in good standing who had never made a late payment found themselves fired as their death dates approached. It was determined by customer service that two months prior to death was the ideal time to fire a customer. Any earlier gave them too much time to launch a lawsuit; any later and questions were sometimes asked by nosy relatives who wanted to know how the insurance company could toss old granddad overboard just after the oncologist had predicted his death. Two months was the right amount of time for the letter of cessation to find its way into the wastepaper basket and out the door prior to any lawyer picking over the decedent's estate for cash opportunities.

But the most publicized reform was Gormley's adoption of the new regularized thirteen month calendar. As quarterly profits grew and the first two reforms were necessarily kept secret, Gormley's calendar was given credit for the success. "Our accounting staff has the amortization tables memorized," Gormley boasted in a famous business weekly. "Everything is easier, and mistakes are caught before they are made." The new month was called Chester. Seals left the difficult fiscal position of the Dean Darwin era behind and charged into a new bull market. Soon other insurance companies as far away as Australia and Singapore began experimenting with "the Seals fiscal model," as business textbooks of the time referred to it.

Gormley took a short leave of absence to promote his novel, *Death Comes to Broadway*, an autobiographical mystery. He returned, but the company was doing so well that he retired to spend more time promoting his book, and the board voted him a golden parachute in the form of an $800,000 annuity. The novel was made into a movie, and the movie was made into a Broadway musical, and Gormley's straightened teeth gleamed and stood like soldiers in his pink gums.

Things did not go so well for Scratch. Although he was, as he had planned, able to change places with Cooper during his Easter holiday, he spent long months in the hospital recovering from the gunshot wound inflicted by Maconochie's ricochet.

Although Maconochie lost Cooper, he did not lose Scratch. Cooper's erstwhile neighbor had a shoebox full of bank statements from the Isle of Man bank, and there was plenty of evidence that he was a money launderer, deeply involved with illegal drug and weapons smuggling besides consorting with hitmen and pharmaceutical frauds. Maconochie was promoted to a full-time lieutenant in Special Ops and given a medal in a ceremony attended by the archbishop.

"The problem," Scratch explained to his lawyer, "is that things like this didn't used to happen to me on account of my supernatural powers."

"The problem," said Goohan, "may be more succinctly stated: From where is the money to pay me coming?"

But Scratch had put aside enough money to pay his lawyer. Goohan found the case surprisingly easy. Scratch was so famous an evil-doer that no jury could be seated that did not already have an opinion about him, and so, over the course of eighteen months, three mistrials were declared. After another year of motions and changes of venue and challenges and counter-challenges, Scratch was released on the grounds that, as an extra-national mythological character who was part of the world's heritage, Canadian courts did not have jurisdiction over him. The case was punted to The Hague. In Europe, Scratch was feted as the only good thing ever to come out of Christianity, the sole voice for freedom in a religion that had repressed the European continent during its darkest times. Wiccans and Druids and New Age converts of every shape and description cheered Scratch wherever he went, and the public mood was much in his favor. People came to him seeking new contracts, new favors, revenge on their enemies or true love, or the always elusive B+ in Organic Chemistry 220.

"I'm retired," he would say and refer them to Cooper. But, like any retired popular leader, he could not resist the urge to give advice. He suggested a deeper commitment to seeing the good in people, or more time for reflection and prayer, or a plunge into public service. He would drink his tea in the hotels at Innsbruck or Baden-Baden, and women (and, this being a progressive century, men) threw themselves in his path, their requests for counsel a smokescreen for carnal intent. If he sometimes accepted their offers, what of it? The usual suspects lined up against him—the Catholic church, evangelical Christians, Muslims—but their inarticulate frumpiness was overshadowed by the pizzazz of Scratch's fans, who included movie stars and rock musicians.

Abby Bruler, part of a panel discussion that included a comedian with a new movie out and a soccer player who had scored a goal in a winning World Cup match, almost felt sorry for the other side of the debate: an aging priest who looked like the man who answers the door in a horror movie; a pear-shaped housewife-turned-lobbyist, the sort of serious-minded woman who at the age of fifty-two still had never used makeup and whose hair resembled Gormley's before his permanent; and a former judge who had lost his job when it was found that he frequented anti-Semitic websites. The side aligned against Scratch was so unattractive in their appearance and attitude that the moderator ignored them for the last twenty minutes of the debate, giving the comedian broad scope for some rather good joshing, allowing the soccer star to give his own account of some bitterness between Manchester and Chelsea, and allowing the camera to linger on Abby who, with the help of the show's makeup artist, was not merely stylish but devastating. She was invited back several times, and within two years was hosting her own magazine show on the endlessly yapping dog that is cable news.

Abby interviewed her old friend Cooper on one of her first episodes. "The rumor is," she said, repeating a theory that had been in the papers, "that you are merely a dupe, and that Scratch never relinquished his power, and that you only appear to be the devil."

Cooper smiled and said coolly, "Then why am I the master in Hell?"

"The idea," said Abby, beautiful and cool herself, "is that Mr. Scratch has broken off a little piece and given it to you, but behind the border is the real Hell, and Mr. Scratch is still king there. He has remained in complete control of everything. What do you say to that?"

Abby was generally considered to have scored a coup with this question because Cooper's ears flamed pink, and he had to start several times before he was able to formulate an answer. "Why don't you come and see?" he finally sputtered, an answer that might have worked as a rebuttal if delivered immediately and with confidence. The moment was a "most watched" on YouTube for several weeks.

Cooper was mortified that people thought him a dupe. Abby's triumph was complete when he offered her camera crew an onsite visit of his netherworld domain. It was taped in time for the January sweeps and garnered an 8.4 share and a 4.3 rating. It made Abby a star.

Though he did not admit it to Abby, Cooper was not necessarily displeased at the notion that Scratch was still ruler in Hell. Scratch denied it. But Cooper spent a good deal of time looking in drawers and under tables and in boxes for souls that Scratch might have hidden there, hoping to find Thisbe again, to stand once more in the regard of those eyes, to be scolded again for his shallowness and lack of imagination, to hold her hand, to beg forgiveness for the wretched way in which they had parted. But he never found her.

Cooper's job began to pick up. It turned out that, while many many generations of the damned had been given their Get Out Of Jail Free cards and discovered that, as Gregory of Nyssa suggests, God's mercy may ultimately subsume His justice, the final trump had not yet sounded. Cooper woke up one morning in Hell to discover that a new family had moved into the Rulen's house across the street. One day he saw a bus going up the infernal Victoria Park Avenue. He went to Parkway Mall and found that doughnuts were once again being made. He went to the border and found the souls of the newly dead splashing across the river, finding their own way to Hell with no help from the Devil, just as Scratch had told him.

Cooper found the job interesting and rewarding. He organized backgammon and euchre tournaments and drilled the children in multiplication tables. The smarter ones he took aside and was gratified by one small girl who anticipated some of the simpler geometric theorems before he taught them. As more and more people came into his kingdom, he instituted progressive reforms, such as the delivery of yogurt smoothies in refrigerated trucks. He bought a programmable thermostat so that all seasons would be found in his kingdom, not merely numbing cold or burning heat.

It could not be all fun and games however. Though embarrassed by what seemed an obsolete tradition, Cooper felt obligated to torment his subjects. On Fridays he tortured people from the hours of nine to twelve and one to four-thirty. Cooper commuted to the torture chambers on the 91C bus through Woodbine Station, and he was always greeted with disappointed respect by the long line that he passed on his way to the dungeons. Cooper had explained that torture was a necessary industry, and by and large the honor system worked. There was some absenteeism, but Cooper was scrupulous about following up, making house calls like a doctor in the days before disease had been disciplined to fit the schedules of medical administrators. The only man who liked the tortures was a former MPP from Saskatchewan who kept trying to take extra turns. He confessed to enjoying masochistic perversions of all sorts. From then on his torture was not to be tortured. He complained bitterly and came to watch Cooper in the dungeons, eyes full of desire and rage. "Creepy," Cooper said to a man who had spent his career designing telephone answering systems, and we all knew what he meant.

As Scratch had foreseen, there were losses as well as gains. The zombie love drug that had first brought Cooper fame and despair in the world above had been perfected, and it was now not uncommon for frosh (as university-minded Cooper called the newly dead) to disappear for a few days, a few weeks, or even a few years, only to return at a later time.

As more people came into Hell, Cooper found himself growing busier, and he was forced to delegate some of his responsibilities. Instead of supervising the tortures himself, he turned the work over to others. Soon there were so many people that they had to start on Thursday night to get through them all by Friday, and then Wednesday, and Tuesday, and Monday. Still more and more people came, all finding their way straight to Hell despite Cooper's allocating no budget to advertising, and soon Cooper found that by starting on Friday night they still had not tortured everyone by the next Friday afternoon. He brought on more torturers, but these were improperly trained, and there were complaints, and it became clear that despite valiant efforts, the entire torture program was on the verge of failure.

"You must have had this problem," Cooper said to Scratch one evening over a game of gin rummy.

"Cooper, you act like it's a cottage industry. Why do you think we instituted the 'all blast furnaces, all the time' policy?"

So Cooper stopped the smoothie deliveries and changed the program on the thermostat.

In his dark times, after lunch on Wednesday afternoons, when nothing needed to be done but much was unsatisfactory, Cooper wondered if he had wasted his life. The memory of Thisbe, of her beauty and of the exalted leaping delight he had felt just thinking about her, faded away. Sometimes he could no longer remember her face, or he would recall that she had a way of laughing that had once delighted him but be unable to hear it. He realized that she had never told him that she loved him and wondered if he had given up his ordinary life for an infatuation that was not reciprocated. But sometimes at night he would wake up and see her standing beside his bed, a vision like a guardian angel, her eyes as deep and sad as they had been in their last unsatisfactory meeting in Scratch's basement. Cooper would remember how pointlessly he had wasted their last minutes together, and long after the apparition disappeared he would lie in bed staring at the ceiling of his bedroom with great tears rolling down his face, and he would say, as if in prayer, "Thisbe, Thisbe."

Time passed. Cooper, in command and full of deeds, passed back and forth from the netherworld to the world of the living, attending to this and that, working here and there. He would return to Scratch's old house, now legally his, and play cribbage with aging Dean and with the cricket-man Tithonus, who had made a full recovery from his broken rib. When Scratch made one of his periodic trips back from Europe, they played euchre. Dean had recently purchased Cooper's old house and moved in next door.

Cooper called trump. "How much did you pay for it?"

Dean told him.

Cooper whistled.

"Do you think I made a bad deal?" Dean asked nervously. "I didn't even negotiate."

"That's a lot more than I paid for it," was all Cooper said. Property values had held up pretty well after all.

Cooper left the game and traveled to the border of Hell. He remembered that when he had started, he had thought of the river as a barrier. He felt it would keep people out. He had been naïve, he realized: in those days he still had the idea that people would avoid Hell if you let them. Now he knew better. People will find their own way to Hell even if you beat them with a stick to go the other way. It occurred to him that he might set up a ferryman as Scratch had. He imagined a fast ferry, a large flat three-tiered launch that could cross the river many times a day, perhaps helping to defray the cost by concessions that could be sold during the trip: gumballs, chocolate bars, souvenir pennants, and baseball caps. T shirts with witty slogans: "My parents went to Hell, and all they got me was this lousy T shirt." "Go to Hell. I did." "Hell. Like Scarborough, but warm." He would have to contact a marketing person.

While he stood on the bank turning his mind to these clever money-making ideas, a man splashed up the river bank, and Cooper saw a familiar walk, and a familiar way of holding his head when he walked, and, as he came closer, Cooper saw the pockmarked face, and he realized. "Julius!"

"Hello, Cooper. Fancy meeting you here."

"How are things?" Cooper asked.

"How should they be? I'm dead."

"I'm sorry to hear that."

"Heart. Took me out quickly." He looked back at the river. "I guess I should have crossed myself out in your book."

"Why didn't you?"

"For one thing, I didn't see my name. But you know how it is. I believed it, but at the same time, I didn't really believe it."

"Death is like that."

"Yes. You somehow never really think it will happen to you."

"That's true."

"And then it does, and there's not a lot you can do about it."

"No."

"So here I am."

"Yes." They stood. Cooper said, "You get used to it."

"Well, what can you do, eh?"

"Exactly."

They regarded each other.

"I suppose you're still mad about me killing Thisbe."

"You? Dean killed her," said Cooper.

"Dean? I don't think so."

"You?"

"Yes, me. You didn't know– ? You didn't?" Julius whistled.

"How?"

"When we saw her name, she was all in a tizzy and left me holding the book. I was angry. Jealous. I changed her date and then followed her to your house." He peered at Cooper. "Funny you thought it was Dean. It was partly your fault I did it. You sleeping with her and all. When she was living with me."

"I never slept with her," protested Cooper, trying to remember the night Thisbe died. He was flattered that Julius assumed he had slept with Thisbe. "I didn't sleep with her," he repeated.

"Oh." Pause. "Well, someone told me you did." They looked about. There was not much to look at. The dark river behind, the orange glow of the city in front, and the long dreary riverbank stretching out from side to side. "I really didn't know it was going to work."

"I understand." Cooper nodded.

"It was embarrassing if you want to know."

"I imagine it would be."

"No one found out, though. I mean, the police."

"They didn't find much out."

"Neither did the papers."

Cooper snorted derisively. "The papers."

Julius laughed.

"Abby," Cooper said.

"Abby," said Julius, but fondly.

"How was the river?" Cooper asked.

"Cold. I didn't like it," said Julius.

"You'll appreciate that once you get into the fire," Cooper said. He added, "I'm thinking of a ferry. A big one."

"Yes, that would be nice. Where will you put the docks?"

"I hadn't thought that far."

"That outcropping there might work."

"Hm."

"Deep there. The boat will have a draught."

"Yes. Yes, good point."

"Mm-hm," said Julius.

They stood beside each other on the river bank. Another soul splashed up beside them and wandered away over the ridge and into the fire. "Torture starts at eight," said Cooper. There was a new schedule out.

"I'll be there," said Julius. He walked away from the border towards the flaming city and was soon lost to view.

The Last Chapter:
An Equation of Almost Infinite
Complexity

On the day he had predicted his own death, Vishwas dropped his daughter off at school and began the walk home. It was twenty years since Dean Darwin resigned. Twenty years ago, Vishwas had been walked to the door and not allowed to retrieve any of his files. It didn't matter. By that time, he had been working for months almost exclusively on his home network, which was more powerful and better than the computers the Seals insurance company supplied. For Vishwas was a hacker, in the best sense of that word. He loved computers, he loved to write programs, he loved puzzles of all sorts.

He had perfected Cooper's equation of almost infinite complexity two years ago, a hobby that he finally completed, like people who build ships in bottles, or work through the possible permutations and combinations of a particular chess endgame, or build scale Lego replicas of the CN Tower or University College. The last thing that he had trouble with was people who died in bus accidents—not car or train or plane, not cancer or AIDS or old age, just bus accidents. He discovered the problem when a school bus carrying an entire hockey team lost control near Timmins one winter and three children were killed. But he had figured out where his error was—a small but incorrect assumption, something in fact that Sridhar had mentioned to him years before in a Thai food place in the basement of Commerce Court, poor Sridhar. Vishwas corrected the error one rainy April afternoon two years ago. Since then, he subscribed to several newspapers and read the obituaries with satisfaction every morning, much as a baseball fan wakes to read the box scores.

The one thing he had never been able to figure were the exact times the way Cooper had gotten them. That man was a genius. Vishwas had tried to find him after the layoff, but it was as if Cooper had fallen off the face of the earth. Then one night he saw Cooper on the news and realized that he had become a god. This seemed reasonable to Vishwas, and he wrote his old boss a congratulatory letter and asked about two or three strategies he thought might help find the exact times of death. His letter was answered by a signed photograph of Cooper and a form letter. Vishwas had to content himself with predictions that were good only to the date of death. He had done the best he could.

It occurred to him many times that perhaps he should publish his findings. How many might be saved if they knew the day on which their death was predicted? But he knew such things never helped. In school he had read that Oedipus's father had exiled his son to avoid the prophecies of the Oracle, but the Oracle's predictions came to pass anyway. It was a true story. The gods would have their way. Contrary to every impulse of his adopted country, Vishwas believed that there were secrets that ought to remain secret. It occurred to him that this could be expressed as a corollary of the Heisenberg principle.

And tomorrow, or perhaps it would take a few days, his own obituary would appear. His affairs were in order. His wife—who would not die for another seventeen years—would be well provided for. He wondered if she would marry that Prakash who was always smiling at her at temple. There was nothing he could do about that. Prakash was a good man, not perhaps as good a man as

Vishwas's own father, but then, who was? Prakash was a widower, a prosperous man. He would take care of the family. Vishwas's daughter was twelve now and consumed with soccer practices and the school play. She showed promise as a mathematician, just like her father. She would grow to be handsome like her mother, not a beauty, but a handsome woman, with a strong open face that saw the goodness that the gods spread with so much love throughout this wide sad world. He wondered how she would remember him when she was old, if she would think of him with the reverence he had always felt for his own father. She would live a long time, more than twice as long as he would. He was sorry that he would not be a bigger part of that life. He felt that she was already something more wonderful than he could imagine.

He was consumed with such thoughts when the embolus, finally free of the blood clot in his leg, completed its journey to his lungs. A pain in his chest swelled up, and he fell to a knee. He found that he could not breathe. He lay on his back on the sidewalk and looked up. Many suns danced before his eyes. His brain performed its final task, flooding his system with a last gasp of endorphins, and he felt neither fear nor anxiety. He saw his father's hands reaching out to him, felt his father take him in his arms, and together they flew away on the early autumn breeze.

Ite, liber est.

Acknowledgments

Country songs Julius and Thisbe listen or refer to are:

- *Flushed from the Bathroom of Your Heart,* Lyrics by Jack H. Clement.

- *Songs About Me,* by Shaye Smith and Ed Hill.

- *Kissing You Good-bye,* by Waylon Jennings.

- *Believe Me, Baby (I Lied),* by Kim Richey, Angelo Petraglia, and Larry Gottlieb.

Broadway songs Gormley sings are from:

- *Annie Get Your Gun,* by Irving Berlin.

- *West Side Story,* by Arthur Laurents, Stephen Sondheim, and Leonard Bernstein.

- *Oklahoma,* by Oscar Hammerstein II and Richard Rodgers.

- *My Fair Lady,* by Alan Jay Lerner and Frederick Loewe.

The author is grateful for permission to reference these works. Other musical references are Public Domain.

CASTALIA HOUSE

FICTION
The Missionaries by Owen Stanley
The Promethean by Owen Stanley
Brings the Lightning by Peter Grant
Rocky Mountain Retribution by Peter Grant

NON-FICTION
The LawDog Files by LawDog
Collected Columns, Vol. I: Innocence & Intellect, 2001—2005 by Vox Day
Collected Columns, Vol. II: Crisis & Conceit, 2005—2009 by Vox Day
Clio and Me by Martin van Creveld
SJWs Always Lie by Vox Day
Cuckservative by John Red Eagle and Vox Day
Equality: The Impossible Quest by Martin van Creveld
A History of Strategy by Martin van Creveld
Between Light and Shadow by Marc Aramini
Compost Everything by David the Good
Grow or Die by David the Good
Push the Zone by David the Good

FANTASY
Summa Elvetica by Vox Day
A Throne of Bones by Vox Day
A Sea of Skulls by Vox Day
The Green Knight's Squire by John C. Wright
Iron Chamber of Memory by John C. Wright
Awake in the Night by John C. Wright

SCIENCE FICTION
The End of the World as We Knew It by Nick Cole
CTRL-ALT REVOLT! by Nick Cole
Somewhither by John C. Wright
Back From the Dead by Rolf Nelson
Victoria: A Novel of Fourth Generation War by Thomas Hobbes

MILITARY SCIENCE FICTION
Starship Liberator by David VanDyke and B. V. Larson
Battleship Indomitable by David VanDyke and B. V. Larson
The Eden Plague by David VanDyke
Reaper's Run by David VanDyke
Skull's Shadows by David VanDyke
There Will Be War Volumes I and II ed. Jerry Pournelle